The Donation

by

Michele A. Fabiano

KCM PUBLISHING

A DIVISION OF KCM DIGITAL MEDIA, LLC

CREDITS

Copyright © 2021 by Michele A. Fabiano
Published by KCM Publishing
A Division of KCM Digital Media, LLC

All Rights Reserved.

The Donation by Michele A. Fabiano

ISBN-13: 978-1-955620-05-5

First Edition

Publisher: Michael Fabiano
KCM Publishing
www.kcmpublishing.com

*This book is dedicated to Bill Jarnigan who challenged
me to write every day.*

Acknowledgements

Special thanks to Dr. Ken Ostrand, who by plane, bus, boat, camel, foot, and felucca…brought the past to life as we explored some of the greatest mastabas, tombs, temples, museums, and pyramids throughout Egypt! What a great feeling it was to be able to roam around where man built some of the most impressive monuments, hid riches, pushed sarcophagi, and robbers plundered.

And in the middle of the hot Egyptian desert, while bargaining to ride camels to St. Simeon, Dr. Ken slowly turned as he heard the familiar click of my camera as I catalogued yet another important part of the trip, *the art of the deal.*

"What another photo?" He laughed. "Of all the groups I've traveled with I've never seen someone take so many pictures!"

Digital photography was not yet at its pinnacle and most of the group had 35 mm cameras. I carried one hundred rolls of film! Each of the thousands of photos taken, have stories that have been shared endlessly.

The journey, and knowledge imparted, has been an inspiration that lives in the story. I will *always* be grateful to Dr. Ken for the incredible trip *and* allowing *me* to *lecture* in the Egyptian desert in front of the *Stepped Pyramid of Zoser*! My fifteen minutes of fame and glory all under the hot Egyptian sun with the backdrop of a pyramid that foreshadowed the Great Pyramids of Giza. What an experience, time, and incredible journey! Many thanks for an awesome trip!!!!

As always, I am most grateful for my mother, who introduced me to art and photography. Many, many cameras later and I'm still taking pictures, and leaving memories and a piece of myself with everyone who receives photos, memory books, and albums!

Deepest thanks to my friend and colleague Pam Walker for reading *The Agony Continues Michelangelo's Search for Art in 20th Century NYC*. I cherished our conversations as you completed each chapter. So glad you were able to learn more about art. It was you who inspired me to dig this manuscript out of the closet and start again. Your love for the arts combined with your friendship was like a beacon of light on this journey. Much, much gratitude!

To my friend Laura Coffey for her continued friendship, encouragement, feedback and passion for reading. How many books have we've read this year, I lost count!

Special thanks to the team at KCM Publishing for sharing another journey! The behind the scenes work and processes are fascinating and like a painting I truly, truly appreciate what it takes to bring the written word to life. Thank *you* for making *The Donation* a reality.

As always, deep gratitude to my husband Joe who never hesitates to assist by consulting Siri! He puts up with my creative spirit, provides inspiration when he doesn't know it, and is always worried if I really am going to make him a character in one of my stories! As always, *thank you* for the love, laughter, and putting up with it all!

Contents

Introduction

*I*n 1998 I moved from Alabama back to New Jersey with two large dogs, no job and of all places – with my parents.

When I mention I am from New Jersey, most who know anything about the state, from either living, visiting, or hearing about us from a host of comedic jokes will ask, "What's your exit?"

In New Jersey, telling someone the exit you live off of from the two major roadways, the Garden State Parkway or New Jersey Turnpike, automatically pinpoints the location or the area of the state you live in - North, South, or Central.

"Exit Identification" is extremely significant as it gives one a host of additional information about how one may speak, potential tax bracket, what sports team you may be a fan of, and whether or not you refer to a common breakfast food, as *"Taylor Ham* or *Pork Roll."*

This unique system of classification is part of the many cultural idiosyncrasies of the state and brunt of many jokes!

Why do I feel it's necessary to even speak of any of this?

Living off Exit 80 now classified me as residing, *"down the shore!"* Translation: near the beach, boardwalk, and more of a reason for friends to come and visit! *This summer was going to be bursting with fun!*

My parents saw things differently! The boardwalk, jet skiing, beach and the nightlife were *not* on their radar. They wanted to know *what* was I going to do with the *next* chapter of my life?

My mother suggested I take a computer course. Not my skill set or interest, I would later enroll in the Museum Studies Program at Seton Hall University in the fall of 2002. I was working full time in retail, teaching art history courses as an adjunct, and now traveling over an hour north to exit 144 just to take this class!

The course included extensive field trips to view art in New York, which added more time to my already jam-packed work schedule. The trips turned out to be magnificent and allowed me to see some of the world's greatest paintings up close.

The final outing of the semester unrivaled the rest – it was to the conservation lab at the Metropolitan Museum of Art in New York, where the work really happens! Statues, centuries old, greeted our group as we watched conservators and learned what it took to restore some of the world's greatest art treasures.

The final assignment was to write a paper regarding the process of how art gets into an exhibit or a museum.

Instead of regurgitating facts and formal terms, I found myself writing an actual story entitled, *The Donation*, for the assignment. A story-as if you pulled a book off the shelf from the library. What the *hell* was I thinking, I pondered as I completed the assignment. I didn't set out to do this, it just happened. Writing was what I really loved and wanted to do.

While I received and A- *with* comments, I already knew I would *not* be finishing this program. *The Donation* focused on a collection of Egyptian artifacts, specifically canopic jars that were bequeathed to the museum. After the course ended *The Donation* sat in a box on the shelf gathering dust.

Why canopic jars? I became intrigued with canopic jars after I took a class in Egyptian art while studying for my master's degree. In January 2000, I travelled to Egypt and was mesmerized by the canopic jar collection at the Cairo Museum. Not only for their artistic development but their purpose – the eternal resting place of certain organs (stomach, liver, intestines, lungs) during the mummification process and the *lengths* the Egyptians went just to preserve organs.

I collected canopic jars as I travelled through Egypt. The market in Cairo was my greatest find, as I would later use them as pedagogical devices for teaching.

As they sat on my desk and shelf, I began thinking what if…what if the canopic jar with the Jackal head or the Falcon held the key to some power…and *The Donation* was born.

It was years later, now living off exit 74 when I pulled that final paper off the shelf and started to revise it. After years of sporadic writing The Donation ultimately wound up being divided into three parts. I hope you enjoy the journey!

"The only impossible journey is the one you never begin."

Tony Robbins

The Donation

PART 1

The Gift

Chapter 1

New York City
September 2012

Sounds from the computer keyboard echoed through the room. A soft glow emanated from the desktop lamp providing the only light in the dark office. Excitedly, the man pounded away quickly as he couldn't type his thoughts fast enough. He had but an hour or two of sleep and was awake before the sun had begun rising.

His insomnia, coupled with the success from the benefit he attended hours before, left him restless. He had later spent the evening with model and socialite Charlotte Newberry. She'd been seducing him for months. He avoided her, as her wealthy father was a fellow board member. A few too many drinks, the Dolce & Gabbana black strapless dress, and slit that revealed her shapely legs, left him wanting her more than ever. He quickly forgot about her father and the ramifications of his rendezvous.

She slept peacefully as he departed her lavish apartment.

His doorman, accustomed to his late hours, smiled and offered cheerful greetings as he entered his building on the Upper East Side. He showered, changed, and headed off to work.

His office was his cure; his safe haven away from the realities of a life he had long buried. He worked to leave the past behind.

His Armani suit was neatly pressed and hugged his wide shoulders. Not a wrinkle was present on his starched white designer shirt also by Armani. He jumped in his chair, startled by the ringing of his private line. He backspaced, corrected the phrase, and continued typing. The ringing of the phone persisted.

"Who could be calling at 5:30 a.m.?" he muttered as he glanced at the antique grandfather clock across the room. He had hoped to finish his report to the board of directors regarding his latest acquisition and monetary donation before the office staff arrived.

The ringing echoed loudly in his spacious office. He misspelled two words and typed another sentence incorrectly. "Damn." He shook his head annoyed and yanked the black phone from its cradle. "Hello," he hollered tersely into the receiver.

"Ah, Boudreau, I knew I'd find you at your office," the voice laughed. "Don't you ever stop working?"

Chapter 2

ohn Pierre Boudreau recognized the voice immediately …Montgomery Rutland. He switched the call to the speakerphone before dropping the receiver into its cradle.

"Rutland, if you worked harder, your museum would have a better collection. Why do you feel it necessary to disturb me so early? What do you want? To borrow more art for another exhibit?" he taunted as he scratched a day's growth of facial hair he neglected to shave. The women loved it and he didn't care.

Montgomery rolled his eyes in annoyance. "And give you another reason to mock me and my museum. The media coverage, courtesy of you no doubt, was enough at our last show," he chuckled.

Boudreau smiled wickedly and leaned back in his expensive, black leather chair. It was ergonomic and designed especially for his body movements. The comfort it provided made him forget about his old shoulder injuries and fractured bones from years of excavating and climbing.

"Now, Montgomery, you know I had no idea regarding the extent of the media attention you would receive. I only donated some pieces from my collection to your show. Which *you* requested!" he stated firmly making sure to put extra emphasis on the word "*you*" to remind his rival of the debacle months earlier.

"Come off it, John Pierre, that media circus was perpetuated by *you*. They highlighted the art from *your* institution so much that it overshadowed our exhibit."

"Again, did you forget it was art that *you* requested?"

"I'll keep that in mind next time I plan another exhibit," he interrupted. "If it wasn't for these new customs procedures at the airports, the objects would have arrived on time."

"Well that's what happens when you don't plan and research, old friend. Now I'm sure you didn't phone to re-evaluate your failed exhibition so state your business."

"I guess you haven't heard?"

"Heard what?" Boudreau snapped gruffly.

Chapter 3

The voice on the other end chuckled as if he knew a secret. "I'm surprised. The great John Pierre Boudreau, director of the infamous New York Museum of Art hasn't heard. You must be losing your touch?"

John Pierre raked his fingers through his brown hair. At the age of forty-two it was lightly streaked with gray. He had thought about dying it. The older women said he looked distinguished. He really didn't care what they thought as long as they donated money. And they did. Like the Nile River that runs through Egypt, staggering contributions flowed from their wealthy coffers into the museum.

He was getting agitated and disliked being out of the loop, especially when it came to the art world. Montgomery was the director of the Museum of Ancient Antiquities in New York. They both were competitors, adversaries and even after what had transpired between them, still managed to remain civil colleagues. The friendship they built long ago had been torn apart, but he knew he was to blame. Montgomery never believed his story. He sighed heavily and shook his head as if the memories from the past would erase themselves for eternity.

If Montgomery was calling this early the news was surely important. He reached for his coffee and took a sip. "Enough with your riddles. I know how much you enjoy tormenting me, but I have no time for your foolishness. I have a full agenda so spit it out or I am going to hang up!"

"John Pierre, have you seen today's newspaper?" Montgomery questioned. His voice was quiet and calm.

John Pierre recognized the seriousness in his tone. He put down his morning coffee and shuffled through a pile of papers on his desk. He was so excited with getting word to the board regarding the success of his latest acquisition he neglected to look at the morning papers. He had thrown them into his leather briefcase as he hurried out the door of his penthouse suite.

Montgomery heard the rustling and waited. John Pierre raised his eyebrows in shock as he gazed at the headline on the front page.

John Chesterfield Whetherbee III. Dead at 62!

Chapter 4

Stunned, John Pierre scanned the article – **death in plane… crash… pilot…killed on impact…billionaire oil mogul… returning from business trip overseas…unwavering community service…supported groups…donated…also known for impressive art collection…body not recovered….**

Chapter 5

"*B*oudreau, are you still there?"

John Pierre laid the paper on his desk and felt shivers run through his body as he shuddered in disbelief. "I can't believe it," he whispered as he leaned back in his chair.

Still in shock he could feel the blood draining from his face as he recalled their most recent visit. "I just saw him last month during my visit to Paris. We dined together after our trip to the Louvre."

Montgomery knew how close John Pierre and Whetherbee were. They both met John Chesterfield Whetherbee while in graduate school. No one ever called him by his first name. He was simply known as Whetherbee.

Montgomery and John Pierre were roommates and best friends. Whetherbee had been a guest speaker for one of their courses and changed both their lives. Life events would challenge their friendship and history together. Despite their differences, Montgomery knew his old friend was hurting. "I'm sorry J.P., I know how close you were."

John Pierre was speechless. He stared at the paper dazed. His friend and mentor, was gone? He was like family. Dead? He couldn't believe it.

John Pierre could feel the tears burning in his eyes. He swallowed deeply, took a deep breath, and composed himself. "Whetherbee was an extraordinary man. Not only is he a great loss to the business and art world, but the philanthropies he supported will suffer too. Why, he was my biggest donor and benefactor. But you knew that, of course, and that's why you're calling isn't it, Montgomery?" he snapped curtly.

Montgomery knew his old friend was distraught and ignored the comment. He closed his eyes and stretched his shoulders as he leaned back in his chair. His voice was barely a whisper. "He was my friend too J.P., despite our differences. Maybe you can erase the past, but I can't. The reality is…he's gone, and his collection is massive!"

John Pierre Boudreau or J.P., as he was often called, had become one of the shrewdest men in the art world. He had contacts all over the continent. His striking looks and charm helped him convince potential donors to sell even when they weren't considering it! Under Whetherbee's tutelage, he had become a remarkable businessman, and known for his ability to procure art from across the globe. They often battled over pieces. And bested one another on many occasions.

Like the threads of an ancient tapestry, he was also part of Whetherbee's circle of friends. He knew who had money and possessed the resources to negotiate. Endowments were plentiful.

Whetherbee was not only one of his biggest supporters but his closest friend and confidant. Whetherbee's death would certainly be disastrous to the art world and John Pierre's museum.

"Have some respect Montgomery, the man is dead."

"Dead or not J.P. I know you *too* are thinking about his collections and who is going to get what. What do you think he left to our museums?"

"Well, I'm sure we'll find out soon enough," he retorted a bit tersely. Annoyed at his friend's comment and furious at himself for the truth it held. He hung up wondering about the next recipients of the billionaire's celebrated art collection.

Chapter 6

Five Months Later
February 2013

"Muriel," John Pierre barked into the intercom. "Cancel all my appointments for today," he said quickly.

"All of them?" she questioned a bit shocked. Her boss *never* cancelled a full day of meetings.

"All of them," he snapped.

"But sir," she stammered, her voice rising an octave in surprise. She stared at the phone perplexed before pushing the speaker button again. "You have a full day. A press briefing for the new exhibit, meetings with the curators from the Egyptian, Greek, and American wings, a conference call with the Louvre, a meeting with the board …"

"I appreciate your concern Ms. Cambridge," he interrupted abruptly as he retrieved his suit jacket from the coat rack near the door. "I have been summoned for a legal matter that is unavoidable so please re-schedule everything!"

Chapter 7

John Pierre was seated next to Montgomery in the prestigious law firm of *Winston, Toby, Chester, & Princeton*, with other inheritors for over six hours listening to the reading of John Chesterfield Whetherbee III's last will and testament.

He was a generous man. The billionaire had no surviving heirs and had never married. He left parts of his fortune to loyal friends, organizations, and charities he supported. His vast collection of paintings, sculptures, and artifacts was given to museums and galleries across the globe. Montgomery received a collection of ancient art and antiquities worth millions.

They were shocked when the executor had read the next paragraph. "The sum of twenty million to the Museum of Ancient Antiquities." Montgomery's mouth hung open. He never anticipated such an exorbitant amount.

"And finally, to my friend John Pierre Boudreau, director of the New York Museum of Art..."

John Pierre stood on Madison Avenue and dialed his executive assistant from his cell phone. "Schedule an emergency meeting with board for tonight."

Chapter 8

The Board

John Pierre greeted each of them and exchanged pleasantries as they filed into the boardroom. It was a strange cast of characters, who despised his youth, confidence, and the monetary endowments and art that he brought to the museum. No matter what he did, it was always a battle to get something accomplished.

They preferred the old ways and tried to stifle the growth of the museum. He learned to play their political games, but he knew they hated his success and relationship with Whetherbee, who was even more financially powerful then all of them. They tolerated one another. But he knew with Whetherbee gone, things could change.

"John Pierre," Robert Buckingham III acknowledged a bit brusquely as he entered. He was the CEO of a major clothing conglomerate, Milano. A traditional man, he often clashed with J.P. for the unconventional way he fell into the position of museum director. The plan to nominate his friend, LaChance Davidson, a prominent director at the Louvre Galleries in Paris, was surprisingly halted before he knew what had occurred. He hated the fact he was forced to vote for John Pierre instead.

Robert arrived with George Newberry, the CEO of *Commerce Financial*. They were two powerful titans in the business world and fellow art lovers. George scowled at John Pierre as he entered. He and Robert grabbed coffee and chatted with the other members as they arrived.

John Pierre already knew why George was pissed.

Mary Douglas Rockefeller Harding not only was born with money, but she married into it as well. She was a descendent of the infamous Rockefeller family. Recently widowed, she spent most of her time involved with a multitude of philanthropic ventures and sponsoring art exhibitions. John Pierre was surprised to see her after the reading of the will.

Anthony Meyerson was the former mayor of New York. He seated himself next to Jocelyn Stevens Dowing, whose husband was a congressman who spent most of his time in Washington. She was also exceptionally wealthy and funded many exhibits and acquisitions. Their body language suggested they were more than friends.

Leo Thomas Winterberry was the president and CEO of the famous jewelry syndicate Napoleon's. He also worked with the insurance companies supported by the museum and made sure appraisals were accurate. George Newberry had appointed him. They were acquainted in the business world. He never said no when George wanted something. He loathed John Pierre's contacts and relationship with Whetherbee.

Nicholas Stockport was a well-known architect and decorated the world with his buildings. He was also professor and dean of the humanities department at the prestigious Columbia University. His blond hair, blue eyes, and charismatic charm made him a magnet for all the ladies, including his students.

He sat next to young Lindsay Tavistock, the new curator of the Egyptian collection, recently hired, hopefully to bring some fresh perspective for the younger crowds. John Pierre watched as they smiled and whispered together and wondered how well they really knew one another before she was hired.

The last to enter was Victor Ray Marshall, the founder of the world's leading Software Company – *Razor* and Monroe Saxton, the museum's head conservator.

Chapter 9

John Pierre spoke about nothing important with the members as they arrived. Lacey was not present, and he didn't question anyone about her whereabouts.

While he and the board despised one another they all had *three* things in common.

The first was their mutual dislike for one another. Enemies were made and lines had been crossed as the years passed. The politics and infighting continued like an athletic event.

The second commonality was money. Each possessed financial wealth. They were born with extensive portfolios, married into families of monetary wealth, or increased their family fortunes tenfold from lucrative business ventures. John Pierre had his own money, but because his lineage was questionable, he wasn't considered one of them.

With money came connections. They knew the right people, associated themselves with the celebrity world and helped convince others, including their wealthy friends to donate. More importantly they were passionate about art and the decisions made at the museum.

The final common thread of the group – they all had *secrets* and reasons for disliking John Pierre. With Whetherbee's help, John Pierre had become a force to reckon with in the art world. Without Whetherbee, John Pierre knew his job was at risk.

Chapter 10

"*T*his better be good Boudreau," George called. "I have investment bankers, from all over the world flying in."

John Pierre raised his hand to silence the older gentlemen. "I apologize to everyone for the short notice. The timing is unavoidable, but I have called you together this evening to discuss the recent bequeath to the museum from John Chesterfield Whetherbee III."

Chapter 11

" *F*inally! It's about time! Those damn lawyers… You would think they were protecting a flawless diamond. The way this was handled was a disgrace," Leo snapped.

"He actually left us something even after you stole that entire collection of rare Greek vases out from under him? After that, I thought he'd cut all ties with you and this museum," Anthony expressed, shocked that Whetherbee left a gift.

Victor Ray agreed. "And what about when you out bid him for that Renaissance statue and the Minoan bronze?"

John Pierre laughed. "Gentlemen, Whetherbee held no grudges. You misunderstood him and his affinity for art. It was a game to him, always a competition. He had more money than he knew what to do with. He could out bid anyone or purchase whatever he desired. But what purpose would that serve?

"He knew that art belonged in museums for all to enjoy. If he amassed an enormous collection, nobody would see it. He once told me he would have to spend more time wondering how to keep it all secure and safe from the threat of thieves! It wasn't worth it.

"He enjoyed the sport of hunting for treasures and antiquities. He relished in the bidding process, and keeping others including myself in the field alert. Sometimes he purposely created bidding wars just to ensure the seller would receive more than he asked for! He found the entire activity amusing!"

"Well let's get on with it. Tell us *what* that crazy old man has left *the museum*," Mary Douglas Rockefeller Harding smiled, as she purposely emphasized her words.

John Pierre knew she was sending a message to him. Mary wasn't happy about the recent distribution of Whetherbee's foundation. After learning Whetherbee was not going to continue supporting one of her philanthropies, she left the lawyers office irate.

John Pierre knew she would remain cordial and try to get the money from him or one of his connections to continue her charity.

Chapter 12

*J*ohn Pierre smiled and proceeded to read the letter.

Dr. John Pierre Boudreau,

To my friend and favorite of all my museum colleagues - I have enjoyed debating with you about art and engaging in our marathon contests to procure some of the world's grandest artifacts. I took great pleasure in snatching away from you many objects and collections or making sure the bidding was out of your reach so the artifacts would land in someone else's stuffy museum as yours was already bulging from its foundations with art!

As you are aware, I have always had an affinity for Egyptian art and antiquities. You once asked me of all the pieces I owned, what I treasured the most? Well, what I give to you is the <u>most cherished and prized possession of my life and entire collection</u>. They are one of the few items I have enjoyed obtaining and gazing upon over the years.

I am bequeathing to the museum a crate of canopic jars. What is so spectacular about this collection? Again, I must reiterate, what I am leaving you are a set of <u>my favorite</u> and <u>most beloved possessions</u> – a set of solid gold canopic jars! You are the only person who would understand and know *what to do with them. Where I obtained them – well their provenance doesn't matter.*

There are an additional one hundred crates, which contain mostly canopic jars and artifacts from the tomb of King Tutankhamun. They have never been displayed to the public. A complete catalogue list of the contents is enclosed.

*The entire collection must **<u>always</u>** remain in the museum.*

I want this collection to be exhibited not only in the most prestigious museum, but also, to be protected and placed in the hands of someone who is as passionate about art as I was. I know you will produce a conspicuous and grand exhibit as you unveil my gift to the world. Oh, there is one other thing. The reason the gold jars have never been displayed is due to the Curse of Anubis.

I am sure this gift will complement your collection of Egyptian art. If you choose not to accept the gift, my attorneys will take care of their placement. Please advise them accordingly. If you choose to accept the jars they must forever remain in your museum. They must never be sent on loan. My attorney will present you with legal documents to ensure their final home will be with you my dearest friend.

I hope you enjoy them as much as I have. They represent a culmination of my life's work.

Fondly,

John Chesterfield Whetherbee, III

Chapter 13

" **W**hat the *hell* is a canopic jar?" Victor Ray demanded. Lindsay sighed. As the new curator of the Egyptian collection, she couldn't stand these board meetings. She understood that the members were important and valuable for their financial support, influence, and standing in the community, but they rarely knew much about the historical aspect or significance of objects and paintings. It was mentally draining, trying to explain their prominence.

She removed her glasses and rubbed her eyes. "A canopic jar contained the organs from a dead body and was placed in the pharaoh's tomb after he was mummified. They were constructed of a variety of materials including limestone, black clay, wood, basalt, alabaster, or faience, to name a few, and have a long history of development.

"Eventually the lids were shaped and molded to represent one of the four sons of the God Horus. Each son protected a specific organ. Duamutef took the likeness of a jackal and protected the stomach. Webehsenuf, the falcon-head, was responsible for the intestines. Imset was a human-head and safeguarded the liver while Hapi, the baboon-head, cared for the lungs.

"The sons of Horace were protected by four powerful goddesses, Neith (Duamutef), Serqet (Webehsenuf), Isis (Imset), and Nephthys (Hapi).

"There were also associated with the four cardinal points north (Nephthys), south (Isis), east (Neith), and west (Serqet).

"What makes this donation so impressive is that it contains a set of *solid gold jars*. It's a one of a kind and probably is the *only* set in the world. There is no museum currently on record as having such artifacts in their collection."

"What an incredible donation," Jocelyn said cheerfully. She clasped her hands together and added, "Just think what it will do for the museum! The ownership and the value of the objects will strengthen our prestige. Subsequently enforcing the museum's status as one of the foremost art institutions in the world. Where do you think he unearthed such items?"

Leo, the jewelry conglomerate, laughed and said, "Whetherbee was a billionaire with a lot of time on his hands. He had friends everywhere." Leo didn't care what the decision was, he would do what George wanted.

Anthony chuckled. "Perhaps he won them in one of his famed card games! You know how much he loved poker."

Robert rolled his eyes. "How absurd, Anthony. He was a lover of the arts like all of us. Why is it so difficult to believe that he obtained these legally?"

"You really think that? I've seen a lot over the years and never trusted that guy. He was one shady character!" huffed Anthony.

Leo shook his head in disgust. "I agree. Whetherbee was a con artist. How could he possibly have acquired such treasures? I never *trusted* that eccentric oil magnate! Always showing up with art, artifacts, and undiscovered treasures as if he snapped his fingers and they appeared from decades past."

"Who cares? He left them to us. Consider the publicity," Jocelyn gleamed. "If our exhibition and marketing strategy is executed flawlessly, a display as such would bring more people to the museum increasing our revenues and leaving us money for future exhibits and acquisitions."

George shook his head annoyed. His eyes darkened as he glared at John Pierre over his glasses. "I can't believe that bastard left crates of jars and *not a dime* to this museum! This is your fault J.P! You and your *damn games* with Whetherbee!"

John Pierre swallowed hard. *Like he needed to be reminded.*

George was a financial man. He needed to see reports, proposals, and where the profit was going to come from before he made any decisions, but something else was bothering him. Newberry slapped his hand on the table for emphasis. "What you say may be true, Jocelyn, but I agree with Winterberry. It's too suspect. We don't know anything about these jars. And, furthermore, I don't like this idea of a potential curse! It could lead to disaster."

John Pierre didn't like Newberry's tone. He could sway the board members to vote no. He also didn't like the way he scowled at him earlier. He was afraid he already knew about his escapades with his daughter Charlotte.

"What kind of disaster?" Meyerson asserted.

Chapter 14

"*L*ook, Meyerson," George gestured, "people don't like witchcraft. It could keep them away from our doors. Our goal is to create exhibits that would attract people to the museum. The last thing we want to do is discourage and scare people away."

Inconsiderate bastard! George had a habit of calling the men by their last names, a habit from his days in the service. John Pierre had politely asked him to address people appropriately and he laughed and told him it was the best way to keep people in line and to remind them who was in charge.

Anthony dismissed him with the wave of his hand. "Anyone who believes in curses is foolish."

Mary Rockefeller Harding had been quiet and finally spoke. "Foolish or not, Anthony, there are people who don't believe in black magic and sorcery. They could protest. I can see it now…the public lined up outside the museum, picketing the exhibit. Such a spectacle could ruin this institution!" she finished.

"Oh, you're being overly dramatic," declared Jocelyn.

"You," Mary directed as she pointed her finger, "are just worried that it would be difficult to convince those snobbish and egotistical friends of *yours* to support such a program."

Jocelyn ignored the comment. "Mary, consider this curse for a moment. Why…it adds a sense of mystery to the jars. Think of the enhanced publicity and media hype. And with John Pierre's marketing expertise he would create a suspense-driven campaign that surely would cause people to come just to see these jars. Further, combined with the exhibit Lindsay and her staff would develop around the jars, I can only imagine the revenue it would generate."

Chapter 15

ocelyn smiled smugly. Whetherbee had left money to her family's foundation and Mary had received nothing. She was still gloating and knew Mary was livid. She had decided she would support John Pierre tonight just to spite Mary.

"Curse or not, we still need numbers to look at," George claimed.

Mary wasn't convinced. "This is absolutely ludicrous," she cried in disbelief. "Don't you see how this curse could have an adverse affect? Remember what happened when they opened Tut's tomb? Look at all the terrible things that befell those associated with that discovery."

Anthony regarded the older woman and laughed. "Mary, you have seen too many movies." He looked at his watch. The truth was he could care less about the donation; the only thing on his mind was his meeting later with Jocelyn at the hotel. Whatever she wanted he would vote for. His resentment toward John Pierre hadn't abated.

He was furious when John Pierre didn't support his bid for re-election. Whetherbee stepped in and reminded him of some incriminating photos of him and some model that would be distributed if he didn't leave John Pierre alone. In return, he received a seat on the prestigious board. Whetherbee alluded to the fact that John Pierre knew the location of the photos when he challenged their whereabouts. Since he wasn't sure if John Pierre knew about the photos or if they still existed he would probably vote in favor of the jars; unless George told him to vote no, he would support him.

"Anthony's right. Those incidents were attributed to radiation or mold spores that may have attacked ailments the people already had. It's still inconclusive," Lindsay said nonchalantly.

Anthony stood up and removed his suit jacket. "I think the curse would enhance an exhibit. As a former mayor of New York, I can tell you that this city has it all. There are the voodoo spiritualists throughout the boroughs. Numerous telepathic, clairvoyants, and those who claim they have extrasensory abilities litter the yellow pages of the phone book. Psychic and tarot card establishments exist throughout the city. Mediums with their crystal balls, divinations, wizardry, and sorcery have assisted the police department on innumerable instances. The local and national television stations host psychics and mediums that converse with the dead. And cursed art, well why not? It just adds something else to the plethora of entertainment and activities the city has to offer. It's mysterious and New Yorkers and tourists would go for it!"

"Of course they would," shouted Jocelyn. "Just think curses and lost jars, especially ones of pure gold, never seen before. And then there are the items from the King Tut's tomb. Relics - from the tomb of a pharaoh, who is shrouded in mystery, puzzlement, and doubt? Who was he really? How did he assume a throne at such a young age? How did he die? Was he murdered? If so, who did it? Then there is the disastrous display of his body? The peculiar preservation attempts contradict the established mummification principles.

Perhaps the jars are another piece of the puzzle? By simple ownership, our museum may provide answers to some of the aforementioned questions. This discovery and the publicity… why the financial impact for the museum is incomprehensible. And think, of the jars of solid gold, they are probably priceless!"

Chapter 16

"I agree with Anthony," Nicholas quickly added. He had remained silent, letting everyone express his or her opinions. He had his own reasons, but he wasn't about to reveal all of them.

He was angry that Lacey was absent. They spoke earlier. She had a new assignment and was going overseas. She would be sorry when he told her what she was missing. He was trying to send her a text, but it was returned as 'unavailable at this time.'

"And why do you agree with Anthony, Nicholas?" John Pierre questioned annoyed that he was playing with his iPhone.

"The very presence of the jars would promote increased scholarly research. This museum already has achieved national recognition as a place of erudite study with our library, conservation labs, and impressive collections. Such a rare and mysterious acquisition is sure to promote, encourage, and attract an abundance of academic activity. The Egyptian collection will continue to be a place for learning and study for young school children and high school and college students.

"Furthermore, our Egyptian collection contains one of the foremost and impressive assortments of objects in the world. The jars and their secrets will only enhance the existing collection by creating more awareness of the Egyptian culture and its burial practices. We can't ignore the influx of scholarly exploration, visitors and students, which will generate the monies that George keeps reminding us that are needed and necessary."

Nicholas folded his hands and smiled confidently, challenging John Pierre to retort. *As he answered a text from one of his students agreeing to meet her for a late dinner he thought, how dare he doubt my knowledge or think I'm not paying attention.*

Leo rose from the comfortable maroon leather chair and began pacing around the room. "You're all forgetting that publicity of this nature, positive, negative, or both, is equivalent with heightened-security. And jars of solid gold, that we can't even determine a dollar amount for, opens up new discussions regarding security.

Victor Ray, Robert, George, and I all operate big businesses. A major component of our daily operations *is* security. Victor Ray spends millions protecting his latest software secrets from the hands of hackers and insider theft."

George huffed and added "Leo spends billions on keeping those expensive baubles that I am forced to purchase for my wife safe from thieves. Robert is protecting the potential embezzlement of his unique clothing apparel empire from other couturiers and garment makers. And, like them, we would have to spend money constructing special showcases to guard against the theft of these cursed jars."

He took a sip of his coffee and continued. "More guards would be required for the duration of the exhibit. A higher payroll can be anticipated. This need for continuous security and increased staff would persist after the exhibit ended due to the very nature of the gold and their unknown provenance. Think of it, people, twenty-four-hour security! More money! Money we probably can't afford.

"Our payroll is already astronomical and is getting worse with all the other priceless acquisitions John Pierre has been collecting lately. The salary appreciation alone over, say ten years, and the continuous maintenance for the security systems to ensure we keep current with the technology is going to cost *more* money!"

"George is right," Leo stated. "I've spent my life in the jewelry business implementing new security systems and researching ways to guard against theft. And once you install a system, it needs constant upgrading. We currently spend an enormous amount on our high dollar computer and security system for conversions and modifications to revolutionize ..."

Chapter 17

"Technological progress is unavoidable Leo," the architecture professor interjected.

"Thank you for reminding me, Nicholas," he spat. "Of course I know it's unavoidable and necessary," he shouted. "That's my point it's still going to cost *money*! Victor Ray will agree with me. And if it weren't for his knowledge in the software business, we'd probably would be spending more money!"

Victor nodded his head in agreement. He wasn't sure which way he would vote, but he was angry that his daughter Rachael wasn't hired for the curator position. It forced her to take a position at a museum in Germany. His wife was constantly flying back and forth just to visit. John Pierre's vote was the vote that decided her fate.

"So what?" Jocelyn spat. "So we have to spend more money. That's what this business is about. Our mission is to raise the money to increase awareness and provide continuous art exhibits. Look at the Louvre. How do they do it? The *Mona Lisa* is priceless. Nobody can assign a monetary value to the famous Renaissance portrait, which has its own private guard. It has a multitude of security systems constructed into the bulletproof glass she is encased in. Their program seems to be working and they haven't had any calamities since the Vincenzo Perugia episode in 1912."

Nicholas chuckled. "She's right, Leo. The *Mona Lisa* draws millions. She is perhaps the most visited female in the world."

Leo sat back in his chair and gestured furiously at the architect professor. "That painting has an aura of its own, Nicholas. You can't compare da Vinci's work to the acquisition in question. The *Mona Lisa,* was created in a period and culture of high art. Its theft in the nineteenth century was during a period of great vicissitude."

"Technological advances helped contrive an expeditious outpouring of information. This created an unprecedented awareness of the painting and the artist that continues today. You can't compare the paintings rise to fame with the canopic jars," Leo said indignantly.

Nicholas laughed at the old man's antiquated view. "Why not? Are we not more technologically advanced? The dissemination of information is quicker than ever. I'm sure our media campaign will be grand enough to call attention to the exhibit and draw thousands. The curse will only enhance the show. It will attract more people to the museum. Teachers will return with their students each year. People will tell others. You know the power of information by word of mouth. More people, scholars, documentaries, literature, merchandise…it all equals more money!"

"You're forgetting one thing, gentleman." They all turned to the soft voice.

John Pierre was worried if she would approve of the gift. Mary was from old money and preferred traditional art. She had a strange relationship with the playboy Nicholas Stockport. The family had many skeletons and John Pierre suspected Mary had a few too.

Mary had remained silent but listened carefully to the arguments of the board members. The art world had changed. She may be old, but she had enough sense to know that all the debates had merit, but it was difficult for her to accept.

She came from a generation where people wanted to come to the museum to view art. Acquiring art was simple as was planning an exhibit. There was no pomp and circumstance. People just came. But those people who came were affluent. They had money.

Today the audience was different. The media and computer world could reach any demographic public at a moment's notice. And if the exhibit was big or fascinating enough it could draw crowds of thousands. Technology was so advanced that new discoveries had changed old theories. Planning exhibits and acquiring art was a complex business. If not carefully considered, tested for authenticity, the potential for mistakes could disgrace, discredit and bring scandal to the institution within minutes. Museums now functioned like big companies. They were corporate giants who were in the business to make money for the continuation of education and the display of art.

Chapter 18

"What is it that we are forgetting, Mary?" Anthony asked. "How do we know the jars are authentic?" she replied.

"Boudreau," Buckingham called; like many, he also called him by his last name.

John Pierre stopped writing and looked up from his legal pad. All eyes had turned toward him. He was barely listening to the conversation, for it was the same every time new acquisitions were in question. He was wondering why Lacey wasn't at the meeting. She would have convinced them of the importance of the gift.

"Boudreau, are *you* listening? In your opinion are the jars genuine?"

John Pierre sat quietly for a moment. The corners of his lips rose slightly. His eyes twinkled. And as if someone had bugged the room, he quietly whispered, "I am *sure* of it. I had the unique opportunity to examine them at the law firm in a private room. They are authentic. The gold…it gleams like it was made yesterday in Leo's jewelry factory. The curse is written on papyrus. The ancient hieroglyphic text on the document is also well preserved; it's as if it was made yesterday. I couldn't believe it."

They all stared at John Pierre as he talked about the objects. They knew that look. It was one of awe, and disbelief. His face was resplendent. His eyes illuminated his desire for the canopic jars. They knew he wanted the objects for the collection.

Chapter 19

*A*nthony was the first to speak. "In regard to cost, we may be able to save some money. John Pierre, you said the jars are complete. If there are no repairs necessary, no conservation will be needed. We would only need to build appropriate display cases and monitor them for future deterioration. The jars would become part of the continual preventative maintenance analysis with the other objects in the existing collection. What is your opinion, Monroe?"

Monroe was apprehensive. As chief conservator, she was excited about the donation but didn't like to make mistakes. Mistakes in one of the most prestigious museums were not only costly but could ruin a career. She wasn't about to take unnecessary risks. She rubbed the back of her neck. "You think it's so simple. You all seem to have forgotten some of the most important questions. We don't know where these jars came from. We don't know how they were stored. In some tomb, the sand, or perhaps in Whetherbee's attic? We don't know if they've ever been used. Were any organs ever placed in them? There are too many unknowns! Their changing environments could adversely affect the integrity of the materials they're constructed of. While we are aware of the conservation needs required for these types of objects from the existing canopic jars in the permanent collection, we still need to evaluate and study moisture, relative humidity, and the appropriate lighting. If there is any indication that they have been buried in the ground then we will need to examine salt efflorescing…"

"Save the scientific gibberish for the laboratory, Monroe," George snapped. "The end-result is once again *money*! If we choose to accept this acquisition you had better be prepared to look for ways to cut costs! You can start by utilizing the million-dollar conservation lab in the museum to find ways to save money," he roared.

Chapter 20

" *I* mpossible," she said acidly. "For a show of this magnitude, a complete analysis will be necessary so that the appropriate measures will be taken for authentication, display, and to ensure preventative maintenance…"

"Yes, I believe the board is familiar with the conservation routine. The bottom line is that it's going to cost money!" George stated testily. "I don't understand why Whetherbee couldn't just leave the museum money! Instead we get crates of dusty old jars – something that is going to cost this museum additional monies to prove they're genuine!"

He shook his head and pointed at John Pierre, "This is all your fault. You and your outlandish schemes and games with Whetherbee have once again cost us *money*! I think its Whetherbee who is getting the last laugh!"

Monroe huffed. She looked at Lindsay and they shook their heads in disgust - annoyed with their lack of scientific knowledge and refusal to understand the importance of preserving objects for future generations; they were already worrying about the cost and looking for short cuts.

"The philosophy is the same every time we acquired new artifacts. If it looks good, then just display the object in the museum!" Lindsay returned icily.

"Is money the only thing that you're concerned about?" Monroe added. She was sorry she said it. The words just came tumbling out. She was irritated because John Pierre just rearranged some of the exhibits and she now had to rush to complete the projects. The last thing she wanted to tackle was these jars. It would be another vacation put on hold. She had just cancelled her last trip to Paris to see her boyfriend LaChance. She was hoping he would find a job in the States, but nothing was happening. She knew with Whetherbee's death the board may try to get rid of John Pierre. If that were the case, she would petition for LaChance to apply again. She'd heard he lost the job to John Pierre years prior.

George's eyes bulged from their sockets. His jaw tightened. "Listen here," he gestured toward Lindsay and Monroe. "You both forget that money is my business. And I must be doing something right or I would not be the CEO and president of the largest financial network in New York, the United States, and internationally. As curator and conservator," he pointed toward them, "I understand your passion for art and your roll in the museum but there are other factors we must consider. How quickly you forget how your exhibits are funded?" He snapped sharply. "Do you forget who pays your salaries or who buys the chemistry and machines that clutter your labs? The donors and the public that's who…."

"Don't be ridiculous, George. Of course we're aware of where the money comes from," Monroe interrupted. "And if we endow or ask people to invest money and it turns out to be a hoax – our credibility as a business will be ruined! Wouldn't it? I'm sure you will agree that complete research will be necessary in this situation," she finished vehemently.

"Look, ladies, I mean no disrespect to your areas of expertise," George spat. "I understand the need for research and its importance. Do you think I put together successful billion-dollar deals without research? And when an item needs to be eliminated due to budget constraints, compromises must be made. I've listened to your arguments but for an exhibit of this magnitude I'm sure there will be some compromises! And those compromises may begin in the conservation department! But that's why we're here to discuss and arrive at the best possible business plan that meets the needs of all parties involved! I also understand that, in this case, there are no room for errors!"

Victor Ray nodded in agreement. "He's right. And who would be waiting in the wings? John Pierre's friend Montgomery! He would capitalize on our misfortune with publicity and steal our donors."

"I apologize for my comment. I just think that you are being overly dramatic."

"Monroe," Mary said sharply, "money is the backbone of this museum and *your* research. George, Leo, and Victor Ray have raised important issues that we need to consider. Additionally, we need to talk about the publications necessary. There are the brochures, exhibition catalogues, literature, and promotional items! Think of the money that would be wasted on such preparation if the objects turned out to be fraudulent. I do not claim to be an artist, but the Rockefeller family has donated, supported, and collected art for countless decades. And I can't say that I've ever heard of gold canopic jars."

Chapter 21

"*O*f course you haven't," laughed Jocelyn. "Your family has been looking at too much stuffy art over the years. That's all you're accustomed to viewing." Jocelyn was having second thoughts on how she was going to vote. She was afraid she had been spotted with Anthony through an acquaintance of John Pierre's.

To further complicated matters, John Pierre politely rejected her advances at a social event month's prior and she was further humiliated when he left with a younger female. The incident still stung.

Laughter echoed throughout the conference room. Mary ignored the comment and continued. "Lindsay, you are one of the foremost experts on Egyptian art, are you familiar with these lost jars?"

Lindsay sighed. "I can honestly say that I'm not. However, I have a cadre of contacts and colleagues to consult with, so it won't be too difficult to research."

Unlike Mary and despite her issues with John Pierre, Jocelyn secretly liked the possible acquisition. There was a sense of mystery about it that was intriguing. "Look," she said as she studied the group. "You all must agree that an acquisition as such meets the mission statement of the museum – education, creating awareness of art and other cultures for the public…"

"Yes, that's true but at what price?" George interrupted.

"Meeting the goals of our mission statement could be rather costly. And then we'll be stuck with these objects," he added gruffly.

"This museum is already bulging from its foundations with art. Storage space is at its maximum capacity. And now you want to add one hundred crates packed with pottery? Look at all the stuff listed on this manifest! Remember that crate of ancient Greek vases that Boudreau just *had* to have? Where are they *now*? *Still* packed in the crates awaiting restoration and taking up space! The space constraints, cost of the security, the required climate control, appropriate storage conditions needed, the added staffing…"

"George," Anthony interrupted sharply. "Think of it this way…after ten years, the jars will have appreciated in value and you could sell them and use the proceeds for another acquisition, exhibit, or perhaps to build a wing to the museum in your honor."

"Not really. The stipulation was that none of the collection ever gets loaned out," Nicholas reminded everyone.

Jocelyn shook her head in disgust. "Gentlemen, let's not lose our focus. I think we are all in agreement that the philosophy of the mission statement would be satisfied, so let's hear some dialogue from Lindsay about a potential exhibit. What do you think it will take to put it together?" she asked.

Lindsay turned toward Jocelyn and shrugged. "The possibilities are endless. We can focus on burial practices, or customs in Egypt, mummification, or concentrate solely on the canopic jars. I would like to consult with my staff. Whatever we decide, we have a complete collection here and could relocate the required objects into one of the exhibition rooms or incorporate them with the permanent collection. I doubt we would need to borrow objects from other museums, as our own collection is quite comprehensive; hence, we could save money!" she finished as she glanced at Newberry.

"Well, Boudreau, it's getting late. What are your thoughts?" snapped George, who was furious with John Pierre and his escapades with his daughter. It had been eating at him every time he looked at John Pierre.

John Pierre had been silent as he listened to the board and two of his most respected staff members debate over the positives and negatives of the gift. He scribbled notes, watched, and listened carefully to the arguments. He only spoke when called upon. He didn't like to offer his immediate thoughts for fear he might sway someone's opinion. This was just a preliminary discussion. The dialogue was necessary for everyone to start thinking in terms of why or why not the gift should be accepted or declined. There would be a final vote after pertinent reports were submitted.

Chapter 22

" $\mathcal{I}$ 've listened to the arguments and each of you has cited important issues. Although the financial costs and the dubious origins of the canopic jars appear to be the top considerations, I have no doubt the acquisition is worthy of further study. So I recommend we take action for a full analysis of the jars. But this is an incredible donation and I think we should keep it."

It was clear to everyone he wanted the collection and they had better start thinking how they would vote. George voiced his dismay once more, but surprisingly changed his opinion and agreed more analysis was needed.

John Pierre seethed when it was announced that Lacey had given her vote to of all people - Nicholas Stockport.

George confirmed it.

He and Nicholas stared icily at one another. Lindsay noticed the exchange and began wondering what was going on between the two. She was new to the museum and met Nicholas on an excursion in Paris last year.

"After viewing the reports we will finalize our decision. Lindsay you and Monroe will naturally work together. I will need the following reports: condition, historical, authenticity, exhibit, and financial. Work out of the conservation lab and use the current pottery area for storage. Call over to the design team and get a preliminary estimate on the exhibition cases. Consult old and retired scholars about these jars and track down any colleagues who may be familiar with Whetherbee's hidden treasure and its origins.

Contact Habid Sharig at the Cairo museum and ask if he'll permit access to Carter's original notes to see if we can find any more information on the artifacts and jars in the crates. Perhaps someone missed something. Phone Zawai Hawais, the inspector of the Great Pyramids. He may provide information. Abdoo Kamal is in charge of the Valley of the Kings and Tut's Tomb. Other scholars whose contributions may prove valuable include Rafi Mallah, Ahmad Nasir, and Hashim Farukh. I don't know their whereabouts but Hawais or Kamal should know. Don't forget about the German scholar Friedrick Kubek and French scholar Mark Lemieux. They are leaders in the field of Egyptology and may know something about the origins of the jars.

He stopped talking and poured himself a glass of water from the crystal decanter in front of him. He took a drink and sighed deeply as he returned the glass to its coaster. Everyone waited patiently before he spoke. Anxiety and apprehension were reflected in his eyes. He felt the pain deep in the pit of his stomach as he stated his next request. "And lastly…locate my ex-wife. As you know she is the leading authority on Egyptian funerary practices."

Chapter 23

*L*indsay had stopped writing. She hadn't made the connection until now. Her eyebrows shot up in surprise. She gawked in disbelief. "You mean *Lacey Windsor Boudreau,* the one who works with *National Geographic* and has made all those recent discoveries in the Valley of the Kings…the one that wrote that best selling book…the one that…"

J.P. cut her off. "I am well versed with her impressive resume." His voice was loud, brisk, and business-like. Everyone in the room held their breath. John Pierre never raised his voice to staff or his peers. He was fair and tough but kind-hearted. His demeanor changed at the mention of his ex-wife. "Unfortunately she is the one person that may be able to help solve this mystery."

"Nicholas," Mary said softly. "I ran into you guys at Stella Luna's in the park last month, you were having lunch and…"

Nicholas cut her off before she could utter another word. "We are friends Mary. I'm not her keeper. I heard she was on assignment and I have no idea where she is," he spat tersely. Nicolas was pissed she brought it up. Their relationship was private.

Mary smiled politely and thought to herself. *I saw you holding hands in that restaurant. Don't take me for a fool, Stockport, I facilitated your spot on this board and I can just as easily get rid of you.*

Upon hearing the news, Lindsay silently fumed. She thought her relationship with Nicholas was different. Apparently, he was dating John Pierre's ex-wife! She would deal with him later.

John Pierre seethed at the thought there was someone else and of all people, Nicholas Stockport. He disliked him. He was a playboy with a reputation of sleeping with students. The university didn't care to comment on relationships with consenting adults. Nicholas came from money and his family had donated millions to the university and supported their philanthropies. They didn't care what he did in his spare time.

John Pierre also heard Nicholas was after his job. John Pierre tolerated his presence due to his connections. The board liked him for his money and charismatic charm. For some reason Mary always supported him and J.P wasn't about to make waves with anyone from the Rockefeller family. He knew her importance, but never could put the connection with her and Nicholas together.

He shuffled the papers in front of him and stuffed them into the file and closed it abruptly; a clear signal that any more discussion on that topic was over. The knot in his stomach tightened at the thought of Lacey and Stockport together; well, it didn't matter. While he had no involvement in her life, just the thought of them together infuriated him.

He shook his head as if he could just shake away the past and spoke firmly to Lindsay and Monroe. "We will meet tomorrow promptly at 9:00 a.m. to discuss subsequent details. I will contact the lawyers and arrange for the reports or temporary possession of the jars for study. We have six months to make a decision on whether or not we desire this acquisition. If everyone is in agreement we will adjourn until further notice.

George waited for everyone to leave the boardroom before he confronted John Pierre. He pointed his finger at him. His eyes were like daggers. "I'm warning you J.P.; if this turns out to be a disaster, I will do my best to make sure *your* reputation is ruined and have you *fired*! And *don't* think I don't know that you were with *my* daughter last night. I suggest *you* stay away from her. I heard all about what happened with Lacey and what *you* did to her. I won't have you ruining my daughter's life!"

J.P. sighed heavily. George was a powerful man and John Pierre knew he was playing with fire.

Chapter 24

Six Months Later
August 2013

"*I*'m sorry, Mr. Boudreau, nobody will give me details on Lacey's location or what project she is working on," whispered Muriel. "The magazine only told me she is on a remote assignment."

John Pierre nodded. His facial features twisted in frustration. He wanted her input. They could get in touch with her if they wanted. He really needed her feedback.

Nicholas had overheard the conversation on the way into the meeting but acted as if nothing was amiss. Lacey sent him a few e-mails but gave no clues as to what she was doing or where she was. He didn't like their last conversation.

John Pierre refocused. "Welcome everyone. We have much to discuss today. You have had ample time to review the preliminary reports and we need to take a vote on whether or not we will accept the canopic jars left to us by our departed friend John Chesterfield Whetherbee. The deadline for our decision is tomorrow. I must contact the lawyers and make the necessary arrangements to accept or reject the gift. The floor is open for discussion."

The group discussed items cited on a memo from Lindsay Tavistock, the Curator of the Egyptian Department with input from the respective departments involved in this undertaking.

After an intense discussion of the preliminary and condition reports, the board *surprisingly* voted in favor of accepting the canopic jars into the collection. John Pierre was *positive* that some thing was amiss, but he didn't have time to dwell on what the board members were up to.

Chapter 25

May 2014

John Pierre was seated at his desk reviewing his notes for tomorrow's board meeting. They would be discussing the final details for the new Egyptian exhibit set to open in June displaying the canopic jars. His concentration was broken by boisterous voices in the outside corridor. Muriel was greeting someone and like schoolgirls they were squealing shouts of hello.

He jumped, startled by the banging of his office door as it swung open and connected with the framework and molding.

Sauntering through was Lacey Windsor Boudreau, his ex-wife. She was grinning like a Cheshire cat. She plopped down in the leather chair in front of his desk.

He skipped the preliminary greetings and got right to the point. "Well, it's about time you surfaced, Lacey. Where the *hell*, have you been? You know we have been trying to contact you since last August? Your assistant would not cooperate and said you were involved in a project overseas."

"Yes, so I've heard." Sarcasm apparent, she sat straight, shoulders back, confidently trying to sound as if she didn't care.

"I know you received my messages. Why haven't you returned my calls?" he asked, annoyed, as he threw down his pen.

"Well it's good to see you too, J.P. I hope you've been well…"

"Ok, Lacey, you know my schedule is hectic," he interrupted, cutting her off before she could utter another syllable.

He was furious that she appeared now. "I have been attempting to communicate with you. I thought for sure you would be interested in my latest acquisition."

"What, those silly jars?" She smirked, interrupting his story as he had done to her.

They stared at each other like two animals, sizing up their competition as they prepared for battle. Each fighting the distraction as one another's presence was wrecking havoc with their emotions.

Lacey was confidant she could face him after being away so long. His expensive suit could not hide the muscles of his well-sculpted body… Still perfect. He reminded her of a classical Greek sculpture that had miraculously come to life. He was a cross between the actor Harrison Ford's character Indiana Jones, Hugh Jackman, or Gerard Butler. His rugged handsomeness caught her eye on their first archeological expedition. He cleaned up nice in his suit and fine clothing but…

His eyes roamed over her like a laser beam. Her wavy, brown hair tumbled down her back and shoulders. Breasts and cleavage blatantly revealed through a crisp, white blouse that hugged her shapely form that she couldn't cover with the black blazer. He was grateful for the desk that separated them which hid his growing desire. He shifted in his chair. He had to focus.

"Ahh," he murmured shaking his head. "I see word travels fast. How could you dismiss my latest procurement? This is your area of study. Your love! What possible reason could you have for not responding to a discovery as such?"

She smiled confidently. "I am only interested in authentic art, genuine, or original art, like the objects that fill your museum. I have no interest in *fraudulent* art."

"*Fraudulent*," he snapped as his body straightened in his chair. He grabbed the desk with both hands. His eyes were wide open in shock. "You can't be implying that my jars are imitations?"

"Fake, phonies, call them what you like, but unfortunately that's what they are," she stated, innocently.

Chapter 26

ohn Pierre looked anxious. "Impossible," he whispered. Secretly he was nervous. Sweat was already dripping down his back. Knots were forming in his stomach. He sat at his desk staring deep into the brown eyes of his ex-wife. She was a well-respected scholar. She would *not* joke about something like this or, would she?

"*Verify* it, Lacey," he demanded. "Prove to me that they are fakes! Teams of experts and sophisticated machinery studied the jars in detail. How do you know this for sure? How can you confirm it?"

Lacey smiled wickedly. "It's in Carter's notes you fool. It's all right here," she said as she slammed a file on his desk.

He looked at the manila folder with contempt before he snatched it. He quickly read through the notes. He ran his hand through his hair in frustration. "I don't see any scholarly evidence, Lacey."

Lacey shook her head in disgust. "Of *course* you don't. You've *lost your touch*! You were once intrigued and interested in scholarly interpretation and the preservation of art. You were once an intense observer of objects. Now you're a businessman, who spends most of his time fund-raising, surrounded by and fancying the companionship of the rich and famous. Raising capital for exhibits and projects, you probably don't really have time to view or appreciate.

"You go from one party or press conference to the next and are no longer involved with the study of art, its history and discovery. You may be a noteworthy and exceptional executive, but at what sacrifice? I hope you are happy with your celebrity status and find what you were looking for with all *those women,*" she spat angrily, putting extra emphasis on those women.

"You don't know what you're saying, Lacey. If you would just…"

"Save it," Lacey interrupted as she quickly held up her hand indicating she refused to discuss the past or listen to any more of his explanations. "It's too bad, the art world has lost a great scholar to the business of running an institution for the protection and placement of objects." She folded her arms across her chest. "Look on page five of my notes, John Pierre."

He ignored her comments and began ruffling through the papers.

"At first glance, the hieroglyphic text on the bottom of the jars can't be deciphered. The script is unique, but I later matched it with the same scribble I found repeated in Carters notes.

"Since we can't decipher it, I'm sure your people just assumed that the remainder of the language is associated with this so-called *legendary curse*, which I've heard came with your gift from, Whetherbee. But I've done further investigation. You know…talk to the ancients, the elderly, the people on the street."

He silently smiled. Despite the abundance of technology, it was a methodology he adhered too and instructed his curators to do as well. He taught it to Lacey many years ago - when they traveled together - but that was a long time ago.

"Well, do you want to know?" She asked a bit too smugly.

He had stared at her a second too long as flashes of their life sped through his brain like a freight train.

She quickly looked away and ran her hand through her thick, brown hair.

He sighed heavily. His voice was soft and quiet. "What did you discover?"

"It's an ancient and rare dialect. I had discovered it in a remote spot not too far from the Giza complex. My team and I are still putting the pieces together but look at my notes and the translation of the characters. The word *curse* and the other numbers surrounding the text are speculative. Perhaps a map of some sort, or just scribble to confuse scholars.

"But when you decipher the language backwards the words translate to, *Made in Egypt Curse of the Pharaohs*," she demonstrated as she pointed to the notes. "The dialect is written backwards. We are still authenticating the letters but I'm positive it's a rare and specific dialect."

Chapter 27

ohn Pierre's face turned white.

"What's wrong? It looks like you've seen a ghost. Shall I continue?"

John Pierre removed the handkerchief from his shirt pocket and blotted the sweat from his forehead and neck. "I can't wait to hear the rest," he whispered solemnly.

"We also found some notes, ironically, from Howard Carter. Why they are at this particular site is perplexing since Carter's discovery of KV62, the Tutankhamen tomb was in 1922.

"King Tut dated to the 18th dynasty or the New Kingdom. The KV62 discovery was not even near the Giza complex. I speculate theft, he left them somewhere or someone else took them. I doubt we will ever figure out how they got there."

John Pierre was intrigued. "I agree. Anything is possible, the way tombs were plundered and with the multitude of archeologist's exploring the Giza site, who knows perhaps they were stolen, misplaced, left behind or maybe it was one of Carter's brothers?"

For a moment they spoke like two archeologists trying to put the pieces of the past together. It was like old times. Lacey was first to break the silence.

"An in-depth analysis of Carter's own notes indicate the *possibility* of the jars provenance to the Tut tomb. There are drawings of five canopic jars scattered across his pages.

"But these jars can't date back to the Old Kingdom due to their style and design as they have hieroglyphic text on the front and the lids are fashioned to the Four Sons of Horace. So, again, they have to be from a much later period. King Tut ruled in the 18th dynasty. So, at first, one would think your gold jars came from Tut's tomb."

John Pierre nodded in agreement.

"I heard you received one hundred crates of other artifacts from the Tutankhamen tomb. There are also various drawings of geometric shapes that match some of the hieroglyphics in the tomb of King Tut.

"I do *believe* Whetherbee gifted you canopic jars and artifacts that are most likely from the King Tut's Tomb. You would just have to match up the collection and hieroglyphics. Not a bad gift, but the museum already has an impressive collection from the King Tut discovery.

"But let's get back to the drawings of the five jars, which are all over his notes. Five jars and one with a question mark? What does it mean?

"Another section of notes discusses a need for money and problems for future funding. He also lists different mediums, alabaster, limestone, faience, clay, basalt, and gold. Probably deciding which medium to craft copies.

"There are other miscellaneous doodles, numbers, and the words - Curse of Anubis, Pharaoh's Curse, Made in Egypt repeated on the pages."

John Pierre examined the notes closer while she spoke.

"At first glance scholars may dismiss all this and attribute the doodles to a man scribbling while he recorded his thoughts as he was perhaps cataloguing the Tut collection."

"Or trying to figure out how to fool people by making fake art," John Pierre added disappointedly.

Lacey agreed. "Correct. I also recently uncovered some new documents written by family members who can confirm this theory of making and selling fake art. We also have to remember Carter himself *may* have discovered the tomb earlier and took some of the treasures before and after the discovery.

How could he resist? He probably figured a few items would never be noticed."

"Hmmm. He was like a modern-day tomb robber," John Pierre added.

"So how do the jars fit into all of this?"

Lacey stopped to shuffle the papers in the file and pointed to drawings of jars strewn about the page. "I have no idea what all the numbers are about. But he or someone kept sketching versions of the jars. On this last page he marked a fifth jar with a question mark. It was like a riddle. He was probably deciding to make four or five? Who knows?"

"But I only received four jars? So where is the fifth jar? Wait a minute? How do you know so much about these jars?" He scrutinized her face for clues. His eyes narrowed as he now stared at her accusingly. "The only way you could have known any of this is if you had seen the jars previously."

He saw the triumphant gleam in her eyes. "You *have* seen these before! But *where*?" he demanded.

She smiled wickedly as she recounted the story. "My husband…"

Chapter 28

"*Husband*! *You're Married*!" He shouted in disbelief. The moment she spoke the words, it was like someone punched him in the stomach.

"Since when? I heard you were involved with Nicholas but *why the hell would you marry him*? I *don't* see the connection?"

"Sorry, John Pierre, but my personal life is none of your business," she huffed.

When the hell did she get married?

"As I was saying, my husband, well he wasn't my husband at the time, but that doesn't matter now does it? Anyway, we ran into Whetherbee in Rome. He invited us to his yacht for dinner."

"Whetherbee's yacht! He is very careful whom he invites on his precious yacht. I can't believe he would have that *scoundrel of a playboy like* Stockport aboard. He loathed him!"

Lacey rolled her eyes in disgust. "As usual you're not listening. It *wasn't* Nicholas. I married *Montgomery Rutland*," she spat as if to intentionally hurt him. By the look on his face she knew she succeeded.

"Montgomery never said a word to me," he whispered.

"I asked him not too. It was a small and private ceremony. We never had the chance to announce it due to Whetherbee's death, and then I took an assignment," her voice trembled as the words flowed out.

"But Stockport? Mary Rockefeller said she saw you…"

"We were talking," she interrupted. "He wanted a relationship. I had already *decided* to marry Montgomery."

John Pierre closed his eyes and rubbed his temples. He felt as if she stabbed him in the heart. Now it all made sense. How could he not see this coming? *Montgomery* was always there. He was part of the group but always in the shadows. He was there that night. He had heard she spent time with Montgomery, but to marry him?

Lacey scrutinized his face and body language and knew she succeeded in hurting him. He deserved it for what he did to her.

"Where does Whetherbee fit in? Let me guess, he concocted some sort of scheme," John Pierre interrupted angrily as he threw the handful of her notes down on the desk.

Lacey laughed. "Well, sort of. I actually *never saw* any of the jars *or* artifacts you inherited. Whetherbee claimed he already had the merchandise. It's been in his family for centuries, passed down from one generation to the next. Ironically, Whetherbee was a descendent of one of the brothers of Howard Carter, the archeologist who discovered King Tut's tomb!

Whetherbee a descendent of the Carter family? Unbelievable. Why did I not know this? Then the jars could be authentic. John Pierre remained silent as she continued.

"No, they are fakes," she said reading his thoughts. "They had fake artifacts fabricated from the Tut discovery and sold them everywhere. They made a fortune. It was believed Carter and company purchased and melted items from local bazaars to create and pass them off as artifacts from the Tut discovery to continue to fund the project.

An intense interest in Egyptian antiquities followed the Tutankhamen discovery. Everyone had to have something, so why not produce fakes for money?

Their success prompted them to take their discovery a step further. Carter and his financial patron, Lord Carnarvon, and others perhaps contrived to fool the world centuries later. The scribbles in his notes are clues to the impending deception. One of Carter 's brothers or someone else must have continued the process."

"But I've had the jars tested. I saw the jars Lacey; they're solid gold. The reports concluded…I read them…"

Chapter 29

*J*ohn Pierre could feel the blood draining from his face. First, the news about Montgomery, and now this. *He read that report; it said, "solid gold."*

"They went as far to melt down some of the ushabtis; you know, those little figures the Egyptians put in the tombs to help with tasks in the afterlife. There were thousands of those little figures, and a few wouldn't be missed. The other jars were re-sculpted from the damaged objects that were already destroyed and scattered throughout the interior when they entered the tomb or from metal from the local bazaars and who knows what else they mixed in."

He reluctantly pressed on for more information. "So the gold is of a different time period, not provenance to the King Tut discovery. I'm guessing nineteenth century."

Lacey nodded in agreement.

John Pierre was in shock. "But the papyrus," he protested.

"The papyrus was Whetherbee's contribution. The papyrus is actual scraps from Tut's tomb, written from preserved ink that was found in the tomb. The pressed plant was a gift to Whetherbee from one of his billionaire sheik's buddies in Cairo who actually own some artifacts from the Tut collection."

His eye's narrowed with disgust. "And the riddle?"

"Ah yes, the curse of Anubis. A collaboration courtesy of me, my husband, and Whetherbee over a hundred-year-old bottle of red wine one evening! Something I *interpreted* from some scraps of papyrus from Whetherbee's Egyptian collection. I have no idea where he found them."

John Pierre read the translation she had scribbled in her notes.

Speak my words and take me home
The world awaits - for me to roam
Through zones and dimensions riches await
Unimaginable power is my fate
Armies will rise – the die is cast
Only I will be the last

"It's a rare dialect. I'm still working on its origins," Lacey added.

"But when did you see the jars?"

Lacey shrugged and shook her head. "I told you I *never* saw your jars until Monroe sent correspondence to my office. Which was emailed to me in Egypt. I was able to translate. I called Monroe to inquire about the jars and she told me about the exhibit and the gift from Whetherbee."

John Pierre glared at her suspiciously.

"It was only later when I began deciphering this unknown language, from the recent tomb discovery, that I knew what was written on the jars. Ironically it does translate to *Curse of Pharaohs* on the bottom, but also *Made in Egypt*. It was perhaps a rare dialect of a small group of people that manufactured the jars, perchance as a joke. So conceivably the jars *are* cursed in some way. You look a bit ill, John Pierre, shall I pour you a drink?"

John Pierre swallowed hard. He felt sick. His stomach was in knots. He shook his head no.

Lacey grinned and continued. "Carnarvon and Carter or others set out to fool the art world. They were making money from their production of fake art and wanted to see if they could deceive future generations. They anticipated technological achievement but had no idea what type of technology would be invented. The melting of the ushabtis provided the trace elements needed to perhaps mislead even *your* people. I don't know how it was possible that you missed this in the reports."

"I'm *telling* you Lacey that report said, *solid gold*. I read it myself! I'll prove it to you. He bent over and rummaged through the file drawer in his desk and handed her the file.

Lacey began laughing as she skimmed the report. "Really, John Pierre, it says it right here *not conclusive*…not real…trace elements…"

She closed the file and handed it back to him.

As if stricken with pain, John Pierre shouted, "I'm telling you I read that report…"

Her eyes narrowed as she interrupted him. "That file is from *your* own insurance company. I don't know what *you* read, and I don't care. I'm telling you the jars are *not* real Egyptian artifacts! Whetherbee said so himself. And don't worry; my lawyers have proof of my discoveries and full documentation regarding Carter's and Carnarvon's partnership. You can read about it in my next article!"

Chapter 30

"But why *me* Lacey. *Why did you go and marry Montgomery? What was that crazy old man after?"

Lacey sighed as she recalled the memory that evening in Rome over dinner. "The conversation began over the recent discovery of that fake painting at the Louvre."

"Whetherbee joked, what if I gave John Pierre fake art, would he be able to tell if they were real? He then spoke of jars and other artifacts he could potentially gift to you. His mission was to bestow the jars to someone whom he knew would not only be intrigued but also accept them as authentic. It all began as a joke."

"And you knew that if I tracked you down and questioned you further, I would have discovered the game instantly so that's why you remained so elusive..."

"I was on assignment," she shouted. "I knew nothing of this until I heard about it through Monroe."

"This is ridiculous! You married Montgomery and he said nothing to you?"

"He did, but I never thought about it until I made the discovery and then Monroe reached out to me. I just figured it was best to protect myself and keep my name out of the newspapers and avoid the ruin of my reputation if this came full circle. I wanted no part of Whetherbee's game, you, or this museum. At least I had the courtesy to come and tell you in person when I was sure of my facts and was able to decipher the writing on the bottom of the jars."

"Why are you still on the board of directors?"

She knew why but refused to admit it.

"Tell George to replace me. He should have done it already. I want no part of this place anymore!"

"But…your research and the lab you helped design?"

"Just let me keep my credentials and come in to use the lab."

They stared at one another, each haunted by inner pain that had fueled their anger. Lacey broke the silence first.

She sighed heavily, "Honestly, John Pierre, I never thought Whetherbee would go through with this. It was just a hypothetical conversation at the time. It began as a joke…it was a discussion over dinner and too much wine, which somehow took a life of its own. I *never thought* Whetherbee would go to such *lengths*!"

John Pierre wasn't listening. "Lacey, I could *ruin* your career by explaining to the press your roll in this repulsive conspiracy," he shot back.

She shrugged unaffected by his threats. "Go ahead and try. Try to prove it! The fact is Whetherbee left you some artifacts; you wanted to have an exhibit and some, if not all of the pieces, turned out to be fraudulent! *Your* reputation will be ruined not to mention *you* would be perceived as sounding like an embittered ex-husband. I have proof and have been working on this article and research. When the board of trustees gets through with you, they will see to it you never set foot in the museum again!"

"Lacey, I read that report and I'm telling you what it said!"

"I'm sure your impatience and exuberance for the show caused you to *miss* something," she interrupted.

"I would *never* miss a fact as important as that."

"Really? Well, that reminds me…" She bent over and pulled an envelope from her bag. "This is addressed to you, but it came in my mail. I wasn't paying attention and opened it." She placed the large manila envelope on the desk. "Apparently, it's the *final* report regarding the authentication of the jars."

He grabbed it and his eye and face contorted reflecting suspicion. "Why do you have it?" he growled.

"Really, we were once married. I often get your mail, and just put return to sender. Unfortunately I opened it by mistake. Due to the importance, I thought you'd want to have it immediately."

"This is impossible," he said nervously as he rapidly flipped through page after page as if there was some error. "There must be some mistake!"

"Well, if you don't believe my discovery, its all here in black and white." She laughed and ignored him. "Ha! To think you thought you had something. This was going to be the big one. The big breakthrough that was going to make you so famous and solidify your position in the art world! Even I can't believe you want to be remembered for being the master director of this stuffy old place!"

Her hands cut through the air as she continued to gesture wildly to emphasize her point and pent-up anger. "You were always so impatient, John Pierre. That's your downfall. What a waste of time," she laughed. "I can imagine how much *money* you have invested in the planning of this exhibit. I wish I could be there when you have to break the news to the board members and explain yet *another* disaster and *reckless* spending of money!

John Pierre was seething. He gritted his teeth and glared at her.

"Do you loathe me that much, Lacey?"

Lacey turned her head and stared into the distance. She could not look him in the eyes. Even now the pain was too raw. He was extremely handsome and still moved her and she didn't understand why. No, she was not going to do this. Her head whipped around, and she stared at him defiantly.

He could see the tears forming in her eyes before they turned into daggers as she lashed out at him.

"If you only had paid attention to *my* interest in Egyptian art and attended *my* lectures or read *my* books or papers, you may have learned something. But no you were too busy with this museum and catering to *all those women* and white-haired old biddies. This museum…" she gestured widely, "it has ruled *your* life! Our marriage…*you* destroyed it…something happened to *you* when *you* took this position," she shouted.

She glanced sideways to hide her mounting distress and then back to him. "The day *you* took over is the day *you* became married to me in name only. It's the museum *you* love and the artifacts in it! It's this musty old building, filled with some of the world's greatest antiquities that *you* are devoted to," she pointed at him angrily.

"This place and all *those women* ruined *you* and *us*," she shrieked. "I devoted my life *to you* and that night when I witnessed you with *them it* was the final…"

She threw up her hands in defeat. She could not go on. The arguing was a waste of time. She had nothing left to say.

Chapter 31

Exhausted, he leaned back in his leather chair and loosened the knot from his tie. He was not in the mood to reminisce about his failed marriage. But for the first time he realized how deeply hurt she was. The love they once shared...it was killing him to see her and listen to her pain…there was so much he wanted to say…he didn't even know how to begin. Nothing had ever been resolved between them. He couldn't even deal with his own guilt. Even as she stood yelling at him, he still wanted her. He removed his glasses and rubbed his eyes. "What is the point, Lacey? What did you hope to gain?"

She glared at him. Her body was on fire as the adrenaline surged through her veins. She hated herself for still wanting him and hated him for what he had destroyed between them.

She threw up her hands in disgust. "As I was saying, if you would have paid attention to me you would have learned that the Egyptians did not craft canopic jars of solid gold! They're fakes! Your own insurance company confirmed it."

John Pierre shot up out of his chair. His arm reached out to grab it before it hit the floor. "A joke is a joke, I get it, but this is my livelihood, my career – why would you even consider such a game? You could ruin me!" He shouted as his arms gestured in utter exasperation. Now he was furious. He ran his fingers through his hair in frustration as he spoke. Fueled by anger partly by the situation and also by years of unspoken words and failed attempts at communicating, he continued shouting, "What the hell has gotten into you? I would never play with your career like this! I know I hurt you, but you refused to listen to me. You didn't give me a chance to prove my innocence. To do something like this is unjustifiable."

The thought of her with Montgomery was making him ill.

Lacey felt sick to her stomach. He was right; it wasn't her style. The joke had somehow taken a life of its own and truth be told, she *never* imagined Whetherbee would actually proceed with the silly game and take it to such an extreme. John Pierre interrupted her thoughts before she could explain.

"Ha! I know exactly what this is about!" He walked around the desk and sat on the edge hovering over her like a hawk. He smiled and began laughing. "You're retaliating for when I spent so much time on that book I wrote about fake art!"

"You're impossible," she spat angrily as she shoved the chair back and stood up. She could feel the electricity between them ignite from the proximity of their bodies. She could feel the blood coursing through her, hot, as her adrenaline peaked once more. "I swear I knew nothing about Whetherbee's deceit. You don't get it do you? Laugh all you want if it makes you feel better… You have to live with yourself."

He scowled as his eyes narrowed. His tone was loud and icy. "Well, I guess I can say the same for you! You didn't waste anytime taking off with *Stockport* and then of all people my former best friend *Montgomery*…and who knows what you were doing with him before. That bastard was always around lurking quietly in the background just waiting…and now, *just like that,* you're *married* to him? *I can't believe it*!"

Lacey slapped him hard on his right cheek. The words and sound hung, like the dense fog that settles around the park in the morning after a heavy rain.

She gasped and brought her hand to her mouth. The tears filled her eyes like a dam ready to burst.

It was a low blow and he knew it. He had no business criticizing her choices. Who the hell was he to dictate what someone else did? He was sorry he said it. The pain in her eyes was evident. The words…their anger had gotten the best of both of them…

"Lacey, I'm sor…"

Just then Muriel's voice came through the intercom, "John Pierre, you have an important special delivery from the insurance company, also one of their representatives has been calling and needs to speak with you immediately, and Charlotte Newberry is on her way and she said to remind you the car would pick you up at 7:00 pm sharp!"

John Pierre forgot all about his date with Charlotte. He closed his eyes and rubbed his forehead. His expression spoke of despair and his voice was distant. "It's not what you're thinking, Lacey."

Lacey smirked and her eyes narrowed with disgust. "Really, John Pierre? Charlotte Newberry, why I thought you had better taste," she snapped bitterly. "You'll be out of a job when her father finds out."

"First Stockport and then Montgomery, who are you to tell…"

Lacey held up her hand as her voice increased an octave. "*How dare you*! You have no right to tell me what to do or whom I can spend my time with."

"But, Lacey, if you would only listen to the truth," John Pierre implored.

"Save it, John Pierre." She cut him off sharply. "What the hell happened to you? When did you become such a ruthless bastard?"

He closed his eyes as she slammed the door and departed with tears streaming down her face.

Chapter 32

The silence in the room was maddening. Their words hung in the air and gave him a headache as he replayed the conversation over and over again in his head. Charlotte had called again: her car was in traffic, but she would be arriving shortly, and he needed to be ready. He told the security staff to tell her he'd be right down.

He was in his private bathroom getting dressed when the ringing of the phone cut noisily through his quiet office. It was Montgomery. He sighed heavily. Montgomery was the last person he wanted to speak with. He couldn't let go of the past so easily and they had managed to remain civil to one another over the years. Montgomery was her friend too. He knew they spent a lot of time together, but he *never* imagined she would marry him.

"Yes, she just left," he barked into the receiver. "I believe congratulations are in order for you as well Montgomery. *You finally got the girl.* I'm sure I deserved it. I must compose my thoughts and think about how I will deal with the present situation. By the way, may I ask what your reason in this escapade was?"

Montgomery laughed. "Pay back, old friend, for when you stole that Picasso collection at auction from me in France! But seriously, J.P., I *never knew* what Whetherbee was really up too. It was a strange conversation that night. I *never* thought the discussion would become reality. I never understood what his motives were. He was a complicated man. You knew him better than anyone."

Perhaps I really didn't know him at all.

John Pierre rubbed his temples. His head was pounding. He reached into his drawer for some aspirin. "It doesn't make sense," he said as he swallowed the pills. "Whetherbee and I bested one another before. Why would he go to all this trouble to bequeath some useless funerary objects to me?"

Montgomery was just as perplexed. Whetherbee didn't leave John Pierre's museum one cent of his money, just the pottery collection. Whetherbee and John Pierre were *best* friends. He thought it was strange not to leave any of his millions or notable artifacts to one of the most popular and largest museums in the world. It was a slap in the face to John Pierre. He knew the board and prominent figures in the art world were talking. Even he had no clue or idea why Weatherbee would exclude John Pierre's museum from his will.

Montgomery cleared his throat. "Unfortunately, Whetherbee never revealed his reasons to me. You probably deserved it for your role in some art acquisition that he wanted. You know how he always wanted to make sure his games were played out to the end. You know how he hated to lose! Perhaps it's a message from the dead. Whetherbee is letting *you* know that even in death he got the last word!"

Chapter 33

"John Pierre, the insurance company…"

"I will take care of it, Muriel," he answered briskly as she held his suit jacket. "Can you tell me all the people who visit me on a daily basis?"

"Is there a specific date you are looking for?"

"The past three years."

Muriel was stunned. "Really, do you think I have time to go back and review your calendar? This is absurd. Do you know the amount of work I do for you and this museum? You can go back and watch the security tapes and that's if they are archived! I have no time; do you think I'm not doing my job?"

"Muriel, please," he interrupted. "Forget about it."

He glanced at his buzzing iPhone. Charlotte was looking for him. He turned the phone off.

"Do me a favor and call Charlotte and tell her I'm on my way down."

Chapter 34

John Pierre

John Pierre adjusted his tie as he looked at the window of his penthouse suite. The tie was silk, expensive, like everything else in his home. He carefully manipulated the material, as he made sure he formed a perfect knot. The view overlooked the museum and the famed Central Park. It was early and already signs of the hustle and bustle of city life were awakening. It was not quite six in the morning. Street vendors rolled their carts down Fifth Avenue to procure the best locations for selling food and drink. They offered an inexpensive alternative to those who could not afford the price of the cafeteria or restaurants in the museum. Still, there was nothing better than a warm New York pretzel or hot dog after a long day walking around a museum looking at art.

Buses, taxies, cars, and limos moved slowly as they drove toward destinations to begin their day. In another hour, the velocity of the automobiles would change. Driving slowly was not an option. People were already moving about to catch mass transit, take an early morning jog, or walking their dogs through the park.

The mobile art merchandisers were starting to arrive. The early risers were the smartest as they secured the best real estate for the marketing of their art to visitors. John Pierre knew them all. He made sure to stop by, say hi, and view what they were selling every day. They were all aspiring artists. First, there were the locals. There was Edgar Michaels, who drew exceptional pen and inks. Joey Rizzoli worked in watercolor. Violet Misty had a vast selection of photographs, and Cassidy Baily sold pastels.

Their themes were all the same: views of the city, famous New York landmarks, or copies of celebrated art that resided in the museum. Artists working with the same or other materials such as oil charcoal or pen passed through from time to time, but they came and went like the tourists who visited the museum.

John Pierre moved away from the window. The early morning sunlight was filtering in. Walking through his spacious living room, he stopped as he absently adjusted a Magritte painting that hung on the wall. An eclectic collection of art was nestled amongst the fine furnishings of the ten-room suite. Photographs, pottery from various centuries, parchment, paintings, drawings, and various souvenirs from his travels all over the world proved to be conversation pieces to those who had the opportunity to set foot in the famous bachelor residence.

John Pierre liked living across the street from his office. He disliked commuting. To him it was a waste of time and energy. He didn't like to rely on mass transit. Funny, it was one of the things that he and Lacey agreed on. They loved their work and wanted to be close to it. But that was a long time ago.

Now in the foyer, he grabbed his keys and wallet, and then he reached for his suit jacket and briefcase. His gray Armani was one of his favorites. It hugged his torso and was tailored perfectly for his six-foot frame. There was not a scuffmark on the leather Versace shoes or a wrinkle in his shirt or suit. He could have been mistaken for a model in GQ or any other of the current fashion magazines.

He was in perfect shape. He had risen early, had already worked out in his home gym, and was now ready for his coffee. He had an important meeting with the board today that he was not looking forward to. His thousand-dollar espresso maker could have brewed him the perfect cup of coffee. But today he was in the mood for Starbucks.

His mornings began with coffee, his newspaper, and reading and responding to e-mails. Between nine and ten, he'd start his tour and meet with his curators.

"Good morning! Hello, Mr. Boudreau," echoed through the various halls and galleries as his staff cheerfully returned his greeting. He made sure to say hi to everyone. Security guards, clerks, docents…nobody went unnoticed. That was the way he was. It was a lesson he learned from his first internship in Paris at the Louvre. His boss Jacque Viet Byront was not well received with the staff when he toured the galleries in the mornings. He was a scholarly gentleman who was Ivy League educated and spoke six languages. His specialty was Greek vase painting. He had published numerous books and was in demand for lectures.

He was also condescending and extremely critical. He yelled if there was even a speck of dust on the floor or walls. His face would turn beet red. It was a sign his blood pressure was up, and an impending heart attack was possible. His staff barely looked at him as he passed. They had their own communication system to alert one another that he was on his way. His employees called him all types of names and laughed behind his back. Nobody wanted to work for him. He was the most hated person in the museum. The request to transfer and turnover in his department was so bad, that the museum director had to assign other departments to cover the Greek galleries in order for projects to be completed on time. His status in the art world was such, that rather than fire him, the director chose to send him on a lecture circuit any chance he could. John Pierre had vowed he would never treat people that way.

Chapter 35

Museum Life

ohn Pierre admired the new acquisitions and collections as he passed through the galleries. He gave comments to the curators and made his own mental notes to have objects moved, cleaned, or added from the conservation lab.

He nodded to Lindsay and smiled as he passed under two colossal statues of Ramses as he entered the Egyptian collection. The statues were recently restored and found by an American archeological team at the Valley of the Kings. The Egyptian government had too many large statues and was happy to send them to America as long as the United States paid a donation to the Cairo museum and the shipping charges.

The Egyptian collection was naturally his favorite. As an archeologist he spent all his time looking for artifacts and evidence of the mysterious culture buried in the sands of the Egyptian desert. It was where he realized his love for his wife or ex-wife and ironically what caused his divorce. He tried not to think about it.

Chapter 36

The Mastaba

*H*e raised his hand in greeting to a docent who was lecturing to a group of eager students who were assembled around a descendent of the great ruler Ramses II.

"Ramses was one of the most interesting pharaohs. His life in politics began at the age of twenty or earlier when he ascended the throne and ruled for over sixty years. Not only was he a great ruler, but had many wives, hundreds of girlfriends, and at least one hundred children. His love of art and architecture is reflected in the magnificent temple built at Abu Simbel."

John Pierre smiled and moved on. The collection was one of the foremost in the world. Mummies, pottery, coffins, papyrus, canopic jars, jewelry, artifacts from tombs, utensils, weapons –thousands of years of history from the Old, Middle, and New Kingdom were displayed in the next fifty galleries.

John Pierre was giving his final tour notes as they departed the last gallery and proceeded to the mastaba. The mastaba was usually the first monument visitors entered, but he usually bypassed it as there were too many people moving in and out. Today he decided to enter the structure. The docent was lecturing to what appeared to be a group of middle school students.

"This is a mastaba – its Arabic for bench. These mud-brick structures littered the desert and from a distance look like benches. They were used to bury the dead and foreshadowed the development of the true pyramid. If you stack mastaba on top of mastaba and fill in the sides it becomes a triangle," she demonstrated.

"These are real stones?" a girl with braids in her hair asked.

"Yes, but you should not touch. The oils from our hands contribute to deterioration and decay, that's why the lower portion is covered in plastic, to avoid the temptation of touching."

"How did the stones get here?" Came another question.

"This was an enormous acquisition. The museum spent lots of money having the stones brought to the United States. They were numbered and reconstructed exactly as found in Egypt."

"What is this mark for?"

The docent sighed. She hated questions about that odd mark on the corner of the mastaba's interior. A replica of the mark was on display before entering the mastaba. It was a fun exercise for the scavenger hunt program for the younger children. She had no answer. "We are not sure. There is much speculation."

"Good morning, Mary," called a voice.

Mary stopped talking and looked up to find her boss, John Pierre, part of the group.

She nodded and held her breath as the museum director moved forward to the front of the group. He was a nice man, but it was a bit nerve-wracking to have the director listening in on your tour.

John Pierre smiled at the group. "Miss Mary is correct. We don't know what it is. We have no clues, only endless speculation by countless historians and scholars. It gives us all something to write about, procure grants for research, and allows us stuffy old scholars to fill journals and magazines with countless theories with the hopes that one of us will discover its purpose. What do you think it could be?"

"Perhaps it's for a post to move a coffin," a red-haired boy called.

"It's a current theory."

"Anybody else?"

John Pierre acknowledged the raised hand of a young blond girl. "How about an alter of some sort."

"Another current theory."

"I think the scribble around it could just be graffiti, like we see on the subway," someone shouted.

John Pierre smiled as the group laughed. "It's possible."

"What if it's nothing?"

John Pierre smiled. "Then we've wasted a lot of time trying to figure it out."

Laughter erupted from the students.

The mastaba or what was left of it was intriguing. It was an anomaly. Who build it and why remain unknown? Even his ex-wife Lacey, who was renown in the field of Egyptology, had no clue.

"If anybody has any other ideas what the marks could mean let Mary know and she will tell me. I hope you enjoy your tour of the Egyptian collection today. Mary is a superb guide and will continue to do her best to answer all your questions."

Chapter 37

The day dragged on. John Pierre was anxious about his impending meeting with the board later that evening. He did his best to keep busy and was grateful his executive assistant had over-booked his appointments.

There were constant conference calls with directors and curators from other museums. Acquisitions to follow up on, catalogues for upcoming shows to proofread, meetings with curators and staff, budget reviews, and an unscheduled luncheon with an investment banker who was thinking about donating money. He was in town for a last-minute business meeting and wanted to meet for lunch.

John Pierre wasn't interested in lunch today, but he'd eat for a potential fifteen-million-dollar donation, especially if it made the board happy. He had his staff set his private dining room with the best china and made sure the chef from the Gold Members Only Club was available to prepare the meal.

The investment banker wanted a gallery named after him and also wanted to sponsor an upcoming show. Name recognition – it was what his donors demanded. It was always the same - *give me something that I can put my name on so people will remember my legacy, and my generosity.*

They were no different from the Egyptians; only they didn't want a pyramid built, just a room, with a plaque bearing their name. John Pierre smiled. Only the people with money knew who was who as they walked from gallery to gallery, and that was only if they looked up at the nameplates as they entered.

The majority of the public could care less. John Pierre assured the banker there would be no problem naming a gallery in his honor. They spent the rest of the afternoon discussing the details.

He had minutes to spare for his meeting with the board as he rushed into the elevator. "I have a fresh jacket for you, sir," Muriel called as the doors opened and he hurried past her desk. "The notes you requested are typed and on your desk."

He didn't know what he would have done without Murial. She knew exactly how to prepare his documents. She knew how to field his phone calls. She knew how the museum operated, the paperwork involved, and who to phone in the art, business, and celebrity world when needed. She knew what he was thinking and needed sometimes before he did. She was five years older than him. He hired her when he first started at the museum. When his troubles with Lacey began and the divorce was finalized, he thought she would leave too – due to her close friendship with Lacey. He offered her the easy way out and said he would understand if she left. She was a true professional and said she never even considered it.

Besides Lacey, Muriel was one of the few people who really knew him.

Chapter 38

The Board

It was after six and John Pierre was exhausted. His meeting did not go as well as he predicted. The board members were furious! They were angry about the canopic jar debacle and the millions of dollars wasted in preparation for the exhibit. Nobody wanted to hear about his lunch with the banker and a *potential* fifteen-million-dollar donation.

George did his best to influence the group over every argument he presented.

John Pierre did his best to change the focus of the exhibit to fake art, but the suggestion was immediately dismissed. He wanted to have the jars retested but nobody supported him. "It's out of the question," Leo and Robert exclaimed.

"If you did your job in the first place none of this would have occurred. I managed an entire city. I don't know how we let you get away with running this institution the way you have for so long," Anthony, the former mayor, shouted.

Mary and Jocelyn both agreed and scolded him, like a child, over the exorbitant amount of money squandered.

To add to the humiliation, George and Victor Ray informed him that all his future expenditures need prior approval. In addition, appraisals and provenance reports would be scrutinized.

They blamed him for his impetuousness. They didn't like the fact that so much time and man-hours were wasted on a project that would never come to fruition. They also blamed him and his antics with Whetherbee as the reason the museum did not receive any money from his fortune. None of his past accolades mattered. The final argument was *how* and *why* Montgomery Rutland, received *twenty million dollars* and an impressive collection of art. Nicholas wasted no time provoking and swaying any decisions against John Pierre with every argument presented.

The board members were right; it was absurd. The museum looked ridiculous.

After the yelling and pointing fingers they spent the last hour warning him that his job was on the line if he didn't do something rather quickly to obtain art for a more substantial exhibit or find someone to donate a large sum of money to recover the monies lost.

To make matters worse, after the meeting George took him aside once again conveyed his unhappiness and not so subtle threats to end his relationship with his daughter.

John Pierre opened his mouth to speak but changed his mind. A retort about consenting adults and age would not have mattered.

Chapter 39

John Pierre sat at his desk staring at the four so-called gold canopic jars. They gleamed in the soft light emanating from the computer on his desk. He somehow convinced the board to let him keep the jars. He claimed it was his only connection with Whetherbee. George, Robert, Anthony, Victor Ray, and Nicholas disagreed and argued vehemently.

Mary and Jocelyn were more sympathetic - citing they were the only objects John Pierre had left from his deceased friend.

He still hoped they could be incorporated as a focal point for an exhibition on fake art.

Lindsey and Monroe were annoyed that he kept the objects on his desk and wanted them returned to storage with the other crates.

"This is a museum with tremendous security. Who is going to take them?" He argued.

He loosened his tie and continued to stare at the ancient artifacts. There was something about them that intrigued John Pierre. He still couldn't fathom the attraction.

He read Whetherbee's letter over and over — *"my most cherished and prized possession of my life and entire collection. They are one of the few items I have enjoyed obtaining and gazing upon over the years."*

It made no sense! There had to be a reason for this gift I'm sure of it.

For now he was content to look at them on his desk as they reminded him of his dear, departed friend, John Chesterfield Whetherbee III.

Chapter 40

ohn Pierre took a sip from the brandy he poured earlier from his personal bar. He hoped the warm liquid would help him relax. He sighed heavily, knowing that it would take more then a drink to clean up his mess.

John Pierre was convinced Whetherbee would not have sent these jars to him as a silly prank. And getting Lacey and Montgomery involved, well that was odd too. Whetherbee knew their history. He knew it would open old, painful wounds that he did not want to think about. Only Whetherbee knew the guilt he was suffering.

Although they both bid on art, they never set out to hurt anyone or cause damage to one another's career, and to play a prank of this magnitude that included both Lacey and Montgomery, it didn't make any sense!

He knew Whetherbee had more respect for him, this he did not doubt. They were colleagues and friends. There was something else that continued to bother him – why would Whetherbee bequeath useless pottery to one of the most prominent museums in the world and not leave any other art or monetary gifts? None of it made any sense. There were other reasons for the gift. He would make it his mission to figure it out.

For the first time in his career he felt empty and tired. Tired of listening to the board members and what they liked, didn't like, wanted, didn't want, and how much money it was going to cost. Money, money, money! It was always about money. He shook his head as he reached for the shiny canopic jar. He fingered the falcon head and removed the top. Lacey was right, he was losing his touch. Phony jars. If he were paying attention, he would have never missed something as significant as a fake artifact.

Why wasn't he paying attention? Because he was too busy! His schedule was hectic and demanding. He barely had time to read his mail. Endless meetings, conference calls, press conferences, luncheons, parties, and other events where he was boundlessly cultivating relationships and spewing the importance and prestige of donating money to the museum collections. He was too busy telling women with money how beautiful they looked. Too busy spending time with them. Too busy being charming. And for what? Money, money, and more money!

In the beginning, he liked the power. The power to acquire art, suggest and realize shows that he felt were pertinent to the growth of the museum and the art world. Eventually he became known as the celebrity art director. At some point the politics of it all had become a tremendous burden. When it happened, he couldn't recall. It just happened. He put the falcon lid down in front of him. He brought his hands to his face and rubbed his eyes before sipping more brandy.

The jackal headed lid stared back at him, grimacing, almost laughing at his predicament. John Pierre reached out and plucked the jackal headed lid off and twirled it between his fingers. "What are you trying to tell me? If only you could talk, what would you say to me?" His fingers continued circling the indentations and ridges of the lid. They were not perfect, and the bottom was not a perfect circle either.

"Damn you, Whetherbee! What is this all about? Why did you send me this collection?" He muttered.

Light suddenly illuminated his desk and the objects on it. The heads glared back ominously. He slowly turned in the expensive leather chair and looked out the window as another flash of lightening flickered brightly. He had been so wrapped up in his museum debacle he didn't even realize there was an impending storm.

The moon was full and glowed brightly in strange hues of orange and yellow. He held the jackal head and stretched his hand as far as he could in front of him. A shiver ran down his back. It looked sort of spooky with the moon illuminating it – almost as if it were going to come to life. John Pierre scratched his head in frustration and turned back toward his desk. The more he thought about it the madder he got.

He picked up the photo of him and Whetherbee in front of the Great Pyramids of Giza that sat on the far corner of his desk. Memories flashed through his head as he stared at the picture and thought of his friend. Drinking the best wine on his yacht in the south of France, trekking through the desert on camels in search of ancient archeological burial site's, dinners with his wife in Italy and all over the world. Their love for art was notable in every adventure they shared.

"Even for you this is illogical," he said to the photograph. "You couldn't just bequeath the museum some of your wealth. No that would have been too easy. Instead I get stuck with counterfeit old jars. I have the board breathing down my neck threatening my position as director. How could you do this to me? I thought we were friends?"

John Pierre sighed. It was late. He threw the photograph across the desk. It slid next to the other canopic jars. "Damn you, Whetherbee," he cursed loudly. "What are you trying to tell me? I know you. These jars have to mean something!"

Chapter 41

Thunder rumbled in the background. Lightning flashed illuminating the room. "Looks like we're in for a good storm tonight," he spoke to the jars as if they were his friends.

John Pierre was not ready to go home. He was agitated and felt extremely unsettled. He loosened his tie and wandered over toward the window.

The full moon radiated a mixed palette of orange hues in the now darkened sky. He watched as vendors and pedestrians ran about seeking shelter from the impending squall. He was restless and needed to clear his head. When something was on his mind, he knew the one thing that helped provide him with some perspective – a walk through the museum, specifically the Egyptian collection – his favorite.

He grabbed his jacket from a near by chair and absently slipped the jackal head in his pocket as he searched for a flashlight in his desk drawer.

It was ten o'clock. Between the emergency exit signs and the illuminated display cases an eerie glow was cast on the mummies and ancient sculptures in the Egyptian wing making everything seem a bit ghostly.

Thunder rumbled in the distance. Lightening flashed on the Temple of Dendur as he moved through the wing that overlooked central park. The raindrop's thudded loudly as they struck the roof. He ignored the monsoon that was brewing outside as he sauntered through the galleries. Lightening flashed and the thunder crackled loudly causing him to jump. He didn't know what he was doing as he moved through the exhibits.

Lightening continued to illuminate the galleries and the thunder was unusually loud. He immediately remembered the jackal head as he thrust his hands in his pockets and his fingers came in contact with the cool stone. He had to admit the thing looked menacing in the shadowy gallery. He held it up to the light. "What do you want with me? Why did Whetherbee send you and the rest of that damn, dusty pottery to me?"

John Pierre was so frustrated he could scream. He was normally calm and collected. But this entire ordeal had taken a toll on his emotions and rational thought process.

He stopped in front of a display case of other canopic jars. "Are these your friends? Do any of you know this sinister looking jackal?" he asked the jars in the case.

Nothing. All the heads of the other jars stared back at him. John Pierre sighed and muttered, "As if they're going to respond!"

He continued through the gallery, stopping at some of his favorite pieces of sculpture, pottery, and jewelry, and posing questions to the ancient treasures. "What about *you*, you ancient mummy, perhaps this jar was part of your tomb?"

To a headless statue from the Middle Kingdom, he laughed and said, "Or perhaps we have it all wrong and *you* have something to do with these jars that now haunt and fill my thoughts so much that I am unable to concentrate."

John Pierre rubbed his temples as he stared at his reflection in the display case. His headache was imminent. "Really, Boudreau, now you are losing your mind," he mumbled.

He was thoroughly disgusted. He had reached the main entrance of the Egyptian wing and was about to exit when the next round of thunder came. It was earsplitting. John Pierre stopped walking. His hands unconsciously covered his ears. He could have sworn the building was hit. He listened again and waited to see if the roof was collapsing somewhere in the building. It was then he noticed the mastaba.

Chapter 42

A ray of light illuminated the entrance. That was unusual. He went over to investigate. The lights were off, but the mastaba was lit. "What the hell?" He whispered as he tried to make sense of the electrical issue. His eyes scanned the floor and stones for some hint of an electronic device.

The light was quickly forgotten when he caught sight of the unknown carving in the corner.

"So, ancient jackal, do you have knowledge of this symbol?" He laughed as he held the lid toward the ancient markings.

That's when he saw it. The strange markings were similar to the ones on the inside of the lid. He silently cursed himself for not recognizing this before. He quickly knelt down and gazed excitedly at the strange lines and back to the jackal-headed lid in his hand. The lid felt warm, probably because he was holding it in his hand.

"Could it be?" He whispered.

He looked at the jackal head in his hand and thrust the base into the indentation in the stone.

It fit. His eyes widened in shock. "Unbelievable," he mumbled.

The enormity of the discovery and prosperity that could befall the museum filled his mind and like a tape player on fast forward he began thinking of the possibilities. But, at the same time, his historian and archeological instincts immediately took over.

Why? For what purpose?

He waited. Nothing happened.

He ran his fingers across the ancient hieroglyphics on the cool stone something he knew was forbidden. What was he doing? He quickly yanked his hand away. He slowly reached out again and tried to pull the jackal head out. It wouldn't budge. Damn. He sighed deeply and immediately thought about the absurdity of his impetuousness.

"What if it doesn't even belong in here? Great, just more ammunition the board needs to terminate my employment. I can see the headline now, Museum Director Lodges Fake Artifact into Prized Mastaba! Ugh!" he muttered. "This can't stay here. I have to get it out."

John Pierre sat down on the dusty floor, forgetting about his expensive suit, and stared at the jackal. "You mock me, jackal, but you have my *word*…one day I *will* learn *your* secrets," he expressed with certainty.

Moments later a smile of satisfaction suddenly crept across his face. "Words," he whispered. "That's it." He had read the words on the papyrus from Whetherbee's donation many times, but in the mastaba they were depicted backwards. The so-called Curse of Anubis!

Speak my words and take me home…the phrase had haunted his thoughts. The hieroglyphs on the stone were the same on the papyrus. He was sure of it. He read the hieroglyphics aloud, one by one and then ran his fingers across the jackal head. As he touched it, suddenly it turned like a well-oiled hinge as if he was opening a door.

Thunder boomed and darkness descended upon him.

PART 2

The Journey Begins

Chapter 43

ohn Pierre groaned. His eyes fluttered and he began coughing. He slowly rolled over. His muscles ached. He stretched and leaned on his elbow for support as he attempted to rise. His head was pounding. It was pitch dark. He recalled the mastaba and assumed the power had gone out. He was able to push himself upright and felt the cool stone through his clothing as he leaned back against the wall for support.

He rubbed his neck and moved his head from side to side as he attempted to massage the soreness of his muscles. He took a deep breath only to start coughing again from the thick, musty air.

He felt for his watch and pressed the light. His Rolex flashed four p.m. Impossible. I could have sworn it was around ten in the evening when I started walking around the museum, he thought to himself. "Don't tell me my expensive watch is broken. This watch has never failed; now I have to take it to the jeweler," he muttered, aggravated.

"What the hell happened?" He could immediately smell the dirt as he lifted his hand and started to rub his head then eyes. "I can't believe I was so tired that I fell asleep in the mastaba," he whispered in between fits of coughing. The thought of the museum staff finding him like this was alarming.

But why didn't they find me if it's four p.m.? Impossible that an entire day passed, and nobody came in?

It was pitch dark. He searched in his suit jacket, pulled his flashlight from the inner pocket and turned it on. His eyes followed the beam as he moved it along the wall. Surprised as the light hit the stone, he pressed his body back into the wall, frowning, and uttered, "I don't remember the hieroglyphics looking so crisp and clear. The colors are so vibrant. It looks as if they were painted only yesterday."

He made a mental note to congratulate the conservation team. The low relief carvings were just as sharp. It must be a new addition to the exhibit he concluded.

Arching his back he stretched again and started to get up, wanting to get a closer look, when his eye caught sight of a statue in the corner. "What the hell?"

The five- or six-foot Ka statue stood on a base in the traditional Old Kingdom style: stiff, formal and frontal. There was enough detail to define the features. No arms or limbs jutted forward as was the tradition for fear of breakage. One's spirit certainly couldn't exist in the afterlife with a broken body.

John Pierre rubbed his temples again. He was feeling disoriented as he could not recall a Ka statue ever being placed in the mastaba. Perhaps the curator added it for ambiance. Even from a distance he could tell something was amiss as the light from his flashlight moved up and down the stone. It was the stone; it was too shiny – something was terribly wrong.

Upon closer examination he realized there wasn't a mark on the stone. Not one nick, dent, or scratch. It was as if it was newly carved. He couldn't ever remember seeing this statue in the basement storage. There was even a fresh basket of fruit at the foot of the figure. He smiled bent down, picked up an apple and bit into it. It was real. It was a nice touch, but he made another mental note to remind the curator about the cost and to use wax fruit. "And they tell me I'm wasting money, humph," he grumbled.

John Pierre was ready to go home. He was tired and felt drained. He had a pounding headache and his muscles ached, which he attributed to falling asleep on the floor. He couldn't fathom how this could have happened to him. He continued to follow the beam of light from the flashlight. The dirt on the floor was concerning. He could not remember the mastaba having such a long, passageway, as the museum only had a small section of the ancient architecture.

As he rounded the corner an intense ray of light hit his face. He immediately brought his hands to his face to shield his eyes from the blinding beam. He looked away and turned off his flashlight before deciding to follow the light.

"What the hell is going on?" he screamed as he found himself on the ground. Again, raising his arms above his face, his eyes squinted as they tried to adjust to the glaring light. The ground was soft beneath him. He was having difficulty getting up.

"Sand!" he shouted.

As he tried to rise, he sank further into the soft earth. It was everywhere. Like a child his arms flailed about him as he attempted to rise. Once upright he began dusting himself off. His four-hundred-dollar Armani suit as well as his Italian leather shoes were ruined. "What the hell kind of exhibit is this? And who the hell put this sand here," he yelled harshly. "This is a disaster! It'll be tracked all over the museum!"

The light was blinding, and the heat was intense. But as John Pierre squinted and his eyes began to adjust to the dazzling sunlight, he gasped at what he observed before him. People, thousands of them working on what appeared to be the Great Pyramids of Giza.

He closed his eyes and opened them again. He must have hit his head really hard for the scene before him had not changed. His feet were unsteady as he took a few steps forward. He had emerged from the mastaba and was looking at the Giza plateau. He stood, staring wide-eyed at the fantastic site looming in the distance.

Chapter 44

$\mathcal{H}$is eyes squinted as he tried to adjust to the blinding light. In the distance he saw people - thousands of them. They filled acres and acres of what he knew as the Giza Pyramid complex. They were in the process of constructing the pyramids. Ramps, just like scholars had suggested, wound their way around the limestone structures. Animals and people were engaged in moving the stones. Ropes were tied to giant boulders while men pushed and pulled. Everyone was working. Like radar, his eyes scanned from right to left a few times as he tried to make sense of the apparition.

Mastaba after mastaba cluttered the landscape like a modern day fifty-five and older development. Giant temples with brightly painted pictures rose in the distance and around the complex. There was so much to see that John Pierre didn't know where to look first. Stunned, unbelievable and impossible was the only way he could describe what he was feeling and viewing.

He could hear his heart pounding loudly against his chest as his body trembled from the adrenaline that electrified every limb and vein. How could this be possible? Either it was a dream, or he was having a nervous breakdown.

John Pierre reached down, grabbed a fistful of sand and let it trickle back to the ground. The grains were soft and hot. It was real. He searched in his pocket for a handkerchief to wipe the sweat that was now dripping down his face. His fingers brushed the jackal head. "The canopic jar lid," he muttered.

Shivers ran up and down his spine. It was all coming back to him. The museum…the mastaba…the canopic jar…the lightening…the lid…the unknown hieroglyphic's…Whetherbee…

Chapter 45

The lid was quickly forgotten as strange grunting and snorting like noises interrupted his thoughts. He tried to focus on the sound coming somewhere from the left but was having difficulty making out the image as brilliant rays of sun were blinding him. He turned and ran back inside the mastaba to observe. Using his suit jacket as a shield he pulled it partially over his face, unsure of what was coming toward him.

"You can come out. I will not hurt you," the voice called in broken English.

John Pierre poked his head slowly around the entrance. Mastabas, pyramids and now a young boy on a camel stood before him. "Yes, you," the boy pointed. "Come forth. 'Tis ok. Do not be frightened."

John Pierre was cautious. He had no idea what was going on. The boy was dressed in a white tunic that draped around his body. More white cloth was wrapped around his head. Even through the clothing, he could tell he was thin. He looked to be approximately twenty years old. Scenes from movies like *The Scorpion King, The Mummy,* and *Cleopatra* flashed through his head as he studied the young man sitting on the camel. His smile was not threatening but welcoming.

The camel started grunting and spitting.

The young man chuckled. "Do not be afraid of Arthur. He is very old and does not like the fact that he is in the hot sun. Come out. I have been waiting for you. Whetherbee said you would come one day."

John Pierre stood up at the mention of Whetherbee's name. "What do you know of Whetherbee?" he shouted as he emerged from the mastaba.

"Come, come, we must get you out of the hot sun, and you can't go around dressed as you are. You will be *killed* if discovered!" He waved his arms feverishly. "You must come *now*, 'tis not safe." He then spoke sharply to the camel in an unknown dialect John Pierre did not recognize and the camel immediately sat.

Eyes wide in shock, John Pierre continued to stare.

"John Pierre, you must hurry; I will tell you all, but we must go now. Come, Arthur is old and cannot sit for too long."

The sun was blinding. John Pierre inched closer. "Who are you and how do you know my name?"

The young man glanced about nervously. "All will be explained but we must go, the pharaoh's men...they are everywhere...there is no time to talk...I will reveal all to you... Whetherbee said you would come...I knew it...you must come with me," he demanded.

"What kind of joke is this? What has Whetherbee gotten me involved with now?" John Pierre demanded. "I'm not going anywhere with you. You're a complete stranger. How do I know you are not going to abduct me?"

Arthur grunted. Abu was losing his patience. He spoke rapidly in his native tongue as his hands gestured impatiently. Although he could not understand the language, John Pierre was positive some of the words flowing from his mouth were expletives. "The only abduction that will most surely happen will be by the pharaoh's guards if you don't come with me now!"

"I don't care who you are. I'm not going anywhere with you. Not unless you give me some proof that you know who I am."

Abu sighed. "You want proof? I give you proof then you will get on Arthur?"

John Pierre nodded.

"Whetherbee said you would be difficult. Apparently, you have a multitude of scars across your back all resulting from an unfortunate incident at the Red Pyramid…"

"It's public knowledge. I spoke to a reporter about it last year," John Pierre interrupted.

"Did you include how you stole some important ushabti and other artifacts from the Red Pyramid and you were *stabbed* by one of the guards? Your wound healed into the shape of a triangle and Whetherbee said the guards fled, frightened. I understand the items you stole they sit on your desk in a muu-sm-em," Abu pronounced slowly.

"Museum," John Pierre immediately corrected the mispronunciation as he tried not to look stunned. The only person in the world that knew this was Whetherbee. Not even his ex-wife Lacey was aware of the unfortunate altercation he was involved in.

The archeologist in John Pierre took over, as did his curiosity. It was obvious the boy knew Whetherbee, and he needed answers. He headed toward the camel and climbed on. Besides, where the hell else was he going to go?

"'Tis good. Here you must put this wrap around you. You will frighten the people. Dressed as you are, they will think you are a demon of some sort. Hurry, my friend."

John Pierre took the cloth from the extended hand and did as he was told wrapping the thin, white material over his head and body. He certainly did not want to evoke any trouble.

"My name is Abu. Welcome to Egypt. Come, we go, and I will tell you everything."

John Pierre barely listened as Abu yelled commands to Arthur who immediately rose and started moving. He was more confused as he tried to grasp his surroundings and what was happening.

He was riding a camel in an Armani suit, and Versace shoes, in the Egyptian desert, supposedly in the Old Kingdom of Egypt. It was too surreal.

The Old Kingdom of Egypt…could it be possible?

Chapter 46

Abu was yelling and waving his arms at Arthur who had deposited them in a complex of small mud-brick structures that littered the desert sand. The site over-looked the Giza Plateau.

"What is this place?"

"'Tis my village. Come, it will be ok."

Arthur spit before he meandered toward the corral with the other camels. John Pierre ducked to avoid the flying discharge and followed Abu who had motioned for him to hurry.

They descended underground. He counted twenty steps of stone. The change in temperature was apparent with every step. He welcomed the cool air as he stood trying to get his bearings while Abu unlocked a door and ushered him in. While he could not see, he could hear Abu rambling about the cool room, mumbling, as he seemed to be searching for something. He was about to procure his flashlight, when light filled the room. "Ah, 'tis good. You see," Abu smiled proudly as he pointed to the lantern on the table.

John Pierre stared at the battery-operated lantern. He turned and glared at Abu. "The Egyptians did not have electricity or batteries, so tell me where we are because it is clearly not ancient Egypt. I am sure Whetherbee is behind this trickery. Explain yourself," John Pierre demanded.

"I tell you no lie, you are in Egypt," Abu replied calmly.

John Pierre chuckled at the absurdity. "Really? I saw pyramids; it would make this the Old Kingdom or the fourth dynasty of ancient Egypt. Tell me what year is this?"

Abu shrugged, "I do not know, Whetherbee told me once about your system of dating but I get confused with the math, so I think it is somewhere perhaps 2520, I am not sure."

Frustrated, J.P. threw up his hands. "Really. You don't know the date?"

"I am not a scribe so 'tis not significant. If you know our way of life you understand survival is more important and what class you are born into 'tis how you *serve* the pharaoh."

J.P was going to explode. He rubbed his temple and took a deep breath for he could not believe what he was going to ask next. "Who is your pharaoh?"

Abu smiled, "Oh, 'tis easy. I serve Khafre."

"*Khafre!*" J.P. shouted.

"Yes, yes," Abu responded excitedly. "Do you know of him?"

J.P. smirked as he waved his hand through the air, "Oh sure, we are best friends. I had dinner with him last week!"

Khafre was one of the great rulers of the Fourth Dynasty, which was the height of the building of the Great Pyramids. The dates when he ruled are suspect as are the dates of the dynasties and kingdoms.

"Explain how this is even possible? And where did you get that lantern?"

"You like my magic? It was a gift from my friend Whetherbee."

"Whetherbee. Humph. And what did you have to give him in return?"

Abu turned from the pot he was filling with water from what appeared to be a plastic water bottle and shrugged, "I show him where to find Egyptian artifacts. 'Tis all he wanted. I tell him it will bring great trouble, but he say to me, "Don't worry, Abu.""

John Pierre watched as he pulled of all things a box of matches from a niche in the wall and started a fire in an area that looked to be reserved for cooking. There was a selection of pots and pans in niches and in well-constructed counters fashioned in wood. Nothing made any sense.

"I show him the art, and every time he comes, he brings me more magic!"

If he wasn't dreaming and what was happening to him was real, then Whetherbee's acquisitions now made sense. Whetherbee was quite secretive and always managed to collect art. No scholars knew how he attained the pieces. Since he was able to provide provenance reports, which seemed genuine, nobody questioned him. He also had money and could afford to purchase anything, so nobody ever challenged him. Was this possible?

Impossible. He must be hallucinating or dreaming. He used both hands to wipe the sweat that was dripping down his face. His heart was racing, and he was sweating profusely. Nothing made sense.

He immediately removed the white covering and took off his suit jacket. Abu moved quickly about the room that was filled with wooden trunks, tables, chairs, and what could be considered a couch. Hay served as bedding for the wooden cots in the corner. Abu had taken a pillow and stack of blankets out and laid them on top of the hay. The interior of the mud-brick structure was sparse.

"Come, sit here. You will find more comfort on the soft cloth. I prepared us food and beverage."

"You have a Martha Stewart comforter and pillows and yet no real furniture or other things in this place," John Pierre stated suspiciously as he read the tag and ran his hand over the luxurious blue comforter.

Abu laughed. "Ah yes, Ma..tha St...w...at," he stumbled over the name as he tried to pronounce it. "Whetherbee said she is famous, like god of man-u-fact-uring...he give it to me...I like the colors...it brightens up the place. Come sit at the table."

John Pierre's eyes scanned the room. Brightly painted hieroglyphics and bas-relief sculpture covered the walls. It was unbelievable.

Abu placed some hot tea and pita-like bread in front of him. "I make this for you. I knew you were coming. You must eat to keep your strength. I assure you, you will need it, John Pierre."

John Pierre needed answers. "This is absurd. I don't believe it. How did I get here? What is this place? How do you know my name? What does Whetherbee have to do with all of this?"

Chapter 47

Abu smiled and raised his palm, gesturing and nodding. "Yes, yes, I tell you everything. But you must eat. You need your strength, or you will not be able to continue."

John Pierre sipped the tea and took a bite of the bread. It was tasty, filled with herbs and garlic.

"Whetherbee said you would come. And I have been waiting. Arthur and I check the mastaba every day. You are finally here," Abu rambled excitedly. He stopped talking and took a sip of his tea.

John Pierre frowned. "And where exactly is here?"

"Why, Egypt of course. 'Tis what I try to tell you."

John Pierre rubbed his temples. His head was still throbbing. "What year is this?"

"'Tis 2520 B.C., I think, but cannot be sure!"

"There you go again with that 2520 B.C. nonsense. So what you are telling me is that I have been transported, thousands of years back in time, to the ancient kingdom of Egypt."

Abu smiled and nodded, as he continued to eat his bread, shouting in between bites, "Yes, yes, you understand!"

"I don't believe you. Do you know how ridiculous that sounds?"

"Ah. Whetherbee said you would be difficult…"

"I am not difficult! I do not believe it! It's impossible!" he interrupted.

Abu shrugged nonchalantly. "Do you not have the canopic jars…the lid…then yes, 'tis possible? You have finally uncovered the secret. It is about time too. I was getting tired of looking for you every day and waiting!"

"Waiting…for me…you can't be serious…I demand you tell me where I am. I don't know what kind of prank he is pulling but this time he has gone too far…damn that bastard and what is your involvement?" John Pierre spat angrily.

Abu scratched his chin and laughed. "Ha! Whetherbee said you would call him a bas-tard."

John Pierre threw up his hands in frustration. "Listen here. Not five minutes ago I was in the museum and now, I am… well…quite frankly…I have no idea where I am and that is not good for me because I always know where I am and what I am doing…so if you know what is good for you I suggest you tell me what is going on," he yelled.

"Ok, Ok. John Pierre. I will reveal all. But first you must relax, 'tis not good for you. You need to adjust to the climate. I promise I will tell you what you need to know. But you must stop yelling."

Abu pushed a plate of food and tea toward him. "You must eat to keep your strength. Please!"

John Pierre took a deep breath. He was hungry and could use some food.

"'Tis good. No?"

John Pierre had to admit the bread was tasty. "Just tell me where I am."

"According to history, my grandfather, great-grandfather and all those who came before me were very powerful men." Abu smiled with pride as he spoke while gesturing with his hands. "They were great seers, shamans, or what Whetherbee referred to as ma-gee-cia-ns."

"Magicians," John Pierre interrupted correcting his pronunciation again.

"Yes. Yes. Thank you. I have difficulty with that word. Anyway, there were many, but my mother told me about one in particular. He had lived alone on the other side of the Nile and eventually was forced to move during the great flood. He had a mastaba built near the pyramids where they made potions that could cure ailments. He knew the answers to many things. Through the centuries the mastaba was passed to others in the family who possessed the craft. They became known as healers."

John Pierre eyes widened in surprise.

"Through the ages the pharaohs called upon these healers many times for assistance. This one healer, he made the mistake of talking about travel to foreign lands. And soon the pharaoh began to fear him. He was afraid he was becoming too powerful. Some say his magic was *too* dark. Others said he was even more powerful than Ra, the Supreme God and Ruler. Afraid to kill him, the pharaoh put a price on his head and promised a great reward for someone else to murder him."

John Pierre was stunned as he listened to the outlandish tale. He was about to speak, but Abu held up his hand, indicating for him to wait.

"One day he disappeared and never returned. My family searched and searched everywhere for him. For months they did not know what to make of it. It was *believed* the pharaoh killed him.

"My mother told me the story. When I was older she said the mastaba was passed down to me. It is my legacy she said."

"The mastaba I was found in?"

"Yes, yes! 'Tis my legacy."

John Pierre's jaw dropped in shock. "So what are you using the mastaba for?"

"Well, 'tis a problem. You see, one day I return and find members of the pharaoh's army in the mastaba. They had ransacked the place. They threw everything all over. I had just arrived to see them running and screaming from the mastaba."

Abu stopped talking and shuddered as he recalled the incident. "Something had frightened them, so much so that nobody comes near the structure now. Khafre 'tis terrified and afraid to destroy it. My mother suggested it might be enchanted perhaps for protection."

John Pierre was speechless. Stunned, he could feel his eyes widen as his mouth hung open as he listened to the incredulous tale.

"I return to the mastaba to look for any signs that someone from my family perhaps would return. I always feel drawn to the place but am never sure why. I was very sad, and I started searching thinking perhaps I would find something that would give me a clue. You see, I too have powers like my elders but, unfortunately, I have no teacher, so my magic is weak."

Abu paused to take a sip of his water.

"I eventually found a journal and some papyrus buried deep beneath the rock. The journal is undecipherable to me. But the papyrus spoke of the travel through other dimensions. Through time forward and back. It was fascinating. I like to think my grandfather or great-grandfather and perhaps others before him journeyed and for some reason cannot return or perhaps they do not want to. Or maybe they are stuck somewhere."

Chapter 48

"Time travel – impossible?"

Abu shrugged and smiled. "Apparently not so because you are here!"

"Where is this journal and papyrus?" John Pierre demanded.

Abu got up and went to the chests and started frantically rummaging through them. One by one, all the while muttering in a dialect John Pierre could not understand.

He was annoyed and his tone was sharp. "How could you be so careless with something so important?"

"Ah, you must be patient. Nobody comes near here. Besides they are afraid of Arthur and this place. Ah, yes, 'tis here."

John Pierre took it from his out-stretched hands. The aged book had a faded leather cover with scroll like designs embossed in gold. It was about five and a half by seven. He started flipping through the yellowed pages of ancient papyrus.

It was evident some pages were missing. He could tell from the corrugated edges revealed between the pages they had been torn out.

"Do you know anything about the missing pages?"

Abu shook his head no. "'Tis that way when I discovered it."

There were maps he did not recognize but the notations of the Nile River and now famous monuments were proof they were drawings of Egypt. He gasped as he turned the page and an additional piece of papyrus fell out.

"That is the other piece of papyrus I was telling you about," Abu pointed.

"I know this translation; it's the Curse of Anubis! It's on a piece of papyrus I own, from Whetherbee. "It's a rare dialect," he described as he read the words.

Speak my words and take me home
The world awaits - for me to roam
Through zones and dimensions riches await
Unimaginable power is my fate
Armies will rise – the die is cast
Only I will be the last

John Pierre leaned back in his chair. The color drained from his face.

"What…what is it?" asked Abu.

"It's also the text I read on the mastaba. It's the Curse of Anubis."

Abu shrugged. "I'm not sure about a curse, but it speaks of travel to other dimensions. 'Tis what I try to tell you."

John Pierre put the papyrus down and continued flipping through the worn book. Text written in hieroglyphics and sequences of numbers also filled the pages.

He stopped when he caught site of what appeared to be the gold canopic jars that sat on his desk. The text below and on the pages following was unrecognizable.

"What can you tell me about these canopic jars, Abu?"

"Ah, yes, the jars. You have the lid, no?"

John Pierre nodded.

"Whetherbee somehow acquired…"

"You mean stole," John Pierre interrupted.

"Well, call it what you will, 'tis safe to say he *obtained* the pharaoh's golden canopic jars. The pharaoh was outraged, for they were part of his prized collection and going to be used at his final resting place in his pyramid. Legend says the pharaoh hid the jars to make sure they were not found."

Abu stopped talking and poured more tea for John Pierre before continuing. His voice was but a whisper. "The jars never made it to the pharaoh's tomb for he was killed by his own people. Mysteriously murdered, in his temple. Found by one of his concubines!" Abu threw up his hands in disgust as he continued talking. "The fool died before telling someone where he hid the fifth jar."

"I still don't understand what all this has to do with me, Whetherbee, or my presence here."

"The canopic jars have magic. They apparently have been in my family for centuries, possibly crafted for the legendary ruler King Menes who united Upper and Lower Egypt."

"That would be King Narmer as we know it also," John Pierre interjected.

"How King Menes or this Narmer obtained them it is unknown. Who crafted them is unknown. Some believe descendants of *my* family hid the jars for centuries to protect their secret. Some believe they are a gift from the gods above…"

"The *lids* allow you to time travel," John Pierre finished. "That is why Whetherbee left them to me. Its not the *jars* that are important, but the lids."

"Yes, yes. Now you understand," Abu clapped his hands together excitedly. "The entrance is from a portal in ancient Egypt – according to Whetherbee 'tis what your people now refer to as the Old Kingdom."

"The mastaba is the portal?"

Abu whispered, "Yes."

"What pharaoh were these jars stolen from?"

"I am sorry, John Pierre, I do not know."

Chapter 49

John Pierre shook his head in disbelief. The story was more and more ludicrous as Abu spoke. He scratched at the stubble forming on his chin. "You seem young to be roaming about? Where are your parents? I need to speak to them."

"Ah, I see," Abu nodded. "You do not believe me? My parents will be of no help to you," he stated matter-of-factly.

"And why is that? You look too young to be living alone."

Abu shrugged. "'Tis way of life here."

"If you are alone, how do you survive? What do you do for money?"

"I have small camel farm. You can meet them all tomorrow. Jahara, Safiyah, Zohar are the females and the males are Quamar, Yasir, and Arthur."

"Arthur?"

"Whetherbee named him. He said 'tis after the Arthur of the King and the Knights at the Table."

"I think you mean King Arthur and the Knights of the Round table," John Pierre corrected him. "It was one of his favorite books," he reminisced.

John Pierre sighed heavily he was getting tired and was having trouble focusing. Abu was his only link to Whetherbee, and he needed as much information as possible to get out of this mess and get home. "Ok, can you tell me anything about your parents? Perhaps it will help solve this mystery."

Abu smiled proudly as he spoke of his father. "My mother told me stories about my father. He was a very clever and smart man, but I am not foolish to think others knew about the secret. I believe my father, grandfather, and family before must have known and perhaps traveled too, but I cannot be sure. Likewise Whetherbee knew and traveled all the time."

"So your father does know Whetherbee! Where is he? I must speak with him immediately!"

Abu shrugged, "Perhaps, but I cannot be sure they have met."

John Pierre's arms flew out in a gesture of annoyance. "And why is that?"

Abu shrugged and looked away. "I am sorry to say I never knew him."

John Pierre could sense the distress. He knew what it was like to grow up without a father.

"Abu, tell me what happened to Whetherbee. How did he do it?"

"Whetherbee traveled all the time. As I grew older, I wake up and feel something. I was drawn to the mastaba. My mother told me it was nothing and to ignore it. One night I sneak out and go to the mastaba. I find a man. 'Tis how I met Whetherbee.

"I felt his arrival. It was the same for you. One day he stopped coming and I know something is wrong. I look for him every day, but I do not know of his fate."

"Well, I'll tell you his fate. He is dead. Died in a plane crash!"

Abu's hands flew to his face in disbelief. "I understand death, but I do not understand this pla..ne...crash?"

John Pierre drew a picture of a plane on the dirt floor with the sun and clouds and explained, "It is a mechanical travel machine, like a giant bird, that is able to fly in the sky like this," he pointed upward and then boom...it crashed."

"'Tis impossible," Abu said confidently. "If he was wearing his amulets, he should not have perished. He should have died his permanent death in Egypt. It does not make sense." Abu shuddered as a he felt a chill run through his body. "He can't be dead 'tis impossible. I am sure he is alive somewhere," he stated positively.

"Well, you better believe it, my friend. I can assure you he is *dead*! I attended his funeral; I gave the eulogy, there were thousands of people in attendance."

John Pierre stopped talking and eyed Abu suspiciously, "Tell me, why is it impossible?" John Pierre shook his head in disbelief. "I can't believe I am even suggesting such a thing!"

"No, no, John Pierre, you don't understand. Whetherbee *cannot* be dead. He wears the amulets…he *must* go to the Hall of Judgment…"

John Pierre stood up and cut him off. He had enough. "This is unbelievable," he stated clearly frustrated as he ran his hands through his hair. "Whetherbee is *dead. Nobody* could *ever* have survived that crash, not even Whetherbee. There was nothing left of his plane. It is utterly absurd that I am even having this conversation with you. I must be dreaming."

Abu frowned. "I assure you, sir, you are not."

"Ok. But why me?"

"I do not know why Whetherbee passed the jars to you. He said if he ever stopped coming, if anything ever happened, he would send his good friend John Pierre who would know what to do!"

"Have there been others?"

"To my knowledge, no. Since Whetherbee, you are the first I know of."

"Something is wrong. I am feeling dizzy."

Abu rose quickly and guided John Pierre to the wooden bed. "Come, my friend. You must rest. It is difficult traveling through time portals. You will need your strength."

Suddenly John Pierre could no longer keep his eyes open. They fluttered and became so heavy. He felt unusually exhausted and lightheaded. His limbs grew weaker by the minute. "That tea…the herbs…what did you…" he muttered as he slowly fell on his side.

Abu covered him with the Martha Stewart comforter as he collapsed.

"You must sleep, my friend. We will talk more tomorrow."

Chapter 50

John Pierre rolled over, stretched, and arched his back. He opened his eyes. The colorful hieroglyphics on the wall were just as bright as he had encountered in his dream. He quickly shut his eyes, took a deep breath, and opened them again. They were still there. What made it worse was that he could read them. The words paid homage to the many gods and goddesses worshiped by the Egyptians.

Swinging himself into an upright position, he vigorously rubbed his head and temples, "This can't be happening. It's not real," he muttered.

"You are very wrong. 'Tis real," the chipper voice called from the other end of the room.

Abu. He was preparing tea and assembling a plate of bread and fruit for himself and placed a plate of what appeared to be granola bars on the table.

"I see you are still in disbelief. We go over it again. You must listen to me and perhaps you will not be like your friend Whetherbee who you claim is dead! Now come you must eat, or you will not last in the hot sun."

John Pierre stared at the plate. "Is this a granola bar? And you have bottled water!"

"Yes, yes," Abu nodded excitedly. "It is your Per..ri. Whetherbee said it was the finest bottled water. I drink it all the time."

"It's pronounced Perrier," he corrected. "Now I know this is a joke. What is Whetherbee up too? You didn't have this in 2520

B.C. Tell me where we are and who you are," he demanded sharply.

"Ah, I see 'tis no reasoning with you. Come I show you instead."

John Pierre followed Abu to the far corner of the room. Abu pushed the table and chairs away and rolled a dusty old silk rug to the side. Even through the dust, John Pierre could see the wooden door that Abu quickly revealed.

John Pierre held the door but only saw darkness. "Come, John Pierre," he motioned with his hand.

"It's pitch black. I'm not going anywhere. And what if there are snakes or spiders? We could get bitten," he argued.

Abu rolled his eyes. "Snakes? Here? I assure you what is below contains *no infestation* of any sort. *The house of Abu is very clean because I have the secret can!*"

"What?" John Pierre asked, perplexed.

"You come and see, or are you afraid?"

John Pierre accepted the challenge and followed as Abu started down another set of wooden stairs. Squeaks from the aged wood echoed through the chamber. Abu fumbled around in the dark and within minutes the room was flooded with light from another lantern.

John Pierre blinked in surprise. It was huge. Cans of food, bottled water, candy, cereal, medical supplies, and other non-perishable items from the twenty-first century filled the shelves. "You have got to be kidding," he stated his eyes wide with awe as he walked around touching the objects. "How is this possible?"

"You can't exist in this time drinking the water or eating the food. Whetherbee said, this was, let me think, ah yes, necessary for surr-vi-val."

"Survival," John Pierre corrected.

"Yes, yes. You are not of this world. You cannot eat our food. Whetherbee brought artifacts back and made sure when he came, he had what he needed to stay here. He told me one day you would come and would need to have all this too," his hand slowly pointed to the shelves.

"But the bread?"

"The bread I make from the flour, water, and spices of your time. 'Tis tasty. I like to prepare for myself."

John Pierre fingered the wrapped toothbrushes, toothpaste, and soap.

"Whetherbee always stressed this thing called hi-gen-e."

John Pierre looked at him with raised eyebrows, "It's called hygiene. If you don't keep clean you will get sick and die."

"Yes, like a plague. Whetherbee told me all about it. I do my best to be clean and take care of my teeth."

John Pierre walked among the supplies. "You have suntan lotion?"

Abu smiled excitedly. "Yes, Whetherbee brought it for me. He said it was to protect me from a terrible plague that will eat at your skin or inside your body."

"Cancer," John Pierre added solemnly, as this is what his mother died from.

"Yes, yes, that 'tis it. I make sure to use every day. This has no scent. Whetherbee told me other types would bring too much attention due to the odor. I understand there are many plagues in your land and many of these things will protect me."

They walked further down the rows of items. "Here is why I have no bugs," he smiled as he pulled a can off the shelf. I have the can," he smiled. "'Tis a great i- ve-tion."

"It's pronounced invention." John Pierre took the can and shook his head in wonderment. "You have RAID?"

"Yes and more," Abu pointed. "'Tis why I don't have bug plague. They do not come!"

"This is incredible. Whetherbee must have dedicated his life to this."

"Whetherbee said to remind you, he make a gift to you," he proudly gestured to the shelves and their items. "There is another room for clothing too, come I show you. You must change, the heat, 'tis hot and you can be sick."

John Pierre continued to stare at the shelves and their contents as Abu continued in broken English.

"When you are ready to return to your time, I give you a list. I have come to like your Fri-tis…"

His eyes narrowed and he glared at the shelves of junk food. "Fritos," he corrected. "You think I'm going food shopping for this?"

"Ah, you must," he smiled. "When you come back."

"I don't intend to return because I don't believe this is happening to me. It's all just a dream and I am going to wake up soon!"

Abu ignored the remarks and continued to give instructions. John Pierre reluctantly changed out of his suit and slipped into jeans and a white cotton t-shirt.

"No, no, John Pierre," Abu yelled anxiously. "You must wear the white cloth. The material you wear to cover your legs is not of this time. People will not understand. They will think you are evil…"

"And the pharaoh will kill me," John Pierre interrupted.

"Yes, yes," Abu stated glad that John Pierre was now understanding. "Further, you overheat yourself in that heavy cloth."

"Then why is it here?" John Pierre grumbled as he removed the jeans and donned the white garment.

"Whetherbee said you would be difficult. He also said your head is…like…I forget the word, but it means hard."

John Pierre glanced at Abu sideways. "It means stubborn. I am neither difficult nor stubborn."

"You will need your Le…vis," he pronounced slowly. "This is what you wear in your time. 'Tis too tight for my taste, but you will need them to return, or do you want to arrive dressed like this!"

John Pierre squinted his eyes. "Let's say I believe you and all this is true and not a dream, then your point is well taken," he spat.

They argued more about his clothing attire before returning to the upper level.

John Pierre sat drinking tea and eating, of all things, strawberry Pop Tarts and granola bars while Abu rambled on about the chips and food he needed replenished.

Chapter 51

John Pierre was barely listening. He was thinking about the Old Kingdom or what scholars referred to as the Fourth Dynasty. If this was true, if he was in Egypt 2520 B.C., there was art, loads of it.

His eyes gleamed as he thought about the treasures he could bring back with him. The board would find favor with him and forget about the canopic jar debacle. He could even sell the stuff and make millions for the museum. Nobody would question where he got it. He had traveled all over the world. He could take a short leave and tell everyone he was going on an archeological dig.

"Abu, stop rambling. You are giving me a headache. You must show me art and then tell me how to get home."

Abu nodded knowingly. "Ah, sir, I know you must return but you must help me find Whetherbee."

"Ok. Ok," he interrupted impatiently. "So say I believe you. What do we need to do to find Whetherbee, who I told you was dead?"

Abu shook his finger. "Do not mock me. I speak truth. Now before we do anything, you must be protected."

Abu went back to the trunk and began rummaging, "Ah here they are. You must wear this."

John Pierre took the amulets from his outstretched hands.

"You must wear the Ankh."

"The sign of life," John Pierre remarked as he rubbed the precious stone between his fingers.

"Yes," it will hopefully ensure permanence of your efforts and long life."

"Funny, I remember Whetherbee always wore this and others. Even underneath his three hundred-dollar shirts. I asked him about it one day and he told me they were his good luck charms. He was never without them."

"Exactly 'tis what I try to tell you, Whetherbee always wore the amulets - this is why he cannot be dead."

"Abu, I was at his funeral…"

"Did you see his body…was he wearing the amulets?" Abu pleaded.

While John Pierre didn't know what was going on, it was evident Whetherbee was important to Abu. "I know this is hard for you, but not even Whetherbee could have survived that accident. There was nothing left at the crash site."

Abu ignored him.

"Whoever travels through the portal must always have this." Abu maintained eye contact as he spoke. *"I warn you now. You must never take it off, ever. Now for the scarab beetle."*

"You're giving me a representation of the God Khephri?"

Abu nodded.

"Khephri was responsible for pushing the sun through the sky through the darkness into the light of day. Rebirth and renewal. He was usually represented as a beetle. The Egyptians equated the beetle with the sun god. The beetle rolled their balls of dung around which their children sprung forth from. To them it made sense as a symbol of rebirth or regeneration. The scarab also became part of the weighing of the soul's ritual. The scarab was placed near the heart during mummification. During one's journey at judgment it was weighed on the scale. Anubis put the heart on the scales where your deeds, faults, sins would be examined. If your life's actions were judged with honesty and integrity, Anubis would accompany you on your final journey to the throne of the God Osiris. If things didn't work out, you were immediately consumed by Ammit, the lion-crocodile-hippopotamus monster and die a second and permanent death! According to Whetherbee, Ammit was like your devil."

"Spare me the history lesson, Abu, I am not wearing this."

Abu stared at him and nodded. Instead of arguing, he quietly said, "Ok so be it, then *you* will die. But before you die you *must* help me find Whetherbee. And if you think about it, what do you really have to lose by wearing the amulets?"

John Pierre pursed his lips and smirked. "Ok, ok. Stop with the reverse psychology. Just give it to me."

Abu looked confused. "I am afraid I don't know of this pc…olgy…"

John Pierre shook his head frustrated. "Just give me the charms."

John Pierre ran his fingers across the perfectly formed beetle carved from alabaster. Shades of green and brown swirled through the stone like veins running through marble. The entire piece was encased in a ring of gold. It was a stunning charm. Its pristine condition would fetch millions at an auction house like Sotheby's. His eyes widened in shock as he deciphered the text on the back. He glared at Abu. "This is my name. Why is it carved on this?"

"'Tis necessary if you do not make it. You will need it during the Judgment of the Gods; it will increase your chance at life or resurrection from the dead. Take this one too. It's solid gold. The spell on the back is from the Book of the Dead. Attach them to the necklace I gave you."

"Nothing like setting me up for failure already."

Abu shuddered. "When it comes to the gods you take nothing for granted. You have been bestowed the special gift of time travel. It is unexplainable. I do not question. I only know you may need to have these items. Do not *ever* remove them."

John Pierre did as he was told and slipped the necklace over his head and under his garment.

"What now?"

"Can you ride a camel?"

Chapter 52

"Incredible," was the only way John Pierre could describe what he was witnessing. If he wasn't in a coma or having some wild dream, it could really be happening. He traveled through time and ended up in the Egyptian Old Kingdom.

He had consented and dressed in the long white robes and sandals as Abu directed. His head was wrapped as well. He rode Yasir, a large male camel, while Abu was on Arthur, and together they slowly meandered toward the Giza Plateau.

Palm trees were scattered about the desert, unlike the treeless space that existed in present day Egypt. Like a mall parking lot packed with vehicles during the Christmas holiday, mastabas littered the landscape while construction activity was set up nearby the completed pyramid of Khufu. Miscellaneous satellite pyramids and mastabas for families and wives surrounded the grand pharaohs pyramid. Colorful temples added to the beauty of the complex.

A second pyramid, belonging to the Pharaoh Khafre was in progress. The smallest pyramid of the Pharaoh Menkaure's had not yet begun. The sun glared radiantly off the polished limestone surfaces making it difficult to see. John Pierre pulled the covering over his head and raised his hands to shield his face from the blinding sun.

He was speechless. Abu smiled. "Amazing is it not? I will give you a tour and then we go to the mastaba to plan how to find Whetherbee."

Each area of the plateau was divided into what John Pierre could only describe as specific workstations. Men dressed in white linen moved stone off pallets of wood that floated down the Nile. Stone was loaded on top of wood sleds with wheels and pulled by men and mules.

Others chiseled, polished, and cut stone with a variety of tools. Men retrieved wooden mallets and other devices, which were scattered on tables of wood in a multitude of sizes and shapes.

As they rounded the corner of the first pyramid built for the deceased Pharaoh Khufu, he could see the massive stones, which he knew to weigh at least two and a half tons, were in the process of being moved up spiral ramps that circled around the half-constructed pyramid for Khafre. Constructed all by man with the help of ropes, sleds, pulleys, and animals.

There were no aliens or spaceships, as some believed had constructed the Great Pyramids. It was all manpower.

The Sphinx was nowhere in sight.

John Pierre was excited. If there was no Sphinx, it was either yet to be constructed or buried under the desert sand as scholars had suggested. However, the mortuary temple where Khafre's body would be mummified *was* in the beginning stages of construction.

"Abu what is that smell?"

"Ah, the people, you know, they must to eat. Bread is prepared all day for the workers. Water is everywhere. Remember, you must not eat any food or drink the water. You will become deathly ill. Since you were not born here your, im… un…system…"

"Immune system," John Pierre corrected.

"Yes, yes that 'tis it, the imm…une system, your body will not be able to fight in…fect…ons…"

"Infections," John Pierre corrected again.

"Yes, 'tis the word. Again, if you drink the water or eat this food you will become deathly ill."

"How do you know this?"

"It happened to Whetherbee. He said he was very sick and did not think he was going to survive."

"What happened? He obviously lived."

Abu shrugged. "I am not sure. I believe he went back to his time but arrived sick and his recovery was long. I did not see him for a long time because of it. Anyway, I have plenty of sustenance for you in my pack. 'Tis from your time. You must bring back what I have written on the list."

"Why should I bring something back that I don't even eat," John Pierre teased.

"Ok, ok! I admit this Fri-tos, 'tis an interesting food and since Whetherbee has stopped coming I fear I am going to run out. You are my only hope!"

"Well savor what you have. Not only am I *not* a delivery man, but I don't intend on returning."

"But, but, John Pierre, I do not understand."

"I must have hit my head pretty hard because when I wake up this will all be just a fantastic dream. But while I'm here I must have the opportunity to see that mortuary temple," John Pierre pointed.

"'Tis too dangerous. You will have difficulty blending in. Look at your skin color 'tis too white. And your hair – there is too much and 'tis too dark. You are clearly not one of us. Although I have wrapped your head, if discovered, you too will be accused of having black magic or an invader from foreign lands."

"Abu, I really don't believe I'm here. This is some intense hallucination and I will have a good laugh when I wake up. So can't you just let me enjoy the dream?"

Abu sighed heavily. "You *must* listen to me John Pierre. This is no dream. Something terrible will happen to you if you do not listen. If you are the smart man as Whetherbee claims, then you should know the Egyptians have a god and goddess for everything. In order for them to understand life, as they know it everything must have an explanation. If you are revealed, you will be taken right to the pharaoh." Abu shuddered at the thought. "I will not be able to help you if that happens."

John Pierre laughed. "Abu. He's just a man. What could he possibly do to me? Besides, you gave me these amulets for protection. Take me out of this hot sun. You were right. I need some water."

Chapter 53

John Pierre removed his white hood wrapped around his head. They were back at the mastaba where his journey began. Drinking water and eating granola bars, he was flipping through the journal, while Abu was making more tea and munching on his chips.

"Lacey just showed me some pages with jars on them, and an ancient dialect she discovered. The hieroglyphics are the same. I am intrigued because I saw them on some papyrus and, once again, I see jars and numbers..."

"What is this La...cee? Does she know of the jars?"

"Lacey is a female scholar..."

"I am not sure I understand this sc...olar..."

"Scholar, someone who studies and is an authority on Egyptian art, the pyramids, or any field of study," he interrupted.

"Yes, yes, ok. I understand. But I see how the light of your eyes comes on when you speak of her...I see she is more to you," Abu interrupted. "Perhaps she can help us?"

"No," John Pierre spat adamantly. "She does not like me."

"Is it because you are difficult?"

Annoyed, John Pierre slammed the book closed. Lacey was the last person he wanted to discuss. "You must take me to find some art. I must explore while I am here. Perhaps if I bring back some artifacts it will be the proof I need that this is all real."

Abu sighed. "You are just like Whetherbee. It was always about the art. You will die if you do not listen to me. The pharaoh will catch you," he said adamantly pounding his fist on the stone table.

"We must decipher the journal. It is my only clue to find Whetherbee. Whetherbee said you would come and help me!"

John Pierre ignored Abu and his outburst. He didn't know how to convince Abu that Whetherbee was dead. He picked up the book and began feverishly flipping through page after page. "The text is rare; I am not familiar with it. There are numbers everywhere, all scrambled. It could be a map of some sort. I would have to return and put the numbers in the computer to get the longitude and latitude coordinates and see if it reveals anything."

Abu looked puzzled. "I do not understand com…utor or 'tis long...tude and la…tud…"

"It's like plotting the course with the sun and stars but more advanced in a machine. Can you read any of it?"

Abu took the small journal from his outstretched hands. "I have looked at this many times, as many as there are stones on those pyramids," he pointed toward the main entrance, "but I am sorry to tell you no."

John Pierre rose and started pacing. "This journal is worthless! I need to return to my time to use resources to help make sense of what is written. I need a computer and books and must consult scholars. If what you tell me is true then I have much research ahead of me. But before I leave you *must* take me to those pyramids. I must have a closer look!"

"John Pierre, I will do as you wish but I must warn you of the precious time we waste."

John Pierre had stopped pacing and had walked over to one of the far walls of the mastaba. He was admiring the colorful hieroglyphics. He turned to Abu. "Abu, this is a scholar's dream, a once in a life-time chance. If you don't take me, I will walk outside myself. The way I see it, I have nothing to lose."

Abu sighed disgustedly. "You are just like Whetherbee. I do not understand this fascination with the sand and stone which in your time surely does not exist."

John Pierre's eyes gleamed brightly as he walked back to Abu. "Ah, but this is where you are so very, very wrong. Would you believe *your* stone monuments are *still* standing?"

"Impossible," Abu stated. His eyes widened in disbelief.

"No, not impossible. Possible and true! They are classified as one of the Seven Wonders of the World. Scholars continue to research, write books, and speculate how they were constructed and who constructed them." John Pierre pointed toward the heavens gesturing, "Why some even believe aliens…you know beings from other civilizations from far away…came down out of the night sky and snapped their fingers and the monuments appeared."

Abu laughed. "That is as you say ri-dic-ulous," he interrupted as he slowly pronounced the word. "The construction… just look outside. You have already witnessed it. There is no-body but men out there," he pointed. "They are responsible for the building. But to still be standing, after all this time, I do not believe it."

John Pierre sat down on a stone bench. "Well then, my friend, we are even, for I don't believe any of this," he gestured with both hands at his surroundings. "I don't believe I am in Egypt. I don't believe I have traveled back in time."

Abu bowed his head in defeat. "Ok. I see your point. How about I make deal with you. We study the journal and I take you to retrieve art. I will also show you how to return to your time and you will help me find my friend Whetherbee."

Chapter 54

"What is this?" John Pierre fingered the burlap sack Abu had handed him. Abu took a moment to wipe the dust from his white clothing. He had retrieved the cloth from a hiding place between rocks deep in another room of the mastaba.

Abu smiled. "You will need it for the art. I collect them for Whetherbee."

The sun beat down on them as Arthur sauntered slowly through the desert sand. The sand was littered with people. John Pierre continued to marvel at the thousands, maybe a hundred thousand and more human beings that worked. He took mental notes as they rode.

The Giza Plateau was divided into sections where workers had specific tasks. Some carved, sanded, and polished stone, while others moved the massive blocks from the river to prepare for transportation to the pyramids. He could tell immediately who the supervisors were as they directed people about the complex and delegated tasks. It was like a giant factory that was extremely organized. The only difference was – it was outside!

"Abu, those people over there, what are they doing to the stone?" John Pierre pointed.

"They sand and polish. The stone must be perfect. There can be no cracks, holes or openings…"

"…they will fit so tight that it will be impossible to fit a piece of paper or what you know as papyrus, through," John Pierre finished.

"Yes, yes my friend. You are most certainly correct. How do you know this?"

"I study Egyptian art and already told you, in my time the pyramids are still standing."

Abu smirked. "I still think you tell a tale. You must bring me proof."

They dismounted and tied the camels to one of the many camel corrals. "Keep your face covered and make sure you do not remove the wrap from your head. My people will not understand all that hair."

John Pierre followed Abu as they walked into the beginning phases of the mortuary chapel. The walls were still not completed. "Can we go to the pyr…."

"Shhh…" Abu hissed. "You must not talk, you sound different. I tell you people are superstitious."

"Tell them I am from a foreign land, just visiting."

"Then they be wary and think you are an invader and that will get us a trip right to the pharaoh. Remember where you are, John Pierre, do not bring trouble upon us," Abu warned sternly. "Now follow quietly."

Chapter 55

"Abu!"

Abu froze in his tracks. He knew that voice. It sent shivers up his back.

"What are you doing here?"

It was Moustafa one of the pharaoh's loyal guards. He was dressed in military attire.

"You have no business on the pyramid complex. If the pharaoh finds out you are here he will not like it. You are a thorn in his side."

John Pierre stepped in front of Abu, rubbed his fingers and a small flame of fire burned from the tips. The guard jumped back, his eyes wide reflecting fear.

"You tell the pharaoh that Abu will cast the most wicked incantation if he bothers him anymore. If you are smart you will forget you saw us. Now, in the name of the great sun God Ra let us pass," John Pierre, whispered in the royal guard's ear.

"Who are you?" growled the guard. "You speak with a strange accent. What land are you from?"

John Pierre stared at the guard never breaking eye contact. "I am Abu's new assistant. Now I suggest you let us pass!" John Pierre then snapped his fingers and fire emerged again.

Eyes wide open in shock the frightened guard stepped aside and permitted the two to continue.

Chapter 56

Anybody associated with Abu was trouble. Moustafa had heard the stories of the black magic that took place at the mastaba. While most of Abu's family was gone, the pharaoh was not going to mess with any descendants, and that included Abu.

It was said Abu did not inherit his family's craft but others were still frightened of him; besides, it was too hot to be chasing after anybody today. He had other things to concern himself with and an audience with the pharaoh was not one of them.

Abu didn't need to be told twice as he started walking away quickly. He grabbed John Pierre by the sleeve, and grinned, "Come, my new assistant, we must hurry before that guard changes his mind."

"Humph. Change his mind. Don't be ridiculous. He was too frightened. I doubt he will bother you again. Are you not even curious about my trick?"

Abu smiled as if he knew a secret. "It is one of the oldest tricks. In fact I use it all the time!"

"Really, then tell me how I did it?"

"'Tis simple. You carry the machine for fire. Whetherbee showed it to me many moons ago."

John Pierre had the lighter in his suit jacket. He picked it up off the ground on his way out of the museum one day and meant to throw it out but forgot. While he was changing, he decided to carry it with him.

Abu hurried after John Pierre. "Where are you going? You may have fooled that incompetent guard but the stunt you just pulled will not allow you access into Khafre's pyramid! Besides, you will not find any art in the pyramid yet. 'Tis still being built."

John Pierre abruptly stopped walking. Abu was right. Artifacts were not brought in until the work was done. At the rate of the current construction, he'd be dead before he would see it completed. "Then tell me where I need to go."

Abu looked around and pulled John Pierre away from the pyramid.

John Pierre grumbled and huffed as he navigated through the hot, heavy sand. His legs were on fire. It was like lifting weights. There was no stone path to follow, just sand.

Abu moved swiftly like a cat. Even with sandals and the white robe he didn't seemed bothered by the hot sun. John Pierre was drenched in sweat.

The building was made of stone with eight-foot columns on the front entrance. It looked like a temple, but as John Pierre got closer, he realized it was another mastaba with a fancy façade. Abu look around nervously. "The guards are at lunch. You must hurry before they return."

"This is one of the buildings used for artifact storage…"

"Artifact storage?" John Pierre interrupted. "I never heard of a temple being utilized this way. It is irregular. To my knowledge, no documentation exists detailing this function."

"Precisely the point. 'Tis where art was stored as it was secretly brought into the pyramid upon completion."

John Pierre didn't need an invitation. He entered.

Abu sighed and followed.

The room was empty. Colorful hieroglyphics decorated the walls. John Pierre started deciphering the hieroglyphics. "The gods will…

"…come after all who disturb the contents. Steal and your fate is sealed forever," Abu interrupted as he completed the translation.

"There is nothing in here."

"John Pierre, I will go bring Arthur and Yasir and return for you. You must walk down the tunnel. You will know what to do next. In respect to the gods, I cannot accompany you."

Abu was gone before John Pierre could comment. He pulled his flashlight from his pocket and followed the light as he carefully walked down the smooth tunnel. The tunnel was not straight. It curved and led him deeper into the structure, eventually bringing him to a dead end. "Gods my ass," he muttered as he surveyed the end of the tunnel. "Remind me to tell him how he would be considered an accessory to a crime."

He removed his hood and wiped the sweat from his face. While it was cooler there was still no airflow. It felt like a sauna and he was having difficulty breathing. "Damn!" He shouted. "What kind of game is Abu playing with me?"

John Pierre took a deep breath while his eyes scanned the walls. Within minutes the corners of his mouth lifted in a huge smile.

"Think like them," he muttered as he started pushing against the walls, looking for a weak panel. "It has to be here somewhere or perhaps I have seen too many movies."

Suddenly the wall moved causing John Pierre to fall. "Abu," he shouted as he tumbled into darkness.

John Pierre opened his eyes. He was flat on his back. The wall had given way and he had slid down a stone passageway. He moved his legs before deciding it was ok to rise. The room was pitch black. He looked around and saw his flashlight glowing in the corner. On hands and knees he slowly moved toward the light.

"Unbelievable," he whispered as he waved the light around the room. His eyes widened in shock as he stared at the treasures before him. Statues, pottery, jewelry, models of boats, farms, animals, and clothing, filled the room. It was all new and worth a fortune. It would take him years to remove and categorize such a discovery that he knew was worth millions.

He took out his sack and started filling it. He felt like he was robbing a museum but didn't know what to take first. Papyrus, jars, tools, statues, pottery of alabaster, faience, precious stones, jewelry of turquoise, soapstone, lapis lazuli, and gold. If this wasn't a dream, it was definitely how Whetherbee probably made his fortune.

Chapter 57

ohn Pierre emerged from the mastaba with the bag over his shoulder and raised his hand, shielding his eyes from the blinding sun. Abu and his sidekick Arthur were nowhere in site. He started walking away from the pyramids and clusters of people. Men in military garments of brown hues with the pharaoh's insignia rode camels or were stationed throughout the plateau. Workers wore white tunics and sandals of cloth were everywhere.

Finding Abu would be like looking for a needle in a haystack for everyone was covered and looked the same. Dehydrated and in need of water, he was feeling the weight of his success on his back, his feet were blistered from the sand and heat and everything around him looked the same. He was on the verge of collapse when something wet pelted his face.

"What the hell…"

John Pierre looked up to find Arthur, like a dog, his tongue extended wiping the saliva off his fur, which had once again splattered on his face.

"I must apologize, John Pierre. Arthur he never spits. I do not know what has gotten into him. I think he likes you."

"Where is the camel I was riding?"

"I loan him out to someone in my village who was working on the pyramids, in return for food. Sometimes 'tis just too far to walk home as the sun is always blazing hot. They return him later."

Abu proceeded to yell at Arthur in his native dialect. Arthur immediately sat down. "Come, come, John Pierre, hop on, we must go."

"This is disgusting. Do you know how many times I have traveled to Egypt and have never been spit on by a camel?"

Abu shook his head and patted the neck of Arthur, "I think he likes you."

"You better control him."

Abu grinned. "Next time you come, I give you a different camel."

Chapter 58

They sat on the cool, stone bench in the back room of the mastaba where John Pierre first arrived.

"Do you have any idea the riches I just saw?"

Abu passed a bottle of water to John Pierre and frowned. "'Tis no concern of mine. 'Tis all going into the pyramid of the pharaoh so he can live in the next world. 'Tis his journey."

"Why are their no guards posted?"

"The penalty for stealing from the pharaoh is death. Punishment from the gods will follow. Nobody would consider it. Guards are not necessary."

John Pierre stared in disbelief. "The stuff in there is worth a fortune."

Abu shrugged. "Like I said, nobody would dare take something."

"Are you not afraid of the wrath of the pharaoh if he discovers something missing? You helped me and are an accessory to the theft," John Pierre laughed.

"I did no such thing! You have free will. You chose to enter the mastaba…"

"You showed it to me," John Pierre interjected, chuckling as he continued to bait Abu.

"You chose to take the items and, once you realize I tell the truth, you will return for more."

"You must have helped Whetherbee over the years."

"No! You are incorrect," Abu snapped. He pointed his finger upward to make a point. "Whetherbee came and went. I did not know what he was up to. He never really involved me."

"But you knew he was taking the artifacts?"

Abu changed the subject for there was no point in continuing the conversation. "Do you have a plan?"

John Pierre gulped down another bottle of water. "Plan? Plan for what?"

"To help find Whetherbee. I must locate him. He has the answers."

John Pierre shook his head. "I already told you he is dead. I need to wake up from this crazy dream."

Abu shook his head knowingly. "You will soon realize this is not a dream and I speak the truth. Yes, I know it is about the artifacts. I do not understand your people's obsession with some worthless pottery and jewelry. This is all many of us do - make things. Pottery, sculpture, jewelry, coins, clothing, items to fill the pharaoh's final resting place. Things he will need to exist in his next life. 'Tis the way of life. 'Tis for the gods. Everything is for the pharaoh to exist in the afterlife. If we help, we go to the afterlife too."

John Pierre was barely listening. He marveled over the objects in his bag and the money it would bring the museum. The board members would forget all about the canopic jar debacle and he could keep his job.

"Abu send me home."

Abu was resting on some colorful blankets and pillows he had pulled out of another hidden storage compartment. "Assistant, this I cannot do. You have the canopic jar lid. You already know what to do."

John Pierre removed the lid from his pocket and rolled it around in his hands. The jars…lids…Whetherbee's gift…it was all about time travel…he still couldn't wrap his mind around the turn of events in the last twenty-four hours. He was hoping it was all a dream or perhaps he had a concussion and he would wake up shortly.

Abu followed John Pierre to the corner of the mastaba where the journey began. "Before you leave, I am giving you a list of things I require upon your return."

"Don't be ridiculous," John Pierre interrupted. "This is it. I am not coming back. I don't believe this is happening. I told you Whetherbee is dead. You need to accept this."

Abu moved away shaking his head. "You will return. Look at you, just like Whetherbee, stealing artifacts. You will be unable to resist - oh yes, John Pierre, I will see you again," he smiled confidently,

John Pierre was no longer interested. Bag slung over his shoulder he stared at the stones in front of him. He immediately recognized the relief carving of the God Anubis, the lord of the underworld. He searched the wall and saw the slight mark on the Anubis throne and inserted the jackal head. "Thank you for your help Abu and stay away from that pharaoh." He threw his lighter toward Abu.

Abu caught the magical light source and nodded, "Safe journey my friend. I will be waiting for your swift return."

John Pierre held on tight to the burlap sack as he ran his hands across the hieroglyphics and recited the ancient dialect. The mastaba shook, knocking Abu to the floor. A cloud of dust filled the room and dissipated quickly, leaving Abu alone with his thoughts.

Chapter 59

"Mr. Boudreau, Mr. Boudreau, please wake up. Are you alright?" The night guard continued shaking his boss on the shoulder. He heaved a sigh of relief when he saw his eyes flutter. "Mr. Boudreau," he called again. "Can you hear me?"

John Pierre's eyes opened slowly. His head was pounding. He immediately recognized his night security guard, Sonny. He was relieved to see a familiar face. It was all a dream.

"Oh sir, thank God you're ok. Come let me help you up."

John Pierre waved his hand gesturing he was ok and started to rise. "Thank you, but I am fine, Sonny."

"Sir, do you want me to call someone. I was making rounds and the thunder was so loud I could have sworn the building shook. I heard a noise in the mastaba, and I came running. I didn't expect to find someone. Are you ok? What are you doing here? Why are you dressed like one of the models in the gallery?"

John Pierre ran his hands across his chest. The texture of the material was rough. He looked down. His suit. It was gone. He was wearing a white cloth and sandals. His eyes then caught sight of the burlap bag at his feet. "What time is it, Sonny?"

"It's around one in the morning, sir. I was just making rounds and never expected to find you here. I didn't know you were still in the museum. Your name is not on the list for this evening."

John Pierre was still stunned. Could this be real? He wanted to look in the bag, but knew he had to convince Sonny he was ok. He cleared his throat. "I was just thinking about putting together a show in the gallery. I wanted to see how it would actually look and must have lost track of time."

Thunder roared in the background while he spoke. "The storm and the thunder were so loud and I saw light emanating from the mastaba and came to investigate. I must have slipped and hit my head."

Sonny's eyebrows shot up. "Sir, there is no light on in here at night. It's controlled with the rest of the morning lights."

"I'm telling you Sonny the light was on and I came to investigate."

Sonny could feel his eyes widen in disbelief. His boss was covered in dirt and his feet were caked with sand. "Sir, you look a bit exhausted. If you hit your head perhaps you have a concussion. I can call an ambulance if you'd like?" He interrupted worried.

"Sonny, I assure you *I am fine*. Please continue with your rounds. I will be leaving the building. And please, I would ask that you not talk about this. I have not yet announced my idea to the staff or the board. I'll be exiting from the private entrance; just buzz me out when I radio you."

"But sir, your bag, you know you can't leave…"

"Sonny, its only my clothes. Do you actually think I'd walk out of the museum with art? If you don't believe me, I will gladly show you what's inside."

Sonny wasn't stupid. He knew that it was his cue to leave. His boss was an important man and he wasn't about to question him and what he was doing. It wasn't uncommon to see him in the museum at such a late hour. What was strange was the clothing he was wearing. He looked as if he just stepped out of the Egyptian desert. "That won't be necessary, Mr. Boudreau. You have a pleasant evening."

It wasn't a dream. It was real. Deep down. He knew it happened.

John Pierre bent over and opened the burlap sack and gasped. It was filled with Egyptian artifacts. How the hell was he going to explain this to the museum curators, staff, or the board? You just can't show up with a sack full of artifacts from Egypt.

He needed to get home and thought about his clothing. Abu, he did this on purpose; he knew it. He felt naked without his suit. He silently cursed himself for leaving his expensive suit behind. He smiled. A four hundred-dollar Armani suit, left in the Old Kingdom of ancient Egypt. Nobody would believe him. He didn't believe it himself. He wondered about the consequences if discovered. Hell, Abu probably had it burned. He was still having trouble comprehending what had actually just occurred. He seemed to materialize right back to where he had started his journey. His watch now read one fifteen in the morning.

Only a few hours had passed as he recalled it was about 10 p.m., when he was walking around the Egyptian collection earlier. He gathered the sack and started to leave the mastaba and gasped, "The lid." He turned quickly to find the canopic jar lid protruding from the base of the mastaba. He bent down and pulled on it. The jackal head came out easily. He smiled and stuffed it in his pocket and headed home.

Chapter 60

The hot water felt good as it beat down on his back. John Pierre closed his eyes and laughed as he recalled the look on the stunned face of his doorman as he brushed quickly past him and headed for the elevator. "Costume party at the museum tonight; I didn't have time to change," he yelled as the doors closed.

He headed right for the shower. The desert sand was stuck to his feet and other parts of his body. "This is amazing," he shouted to himself. "Time travel! It was Whetherbee's secret all along." Laughing aloud, he said, "Ahhh, Whetherbee, the things you must have seen…if only you shared your secret with me sooner...what we could have accomplished together," he muttered.

Not wanting to linger in the shower, he grabbed his towel, threw on a t-shirt and sweatpants, and headed for his study. Carefully he opened the bag and began pulling the artifacts out one by one. The ancient statues, jars, jewelry, and amulets sparkled as if they were just crafted – because they were.

John Pierre slumped down in his leather desk chair and marveled at the discovery in front of him. Pieces straight from the Old Kingdom, even he was having difficultly processing the magnitude of what was staring back at him. He couldn't even put a price tag on them – somewhere in the millions. How could he possibly explain this to the museum? Since they were stolen, then there would be no documentation on any of them, no provenance reports, no history, no proof of where they came from.

Getting the objects out of the museum was easy. He had returned to his office and transferred them to a larger backpack and with his briefcase had just left through a private exit in the back of the building. He told the guards he didn't want to be seen dressed the way he was. He threw one of his spare suit jackets on top and let it hang out of the bag so they would think it was his clothing. They just let him pass. He knew he wouldn't get away with it again.

He took photos of all the objects, scanned them into his computer, and started his search for any evidence of their existence.

Chapter 61

The ringing of the phone echoed through the quiet apartment, waking John Pierre. He had fallen asleep at his desk. He rubbed his eyes and grabbed the receiver. "Hello," he answered groggily.

"Sir, thank goodness you're home. When you did not show up this morning, I was worried sick! Are you ok? Is there something wrong? You have appointments all day today…"

John Pierre was barely listening to his executive assistant, Muriel. The clock on the wall read nine-thirty. He was *never* late. In fact he was always the first one at the museum. He yawned. He felt exhausted, and drained. "Cancel all my appointments. I won't be in today. I think I'm coming down with the flu."

Murial held the receiver away from her as she hung up. "John Pierre with the flu?" Something was definitely wrong. Her boss was never sick, late, or missed a day of work. She put the phone back in its cradle and grabbed her coat.

Chapter 62

$\mathcal{J}$ohn Pierre made coffee and returned to his study to continue his research. It wasn't going well, and he had no idea what he was going to do with the millions of dollars worth of artifacts that sat on his mahogany desk. Thoughts of how to proceed raced through his head. *Whetherbee was always giving me items as gifts...perhaps I can say they were gifts from him and I never opened them until now...but I still need documentation... but how did Whetherbee do it...he always gave me artifacts with detailed explanations of locations, and tombs associated with them...I bet Whetherbee had every document he gave me forged...who would have questioned them?*

"Ah ha!" He shouted aloud. "Anonymous donors! That's it. And the more I think back, Whetherbee, that sly old fox was always bequeathing something, and he was so nonchalant about it too. I can just hear his voice, stating the donor wished to remain anonymous or I'll give it to another institution."

John Pierre leaned back and stretched in his chair. The legal department wouldn't put up with that for too long. He could say he was donating stuff Whetherbee had given him over the years. Hell everyone knew his penthouse was like a small museum anyway.

The ringing of his doorbell interrupted his thoughts. He jumped up, closed the door to his study and headed toward the foyer. He sighed heavily as he looked through the peephole. It was only Muriel. He wasn't surprised that she was able to get past the security guard. He made a note to talk to the building supervisor as he opened the door.

Her scream echoed down the hallway as she stared at her boss. Her hand flew to her face in shock and she shrieked again.

Unprepared for the outburst John Pierre reached for her arm. "Muriel, what's wrong? Are you ok? You look like you have seen a ghost? Don't just stand there gawking come in."

"Oh my," she gasped, "you really are sick. I went and picked up some soup for you."

John Pierre took the bag and ushered her into the kitchen.

He pulled out a chair. "Muriel, please sit. From the way you are looking at me you'd think I had some sort of plague. Thank you for thinking of me but I am going to be fine," he said as he put the soup in the refrigerator.

"But sir," she stammered. "What happened?"

John Pierre looked at her suspiciously. "What do you mean what happened? Nothing; I'm fine. Why are you looking at me so strangely? Do you need some coffee, tea, or a glass of lemon water?"

"Water," she answered meekly. "When I saw you yesterday…your hair…it was…well…I don't know how to say this but…"

"Muriel, I need to rest. So if you don't tell me what is wrong, I'm going to send you back to work." His face and tone reflected annoyance.

"Sir, may I ask why you changed your hair color? I mean yesterday, it was brown and…"

John Pierre shook his head as he cut her off. "Muriel, I have no time for this. This is my hair color. I am fine. Just cancel all my appointments and I'll be back tomorrow," he stated quickly as he ushered her to the door. "And thank you for the soup," he added.

Muriel knew it was her cue to leave. Perhaps this is what he really looked like and was too embarrassed to talk about it.

John Pierre leaned against the door wondering what had gotten into her. "What did she mean when she said I changed my hair color?" he muttered. He ran his hand through his hair and dashed toward the bathroom.

"What the hell is going on?" He screamed as he looked in the mirror. John Pierre stared back at his reflection. He looked as if he had aged ten years. His right hand tentatively touched his hair. It was almost completely gray. And his face! There were wrinkles like a senior citizen! No wonder Muriel had looked at him so strangely.

Chapter 63

ohn Pierre stayed in his apartment all week. He told Muriel to tell everyone he had the flu. He dismissed the cleaning people and had his meals delivered while he worked. The kitchen was a cluttered mess of dirty dishes and stale take out food. His newly acquired artifacts shone brightly around him as he tried to research and find out anything he could about them or the ancient journal.

He tried all different number combinations including longitude and latitude plots and nothing made sense.

He was sleep deprived as he was up at all hours talking to the best scholars in the field of Egyptology. Abdoo Kamal at the Valley of Kings was not interested in the canopic jars and had never heard of an ancient storage area for artifacts before they went into the pyramid. Nor had Rafi Mallah, Ahmad Nasir, Hashim Farukh, Friedrick Kubek, or Mark Lemieux. They thought he was crazy.

He had scanned a page from the journal to each of them via e-mail, but no one had a clue what it said. He crumpled the fax up and threw it across the room. "Hundreds of thousands of dollars in education and scholarly research and we can't figure this out! Unbelievable," he cried, irritated.

He rubbed his eyes, which were red from fatigue. He threw his pen across his desk further agitated that he could not find any anomalies about the pharaoh, whom he had stolen the artifacts from.

"Damn you, Whetherbee," he shouted as he leaned back in his comfortable leather chair. He was tired and knew that even a good night sleep would not erase the dark circles under his eyes. The jackal headed canopic jar lid stared back. It sat on a shelf with miscellaneous artifacts from his travels over the years. Pottery shards, papyrus, and stones from the different pyramid complexes and expeditions sat in front of photographs of him and Whetherbee.

Limestone, granite, alabaster, basalt, and sandstone in a variety of shapes and sizes all had a story to tell. His eyes wandered to the photographs of him Lacey, Montgomery, and Whetherbee all smiling and having the time of their lives on their many adventures. He sighed. They had once been a great team – what had happened?

The jackal-headed jar lid glared at him. He sat upright in his chair. "Those jars. They hold the key. I need to get to the museum."

Chapter 64

$\mathcal{I}$t was late morning. He walked quickly through the museum, nodding or waving his hand acknowledging staff as he passed. He did not stop to chat as he normally did as their facial expressions reflected disbelief. He already saw them bending heads and whispering.

At the elevator he punched the button for level two and sighed heavily when the doors did not immediately open. The security guard saw him punching the buttons and ran over. "I'll get that, Mr. Boudreau," he stated nervously as he too stared in shock at the change in his appearance.

"I guess none of you have ever seen someone with gray hair before?" John Pierre snapped, exasperated as the doors closed behind him. He slumped against the wall, closed his eyes, and rubbed his temples. He was angry with himself for yelling at his employees. It wasn't their fault. He looked hideous.

"Good morning Mr. Boudreau," Muriel stated cheerfully as he breezed by.

John Pierre stopped at her desk and looked at her "Ok, Muriel, we've known each other too long for you to pretend you don't notice," he pointed to his head. "First, don't ask. Second, just help me fix it."

Muriel returned to her computer and answered as if there was nothing wrong. "Right away, Mr. Boudreau." She grinned as the door to his office slammed.

Once in his office he removed the journal from his suit jacket, turned on his computer, and started his research. What he was looking for he didn't know, but he felt the answer was in deciphering the journal passages and looking for anything that resembled the canopic jars. He photographed the jars and recorded the different markings in his notes.

"Roberto can be here at five Mr. Boudreau, or he can come straight to your apartment if you'd like," came Muriel's cheerful voice over his phone intercom.

"Five is fine," he grumbled.

"And Mr. Montgomery Rutland is here to see you. You scheduled a meeting to talk about the benefit in honor of Mr. Whetherbee next month."

John Pierre rolled his eyes. "Tell him I am in a meeting and reschedule it."

The oak door flew open but was quickly slammed as Montgomery stormed into his office. Montgomery's eye's widened as he took one look at his former best friend.

"Ok, get it out of your system. Say what you have to say," John Pierre hissed.

Montgomery chuckled. "Well, you have always had a way with the older women, but don't you think this is pushing it a bit far. You are almost totally gray. What the hell happened to your hair? You can't go to the benefit looking like that!"

John Pierre walked away from his desk toward his coffee bar and poured himself a cup of the fresh brew. "I think I look more distinguished," he stated confidently as he added milk and returned the container to the refrigerator. "Besides, it will go over well with the older group, you know the wealthy ones with the old money. Help yourself to some fresh coffee."

Montgomery dismissed him with a wave of his hand. "Where the hell have you been? You look terrible. I heard you had the flu and Noah told Lacey you were going overseas to do some research. Who is going to take over in your absence?"

Noah worked at the Egyptian consulate. He must have heard it from one of the scholars he'd been talking with overseas he mused. While he hadn't finalized anything yet, it had been on his mind.

John Pierre shrugged. "The board members are breathing down my neck. Newberry, Winterberry, and Stockport are persuading the others. Its either leave or I get fired. Besides, this museum can function fine without me."

Chapter 65

ontgomery's eyes widened in disbelief! "Did I hear you correctly? You? Take a leave of absence? The way you micro-manage this place? I know we have had our differences, but business is business John Pierre; you and I have known each other too long."

John Pierre turned abruptly from the window. "Take a good look at me Montgomery…this…this museum…instead of me managing it, it has some how managed *me* and *my life* and you know it! It ruined my marriage and perhaps my career as a serious archeologist and historian. Unfortunately I have some things to take care of that require my immediate attention!"

Montgomery was speechless. Something was wrong but when John Pierre made up his mind there was no sense arguing with him or trying to figure out what was really going on. Years ago they would have talked but now the relationship was too fractured.

"You agreed to host the benefit to honor Whetherbee and his life of philanthropy next month? Did you forget that you are the keynote speaker? We were to meet today to plan the details?"

Montgomery stopped talking. He followed John Pierre to his desk where he was now seated. He placed his hands on the desk firmly, "Don't tell me you forgot about this?"

John Pierre smiled. His perfectly white teeth matched his now aged white hair peppered with grey. "Relax, we have plenty of time to work out the details. Unfortunately I will have to reschedule!"

"You could have at least called me to cancel the meeting," Montgomery added as he left aggravated.

The truth of the matter was he did forget. Muriel probably reminded him. But he barely glanced at any of her e-mails. As he continued to stare at the canopic jar lids and knew what he had to do.

"Muriel," he bellowed while he grabbed his jacket and keys.

She came rushing in. "Is there something wrong, sir?"

"I need you to call Roberto and see if he can meet me at my apartment."

She followed him out the door. "Shall I confirm your attendance at the University fundraiser on Friday?"

His brow furrowed and he rubbed his temple stunned. "Oh yes, the annual fundraiser." *He had forgotten about that too.* "Leave a message on my machine if Roberto can't make it."

The elevator had arrived, and the doors were opening. "But what about your speech sir, do you have it ready for me to begin typing? And the guest list, you always like to review it…"

He cut her off before she could finish. "Don't worry about it, Muriel, I'm sure it's a waste of time, I probably know everyone. As for the speech, I will figure out what I'm going to say when I get to the podium!"

Her jaw hung open - waste of time! The doors closed before she could respond. He said he would figure it out! John Pierre never went anywhere without a prepared speech. He never went anywhere without studying the guest list either. That was one of the reasons he was so good at what he did. He was always prepared for his audience. Knowing who you're dealing with was the first rule of thumb in business. Know their likes, dislikes, where they're from, their business associates, understand their language, identify the commonalities and the money and donations will be easier to obtain. It was a strategy he lived by, and one he had never deviated from, until now.

She stood staring at the doors, her mouth still hanging open in disbelief wondering what had happened and just how sick her boss really was.

Chapter 66

" What do you mean it will not take?" John Pierre asked. Roberto stepped back tentatively and handed him the mirror. He was a stylist at the prestigious Elegance Forever Hair Salon and had been cutting his hair for years. Mr. Boudreau's hair had turned gray overnight and he had been summoned to repair it only the color was not holding.

He did not understand it. He'd been cutting hair for decades and had never, ever had a problem like this before. His father came to the United States from Italy and had opened a small business. Roberto was born in the States, had learned to cut hair in his father's corner shop in Brooklyn, and eventually went to school and became one of the top colorists in the field. While he had not mastered the English language, he was one of the best colorists in New York.

Roberto scratched his head. For the first time in his life he had no answers or knew what product to use, for nothing was working on John Pierre's hair. It was an anomaly.

"It is like I say to you…the color, it not take. It is as simple as that."

John Pierre pulled the towel from around his neck as he rose from the chair and headed toward his bathroom. Roberto followed.

He stared at his reflection in the mirror. "I look like I'm sixty years old." He began running his fingers through his hair to make sure it wasn't on the verge of falling out. The skin on his face was no longer tight and wrinkles were visible at the corners of his eyes and cheeks.

"No, more like late fifties," Roberto lied. "Think of it like this, you look, I dunno, like distinguished, like me. No? The older ladies you hang with will love you. Gray is like, you know, eh, like the new in style."

John Pierre scowled before yelling, "This is not the new style. This is old. How can I go out looking like this?"

"Mr. Boudreau, perhaps are you taking some sort of medication, eh no? Medications, eh, often interfere with, you know… the entire process of the color."

John Pierre turned quickly, knowing what Roberto was implying and stated rather sternly, "I am *not* doing drugs or on any medication. I am as fit as can be!"

"Ok, ok. I just try to help you figure this out…perhaps you went somewhere…think back to what you were you doing before this happened?"

John Pierre turned and left the bathroom and headed for his closet. If it was true, he knew exactly what he was doing. He knew it wasn't Roberto's fault. What was he going to tell him…that a few days ago he traveled back in time to Egypt? He grabbed his dress pants and dug out his wallet.

Roberto threw up his hands in frustration as he left the bathroom muttering in Italian, cursing about the eccentric and inexplicable antics of the rich and famous. "I should have stayed in Brooklyn and never left my father's shop…catering to this wealthy and celebrity world is becoming exhausting…and ridiculous…"

"Watch it, Roberto, you know I am well versed in many languages and Italian is one of them." He sighed heavily as he thrust a wad of cash into Roberto's hand. "I appreciate you coming out. It is not your fault. You know how busy I am. The pressures of my job are simply making me age. I guess I have been under more stress than usual."

Roberto grabbed his tools, thrust them into his travel bag, and headed for the door. "I am so sorry, sir," he said nervously. "Perhaps you call me next week…we try again and…if something is in your system it will have left and…"

John Pierre held up his hand and smiled politely, "Roberto, it's ok. I will call you and let you know. Don't worry about it."

Roberto left shaking his head in frustration.

Chapter 67

The following morning John Pierre arrived at his office at five and worked until Muriel arrived. To her annoyance he conversed with her by phone and email and did not emerge until noon for a lunch meeting. She, like the other employees, did their best to hide their shock at his appearance but John Pierre overheard the whispers and comments as he walked through offices, exhibits, and the bookstore.

What wasn't said was communicated by the surprised looks on their faces. By the end of the day he was fuming. "Damn you, Whetherbee," he shouted into the mirror in his private bathroom as he knocked some of the toiletries on the sink to the floor.

The commotion brought Muriel rushing into the office. "Is there something wrong, sir? Are you ok?"

"Nothing is wrong. The stuff fell off the sink," he lied. "You may go home for the evening; I'm staying late. I have work to do," he spat tersely.

Muriel apologized and left quickly. She didn't know what was wrong and wasn't sure what to tell the staff. Everyone was talking about how he had aged and how terrible he looked.

John Pierre sighed with frustration. He didn't mean to snap at Muriel. He would apologize tomorrow. Right now he had to figure out how to get back his life.

He tried to contact Lacey with the hope that she would be able to decipher the journal. But she was not available. After their last conversation, he doubted she would return his call.

He had the cafeteria send up some food. The canopic jars stared at him as he ate. All the lids were grinning as if they knew the answer to his situation. He was still in a state of shock every time he thought about the journey to Egypt. Was it really possible? Did he actually travel back in time? Was it all a dream that he was just waking up from? Or was he simply losing his mind? The stash of art in his study implied he was really in ancient Egypt. He would find out in a few hours. He reached for Webesenuf, the falcon, and put the lid in his pocket. He would wait until the museum closed for the evening.

Chapter 68

The night cleaning staff had arrived, startling John Pierre from his work. Unable to concentrate with the noise he decided to take a break. His Rolex read nine-thirty.

He walked straight to the Egyptian gallery. He spent fifteen minutes walking around looking at the statues and objects in the protective glass. He took out a pen and small pad and pretended to take some notes as he moved from gallery to gallery. When he was sure the cameras had rotated past and there was nobody watching, he ducked into the nearby mastaba.

His heart was beating twice as fast from the adrenaline coursing through his body. He wiped the perspiration from his forehead and quickly went to work placing the lid in the indentation and reciting the text. He closed his eyes and waited. Seconds passed and he opened his eyes. Nothing. He turned his head and realized he was still in the museum mastaba.

John Pierre tried to turn the lid again repeating the verse. Nothing happened. He scratched his head in frustration. "What the hell could be wrong?"

"Mr. Boudreau do you need help? Are you ok?" a voice called.

John Pierre held up his hand to shield his eyes from the blinding light. For a moment he thought he had been transported until he realized it was just one of the night security guards who was shining an extremely bright flashlight in his face.

"Mr. Boudreau, are you hurt? Do you need help? Are you injured?" the guard continued to shout anxiously.

"I'm just fine," John Pierre grumbled. "You can stop shouting. I haven't lost my hearing. And get that light out of my face, I'm coming out." He quickly pocketed the lid and made his way out of the mastaba.

"I was walking by and I thought I heard something…you know it could have been like that movie *Night at the Museum* where the statues come to life…can you imagine, Mr. Boudreau, if that happened in this museum it would be a riot…I'm glad it was you because if any of the Egyptian art collection came to life, quite frankly, I don't know what I would do…can you picture the mummies or the giant statues moving about the museum…but I'm ready if it happens…"

"Albert!" snapped John Pierre, "Please! I beg you to stop talking. You're making my headache worse. Let's get out of here; it's getting hot."

"What were you doing, Mr. Boudreau?"

"Nothing, Albert. Just research. I wanted to take a look at the hieroglyphics that is all."

"Well, I'm glad you're ok."

John Pierre eyed the guard suspiciously. "Albert, I thought you worked in the Greek and Roman galleries."

Albert shrugged. "Well, ever since you know…you were discovered in the mastaba we were told to check the mastaba more often and…"

John Pierre quickly held up his hand indicating for the guard to stop talking. "I've heard enough! You can go back to your original post. I will deal with your supervisor and the rest of the staff."

"But, Mr. Boudreau, I'll get in trouble and…"

"Albert! Have you forgotten who I am? I am the director of this establishment," he hissed. "I have spent days researching for other exhibitions in the past and this is no different. I will make sure the departments are notified of my presence. You may tell everyone you report to that I am fine, and I am leaving for the evening!"

John Pierre was sipping a glass of wine while flipping through the television channels. He occasionally glanced at the falcon lid that rested on the coffee table. He spat a few obscenities at the lid and shook his head wondering what went wrong.

He wasn't crazy. He had the art to prove it. The gold glistened as if it was made yesterday. He rarely watched television. He was always too busy but tonight he had turned it on just for a distraction. He continued to flip through the channels – music, movies, commercials, sitcoms, game shows, news, weather, old movies, sports – there was nothing he was interested in watching.

He was about to shut the television off when he suddenly sat upright. "That's it. It's the weather!" He shouted as he flipped backwards until he found the weather channel, which was currently depicting the remnants of a tropical storm in the Caribbean Islands.

He hurried to his office, waited for the sleeping computer screen to come to life before he began typing. "I remember it was raining," he muttered as he typed the date of his first journey. He needed the exact weather conditions, stars, sun, moon phases, and anything else that occurred on his first trip.

Chapter 69

" $\mathcal{I}$ 'm telling you, Lacey, I think there is something terribly wrong with John Pierre."

Lacey took another sip of her white wine. It was one of her favorite Pinot Grigio's at the Mezza Notte Trattoria on the upper west side. Decorated in an Italian Tuscany motif, it was nestled in a quiet neighborhood and family owned. Generations of the Sansosio family cooked homemade meals and recipes passed down from the old country. Tonight they enjoyed the outdoor café as the sultry heat of the summer finally subsided.

Montgomery studied his wife as she took another bite of her fettuccini Alfredo. She was as beautiful as the day they met in Classical Greek Art during their first year in graduate school at Harvard. They were fast friends and he was waiting for the right moment to ask her out, but something always got in the way… the last something was John Pierre. He was assigned to their study group and that's when life changed for all of them.

"What makes you say that?" she asked nonchalantly as she continued to eat. "John Pierre is as fit as could be."

Although she pretended not to care, Montgomery knew her better. "You just can't erase the past so easily Lacey. I saw him today. I tell you his hair was completely gray and his face, well, he has aged!"

Lacey had heard the rumors. If you were anyone in the art world, you knew John Pierre. No matter what she did to escape her former life, he was always hovering in the background like some dead spirit. No matter what assignment she took, someone was always asking about him…how to get an audience with him…if he would be interested in some collection…as of late it was all about the drastic changes in him. It was exhausting. To escape, she worked harder and took more assignments out of the country.

Montgomery complained about her absence. She resented his objections, but knew it wasn't fair to him. Traveling across the globe was not helping her forget about the past. She promised Montgomery she would make some changes in her life.

Lacey put down her fork, reached for her glass and finished the wine. He automatically filled it without asking.

She was getting aggravated. She did not want to talk about John Pierre. "Montgomery, I thought we came here to have a nice, quiet meal. The last thing I want to chat about is my ex-husband," she hissed. The disapproving look she shot him was noted.

Montgomery wasn't satisfied. He poured more wine in his glass. They all had a history together and her refusal to talk was just more evidence that she still cared. But it didn't really matter as legally she belonged to him now.

Chapter 70

The next two weeks went by quickly. John Pierre continued to ignore the whispers and stares from his staff about his appearance.

Nicholas Stockport and Mary Rockefeller stopped by unannounced and demanded lunch. He had no choice as he had been ignoring their calls. They wanted to discuss his current plans for a new show and the internship program. Translation – they had heard about his aging. They couldn't hide their surprise when they saw him. He was sure they were reporting back to the board.

"Did you hear Montgomery got married?" he asked Nicholas.

Nicholas did his best to hide his discomfort. Mary quickly changed the subject to her organization.

John Pierre told her he was not interested in funding the charity Whetherbee left no money too.

He didn't flinch when she mentioned his job was on the line and that she could change George Newberry's mind.

"Then you should ask Newberry for the money. As for my job, it was over a long time ago."

In retaliation, Mary had an emergency board meeting called. George and the others demanded to know what he was doing to make up for the financial loss from the canopic jar debacle.

John Pierre quickly wiped the smirks from their faces as he distributed preliminary photos of his newly acquired art. "The donor wishes to remain anonymous. I am working on getting a catalogue and details together."

George was speechless.

"What is the monetary value?" Mary and Jocelyn inquired.

"What about the authenticity reports?" Leo demanded.

Anthony was not easily fooled. "I don't know how you pulled this off, but if it's real, then my apologies. But if it turns out to be another one of your games, you'll be out of a job."

Robert and Victor agreed.

"What I'm working on is priceless and when I'm done it will be the biggest donation in the history of this museum. Now if you'll excuse me, I have work to do!"

John Pierre knew he left the board members in a state of shock. He might have bought himself some time but knew George and the others would be plotting to get rid of him.

Chapter 71

The majority of his time he spent sequestered in his office. Researching, on the phone with colleagues all over the world, or on his computer trying to find out anything he could about the mysterious journal, canopic jars, and the old kingdom of Egypt, specifically at the Giza complex. He continued to speak to prominent professors and archeologists and claimed he was thinking of taking some time off to do some research.

As usual, they were wary of his questions and knew if he was involved it probably meant he was on the verge of something big.

Muriel continued cancelling appointments and making apologies and excuses for his lack of response in answering e-mails and returning calls. She even rescheduled the board meeting. George Newberry hung up on her while Thomas Winterberry was a bit more understanding.

The only people he did meet with were Lindsay and Monroe, who requested a meeting. Muriel was surprised when he agreed.

The lab was located in the basement of the museum and John Pierre was down there almost every day looking at ancient artifacts under restoration or stored in crates. Every conservator was on edge when they saw him. Monroe wanted to know if there was something wrong. She was convinced he was spying on her, the staff or the conservation projects for some reason. She wanted to know if he needed assistance with something.

Lindsay had the same complaint. "You have walked through the gallery so much that you are like a fixture from one of the displays. You are starting to make the staff nervous. They think you are going to fire one of them."

"Ladies, I assure you that is not my intent. I am sorry for any distress I may have caused you. Go back and inform the staff I am only working on a new project. Now while I have both of you here, I need to ask if you are familiar with these hieroglyphics? Do you recognize this at all? Do we have any artifacts that depict these markings?"

Lindsay and Monroe stared at the photocopy that was placed on the table. Lindsay removed her glasses after staring at the paper for a minute. "Mr. Boudreau, I don't know what this is. It makes no sense. I think you and I both know that what we are looking at is not Egyptian hieroglyphics. Is this a joke? Are you trying to test me? Have I done something to make you doubt my capabilities as a curator?"

When Lindsay finished talking, Monroe continued, her voice filled with apprehension as she spoke rapidly. "Do you have any idea how many conservation projects we are in the middle of? Do you have any idea how many artifacts we have in storage that need to be catalogued? Lindsay is right, what you are showing us isn't even part of the hieroglyphic alphabet! Why are you wasting our time?"

John Pierre closed his eyes and rubbed his forehead. "Ladies, ladies. I mean no disrespect to your scholarship; I am doing research and I only wanted to know if this looks familiar to you. Please do not feel threatened by my presence in the Egyptian gallery or in the conservation lab. I only ask that if you come across any artifacts that have these markings to please let me know."

"Can you at least tell us what medium you are researching? Is it something you saw on stone, papyrus or wood?" Lindsay pleaded.

John Pierre's face lit up at the mention of papyrus. "Thank you for your help, ladies."

He headed for the elevator to his office. Once inside, he moved stacks of paper around on his desk and grabbed his file entitled 'Whetherbee Acquisition.' He rifled through to make sure the piece of papyrus was still in the protective covering. It was a clue he may have overlooked.

Chapter 72

They sat in a quiet corner of an expensive restaurant in the theatre district. "I thought Nicholas was coming?" the male voice questioned.

She shrugged. "He cancelled. We didn't need him here anyway."

He laughed. "He is probably off with one of his students somewhere. More wine?"

She held her glass as he poured. "Do you know how many years I had invested in Whetherbee? Do you know how many dinners, events, and money I spent on his behalf? I spent decades cultivating that relationship! For what? Nothing! The family is still talking about it. It's like a slap in the face to me," she spat angrily and then took a sip of her wine.

"Then you force us to agree to accept that donation from Whetherbee, which turns out to be fake. I just don't understand."

He rolled his eyes and finished his drink. The conversation was getting old and he was tired of talking about it. "What do you want to do about it?"

"I want him out," she hissed. "Just like that he comes up with some monumental donation and he tells me he can't help my foundation. How dare he dismiss me so easily?"

"My dear, you must have patience. The plan has been in place for some time. Your contribution was invaluable."

"I'll believe it when I see it happen."

"Forget about all this; now, do you like your gift?"

She smiled as her fingers gently touched the diamond necklace on her neck. "It's stunning," she whispered. "You always know what makes me happy."

He grinned. "I have a beautiful evening planned for us after the show; let's not ruin it. This will be over soon."

Chapter 73

ohn Pierre stared at the canopic jars on his desk. He glanced at the clock on the wall, which read nine-fifteen. The museum had closed hours ago. He turned back toward the computer and started typing. He pulled up the museums security system and watched as the guards went through gallery after gallery checking for any anomalies. His fingers typed as he waited for the Egyptian gallery to come into view.

He clicked through the frames as he followed them in and out of the different rooms that connected with the galleries. Satisfied, he dialed the security station to alert them he was leaving his office. It was protocol for him and those he gave permission to stay and work in the conservation lab or when preparing for a major exhibit. A list he approved daily of who was in the museum after hours was with the guards. The procedure was to call security, stop by to sign out, and then they would watch him leave and record the time he departed as well. Satisfied with what he saw on the screen, John Pierre grabbed his leather briefcase and slipped the lid of the canopic jar belonging to Webehsenuf, the falcon head that guarded the intestines, into the pocket of his suit.

After signing out, he told the guards he forgot something in his office.

"Are you going to take the elevator Mr. Boudreau," the night guard called from behind the glass. "No, Henry, I think I will walk. I want to take another look at the new exhibit on Greek sculpture before I leave. I will be right back."

Henry came running after him, "Sir, why don't you take a radio with you. Just in case you need something."

John Pierre knew he was being watched. Not because they thought he would steal something, but to make sure nothing happened to him. The staff was still talking about what he learned had been nicknamed the "mastaba episode."

It was his fault. When he stayed home from work for a week, Sonny, the guard who found him in the mastaba, thought there was something seriously wrong with him and inquired his whereabouts to Muriel.

She was immediately suspicious and demanded an explanation. He confessed to her about finding John Pierre in the mastaba. He didn't see the harm in telling the other night staff. Jordan, who was in charge of the bookstore, alerted Muriel to the gossip. She in turn told John Pierre. The "mastaba incident," his newly gray hair, wrinkled skin, and the erratic behavior had put everyone on alert.

He took his time as he made his way to the Egyptian galleries. He knew the location of the cameras and pretended to take notes on his pad as he darted through the new display of Greek gods.

The statues were not against the walls but instead haphazardly placed throughout the exhibit. Hence, a person walking by could enjoy them from every vantage point, just as the artist had intended. The power of Zeus and Poseidon were depicted with bulging muscles, and veins. Zeus was in the process of throwing a lightening bolt while Poseidon raised his trident. Facial muscles clenched one could feel the wrath they were about to unleash. With their twisting torsos, limbs, and bulging muscles, these two Gods looked fierce as the light from the full moon shown brightly through the sky light casting eerie shadows on the ancient figures.

"Sorry, Athena and Aphrodite," he muttered as he ducked between them to avoid the camera as it made another pass around the exhibit.

He quickly proceeded to the coat check area pulled a flashlight from the inside of his jacket and smiled as he aimed the light in the corner. The oversized backpack he left earlier was still there. He told the staff to keep it for some school children that would be visiting the museum and it would be part of their project.

After the security camera passed, he practically ran through the entrance into the Egyptian galleries but stopped before entering the mastaba. Once again the strange light was emanating from inside. He made his way through the passageway.

The sweat was dripping down his face and neck as he secured the pack onto his back. Not only was the air conditioning in the museum turned down, the humidity in the enclosed space combined with his heightened adrenaline, had him on edge.

He fumbled in his pocket for the falcon head. His heart was racing as he knelt and gently placed the lid in the strange notch. He heard the click. Another perfect fit. He smiled as he ran his hands across the wording above, turned the piece, and began reciting the ancient text out loud.

Chapter 74

Abu awoke from a deep sleep in great pain. It was as if someone has stuck a knife in his back. He sat up on his pallet and looked around. It was happening again. He jumped up, quickly dressed, and ran outside to find Arthur.

Chapter 75

The ground was hard and cold. John Pierre's eyes fluttered open as he tried to focus on his surroundings. Everything was blurry. He groaned as he moved and tried to sit up. His head was pounding.

"John Pierre, John Pierre, are you here? John Pierre, John Pierre," the voice shouted loudly.

John Pierre groaned. "Abu." The pressure in his head was so bad he could barely move. "I am over here, you fool," his voice was barely a whisper. "You must stop yelling. Just follow the light from my flashlight."

Abu recognized the familiar ray of light and ran over to him. He knelt down. "I knew it. I knew I was not crazy. Come let me help you up."

John Pierre had no choice. He could hardly move. "Water. I need some water," he murmured.

Abu helped him over to the wooden bench. He then grabbed a lantern from a burlap sack he had brought with him for better light. "I knew you would come. I say to myself, John Pierre will come. Whetherbee told me you would not be able to stay away and that I would not be sorry."

Abu gasped. "John Pierre, you look terrible. What happened? You are an old man!"

"Abu, you have got to stop talking. Help me…my head… it hurts so bad."

"Yes, yes…I am very sorry. But I don't understand, you are old. The last time you were young, well, not real young, but young, and now you are old!"

"Abu, if you call me old one more time, I will bury you in the sand."

"Ok. Ok. I make the tea; it will help."

"Forget the damn tea, open my bag."

Abu ignored him as he quickly moved about the room preparing tea.

"I can barely move. My body aches terribly."

"Here drink this it will help."

"Traveling through dimensions of time is hard on the body but I never saw this before. You look terrible. Something is so very wrong. This never happened to Whetherbee."

Within minutes John Pierre felt his eyes grow heavy. He felt like he was falling. He wondered where he was going to land and if it was going to hurt.

Chapter 76

"Are you feeling better, sir? You are still old but looking much better than when you first arrived."

"Thanks, I think," mumbled John Pierre his eyes half closed. He had rolled over and started to sit up. His eyelids fluttered open. He was staring at Abu who had already begun pouring hot tea into the cup in front of him.

"So it is true? All of it? I am really here? I am in Egypt?"

Abu nodded.

"What is in that tea?"

"A bit of this, a bit of that. Herbs, from your time, 'tis something Whetherbee developed. It helps with the travel. It does not matter. You feel better, no?"

John Pierre nodded. "Whetherbee is trying to drug me."

"I thought you would be here sooner. What took you so long?"

"The weather did not cooperate. I'll have you know I made an attempt…"

"Ah, I knew it! I knew you could not stay away from me," Abu interrupted smiling.

"It seems I can only travel when the moon is full. Didn't you know this?"

Abu shook his head no. "Whetherbee said it was best not to tell me much, but he would reveal all one day. But the first time you were here…"

"The moon was probably still full. I know I traveled on the full moon in my time but when I arrived here it wasn't full until I departed. It must have been a coincidence and I just got lucky," interrupted John Pierre.

"I don't understand. Whetherbee, was always coming and going?"

"Well, something is wrong, and the full moon is what got me here. I guess I have to watch my time, or I will have to wait until the next full moon."

Abu shrugged and changed the subject. "Now tell me, did you bring what I requested?" He sat patiently, his eyes gleaming, like a child at Christmas waiting to open his presents under the tree.

John Pierre grinned as if he had a secret and nodded, "Why don't you open the bag."

Abu was off the bench like a rocket and headed straight for the duffel bag. He pulled open the zippers and out poured bags of chips, Doritos, Fritos, Cheese Doodles, a variety of crackers, Pop Tarts, pens, paper, books, toothpaste, and toothbrushes, a first aid kit, batteries, flashlights, water, coffee, sneakers, sheets, sandals, and other stuff.

"You are a good man, John Pierre," Abu said in between bites of his Doritos. "Whetherbee said I could count on you. This is one of the greatest foods of all time."

John Pierre chuckled. "It's loaded with salt."

"Look around you; there is salt *all over* Egypt."

"Yeah, well it's this *salt* that will eventually cause all your beautiful monuments to erode. And too much salt in your food can cause high blood pressure and a host of other ailments."

"What is this high bloo..od pre...ssure?"

John Pierre scratched his head in frustration. "It's pronounced high blood pressure. Look, this much salt is not good for your organs, you can get sick and die."

Abu was licking his orange-stained fingers. "Salt is what helps us preserve the organs. Have you not heard of mummification?"

John Pierre laughed smugly. "You are right, my friend, but salt is *your* enemy. It is going to eat away the monuments and someday there will be nothing left." He gestured wide with his hand, "All you see…all of them will be destroyed."

Abu shrugged. "Who cares? I already told you. I know thousands of dynasties from now, it will all be gone."

Chapter 77

S haking his head no John Pierre smiled, "That is where you are wrong. I told you it is going to last. The book I brought is about art history. It details history from pre-historic times to the present."

Abu searched the bag to retrieve the book.

"Well, if you want to know a secret, I didn't think they would last anyway. These fools, they keep building one pyramid after another. And bigger than the last one! One colossal structure for *one man*! And that pharaoh, he is not a nice man. He does not deserve it."

"Go ahead, open the book. I didn't have time to get an Arabic translation, but I doubt there will be time to match the dialect you speak to have it translated anyway."

"'Tis ok, I can read…"

"Read?" He interrupted. "What do you mean?"

Abu stammered, "What I mean to say is I can look at the colored pictures and understand. This parchment is so soft, and how do you get the pictures and words to stay on each page?"

"Machines."

It was getting hot. John Pierre rose slowly, stretched and removed his suit jacket and retrieved a bottle of aspirin from his bag. "I will tell you all about progress later. Right now we have work to do. Look at me. Do you notice anything different?"

Abu shrugged. "I already stated you are old, and you do not wish for me to call you old. What is this pill you swallow?"

"Aspirin. It's for headaches."

Abu's face revealed he did not understand.

"For when you head hurts; when you are sick, you feel it pounding. I brought extra for you. I also need you to heat me some water for coffee."

"Co..fee."

"Coffee," trust me you will love it.

John Pierre pulled at his hair. "As you have already pointed out, I have aged at least ten years. I look terrible. My appearance has frightened my friends and colleagues. What has happened? There must be something that can be done."

The crunching of the chips echoed loudly through the mastaba while John Pierre waited for a response.

"Abu!" he shouted impatiently.

"I do not know, John Pierre. But I will say, it was never like this for Whetherbee. I do not know what the answer is." He pointed to the painting on the wall. "Perhaps your presence has angered the Gods. Maybe you took too much art. I told you that if you took too much art something bad would happen, and it did. I tell this to Whetherbee all the time…and look what happened to him…he's missing."

It was all John Pierre could do to contain his anger.

"Look, Abu," he interrupted, "stop rambling. You must help me. There has to be an answer somewhere. The only thing I have is this mastaba and a journal. We must go through that journal page by page. We must find the key to decipher its contents. You need to help me reverse the process," he said franticly as he pointed to his gray hair. "Or if this is my fate then I will take more art."

John Pierre extracted the red, worn journal from the knapsack and put it on the table along with his notes.

"See there you go again, just like Whetherbee, 'tis all about the art. He would say, Abu, you must take me…I need more… can you help me locate this temple," Abu shook his head and waved his hand through the air in frustration. "Look at how you aged…I tell you…you have upset the gods."

John Pierre got up and started pacing quickly. "Abu," he shouted, "if we don't decipher that journal, and I continue to age, I may die. If I die then your link to chips and all this other stuff will come to an end," he gestured at the mess around Abu.

Abu looked horrified.

"That's right. You seem to have forgotten that Whetherbee is not missing but dead! Dead! Dead! Dead! And he is *not* coming back. So I am your only hope!"

"I thought you came back to help me find Whetherbee?"

"Why do you need to find him so bad?"

Abu looked sad. There were tears forming in his eyes. "He was my friend, my *only* friend. I do not have the gift like others in my family. People listen to all the stories passed down over time about my family and think I not tell the truth. They think I am more powerful, so they stay away from me. My mother tried to send me to learn with other children, but other families would not have it. I was made fun of. Whetherbee was my only friend. He helped with my camel farm. I don't believe he is not coming back."

John Pierre understood how he felt. "I know it's hard when you suffer the effects of bullying. The men that run the museum, the board, they try to bully me all the time and it can make life difficult. Whetherbee was my mentor and best friend too. I was devastated when I heard the news of his death. But I know what I saw, and nobody could survive that crash. I am just glad he was in my life for the time he was. Right now we have to figure out this mess he left and how to reverse this aging process."

Abu looked crestfallen and sighed deeply. "Ok, Ok. I see your point, but I still believe he lives. Where do you want to start?"

John Pierre rubbed his temples. "That's just it, where do we begin?"

Chapter 78

bu, you must think hard. I need a starting place. I studied the journal, researched and talked to many scholars. The hieroglyphics are foreign. Not one historian is familiar with them."

Abu sighed heavily. "I do not know how to help you. It all means nothing to me. If only my father were here to help."

John Pierre's head snapped up. "That's it - your father. You said he worked here. This is where you found the journal. Tell me more about this place. Why is it here? Who built it? Just what exactly did your father do here? Where did he find the journal?"

Abu got up and started pacing nervously. Waving his hands briskly. "Stop. 'Tis too much. You ask too many questions. I already told you what I know."

"Well, think harder. Let's start from the beginning."

"The journal I found in the wall over here, come I show you."

John Pierre followed. The wall was brilliantly painted and covered with depictions of Egyptians doing every day mundane tasks of farming, gathering crops, and fishing.

The next section was a typical funeral procession.

"Abu, whose funeral are these people going to?"

"I am not sure, for the picture is not finished. I find the journal here, buried in a false panel in the wall." Abu removed a vase that sat in a niche in the wall, he blew hard and a cloud of dust swirled about.

"You could have told me to step back before you did that," John Pierre said sternly in-between fits of coughing. "I think I swallowed all of that."

Abu brushed off the dirt and sand and cleaned around the outside of the niche. He fumbled with the rock, which projected forward and actually formed the shelf that the vase rested on. After he carefully removed the stone, he stood back.

John Pierre peered in. It was large enough to hold just the book. He felt around the edges, but it was solid rock. He retrieved his flashlight. As he held the light in the niche, he could see numbers on the wall. "Abu, bring me a cloth with some water."

"'Tis a terrible waste of this good water."

"Abu, I see something, just put a little water on the cloth."

"Ok, ok, John Pierre. Here, you are too demanding; what do you see?"

John Pierre was wiping the dust off the wall. "It's those numbers again. They are on the jars, the papyrus, and now the wall. It's a clue I'm telling you. Was this the only thing that was in here?"

"Only the journal and the amulets all of which you are now in possession of."

John Pierre glared at him suspiciously. "How did you know the amulets were for me?"

"Whetherbee left them for you. He told me he was making them and on his next journey he was going to explain a lot of things. He said it was time I knew." Abu shrugged dejectedly. "But he never returned to explain. I told you, I found it all by accident."

John Pierre left the niche and walked around staring at the frescoed walls before heading back to the table. His head rested in the palm of his hand as he contemplated his next thought. "Tell me how you discovered this."

Abu shrugged as he began replacing the stone. "I sometimes come here looking for signs of my father…according to my mother this was his work area…before he died…I was hoping he would leave me something…anything to tell me who he was and what he was like…I was angry and could not under-stand…I sit where you are now and stare at the vase and recall Whetherbee say to me…that I was never to touch it."

John Pierre nodded, "I get it and you went over to investi-gate further."

"Yes, yes. Normally, I would not pay attention…but as I lay staring at the ceiling, my eye wandered to the niche and, like I said, I could hear Whetherbee's voice in my head, reminding me every time I was here never to touch the vase…he would say 'Abu, I warn you never touch the vase,'" he mimicked Wheth-erbee's voice.

"And one day you changed your mind."

Abu nodded excitedly, "Yes, yes. I remove it and nothing happened, but it was only when I was laying down, later and staring at the wall, I noticed the stone shelf was on an angle. That is when I removed the stone."

"And you are positive there was nothing else in the hiding place?"

"Nothing. Just what I give you."

"Ok, so I have a worn journal, in a dialect I can't under-stand, and some amulets. I have the ability to travel back in time and Whetherbee is key, but he is dead, and I seem to be aging and we don't know why?"

"Yes, yes," Abu nodded excitedly. "This is what I try telling you – you are a time traveler."

"I'm going to be a *dead* time traveler if we don't figure this out! Although I don't understand the aging part, something is definitely wrong."

Abu shuddered. "I tell you the gods *are* mad."

John Pierre rolled his eyes. His facial expression clearly re-flected annoyance "Alright, now we are getting somewhere!" He snapped impatiently. "I am not thinking like an archeologist or historian. If the journal was left here with the amulets there must be a reason. Whetherbee or someone wanted *you* or *me* to have them or maybe not at all. Regardless, there must be *more* clues, but why, and where to start?"

Chapter 79

*J*ohn Pierre walked away from the niche to the far side of the room.

"Abu, what was this room used for? Do you know *why* your father, grandfather, or anybody in your family worked in here or what they were doing?"

Abu shook his head. "According to my mother, everyone in our family, were different types of healers. Our people would come for help when they were sick. Drinks were made from local plants and trees to help cure people of illness."

John Pierre started examining the brightly painted hieroglyphics on the walls. There were depictions of the traditional scenes, which read like a resume of someone's life. The larger people were always the most important. There was fishing and hunting for food, gathering of crops, dancing, and young children playing about. The leader was a hunter of some sort who had two sons. One son was depicted in a marriage procession with food and celebration. He was seated, legs crossed, with a scribe. He was smart and would have held an important position in the kingdom of the pharaoh.

The other was too young to have a determined career. He was portrayed between the mother's legs with his hands outstretched toward the older man, presumably his father. It was an odd gesture. The hunter was always shown with his wife and family. There were paintings of them in a garden, on a fishing boat, or at a celebration or festival. He must have loved her so because they were always depicted together. The last scene showed the husband, wife, and both children traveling up the Nile on a boat.

Temples, pyramids, and mastabas littered the landscape. Images of the sun, moon and stars surrounded the boat, signifying some sort of long journey.

"What are these marks in the corner?"

Abu shrugged as he looked at the lower right-hand corner of the wall. "I only see lines, I do not know what it means."

John Pierre looked closer at the seated scribe. "What is this?" he pointed.

Abu came closer. The scribe had some type of tools tucked into his belt.

Abu rubbed his chin. "I never have noticed this before. I am not sure."

John Pierre ran to his bag and dug out his digital camera. Abu stood in front of John Pierre as he fiddled with some buttons and marveled at the shiny device. "Let me see, John Pierre, please what is this?"

"Expensive and not something you can touch," he laughed as he hit the button on the top. Abu jumped back in fear as the light blinded his eyes. "My eyes, I cannot see, there are spots in front of me! What magic is this?" Abu cried in horror. "I now think you *are* some sort of god."

John Pierre moved about snapping photo after photo laughing. "Relax. I can assure you I am no god. This is technology… progress. I will explain later and demonstrate its use. The spots will dissipate in a moment."

Abu was in awe of the digital camera. "The picture 'tis in the box? How do you get it out?"

"It works on batteries; you know, what you put in the lantern. The pictures are made with machines. Now forget about the camera. Who painted all of this, Abu?"

"I do not know."

John Pierre turned to face Abu and eyed him suspiciously.

"The paintings were already here."

John Pierre was confused.

"How long have you known Whetherbee?"

"I come here with my mother once as a young child. I barely remember. She once told me it was my legacy and that is when she told me not to touch the niche. She explained it was a sacred site to some god or goddess that I can't recall. I never come back after that."

John Pierre was confused. "What? That makes no sense."

"Years later, I feel compelled to come, I do not know why. I get this strange feeling inside of me, and I come and find Whetherbee. I hide and watch him come and go. One day he caught me and that is how we became friends." Abu shrugged. "I guess I have known him for as many stones that have been sent down the Nile and dragged up to build the pyramids," Abu stated solemnly. He turned and walked toward the entrance of the mastaba.

"Do you know what happened to your father?"

"That I do not know. You see I never knew him or anybody in my family. My mother raised me. My mother said he died in a hunting accident."

"What about your mother? Where is she?"

"She worked baking bread at the pyramid complex. She, too, recently went missing. I fear one of the pharaoh's men took her, and she perhaps has become one of his wives."

"And this does not upset you?"

Abu shrugged. "'Tis the way of life here. The pharaoh can take as many wives as he wants and have more children. Sections of the mastabas you see are for his wives and other families. Perhaps my mother is there. I have no way of knowing, but 'tis what I heard."

John Pierre sighed heavily. He knew what it was like to be without family. He understood all too well how the boy was feeling. "Look, Abu, perhaps if we search this mastaba from top to bottom we will find a clue. I will have to return soon. I can use the technology of my time to research more. Let's review the protocol for these jars and time travel."

Chapter 80

The Duat - The Underworld & Samir

Anubis sat on his golden throne encrusted with an unknown black stone that glistened as light fell upon it. Doric columns shimmered in gold and silver casting a strange glow in the dark room. His eyes were closed, and he was deep in meditation. "Enter, my most trustworthy servant," he stated aloud his eyes still shut.

A large black dog with deep blue eyes appeared from the darkness and wandered into the courtyard and slowly made his way toward the throne. His ears were oversized and pointed in the fashion of his master, like a jackal. As he approached, he materialized into his human form, standing almost six feet tall, and built of solid muscle.

Jobehar was one of his most trusted guardians. If he took the time to venture this far into the realm of the Hall of Judgment, during his time of reflection and consultation he knew it must be important. "Jobehar, what can I do for you?"

"There is a disturbance in chamber twenty that needs your attention."

The Lord of the Afterlife eyes snapped open. Green light emanated from his pupils like fire. "Chamber twenty," he retorted impatiently.

"Yes, I knew you would want to hear the news immediately."

Anubis stood up quickly staff in hand, the green orb at the top glowing brightly and walked toward his loyal servant. "You

194

have done well. Only *one* person can access *that* chamber. "Is it him?"

"Unfortunately the incident was before my time, but I believe it to be true. Although he has aged, the older guardians say the description matches. The resemblance is frightening. You should also know that he has arrived with someone."

"Impossible," growled Anubis.

"We have separated them. They are unconscious and await your presence. My Lord, you also should know they are not dead but alive!"

Anubis smiled knowingly. "So it begins. Come let us go greet our visitors."

Jobehar immediately shape-shifted back into his jackal form and followed his master into the darkness.

Chapter 81

Anubis stood staring at the figure, who was chained to a stone sarcophagus. The chain was constructed from precious stones, which sparkled like a diamond mine. "Unbelievable," he whispered to Jobehar, who chose to remain in his jackal form.

He followed his master around the body before deciding to sit beside the intruder's legs. "Samir, it is good to see you. It has been a long time. How have you been?"

Samir opened his eyes; his attempts at rising failed as he realized he was tightly bound.

Anubis walked slowly around the shackled figure. "Well, Samir, I guess I should say welcome home? I will also remind you that the more you move the deeper the stones will cut into your skin. The chain is a fission chain from the Goddess Serket. She made it especially for you and it has been resting in this chamber for thousands of stars awaiting your return.

"The stones turn into scorpions and snakes the more you move, biting and sapping your energy and every power you possess. So I suggest you stop moving as each bite becomes more painful."

"Why do you feel it necessary to chain and torture me, my brother?"

"Half-brother," Anubis reminded him sharply.

"Why am I shackled? Please, I beg you set me free."

Anubis laughed. "You have the *audacity* to ask? I am shocked. You have been gone far too long my friend. I sent you out for an errand and you never returned," he clasped his aged hands together and smiled cynically.

"Many moon cycles have passed and like magic," he snapped his fingers for emphasis, "you are here!" His hands moved slowly through the musty air as if he was welcoming some lost followers. "The gods will not take your presence lightly. In fact, it is *disturbing* to them as it is to me."

Anubis removed his small staff from the inner pocket of his black cloak. The stone shone brightly, blinding Samir and causing him to close his eyes. Anubis moved the wand over the limbs and entire body of the bound figure. The black stone turned colors as the wand passed over the body parts.

Samir felt the electricity and sharp pain coursing through his body.

"What are you doing to me, brother?"

"Gathering information for I doubt you will tell me the truth!"

Anubis stared at the stone on his staff, nothing was revealed. It was completely blank.

"Nothing!" He shouted. "It shows absolutely nothing! Impossible!" Anubis thrust the staff into his inner pocket.

"I think you should be more concerned about telling me what the hell has happened to you and where you have been before you meet the ultimate death!"

Samir was shaken. "But brother you must give me a chance to explain. I did what you asked; the prophecy, as you predicted, was true. Through trickery I was brought to the portal. Before I knew what was happening, I was stabbed and my bloody body was pushed into the portal.

"Somehow the atmosphere or something enabled me to survive. I was nursed back by some women of the craft. I have spent lifetimes attempting to return to you. The sun and moon passed as I searched for him, the one who robbed me of the life I once knew."

Samir screamed in pain as he moved, forgetting about the fission chain. The intense pain caused a fit of coughing and his breathing became labored.

"You must believe me. I have been traveling in and out of time, meeting shamans, witches, magicians, and finally a wizard…a wizard named Merlin, who came to my aide…he cast a spell transporting me to another dimension…I have dedicated my entire existence to locating him and ensuring he *pays* for what he has done to me!"

"*ENOUGH*!" interrupted Anubis. The walls shook as he spoke.

Anubis walked closer and was inches from his face. "I am in no mood to listen to your *lies*. After all this time, I can't believe you have the audacity to tell such a tale! Do you know WHY?"

"But brother…I swear…I tell the truth," he stammered.

Anubis' eyes glowed green. "'Tis *IMPOSSIBLE* for *ANY* of us *to TRAVEL FORWARD IN TIME*," he shrieked.

Samir was frightened. He knew how powerful his brother was. "Brother, you *must* hear the rest of my story. I found him."

The great ruler raised his eyebrow with interest.

Anubis snapped his fingers and his emerald throne appeared instantly. He settled himself in and Jobehar followed and lay next to the ornately encrusted chair.

"Ok, Samir, tell me the details and I will decide if you will live," he stated casually.

Chapter 82

Samir sighed. "Once I was in the right time, I stalked him and when I finally confronted him, we were on a giant bird and somehow we traveled through the portal and here I am."

Anubis rubbed his chin. "Interesting. How did you access the portal?"

Samir stammered. "I…I…he tricked me and…"

Anubis tapped his fingers impatiently on the arm of his chair and shook his head. "Really? I just told you '*TIS IMPOS-SIBLE TO TRAVEL FORWARD IN TIME!* Do you have any idea how you accessed the portal? Where is it? Where are the jars?" he demanded.

Samir had no idea. He tried to think of the events of the past. But everything was blurred. Nothing made sense. "Something happened…the flying bird…and then I woke up here. You must release me."

Jobehar growled at the noise from the chains.

Anubis rose from his throne and came face to face with Samir. "You are not only a *FOOL* but a *LIAR*! It is *impossible* for any of us to leave. We are *bound* to this time! *Giant flying bird...do you take me for some type of idiot?* I have business to attend to. When I return, you will tell me the truth and the location of the portal!"

Jobehar turned to his master in silent communication.

"I suggest you stop moving as I have already told you the scorpions and snakes are eating at your flesh. Jobehar and his pack would certainly like a piece of your flesh to add to their power.

Jobehar snarled at Samir. His razor-sharp teeth did not go unnoticed by Samir. He knew the power of a jackal pack and what it would do if they were given his body.

Jobehar looked toward his master, who finally signaled they were departing. He rose and they walked into the darkness ignoring the shouts from Samir.

Chapter 83

"Abu, we have to think like archeologists and look at the clues we have in front of us. We have a journal, that we need to decipher, and jars that allow us to time travel. There are many questions; like, how is Whetherbee involved and how long has he been traveling? I can tell you he has been doing this as long as I have known him, as he was one of the wealthiest men on the planet. He also was a great collector of Egyptian art. Abu, tell me again, how long have you known Whetherbee?"

Abu scratched his head as he thought. Minutes passed.

"Well?"

Abu shrugged. "I do not know. He comes and goes."

"How old are you now?"

Abu looked perplexed.

"How many years have you in this life?"

Abu smiled. "Oh, yes. Now I understand. When we go back to the mastaba we will count. I have it marked on the wall. Twenty something or more marks I counted last."

John Pierre shook his head in frustration. "Ok, it's irrelevant right now. Let us search this area. You said your father worked here and this is where you discovered the journal. There must be more clues. We must be missing something."

After hours of searching and pushing on the walls they found nothing. They sat on the hard, stone floor, drinking bottled water and eating potato chips. John Pierre propped his head up while he stretched out across the floor. He was hot and sweaty and the humidity in the mastaba added to his discomfort.

The cool stone was refreshing on his warm body. He closed his eyes and sighed heavily. He wasn't sure if he was going to solve the mystery and time was his enemy. He stared at the brightly painted scenes on the wall across from him. "Abu, I know I asked you this before, but do you know who painted or designed the hieroglyphics?"

"No, they have always been here."

John Pierre rose quickly and walked toward the wall to get a closer look at the relief carving.

"The entire scene has always been here? Impossible?"

Abu joined John Pierre at the wall. "What makes you say that?"

"You see here" he pointed, "the paint is brighter on this section but, over here it has faded. They were clearly not painted at the same time."

Abu nodded in agreement.

"There are mastabas all over this section," John Pierre pointed.

Abu stared at the illustration.

"Think, Abu!"

"John Pierre, drawings like this exist in every temple, mastaba, pyramid in Egypt. I see this everywhere I go. It all looks the same to me," he shouted. "Water, palm trees, temples, sand, mastabas, and pyramids. I get tired of looking at the same things myself. 'Tis why I do not pay attention."

"Look here," he pointed. "The mark on this building, do you recognize it?"

Abu looked closer. "Ah, 'tis a marking on the artifact storage building. All the buildings are numbered, but this is a marking of the pharaoh. Only the pharaoh's guards or specially chosen men can enter these buildings.

"We are missing something, Abu, and if we don't figure it out my time could be running out."

"Ok. Ok. John Pierre. But what should we do?"

"This symbol is our only clue. We need to explore. Let's head back to the artifact storage. I need you to help me navigate through the complex. And we must blend in and not draw any attention to ourselves."

"John Pierre, you must not go out dressed as you are. We need to get you the proper clothing."

"Don't worry, Abu, I came prepared this time." He walked to the corner and pulled the clothing from his backpack.

"Abu touched the material. "'Tis old. Where did you get it?"

John Pierre smiled. "I am surprised you don't recognize it. It's from your time. I took it from the museum."

"The place where you keep all the art?"

"Yes, that is correct."

"So you stole it? See, you are just like Whetherbee. A *thief.*"

"No. I *borrowed* it and will return it. Never mind. It is for an important cause and I'm going to return it."

"Just like you are going to return the art that you are going to take today?"

"Don't be a wise ass. What I take is going into the museum for people to come and look at. If I don't take it, the artifacts will be stolen by *your own people* or buried and lost in the sand forever."

"Stolen by my own people?" Abu looked horrified. "Never! The gods would not allow it!"

"Abu, through *every* age man has done his best to keep their gold and valuables safe. The constant theft came with a price but also forced great ingenuity – the desire to build or create something that is infallible. I am sorry to report, man is still stealing."

"If what you say is true, then what all my people make will be stolen too?"

John Pierre nodded. "So what ever I take I will give to the museum. It will be a donation from Whetherbee's foundation, in honor of his death. Look, you help me figure out what is outside and perhaps we can try to put the pieces together."

Chapter 84

John Pierre found himself face down in the sand. He had ridden Jahara, one of the female camels, who rudely deposited him in the camel corral and then spit on him.

Abu burst into a fit of laughter as he jumped off Arthur and ran over to help John Pierre up. "You offended her. You should not have told her she smells."

John Pierre dusted the sand off and pulled the white material tighter over his head as he tried to blend amongst the thousands of workers who were, hauling, chiseling, cutting, or moving stone. Nobody was complaining. Everyone was just working.

"Amazing," he muttered as he walked past the different groups of people. The climate demanded the need for continuous breaks for water. Deliveries of fruit and fresh bread were well organized, and the bread was baked on site. He equated the entire scene to the construction of a building in Manhattan.

The only difference – there was no union. People engaged in manual labor because they wanted to. Their goal was to gain entrance into the afterlife. They worked not only for the pharaoh, but themselves as well.

A foreman stood at every station watching the workers and shouting orders from time to time. Abu had told him earlier they were assistants to the pharaoh and only there to make sure the project ran successfully.

John Pierre followed groups of people and darted in between mastabas and stone piles as Abu led him toward the area where the art was made and stored. For some reason he felt compelled to begin looking for clues here.

Just before he reached the entrance he quickly jumped behind a pile of rocks. He could feel the hot stone searing his back as he pushed himself against a stone that was waiting for transport. His head moved ever so slowly as he peered around the gigantic rock with one eye.

"Damn," he muttered. A guard now stood in front of the entrance and seemed to be questioning everyone who entered. They all handed the guard a piece of papyrus. It was like a pass to get in. He quickly darted in the opposite direction.

"You need a special pass to get in," Abu whispered. "They probably discovered the theft and now security is heightened. This is not new. It happened once after Whetherbee took art, but Whetherbee has not been around for a long time. That is probably why there were no guards when you visited last."

John Pierre was desperate as he looked around. Holding up his finger to his lips gesturing Abu to remain silent, he slowly moved around the rocks and grabbed an unattended cart of hay. He pushed it around the backside of the mastaba and, when he was close, he rammed it into a table of stonecutters. The commotion brought the guards running and while everyone was yelling to place blame and checking for injuries John Pierre ran around the mastaba and ducked inside, leaving Abu to deal with the commotion.

The thin cloth he wore stuck to him like glue from the sweat that was pouring down his back. He welcomed the cool air as he slowly made his way through the dark passageway.

He kept his head down as the voices grew louder. He walked slowly as he peered at the scene before him. The gold artifacts glistened in the dim candlelight. John Pierre counted five figures moving newly crafted art from a cart.

"You! Come here and help with this statue," one of them gestured for John Pierre to hurry.

John Pierre hugged and secured the fabric tighter to his body and head and moved quickly to assist.

"Help us move this statue," the leader spoke.

John Pierre grabbed the end of the statue and began to lift. He groaned in pain. Although he trained daily, the aging process had not been kind to his muscle strength.

The men lifted the heavy statues with ease. They could have been the perfect models for any fitness magazine. Muscles sculpted to perfection. He wondered what they would have thought of his society's penchant for spray tanning as he admired their smooth, bronzed skin. If they only knew the medical consequences of life spent in the hot sun, John Pierre thought.

They were laughing at him as he attempted to lift a statue of a seated scribe. The leader waved him away, annoyed, and told him to follow. He muttered phrases to the gods and wondered why the pharaoh sent such a weakling to work this special detail.

"Come, come." He led him to another cart packed with boxes. He watched as the leader removed jewelry. Rings, bracelets, necklaces, and earrings embossed or carved. Some set with precious stones of turquoise, amethyst, lapis lazuli, and gold. Gold and more gold; it was like opening a safe at Cartier in New York. The jewelry was laid out on some type of course burlap on a smaller cart.

Statues, jewelry, relief sculptures, papyrus, and pottery…it was incredible. The craftsmanship was undeniably perfection. Removing anything was going to be difficult. He made mental notes of the room as they unloaded the art.

Chapter 85

$\mathcal{J}$ ohn Pierre watched and followed two of the men to the back of the structure. He set the cart down in front of some sarcophagi that were standing up against the wall. With one push, the top slid open. The sarcophagus was actually imbedded into the wall - like a door.

John Pierre tried not to act surprised as they entered. This was the safe of Cartier's jewelry store only without any locks or combinations. It was all laid out for the taking. The man was talking and gesturing toward the rock shelving.

John Pierre laughed. "Jewelry for the wives, girlfriends, children, concubines," he nodded at the man, smiling.

"Yes, yes," the man shouted, elated that he understood. He went on to point and show John Pierre where to place the jewelry and then departed to help his crew. The other man gestured for him to follow his lead. Although it was a task that one person could handle, John Pierre knew he was being watched.

John Pierre realized taking anything was out of the question. The guard at the exit would catch him for sure; instead, he admired the pieces while contemplating how he was going to remove them. The room was only about 10x10 and the walls were painted. Not carved, but actual paint, almost like a fresco. John Pierre made a mental note to ask Abu about this room when something caught his eye across the room. He put the jewelry down and walked closer to the picture. It was exactly like the one in Abu's mastaba!

The man and woman with children, hunting, and fishing. And of all things there was a skyscraper protruding from the fresco. He gasped; it was the Empire State Building! He followed the scene and it stopped at what appeared to be the Museum of Art in New York!

"Incredible," he muttered shaking his head in disbelief as he ran his fingers over the brilliantly painted fresco. "I was right; the frescos are important. I think they're clues."

The men had returned and were yelling. John Pierre knew they were yelling at him for working too slowly. He pointed to the drawing, and in Arabic muttered, "Strange?"

The man in charge laughed and drew back as he spoke. "'Tis magic. Images just appear and nobody knows how it happens. Nothing new has happened in some time. 'Tis why people are afraid of this building! They think 'tis cursed," he gestured. "Others think 'tis the work of the gods. They believe the pharaoh is blessed and 'tis why they make more art and work feverishly to complete his pyramid."

John Pierre stood and stared at the drawing. The scenes behind the family were clearly of the future. New York City. That was his museum. His eyes widened in shock as he eyed the airplane to the far left. He came closer to read the name on the plane.

There was no doubt in his mind that this drawing and Whetherbee were connected. He was leaving a message – what it was he'd have to figure out. But he knew the only person that had that inscription on his plane was Whetherbee – what it meant, he never knew. Whetherbee avoided the subject when asked. His eye was drawn to the lower left-hand corner of the drawing. It had the same markings as the drawing in the mastaba. It was almost like a signature of some sort. He needed to return to Abu and take a closer look at the drawing in the mastaba again.

Whetherbee was elusive and eccentric. He was always coming and going. But John Pierre's gut told him there was more to the painting. He needed time to take a closer look, but time was not a luxury he could afford to waste.

The men were getting impatient. They wiped the sweat that was dripping down their faces with dirty cloths they drew from their pockets. There was no ventilation and John Pierre was starting to feel the affects of the sultry room. The leader began signaling for everyone to finish unloading the jewelry. He watched closely to ensure nothing would be removed before finally ushering them all out of the mastaba.

John Pierre walked quickly away from the group as they exited. He was hot and starting to get dizzy. He was very disoriented and felt as if he was going to pass out. He needed to find Abu. As he rounded the corner of a pile of rocks, he found himself being pulled to the ground. He rolled in the hot sand as he attempted to upright himself and found himself face to face with Abu.

"You must be quiet. Follow me," Abu hissed.

As John Pierre brushed the sand from his white tunic, some flew on Abu's garment. Abu whispered, "You will clean that!"

"Well, you didn't have to push me. I was on my way back and was starting to get dizzy. How did you find me?"

"The disturbance you created 'tis the talk of the complex. The pharaoh's guards are on high alert for a potential intruder. Hurry, we get the camels and return to the mastaba."

Once settled, Abu thrust a bottle of water toward him. "Look at you….you look terrible…you must have water at all times…this is why you were getting sick…you will become what Whetherbee called de..hy…drat…"

"It's pronounced dehydrated, and I was on my way back to you. I made a discovery in that art building."

Abu stopped pulling snacks from his bag and looked up intrigued. "What…what did you find?"

John Pierre walked to the painting on the wall. There are more hidden rooms for art. Also, there is an almost identical painting in the jewelry room just like this one," he pointed.

Abu's hand flew to his face as his eyes widened in disbelief. "You saw this"?

"That's correct," John Pierre grinned. "Just like this one! The only difference is there are markings or pictures from my time. The men called it magic. They said the images just simply appear. He said people think it is the work of the gods."

John Pierre crossed the room and rummaged in his bag for his notebook and a pencil. "It looked something like this."

Abu squinted and rubbed his chin as he studied the rudimentary drawing. He shook his head perplexed. "I do not know these images," he pointed to the buildings and plane.

"Of course you wouldn't; they are from my century. My time. This is the city I live in. This is Whetherbee's plane, his flying machine. This inscription is foreign to me. I asked him over and over what it meant, and he refused to tell me. He always said it was his good luck charm."

John Pierre looked up at Abu. "Are you listening to me? Your face is white. What is wrong?"

"I know the inscription. I know what it says."

Chapter 86

John Pierre rose quickly. "What is it? Tell me what you know!"

Abu sighed heavily and rubbed his chin.

John Pierre saw the apprehension reflected in his eyes. "Tell me, what is it?" He questioned again.

"*Astiramare*. I was told it was an ancient dialect from a time long ago. 'Tis a name I have not heard uttered since I was a young boy. 'Tis the name of my mother."

"Who?"

Abu looked perplexed. "I am not sure. I heard someone whisper the name when I was a young boy. I cannot be sure who was in the room. I thought my mother was there, but I cannot be certain. I was too young. I never thought about it again."

"*Your mother*!" John Pierre shouted in disbelief. "How does Whetherbee *know* your mother? When is the last time you saw your mother?"

Supporting his arm with his leg, Abu rested his chin on his knuckles and thought hard. "I told you, I don't recall. Life is difficult here, John Pierre. People come and go. The pharaoh is consumed with building his pyramid and will stop at nothing to ensure its completion. I believe he took her. He has many women."

John Pierre could see he was getting upset, so he didn't press the issue.

"By the way, thanks for coming to my rescue. I didn't realize the effect the climate would have on me. How did you know where to find me?"

"I followed the story of the disturbance. There is nothing to do all day except to work on the pyramids. Nothing changes. But when something happens everyone is talking. It was not difficult to find you at all. You must be careful. It will be disastrous if the pharaoh catches you," he shivered.

"Life is very difficult in Egypt. Everybody has a place and responsibility. I go forward every day and never look backwards. It makes life easier."

John Pierre's head shot up. "That's it, Abu. You're a genius!"

"I am?"

Chapter 87

Abu smiled while John Pierre rummaged through his bags and laid the papyrus and his notes on top of the wooden table. "If I write the words Curse of Pharaoh and backwards -

S	H	O	A	R	A	H	P		F	O	E	S	R	U	C
1	2	3	4	5	6	7	8		9	10	11	12	13	14	15

and assign numbers to the letters from 1 to 15. The numbers in the journal are 12, 6, 13, 12, 4 Then if we match the numbers, we get S A R S A! These are also the same numbers in the compartment where the journal was found and on the bottom of the jars. It's not longitude and latitude coordinates but a cipher or code," John Pierre exclaimed.

"Sarsa," whispered Abu. "Now I know what the buildings in the painting mean!"

"Well, spit it out!"

"I think the architecture 'tis the ancient mastaba village of King Menes."

"That would be King Narmer or Menes who unified Egypt. Why would this be important?"

"I thought about what you said, John Pierre, think like an archeologist and so I start thinking. I come from a family of healers, and this ancient site 'tis a place the healers would go to and therefore has some importance."

"Now your thinking, Abu," John Pierre praised. "Whetherbee perhaps knew of it?"

"Sarsa, it is forbidden to the common man. I am not sure how Whetherbee would know about it, especially since he was not a healer. He could never get in."

"At this moment I don't consider myself or Whetherbee common – we are time travelers. So how do we get there?"

"I was afraid you were going to say that."

"Abu, we have no choice. There may be someone there who can help us decipher the journal."

"Ok, ok. But we must go home; we will need supplies. And be nice to Jahara and she will not throw you on the ground," Abu chuckled as if sensing John Pierre's fear.

"I'll carry that." John Pierre reached for the backpack as Abu struggled to balance his treats and the huge pack. "We wouldn't want to leave these behind."

"Absolutely not," Abu blinked, fearful of the thought. "I have waited a long time."

Chapter 88

"You want me to get in that," John Pierre asked.

"Yes, yes, 'tis ok. 'Tis a boat. It will take us up the Nile." John Pierre continued to stare at the thin structure constructed of wood and reeds all haphazardly intertwined together.

"Are you sure this is safe? It looks like it is going to fall apart the minute it hits the water. Do you know what animals live in the Nile? Crocodiles, snakes, and hippopotamuses! Creatures that are poisonous and bite, and an assortment of other vile beasts! Why can't we travel by camel?"

"John Pierre, it will take many moons by camel and you said we do not have a minute to waste. Do not worry; I travel in this all the time. It will be ok. Just keep your hands in the boat and do not drink the water. Remember, you are not of this world, it will make you sick."

John Pierre reluctantly got in the small wooden boat filled with cracks. Abu was right, the paddling was necessary for steering, but the current was pushing them down the river at a much faster pace.

"What took you so long to return John Pierre? I was waiting and waiting, but did not give up. Every night I pray to the Gods that you decide to come back and finally you are here."

"Once I discovered I was aging, I tried to return but was not able to. Like I said earlier, I realized travel is linked to the moon phases. I told you, I can only travel when the moon is full... I think that is the meaning of the full moon in the relief drawings I saw in the mastaba and the artifact storage."

"Whetherbee came and went and I never paid attention. So I am not sure."

Abu saw that John Pierre was a bit pale and could sense the nervousness of his friend.

"Relax, John Pierre, the crocodiles will smell your scent if you are anxious," he joked.

"It's not funny, Abu. If one hippo or crocodile touches this thing you call a boat, our days are numbered."

John Pierre took out his camera and began taking photos. Regardless of what happened he was going to document as much as he could.

"So, Abu, tell me about this place we are going to."

"It is sacred ground. It is not far from where the king united upper and lower Egypt. The legend says he built a city and filled it with confidants, advisors who were allegedly sorcerers of sorts. They were to help guide him and let him know what was going on. It was impossible to rule such a large land and not know what was happening all the time. Invaders attacked and destroyed the city. The healers or sorcerers were never found."

"What happened to them?"

"Legends are different. Some say they were all killed, and others say they fled and created Sarsa."

"Do you think your family knew of this place?"

Abu shrugged. "Possibly. I just did not think about it until you encouraged me to look closer at the hieroglyphics on the wall in the mastaba. My family has been known as healers, but it was a story passed down from generations. What is truth and reality, only the gods know."

Chapter 89

"Abu, the current is getting rougher; are we any closer?"

"John Pierre, it would be good time to start removing some of the water. Relax; we will be there soon."

John Pierre looked down and realized his feet were covered in water. He shook his head, annoyed, and uttered some oaths. "What do you want me to use?"

"Why, your hands or the reed plant cup of course. If you do not we may tip over and then the hippos and crocodiles will be waiting for you," he joked.

"I'm glad you find this funny. If we don't get eaten by the crocodiles, I'm going to die from an infection from the micro-organisms in this water!"

Crocodiles had been following them for some time and swimming around the vessel. It seemed like hundreds of yellow eyes bulged just above the water. It was nerve-racking. John Pierre observed the hippos in the distance. Some were on the shore while others hung in groups, camouflaged as rocks in the water, waiting for a good meal. They were one of the most dangerous animals of the Nile. He grabbed the reed plant cup and bailed faster.

"Abu we are taking on too much water, we must get to shore," John Pierre shouted. "The boat is going to sink!"

Abu paddled faster and then abruptly stopped.

John Pierre was drenched in sweat and breathing heavily, "This is a fine way for my life to end…in the middle of the Nile River, eaten by hippos." He looked toward Abu and shouted,

"Do something!" The water was rising quickly above their knees.

Abu closed his eyes and with his arms outstretched began what looked to John Pierre like he was praying.

"Oh great god Sobok, I thank you for the Nile and its abundance. I ask you to grant us passage to the world I seek and help us reach the Temple of Sarsa."

John Pierre could feel the crocodiles swimming around him. He could feel the ends of their hard tails brushing against the boat as he continued bailing water. "This is a fine time for prayer. If you are going to pray ask for a luxury liner!"

The sky immediately darkened, and rain began to fall. "I thought it doesn't rain in Egypt?" John Pierre shouted. Abu continued to chant in a dialect John Pierre could not understand before answering.

"It does not, but my request has been accepted."

John Pierre closed his eyes and braced himself for the impact of the gigantic hippo that was heading their way. "Hold on, John Pierre."

In the next instant, they found themselves on top of a hippo. The hippo dove below the surface, turned and emerged with him and Abu on his back. Wooden planks and remnants of the timber boat sailed through the air. With the speed of an Indy 500 racer, the hippo sped down the river.

Chapter 90

John Pierre lay in the hot sand gasping for air as he tried to wrap his mind around what just happened. He'd hung on the back of the hippo as it moved like a ship speeding down the Nile. Abu was in front of him yelling commands again in a dialect he could not understand. Suddenly the hippo made his way to the side of the river where the water met the sand and deposited them roughly.

"John Pierre, are you ok?" Abu asked as he waved his arms to dismiss the hippo. "I hope you are not injured."

"Yeah, well you could have made the landing a bit smoother. I may have broken something," he gasped as he tried to rise from the hot sand.

Abu rushed over to help his friend. "I am sorry, but I have forgotten much since everyone in my family is gone."

John Pierre brushed the sand off of him. "Forgotten? What does that mean?"

"Yes, yes, I study too, like a mag…ic…n…"

"Magician," John Pierre supplied.

"Yes, yes that is the word and I was studying but have forgotten much. I have no teacher."

John Pierre studied Abu; there was more to him than he had time to figure out. "I don't believe in magic."

Abu smiled as if he had a secret. "Then how do you explain how we got here," he gestured.

"Luck and prayer."

"Yes, you are correct. I pray to the gods and they answer. I see you learn quickly."

"Ok, enough; time is our enemy. What do we do now, my magician friend? There is nothing out here but sand, sand, and more sand. Oh, but wait a minute, I forgot to mention the few palm trees that are scattered about," he shouted, clearly frustrated at the situation.

"You must be quiet; I need to listen."

Abu began concentrating as he slowly moved his head from side to side. He then began chanting as his hands crossed as they moved in a circular motion getting larger and larger. "Ah, we go 'tis way," he pointed.

Exasperated, John Pierre threw up his hands and followed Abu to the right. They went about one hundred feet before Abu stopped. "We have arrived," Abu stated proudly.

"*Arrived? Arrived where? Have you lost your mind?* Abu, we are in the middle of the desert. There is sand everywhere!"

Abu dismissed him with the wave of his hand. "Shh, I must concentrate." Abu closed his eyes and began chanting in the ancient dialect once again. Nothing happened.

"Now what?"

"It seems I have forgotten the words."

"*Forgotten the words*," John Pierre asked. "What does that mean? Like a password of some sort?"

"*Yes*, yes, 'tis a secret word."

"We are in the middle of nowhere and you can't recall a password. And let's say you did, what is going to happen? Is a door going to appear and are we just going to walk in?" He laughed. "How about I recite the text on the canopic jar lid, and we will see what happens?" He continued laughing at the absurdity of it all.

Smiling joyfully, Abu threw up his hands, "Ah 'tis it. The canopic jar. Yes, yes, I will try to see if 'tis accepted? He immediately began speaking in an unidentifiable language.

"What did you just say?"

Abu shrugged, "'Tis secret; I can't tell you. We wait and see if we are allowed passage."

Before John Pierre could react, the sand began to move and he felt himself falling, falling and screaming and thinking this was not going to end well. Together they rolled and slid through the sand, before tumbling down a steep incline, which deposited them on top of another huge sand pile.

"Ah, we are here," Abu stated proudly.

"And where exactly are we?" John Pierre asked as he searched for his flashlight in the darkness.

"Shh. I will provide the light you need. Give me a moment." Seconds later Abu stood in front of him with a round orb that glowed brightly. John Pierre squinted as his eyes adjusted to the light source.

John Pierre was stunned. They had entered a small chamber decorated with brightly colored hieroglyphics. Realizing he was not injured, he rose and slowly made his way to the wall for closer examination. The hieroglyphics and symbols glistened in what appeared to be gold.

"Incredible. It's stunning. I have never seen anything like this before."

Abu saw the look of awe on his face and knew what his friend was thinking. "'Tis not possible to plunder from here. Wipe the thought from your mind."

John Pierre didn't know where to look first. It was beautiful. It was as if they were freshly created. Depictions of animals, hippopotamuses, cats, crocodiles, snakes, falcons, and frogs were intertwined with shapes and symbols. The text made no sense. Shivers ran down his back. He felt as if he was being watched.

"What is all this, Abu? What is this language? Where are we?"

"'Tis one of the most sacred temples. There is nothing like it in existence. 'Tis where I come to learn," he announced quietly.

"Learn? Learn what? You've been here before?"

"My craft."

"What like painting? You told me you were not a scribe."

"No, no! I told you I am like my grandfather, great grand-father, and those who came before them. I was told I have the gift and someday it will all come to me."

John Pierre dismissed him with the wave of his hand. "I told you I don't believe in magic."

"How do you explain your journey? The hippo ride? This orb?"

"The orb is another trick. The rest of this is all a bad dream and I am going to wake up soon," he smirked.

"You must be confident. It is our only hope to decipher the red journal. If you do not believe, we must turn back immediately or you may be killed."

"Abu who is watching us?"

Abu shrugged. "Everyone. Come, we go and seek my teacher."

Chapter 91

They didn't make it ten feet down the dark hallway before they were both zapped with beams of red light. John Pierre lay on the floor gasping for air. "Abu, are you ok?"

Suddenly the wall shimmered in an aura of gold and a Cobra, as least six feet tall materialized. It was as if it oozed right out of the wall. If fully uncoiled, John Pierre was positive its length would have circled the room a few times. The skin was a combination of patterns of vibrant greens, blacks, and yellows. "State your business," the female voice murmured slow and loud causing the ground to vibrate.

Abu spoke quickly. "Oh, great Meretseger, 'tis I, Abu. We seek the council of the ancient elders."

"Meretseger? The great goddess, the guardian of tombs?"

The cobra ignored John Pierre and laughed. "'Tis impossible. You have abandoned your studies and training. You have been banished. How you re-entered is unknown to me. Be prepared to die!"

"Wait!" screamed John Pierre. "Before you kill us, can you at least tell me where I am?"

The snake hissed loudly causing the entire structure to vibrate once again.

"You did not tell him," she hissed angrily. "Another reason why you have failed us!"

Meretseger hissed loudly and laughed. Her tail swished back and forth. John Pierre ducked and pulled Abu to the ground before they were hit. "Now see here! That was unnecessary.

You could have killed us!" He shouted, annoyed, as he helped Abu rise.

"He is right. I am a failure. My magic is not good. I am not worthy."

Abu stared at the snake and hung his head to the floor in shame. "No, I did not tell him."

"Tell him now," the snake bellowed.

Abu sighed heavily. "This is the great temple of Sarsa. Meretseger is the guardian. It is where I once came to train. I told you I was an apprentice and have spent many lives studying. I abandoned my studies."

"You lie. Tell him the truth!" the snake demanded.

"I was accused of something I did not do."

The hissing from the cobra was earsplitting. "Enough! The truth is *you* or perhaps someone in *your* family stole the sacred amulets from the sacred chambers of learning!"

"It is a lie," Abu shouted. "We would never do such a thing! And for the record, I did not steal any sacred amulets!"

"Then why did you abandon your studies? Nobody abandons his or her studies in the middle of training. 'Tis unheard of!"

The cobra hissed and her tail swished back and forth, and Abu found himself on the floor. The cobra was lightning fast, and John Pierre didn't even see how she struck Abu.

John Pierre reached down and helped Abu up. "What are these amulets, and do you have proof someone in his family or Abu stole them? Perhaps if you tell us more, we can get them back?"

The cobra moved her head back and forth as if in thought before stopping to gaze at John Pierre. Her yellow eyes glowed brighter as she studied him. "Your energy is unusual, and you have a strange aura that is unrecognizable to me. Who are you?"

Chapter 92

Before John Pierre could respond, Abu spoke rapidly. "He is a time traveler; we need help deciphering the language in the journal or John Pierre will be stuck here and could alter history, you must help us," he rambled quickly.

Meretseger's eyes widened at the words time traveler. "Then the prophecy is true."

"What prophecy? What are you talking about?" John Pierre demanded.

"When the time traveler comes, he will destroy everything. He is a thief and will steal the most treasured gifts of Egypt. I could kill you now and we will no longer have to worry about *you* altering history."

"I can assure *you* I have no desire to destroy anything. Perhaps we can help one another. Tell me about the amulets."

The cobra smiled as if she had a secret. "So you want to make a deal? There have been others who have attempted to bargain with the gods. I can tell you it never turns out well," she sneered.

"Tell me about the amulets; perhaps I can help locate them."

Meretseger hissed. "The amulets were kept in a sacred location. No one could get to them without passing the tests of prominent gods, goddesses, and healers. Then they must see the council of elders and pass more tests."

"Its just like preparing for a doctoral dissertation," John Pierre muttered.

Meretseger's eyes narrowed as she glared suspiciously at John Pierre. "What is this dis-ser-ation you speak of?"

"It means nothing. It is like a test. In my world, if you pass the test, you get more money when you work. It's not important. If Abu's powers were weak, then how can you explain how he passed all the tests and made it to this special chamber where the amulets were kept," John Pierre asked.

"It must have been some trick! He was a poor student but perhaps figured out a way in!"

"What can you tell me about my family?" Abu asked quietly.

"Your great-great-great, etcetera, grandfather of many eons ago was the best student; he learned quickly, studied, and was proficient in both the dark and light arts of the great shamans and heelers. The amulets were in the learning chamber and disappeared."

"So how can you be so sure someone in my family from many generations ago stole them?"

More hissing and coiling up and down echoed in the confined space. "'Tis simple. He was the only one in the chamber. He was the only one in the temple that evening."

Abu was shaken. "What happened to him?"

"He was banished from the temple and sentenced to death. But they forgot about how powerful he was, and legend said he killed other shamans and escaped. If he stole the amulets, he may have passed them down to someone in the family. Perhaps now Abu is the one hiding them?"

"'Tis not true. I do not have them! Great Meretseger this is not possible, the amulets were in the chamber while I was studying, you speak in riddles," Abu shouted.

Meretseger hissed and bent her neck forward toward Abu. "Yes, we replaced them with fakes after they disappeared the first time. And then you came and stole them. You are a thief just like the rest of your family!"

Chapter 93

"Abu, keep calm," John Pierre warned. "What is so special about the amulets? What do they look like; perhaps we can find them for you?"

"The amulets are a key, owl, sun, and moon enclosed in a circle. These are the most sacred to the elders."

"Take us to this chamber!" John Pierre demanded. "Perhaps we can uncover clues to help recover them."

The snake hissed and laughed at the same time. "Impossible. 'Tis forbidden. You must get there on your own, but you will not have the opportunity because I am going to kill both of you. Be prepared to die," she taunted.

"Wait," John Pierre yelled as he pulled Abu close to his chest to shield him from another attack from the snake's tail. "Before you kill us, could you at least be kind enough to tell us what this journal says. Besides, are you not interested in the text?"

"Ah, I see you are trying to trick me again time traveler."

"Great God Meretseger, I am well aware our fate was sealed the minute we entered your sacred temple. It's the journal that has brought me through some inexplicable journey through time. I just want to know what it is all about. You're going to kill us anyway, so what does it matter?"

John Pierre laid the book before the great god.

The snake glanced down at the strange journal. As her head moved back and forth the pages turned automatically. The snake looked up at John Pierre and began to laugh.

Chapter 94

"*L*augh all you want but it is only because you don't understand the text," John Pierre provoked.

Meretseger glared angrily as her giant tail pounded on the dirt floor. Before they knew what had happened the angry snake had wrapped them in the center of her tail. Suspended in mid-air they were helpless.

"You are going to die since you took the journey through the portal."

"Abu, remember the gift I gave your buddy Moustafa, I think we should give one to the great Meretseger as well, can you reach into my pocket."

"I try, John Pierre, but the pressure…she is squeezing too tight."

"Meretseger, before you kill us, I'd like to give you a gift, please release us," he gasped.

"Gift? What trickery is this?"

"It's like an offering to the gods; they would be pleased." John Pierre struggled for air as the giant tail of Meretseger squeezed tighter around his torso.

The minute they felt the giant reptiles grip loosen slightly, Abu reached into John Pierre's pocket and grabbed the lighter, pulled and released the igniter.

Meretseger's eyes widened with alarm. "You bring *fire* to the sacred temple? Put it out I say!"

Meretseger moved quickly and, in the process, the flame made contact with her tail and set it afire instantly. The snake screamed in pain and they were released immediately and dropped to the floor. Her tail slashed through the air. John Pierre held on to Abu as the smoke grew. "Keep your face covered with your shirt. Don't breathe, there has to be a way out. Come, Abu, you must think, use your magic. Don't be afraid; you can do it. Think, how did Meretseger get in?"

Abu was coughing hard. The smoke was too much.

"*ENOUGH*," shouted an unseen voice. In between fits of coughing, the voice continued shouting.

The smoke was subsiding. "My tail," wailed Meretseger, "you will pay."

"Well if you hadn't tried to kill us!"

"*ENOUGH*!" Echoed off the walls of ancient stone.

A bearded man in tattered robes emerged from the lingering smoke. The robes, of iridescent colors changed from hues of green, purple, and blue as he moved.

"Rufaaron!" whispered Abu, who immediately bowed. "John Pierre, you must bow now."

"Don't be ridiculous. We almost got killed due to that monster."

Meretseger roughly pushed John Pierre in his back with her smoldering tail, forcing him to the ground before he could utter another word.

"How dare you insult an elder and call me a monster?"

Rufaaron waved them all up with his hand. "Meretseger, I am ashamed of you."

"I was just having fun, my lord. I was going to send them to you."

"Go tend to your wounds; I will deal with you later."

The snake slithered to the end of the wall then vanished.

"Come," he gestured to John Pierre and Abu, "we must go. Abu, you must take us through the tunnel."

"But Rufaaron..."

"No! You must close your eyes and search. Abu, you were able to return…why do you think old Meretseger feared you so? Now take us through the tunnel."

Abu studied the wall and then smiled. He walked toward the drawing of two columns, closed his eyes and held his hand out, and muttered words of some ancient language. He walked toward the wall and disappeared through the two columns. John Pierre's mouth hung open.

Rufaaron turned to John Pierre, "So now you believe in the magic of Abu. After you…"

Chapter 95

"Ah, I see everybody is safe. Come."

They followed quietly through the dimly lit chamber to the end. Rufaaron waved his hand over the stone and muttered some words, "Estafa astan." And once again, they walked through the stone.

"Just tricks," mumbled John Pierre. His eyes scanned the room for a way out. There was no door. Just shelves and shelves of books, pottery, artifacts, and parchments. To the right was a table with more pottery and jars of liquids.

"Who are you and why are we here?"

"'Tis I who should be asking you that question, but I think you already know the answer. Please have a seat," Rufaaron gestured.

"John Pierre, this is Rufaaron, he is or was my teacher. He is a great elder. Others in my family have studied with him and the other elders."

"Elders?"

"You know…like you say mag-i-can."

"Magician," John Pierre corrected.

"Abu when you abandoned your training, you should not have been able to return. But I do not question the ways of the gods."

"What do you mean, he abandoned his training? Are you telling me that Abu knew of this place already?"

Rufaaron shrugged. "The story is for him to tell. But I somehow sense a stubbornness about you and that you are not a believer, he must have his reasons."

John Pierre threw up his hands in disgust. "This is ridiculous. I refuse to have any more discussions about magic!"

Rufaaron laughed in disbelief. "You may want to re-think that! How do you explain your presence and all of this?" He gestured to the room around them.

John Pierre couldn't and didn't have time to think about it. He could not explain many things. "I think this is all a dream and as soon as I wake up life will be exactly where I left off!"

"Was your life really so good?"

"I don't have time to analyze how I screwed up my life," he retorted.

Abu quickly told the story of Whetherbee, the jars, what had transpired with John Pierre, and the clues that brought them to the Temple of Sarsa.

John Pierre smiled secretly as he noticed he left out the part about the art thefts.

"Look at me," he pointed to his face and hair. "Look how I have aged. We need help and are running out of time. Can you help us decipher the journal?"

Chapter 96

Rufaaron gestured to the worn journal and it floated to him and hung suspended in the air. His fingers gently slid across the cover as he marveled at the intricate detail.

"Since it is in your possession, then the prophecy is true."

"Prophecy?"

"Abu had it in his possession long before me."

Rufaaron shook his head in agreement. "Yes, but it is useless to him. Only *you* have the power to decipher its secrets."

"*Me*," John Pierre shouted. "I can't read any of this."

"Then you haven't tried hard enough." Rufarron returned the journal to him and waved his aged hand toward a stone shelf filled with books. The shelf separated and opened to a room. Follow me."

Abu smiled with delight as he gazed at the scrolls of parchment and books scattered about the room and on shelves. It was endless. Abu strained his neck as he tried to see where it ended. "How high does this reach?"

"'Tis unknown to any of us. The elders collected for centuries to keep safe. This contains all the written words as we know it in our time."

"'Tis the most sacred of all the libraries," Abu added excitedly as he was in awe to be in the presence of such wonderment.

"It's a scholar's dream," John Pierre added as he stared in amazement at the history before him.

Rufaaron closed his eyes and waved his hand over the ancient shelves. A manuscript high from above slowly floated down and hovered before him. Rufaaron spoke and the book mysteriously opened.

"Ah, here it is," he stated enthusiastically as he scanned the worn parchment. "Someone will come from a land unknown to us. He will journey and steal…if he does not complete the task…time could be altered and…we will be no more."

"What task?" John Pierre begged. "What does this have to do with me and Whetherbee?"

Chapter 97

"The legend says an ancient pharaoh wanted to ensure his immortality and had stolen canopic jars of gold crafted kept by the ancient seers. They allow for time travel. But you already know the pharaoh was killed and a fifth jar is missing."

"So how does this affect me? Why am I aging? And what is Whetherbee's involvement?"

"To prevent the jars from getting in the wrong hands, they are cursed. The legend says you age with each journey."

"But this makes no sense. Whetherbee appears to have spent a lifetime traveling. He came and went; why did he not age as I have?"

Rufaaron sighed heavily. "This I do not know for sure, but the book and probably the journal you can't read make reference to an amulet."

"But John Pierre now wears the same amulets. I don't understand," Abu questioned. "I gave them to him immediately upon his arrival."

"Unfortunately the pages are torn from your journal and the text for some reason is undecipherable to me. Apparently only those with the power are meant to read the journal."

Rufaaron extended his arm and another book from his shelves instantly appeared in his hands. "This has been passed down from generations in my family; it is a journal of amulets. If you are able to open it, perhaps you will find your answer."

Abu tried to open the book. It didn't budge.

Rufaaron laughed. "The book does not like you. You are too rough."

John Pierre was annoyed. "It's just a book! Give it to me. Let me see that!"

Rufaaron waved him off. He took the book from Abu and placed it on the wooden table. "Only those with the gift can open the texts of the ancients. You must not touch the pages, or you will be harmed."

John Pierre laughed. "I told you I don't believe in this ridiculous sorcery."

Abu gasped. "Then how do you explain your presence or how we made it through a wall of solid rock?"

"Unfortunately, I don't have the time to figure out some common parlor tricks." John Pierre grabbed the book and when he attempted to open it a bolt of energy zapped him to the floor, searing his hands and forearms. He screamed in pain as he lay on the floor.

"I see the book doesn't not like you either as it has permanently marked you." Rufaaron shook his head and smirked at his foolishness. "Impatient, are we?"

"Impatient and difficult," Abu added.

John Pierre rose, rubbing his arms and hands.

"Ok, ok. Just open the book."

Abu focused on the book and moved his right hand over the top feeling its energy.

Rufaaron nodded. "You must touch the corner, or you will never know."

Abu tentatively lowered his hand and let his fingers gently touch the corner. He smiled as the book opened.

Rufaaron nodded in approval. "You must trust your skill, Abu. Remember you would not have been able to pass through the doors to Sarsa once you left."

"What about John Pierre?"

"Your friend, well, I am guessing the gods *allowed* his presence for some reason. They must want something, or perhaps Meretseger *allowed* him to pass as he thought he would be a tasty meal."

"We are wasting time. I just want to stop aging can you two help me or not?" John Pierre asked.

Abu returned his eyes to the book.

John Pierre looked at the pages. "There is nothing written, no pictures. What kind of game is this?"

Abu looked at Rufaaron who nodded to continue.

Abu closed his eyes and concentrated. He began moving his hand about the blank page. In his mind he saw colors of red swirling about. Moment's later words and images appeared and hovered over the pages.

"John Pierre, there is not much time. The images will only last for a moment and then vanish. Study them and tell me if they are familiar to you."

As page after page was turned, John Pierre watched in awe as different images appeared, disappeared, and reappeared. The invisible text and images floated right off the pages. "That's it," he pointed to the ring that hovered above the page. "I recognize it. Whetherbee wore it all the time."

Chapter 98

Rufaaron looked at the ancient text next to the ring and read. "They were crafted with the jars. The wearer of the sacred ring is protected. If *not* worn and time travel is successful, then rapid aging will occur."

"Do you think there are rings for all the five jars made?" asked Abu.

John Pierre looked solemnly at Rufaaron who read another sentence from the ancient text, "Death will come on the last journey without the ring. All cycles must be completed before you can start again. It seems as though your Whetherbee must have found the fifth jar and the ring."

John Pierre looked toward Abu and exclaimed excitedly. "Abu, we *were* missing something; the text said, *'they'* – perhaps there's more than one ring!"

Rufaaron smiled knowingly and nodded. "Crafted by the ancients themselves but apparently stolen, without a ring you will die."

"We don't even know if Whetherbee had the ring. He died in an accident and his body was never recovered."

Abu was confused. "But what about the amulets? They must be worn around your neck. These are needed if you die to travel to the Hall of Judgment. So where is Whetherbee if you say he died? Whetherbee, like you John Pierre, wears the amulets."

"He is correct," Rufaaron offered as he summoned the book and it hovered before him. The pages turned and words floated in the air as he continued to search. "Ah, here it is. Anyone who wears the amulets will and must travel to the Hall of Judgment."

Abu's face lit up. "Whetherbee *has to* be alive. See, John Pierre, I told you Whetherbee must go to the Hall of Judgment," Abu said confidently.

John Pierre looked perplexed. "I can't even believe I'm going to say this, but how is it possible? Whetherbee died in my time, not in Egypt."

"Mr. John Pierre, tell me again how you came here?"

John Pierre sat on a worn bench and scratched the stubble on his chin from lack of shaving and quickly gave the ancient elder the condensed version of how it all began. "I then recited the ancient text and repeated the words." The moment John Pierre repeated the ancient words the book began to float toward him.

Abu and Rufaaron stared, wide-eyed in surprise, as the book floated to John Pierre. John Pierre quickly stood, and the stool toppled backwards. Words jumped off the pages and hovered in the air. John Pierre read them easily.

Speak my words and take me home
The world awaits - for me to roam
Through zones and dimensions riches await
Unimaginable power is my fate
Armies will rise – the die is cast
Only I will be the last

"This is what's on the papyrus from Whetherbee – the so-called Curse of Anubis, that Lacey assured me was a lie. She told me the curse was a fabrication. Perhaps Whetherbee played a trick on Lacey and Montgomery and the curse was real. He must have discovered it with the rings or the jars!"

"Tis possible, but tell me if you can read more."

John Pierre looked back at the book and once again the words floated in the air. "The ring needs to be worn for all time travel. Rapid aging and death occur for those who do not wear the sacred ring. The ring or jars in the hands of Anubis will be fatal to all societies and peoples."

The words vanished as quickly as the book had floated to John Pierre.

"The Curse of Anubis and a warning from the ancients of the dangers if the jars and ring or rings are not cared for properly," Rufaaron nodded, his voice filled with grave concern.

Chapter 99

Abu gasped in disbelief. "You read the book, how is it possible?"

Rufaaron looked a bit perplexed but was seemingly not surprised.

"Abu, I know not what you are involved in, but your friend has started something that must be finished. You have put the fate of this culture at stake. Ultimately, you must face the gods and Anubis. Anubis will want the jars, and he will stop at nothing to get them."

Abu looked perplexed. "Why is this so important to Anubis?"

"Think, Abu. Anubis needs all the jars, all the lids, and the ring to make it through the portal! Just think of the power he would have if he could go back and forth in time."

Rufaaron shrugged. "There is something missing. The gods, *including* Anubis, are all bound to their own time period. No gods can breakthrough or there would be chaos. There can be no interference. Man must make his own mistakes in each time period, without meddling from anyone including the gods. If a portal has been discovered, then not only is there a danger to our world but the world *you*, John Pierre, exist in as well as other worlds. Anubis must have *something else,* in addition to both the jars and rings, that will enable him to travel through the portal."

"Now that would be a sight; Anubis running around the streets of New York," John Pierre remarked sarcastically.

"If he breaks into another plane, another world, he could change that too and the world; this New York as you speak of may no longer exist," Rufaaron added.

"So let me see if I understand all of this. There are five canopic jar lids that allow for time travel, if you wear the ring, you will not age. But I only have four jars. You must complete all the four or possibly five cycles of travel before you can start traveling again. None of this helps because I only have four jars and no ring. So, basically, I'm aging with each journey and going to die, unless perhaps I find the fifth jar and some ring!"

John Pierre looked horrified. "Abu, I must return to my time and search for more clues. We must leave at once."

"Unfortunately, this is not possible," Rufaaron stated. "You already said travel could not be accomplished until the full moon. The next moon is in five nights and when the stars are to the west and at the brightest."

"But I left immediately the last time!"

"Perhaps it was at the end of the full moon cycle? Time is elusive. What happens when you leave one portal and enter another is never the same. Time is dynamic and not static. During the next interval you may stay longer or need to leave within hours. You need to be aware of the moon cycles or you may miss a travel time."

John Pierre threw his hands up exasperated. "This is insane! It's like I must have a lunar map for traveling! Well, that explains why I returned to the museum at a different time."

"Following the moon is easy; we simply track the stars and watch the sky…and then we will…"

John Pierre rolled his eyes, clearly frustrated, and interrupted. "The technology I have in my time is better and quicker. I can just turn on the television or an app or read the paper and know immediately what the next moon cycle phase is or where the constellations will be…this will take too long!"

Abu frowned.

"While Abu and I may not understand the devices you speak of, is your technology so great? It may be advanced or quicker, but do you think ancient civilizations were so unintelligent? Just look at what you have seen thus far. Think about how you arrived here?" Rufaaron disputed. "I am quite confident Abu can track the next moon cycle for you with no difficulty."

"Abu, can you get us out of here? We must leave at once."

"Rufaaron, we must return to pyramid complex. Can you get us there?"

Rufaaron smiled. "Of course my young friend, but I must warn you. The game you play is dangerous; you *must* complete your studies. You *must* understand and overcome *your* difficulties. *You*," he pointed at Abu, "have a great deal to learn. You will *no* longer be allowed entrance to the great temple of Sarsa *unless* it is to complete your training."

Before they could say goodbye, he removed a wand from the folds of his robes and dipped it into one of the canisters on the table. Sand adhered to the tip as he pulled it out. Rufaaron moved it slowly in a circular motion and then backwards in the shape of a triangle, sand began to pour out of the wand. With eyes closed, he muttered unfamiliar phrases in a language long forgotten and the two were gone.

Chapter 100

Abu and John Pierre found themselves back at the Giza Complex, behind a pile of rocks, entangled in one another on the soft ground. They rose and dusted the sand off their garments. "We should have been more specific and told Rufaaron to put us inside the pyramid," Abu stated.

"Abu, before I leave, I must get back inside the jewelry mastaba. I must study that relief again," John Pierre demanded.

Abu smirked. He wasn't fooled. "No, you just want to take more jewels."

"Look, I need to get a closer look at that painting. I'm not going to deny that while I'm there I will take more. The jewelry is incredible. I have a special sack to carry it."

Abu laughed. "There are guards all over, no thanks to you. That mastaba now has twenty-four-hour security as someone discovered the art is missing. Since the guards are stationed there all the time, it will be impossible to get in. The fact that you were able to enter before is a miracle."

"It is not impossible. I got in earlier because I caused a brief distraction."

"A distraction that has not gone unnoticed. Remember, the pharaoh is anxious to have his tomb and everything he will take with him completed. He is taking no chances."

John Pierre laughed. "I will tell you this, Abu, if there is one thing that remains constant throughout history is theft. The desire to steal has challenged man to build bigger and higher AND stronger structures and vaults with better materials throughout the ages. Every building has a weakness. We just need to find it and the right moment; therefore, we must stake out the mastaba."

Abu raised his eyebrows in question. "I do not understand this 'stake out?'"

"We will watch and wait for the right time. They have to sleep sometime, right?"

"It will be difficult. Work does not stop after dark. Men come in shifts. I told you, they are eager to complete the pharaoh's final resting place."

John Pierre threw up his hands. "If it is the only way we are going to solve the mystery, then we must do it. Nightfall will be upon us shortly. We'll return to your home and get something to eat and come back after dark."

Chapter 101

"We are never going to get in," Abu whispered. "The pharaoh's men are all over. We have hidden behind every building, stone, and cart; I think this is a dead end. I shudder to think of our penalty if we get caught."

"Have faith, my friend; I have an idea. Watch! Someone is bringing him something to eat. Tomorrow it will be one of those women over there. Come we'll return to the camels, and I will tell you the plan."

Chapter 102

The following evening Abu and John Pierre crouched behind a pile of stones and watched as one of the women approached the guards and offered them their dinner. Her dress was so low cut that her ample bosom looked as if it would fall out. Abu was laughing. "She is telling him she will take care of their needs after they have eaten."

John Pierre shook his head in disgust. Whores, concubines… whatever you wanted to call them – no matter what century, that relationship between man and woman was always for sale. They paid her handsomely in jewels and coin in anticipation.

The two guards finished their meal of bread and chicken, quickly, eager to give themselves to the buxom woman. As they placed their trays down, the woman smiled and handed them a cool beverage. Abu and John Pierre held their breaths as they waited for them to take a sip of Abu's special tea. Seconds later, the guards were on the floor. Abu and John Pierre sprang into action the minute the guards slumped to the ground.

The woman smiled as a pouch of jewels was stuffed into her outstretched hands. Regardless of the language barrier it was evident from her hand gestures and laughter that she was happy to give the men what they deserved, which was a hard kick between their legs.

Three other women jumped from the shadows and loaded one of the guards in a cart and covered him with hay.

"Where are they taking him?"

Abu shrugged. "Probably going to dump him in the Nile River. Either the crocs or hippos will get him, and he will die a permanent death."

"No need for a fair trial. Just the death penalty," John Pierre joked.

"They must dispose of the body immediately. If the guard is found, there will be trouble. The pharaoh and his men will be on high alert and they will not hesitate to search from door to door. Besides, that guard they say he is one of the worst. He treats women so bad that he often kills them. She called him a pig and thanked us for the opportunity to deal with him."

John Pierre and Abu laughed.

Chapter 103

As John Pierre took a knife and cut off the rudimentary lock Abu asked, "What are we going to do with his friend?"

John Pierre hauled the other man over his shoulder as they made their way deep into the mastaba. "Come, we do not have time to look at everything."

"But this is unbelievable. I never imagined so much art and jewelry were stored in here. If anyone knew about this…"

"Well, someone knew about it and that someone became very rich," John Pierre reminded him.

John Pierre lowered the sleeping guard in a dark corner of the jewelry room laid a few necklaces around the guard's neck and placed vases near his body. He filled the vase and positioned it on its side to make it look like he fell. He looked up when he heard Abu chuckling.

"Ah, I see what you do, you make it look like the guard was stealing. You are clever man."

"What's he going to tell the pharaoh? He decided to steal company time and have sex instead of working and guarding his prized treasures? The pharaoh will kill him instantly."

John Pierre felt bad. He stopped and stared at the man. He didn't want him to get in trouble. He would pay dearly for a crime he didn't commit.

Abu read the distress on his friend's face. "John Pierre, I see you are conflicted. Do not worry he is a very bad man. He is not nice to the women who work in this area. They will be glad to see him removed from this post."

"Shhh. Just help fill the bag with all the jewelry. Be quick. I am going to take a look at that painting again."

"Absolutely not! The gods are powerful and will not approve. 'Tis bad enough I am in trouble with Rufaaron."

John Pierre glanced sideways and smirked. "You do realize you're already an accessory to the crime?"

Abu's shoulders slumped in defeat.

"Don't worry I won't tell anyone," he laughed. "Now hand me that bag and have a look at the drawing," he pointed to the wall.

Abu was dusting the dirt from the upper corner and uncovered the rest of the inscription on the plane. John Pierre joined him when he was finished. "Wow, I really think that is my mother's name. I cannot believe it. Do you suppose Whetherbee knew her?"

"I have no idea, but if I ever get my hands on Whetherbee he has a lot of explaining to do," John Pierre whispered sharply.

"Do you see anything? Is there anything that you recognize?"

Abu shook his head no. "We need to hurry; the air is getting too thick and the pharaoh's guards are going to pass soon."

"I will take some photos and download them to the computer so I can study the images."

Abu threw up his hands in frustration as John Pierre continued to snap photos.

John Pierre changed his angle and continued taking pictures as he spoke. "There is a lot we do not know about your culture due to damaged art by man - the pharaohs, erosion, or missing links from lost, stolen, or destroyed images. Much of it is still buried in temples or deep in the sand. When we uncover artifacts, we must try to put the pieces together. There are no books to tell us how you lived or how you built the pyramids. Until the Rosetta Stone was deciphered, we didn't even know how to read your language."

John Pierre stopped taking pictures. Abu thrust another bottle of water into his hand. "I do not know of this Ros…et Sone, but we must leave at once. It is getting too hot; I can see you are having difficulty breathing. There is not much oxygen the further back we go. Come, it's late. We must leave before we are discovered."

Chapter 104

They proceeded directly to the mastaba and Abu was arguing with John Pierre. "Why must you leave now? You just arrived!"

"It is the night of the full moon, I must go. We have already talked about this.

John Pierre had pulled on his jeans and was tucking in his green polo shirt. "I must download these pictures to my computer. I must see if I can learn anything more. I can't do that without some more help."

"But you must return."

John Pierre grabbed his bag and slung it over his shoulders. "Abu, I will do my best. But if for some reason if I can't..."

Abu rambled on as he hurried after John Pierre. "But, sir, I think you're making a mistake. I will look for you every day."

John Pierre was too excited about his discoveries and the technology that awaited him back home that would help him put the pieces of the puzzle together to even think about the ramifications of his hasty decision. He felt bad leaving Abu, but he had to go. He reached in his pocket for the lid and thrust it into the cold stone reciting the ancient dialect as he turned the artifact and quickly disappeared.

Chapter 105

John Pierre stretched and rolled to his side. Every muscle in his body ached. His head was pounding and the noise around him was making it worse. His eyes fluttered open and he squinted as he attempted to focus on his surroundings. Stone. His hand slowly moved as he reached to rub his eyes. More stone.

"Mr. Boudreau! Mr. Boudreau!" voices shouted in unison.

John Pierre knew those voices - the guards at the museum. He was back. Yes, it was all coming back to him. "Mr. Boudreau, are you alright? What are you doing here?" They shouted.

John Pierre winced as their voices bounced off the wall in the enclosed mastaba.

One of them reached down to help him. His efforts to rise were noted as he struggled to lean up against his duffel bag. The guards looked at one another with concern and gasped when he sat upright. He looked terrible. His skin was wrinkled, his hair grayer and skin paler.

"Mr. Boudreau, do you want us to call someone? What are you doing in the mastaba? Are you injured?"

John Pierre sighed. He forgot about timing and needed to figure out how to return when the museum was empty.

"What time is it?"

"It's just after 7:15 a.m., sir."

He rubbed his forehead and stretched his shoulders. He was exhausted. Every muscle in his body ached. He winced as he reached for and rubbed his upper thighs trying to formulate a story. The lies flowed out easily. "I was doing field work, gentleman. No need to worry. I told you before I am working on another exhibit and thought if I spent time in the mastaba I would learn more about the lives of the Egyptians. Sleeping in here was not a good idea, especially without some type of mattress. He held out his arm. "I would appreciate if you would help me rise."

"But, Mr. Boudreau, you look exhausted, are you sure you are ok? I can call a doctor for you."

John Pierre grabbed the small duffel bag. "Not necessary, but I appreciate your concern. Please go ahead with your duties."

John Pierre tried to walk quickly through the museum, but he was finding it difficult. His entire body felt as if he had been in a fight, and the duffel bag was proving to be an additional burden. He hurried past staff as they stared at him, eyes wide in shock as he passed. He couldn't imagine what he even looked like but from the expressions on their faces he knew it wasn't good. Jumping into the first available elevator he sighed heavily as the doors closed.

"I'm sorry, but Mr. Boudreau is not in yet," Miriam snapped, as she watched someone heading toward her boss's office. So engrossed in her typing she did not hear the elevator close. It was a moment before she realized someone had walked passed her desk. "Excuse me," she said rising. John Pierre knew he would have to face her sooner or later.

He stopped walking and turned. "It's just me, Miriam," he stated nonchalantly as if it was just another day at the office. He quickly entered his office and shut the door behind him.

Miriam gasped as her hands flew to her mouth in astonishment. Her boss had aged at least another five, maybe ten years. She was speechless.

"Miriam," John Pierre barked over the intercom. Miriam raced to her desk. It sure sounded like him. "Yes, sir. What do you need?"

"I don't know what's wrong with me, but I need to do some important research. I need you to hold my calls and cancel my appointments for the week. Make any excuse possible. I also need you to have the conservation department bring me *all* the files on the canopic jar donation from Whetherbee."

"But, sir, I thought that matter was closed."

John Pierre shook his head in frustration. "Yes, yes. I know it was, but I need to review those files again. Tell whoever is down there today to bring the information immediately!" he snapped.

"Sir, George Newberry called again and stopped by to see you yesterday."

"Tell him I have the flu again and I'll call him."

John Pierre took the duffel bag and immediately went into his private restroom. He opened the bag and pulled out a few pieces. They gleamed in the light. Turning over the necklace in his hands, he muttered, "Solid gold, lapis…it's like it was made yesterday." In actuality it was, but how was he going to get the pieces out of the museum with out raising suspicion was another matter. A knock at his door interrupted his thoughts. He quickly put the pieces back in the duffel bag and hid them in his closet.

Chapter 106

"Are you looking for something specific, sir? Perhaps I can help you?" Lindsay stated. She was grateful Muriel had prepared her before entering the office. Her boss looked terrible. His gray hair and wrinkled skin made him look as if he was sixty or perhaps seventy years old. She did as Muriel said and acted as if there was nothing wrong. "If you let me know what part of the research you are interested in, I could tell you what stack of files to start with."

John Pierre was feverishly going though the files on the cart. He was lost and needed help. "I would like to see the research on the piece of papyrus that came with the collection Whetherbee gifted to the museum."

She sighed heavily. That was simple enough. She extracted the file in seconds and handed it to her boss.

John Pierre flipped through the pages as he walked to his desk. "Where is the papyrus?"

"In the conservation lab, sir. Since the exhibit was cancelled, it was put away with the rest of the artifacts Mr. Whetherbee left to us."

"Have the artifacts pulled for me and set up an area for me to work. I will be down within the hour to look at them again."

"But, sir, do you know how many crates there are? We are in the middle of all sorts of projects for upcoming exhibitions."

John Pierre shook his head. He knew she was right, and his request was unusual, even for him.

"I am well aware of the donation and the contents. Just give me a space to work and pull the piece of papyrus for me to examine. If someone could bring the crates near, I will open them myself. Please call Muriel when it is ready for me to view."

Chapter 107

$\mathcal{J}$obeher followed as Anubis entered the Grand Chamber of the Gods and took his place at the end of the ornately carved wooden table. Each sat in their rightful place with their most trusted servant or advisor at their side. Osiris, Isis, Horus, Sobek, Hathor, Khephri, Mat, Ra, Thoth, Sekhmet, Bastet, Geb, and even the despised Seth; they were all there. It was the annual meeting for the top-ranking officials. There was business to discuss and Anubis knew he was in the hot seat.

Osiris, the High Judge, wasted no time getting to the point. "So is it true? Is he here?"

Anubis shook his head. "It seems so. Somehow he traveled with Samir."

Intakes of breath were followed by words of disbelief, "Oh no! Impossible," echoed throughout the room.

"Nobody has seen Samir in centuries. Anubis, you told us he was dead," spat Hathor.

"How was Samir able to get through the portal?" We are all bound to this time. How is it even possible Samir was able to do it?" Horus the God of Vengeance demanded.

"'Tis another one of his lies," Bastet cried out.

Sobek gritted his crocodile teeth. "You sent Samir, that fool, to deal with him. His intentions are wicked. The bastard that he is lost his way the minute he entered the world. He is a vile creature. How could you trust him with such a task?"

Anubis was annoyed. "Look, I don't know *what* happened to Samir or *how* he traveled or *if* he traveled through the portal. I am not sure of anything, but they are both here now."

"Are they dead?"

"No, they are both *alive*."

Stunned, the gods gasped in unison.

"If they are alive, they need to go through the Hall of Judgment, 'tis the rule," Thoth, the god of knowledge and wisdom, reminded him.

"I am well aware of the protocol! Do not waste your breath reciting procedures to me!"

"I hope you have not begun torturing him. If he dies before entering the Hall of Judgment it could be the end of us all," Isis scolded him.

"Enough," shouted Anubis angrily. "I am well aware of the laws. I only gave him a taste of what is to come if he fails to give me what I need. Jobeher will heal and release them shortly.

Osiris took his staff and pounded it into the floor. The room shook like a volcano waiting to explode. "Anubis, you are foolish! I demand you heal both of them now. Your intentions are selfish, as usual. As for Samir, we will deal with him in the usual way. But we must discover *whom* our traveler is and if he is really one of us, or perhaps he is someone from somewhere beyond the portal. The process must begin!"

"Gentlemen," Isis said calmly as she held up her hand demanding quiet. "Unfortunately, if he arrived in chamber 6166, then the Hall of Judgment will *not* be his first journey." She waved her hand and an ancient text appeared in the center of their circle.

Chapter 108

*T*hree weeks has passed, and John Pierre had spent the majority of it in the conservation lab looking at the pottery collection of canopic jars donated by Whetherbee. He was so frustrated.

The only thing he discovered was each of the gold jars, had the mark of the pharaoh that was seen via x-rays on the bottom. The jar was later coated with gold or what material he wasn't sure. Using the equipment in the lab he did an intense analysis.

Other than the markings nothing stood out. He checked the crates and found nothing unusual. It would take him years to catalogue and have everything tested. There was no mention of a ring either.

He did take the time to spell Curse of Pharaohs backwards and match the numbers in the journal and came up with Sarsa again. When he spelled Made in Egypt backwards and matched the numbers, he only got *dagge.* He then added all the letters in the alphabet to the end and smiled when it spelled "dagger."

It was possible if he spelled backwards Made in Egypt Curse of the Pharaohs, then it all made sense; the "r" was a match in the number sequence. Another code.

S	H	O	A	R	A	H	P		F	O		E	S	R	U	C
1	2	3	4	5	6	7	8		9	10		11	12	13	14	15

T	p	y	g	e			n	i		e	d	a	m
16	17	18	19	20			21	22		23	24	25	26

24 25 19 19 20 5   Dagger

The staff in the conservation lab thought he had lost his mind when he asked if any daggers were discovered in the crates.

One day, while doing his laundry, he discovered a piece of papyrus in his pocket. It was another shopping list from Abu, who managed to sneak it in the clothing in his back pocket before he departed. While in the lab he discovered another list left in the journal. "Why that ungrateful…how dare he…if he thinks I'm going shopping for chips, candy and more magazines… well, he can get a subscription for all I care and call a delivery service," he spoke to the jars at his table.

News of his erratic behavior and strange outburst became daily gossip amongst the staff.

Chapter 109

Muriel didn't know what to make of the situation with her boss and was worried. The entire museum was talking, and he wasn't returning any phone calls. She did her best to shield him from the board. She reminded Mr. Newberry and the others he was busy putting together a new collection, as John Pierre had instructed her.

"Muriel, do you remember the people who entered my office recently?"

Muriel removed her glasses and eyed him skeptically. "Is there a problem? You have people in and out all day long. Are you missing something? If you are, then review the security cameras."

"No, I was just trying to remember who I met over the past three years and…"

"Three years?" she shouted bewildered. "You *already* asked me. Do you have any idea how many people you meet and speak with daily? I already told you if it's something specific, I'd have to review the calendar or the security footage, but the footage is archived. It would take years to review the tapes. I don't have the time."

John Pierre shook his head. He could see by the look on her face that Muriel was getting suspicious. "Never mind, it's not important."

He was feeling the effects of aging more than ever and the next full moon wasn't for another five days.

His home office looked like a crime unit in a police station. All his computers were open to various ancient web sites.

Reference books were strewn across the desk and floor. Dry erase boards were filled with notes and speculations from his findings. Photographs were laid out on the table. He moved them around as he tried to find similarities between the photos and drawings from Abu.

If Whetherbee *was* a time traveler, he could see him leaving clues, as was evident by the building in New York drawn on the wall and his plane with Abu's mother's name written on the side. Perhaps they knew one another. Abu was not sure.

The photos from both drawings were laid out side by side. He sat in his leather chair and looked up at them and his eyes widened.

The moon was full in both paintings, as they had already discovered that clue, but one of the skyscrapers was not the building that should have been next to the Empire State Building. John Pierre scanned the photo into the computer and did a search of the buildings by address since he could not make it out on the screen.

He wasn't surprised when Whetherbee's Park Avenue address appeared. "I was right. It is a map. Whetherbee is telling me to go to his penthouse."

He showered quickly and put on one of his best suits. He had a meeting with the board this evening. Anthony the former mayor insisted on it. Muriel didn't know what it was about. After the meeting, he would stop at Whetherbee's apartment.

Chapter 110

The Duat

Anubis walked slowly down the long, dark corridor of stone. His trusted companion Jobehar was at his side. The stone on his staff illuminated the passage and brightly painted hieroglyphics on the wall. While he was powerful, he wasn't sure what or whom he was going to encounter in chamber 6166. He and Samir had arrived together but in different chambers. The situation occurred many moons ago, but time was so elusive, even he couldn't recall when it began; nonetheless, it was of grave concern and he did not want to admit that even he, the Great Anubis, was not sure how to proceed or what was to come.

Anubis held up his staff and the door of the stone chamber automatically opened. With a wave of his hand the torches on the wall automatically came to life. He scanned the small room and found his prey leaning back against the wall, shielding his eyes from light.

The man was stunned as he looked at the imposing figure before him – Anubis. The almighty jackal, king of the dead, was standing before him. The legend was reality.

Jobehar shape-shifted into his human form and waited for direction from his master. With the wave of his hand, his throne appeared and Jobehar adjusted the flowing, black cloak of Anubis. He shape-shifted again and took his place at his master's side. If the man thought of doing anything, he was ready to restrain him.

"So we finally meet. I must admit I never thought it was possible. But here we are. You must tell me how you have managed to exist."

"I do not know what you speak of."

Anubis smirked and leaned forward. "Really? You will cooperate or those you love will be killed, including her. Tell me your name."

When the man did not answer, Anubis shrugged, "So be it." His right hand moved slowly through the air and the man began to choke. He struggled to breathe as his body floated into the air. He saw Anubis shift his palm and he immediately dropped to the floor.

"Now, as I was saying, due to my half-brother's carelessness, you have upset the balance and order of life in Egypt."

The old man looked perplexed. "I don't understand. I have done nothing wrong. The last thing I recall is I was attacked, and I awoke here."

Anubis folded his hands across his lap and chuckled. "I do not know what trickery you used on Samir, for I have not seen him in so many moons that I have lost count. We thought he was dead. Out of nowhere you both materialized and apparently together."

The older man was stunned. He thought Samir was dead.

"Impossible. Samir is dead. I killed him with the dagger from the ancient Temple of Sarsa. I watched him die. That is the last time I saw him. I tell you the truth," he whispered.

"*More lies*," Anubis roared. "Only the greatest shamans have access to the dagger and secrets of the Temple of Sarsa."

"I am te..lling you the tr..uth," gasped the man as an invisible force was grasping his neck causing him to gasp for air.

Anubis let him breath again. The old man suffered a fit of coughing and massaged his throat. "I am telling you Samir can't be alive. I saw him die," he whispered.

Chapter 111

Anubis eyes blazed shades of green in anger as he studied the old man. "Perhaps, but nonetheless he is alive. Don't look so shocked. Samir may be dumb, but he is not stupid. He claims he spent ages searching for you and in the process figured out something about the portal but unfortunately made the mistake of attempting to kill you. And as for the dagger, it would be *impossible* for you to have in your possession. The elders guard it. The location is unknown, even to me. Now if *you* don't cooperate, I *will* kill you."

"What do you want?"

"You stole the golden canopic jars and rings and I want them returned. I also want the location of the portal revealed."

Whetherbee laughed. "That's it. Those jars are all you want."

Anubis raised his palm and the man felt himself floating up in the air. He was suspended upside down as if he was hanging from an invisible tree. "I have heard the stories about the plundering of the art from those who have passed through the Hall of Judgment. I believe you and Samir are somehow connected to the thefts."

The man fell hard as his body dropped to the floor. He must have fallen at least eight feet. Thankfully he used his arms to shield his head to avoid a concussion. His entire body ached. "Why now? Why come for me now."

"Believe me, I have been looking for you, but you have been elusive."

"The only way I can get what you need will be to return to the portal," the man coughed.

Anubis roared with laughter. "Do you actually think I am going to believe that story? Do not take me for a fool, sir. I know you are a clever man. Jobehar show our guest what you will do to him if he fails to cooperate."

Jobehar immediately approached the man and bit him in the leg. Whetherbee screamed in pain.

"It's painful isn't it? His saliva is filled with a deadly poison." The old man could feel his body getting cold. "It literally sucks the life out of you while inflicting pain at the same time." He was shivering and it felt like someone was sticking thousands of daggers through his body.

He could barely utter the words. "You don't un..der..stand. I thin…k Sa..mir ki…lled me and re….moved the a….m… from m..nec…"

"Enough," Anubis shouted. He rose, walked toward the man and stuck the tip of his wand in his left shoulder.

The man screamed in pain. It was as if hundreds of needles were plunged in his arm. The pain subsided.

"I have given you an antidote for Jobeher's poison. You see, I am really not such a bad person. Now you were saying," he said as he walked back to his throne.

"Something happened with Samir; we fought, and he took the amulets from my neck. I don't have the jars. I can't return."

"Well, we have a problem my friend…let us just say you and everyone connected to you, including *her,* will die. I will make it my mission to find *her*. I heard about the strange relief with the name *Astiramare* from a man passing through the Hall of Judgment. 'Tis a *very* ancient name. I already set the plan in motion. I will have all the women raped and killed by the pharaoh until she is found."

The color from the man's face drained.

"Ah. I see I have your attention, old man. Ammit will do it slowly; she will suffer a permanent death, and your souls will *never* reunite no matter what. How does it feel?"

Anubis rose and his throne disappeared as he waved his hand. "Come, Jobehar, we have preparations to make, but before we leave you may drain some blood from his legs."

Whetherbee had one last card to play. "The child is alive."

Chapter 112

Anubis stopped walking and appeared instantly before Whetherbee.

Whetherbee tried not to be impressed. He swallowed hard. "That's right, you heard me – the child lives. If you kill me your chances at finding any answers will die too. Do you think I would not have another plan? He is alive. Go ahead and ask Samir," Whetherbee lied.

Anubis stood up straight. "It seems I have some time on my hands. I will consult with Samir, and then we will see how astute *he* really is. But no matter what, the end result is death. It always is."

Chapter 113

John Pierre sat in the board meeting and was barely listening. Nicholas, Victor, Anthony, and George wanted him out and had convinced the rest of them to vote him off the board and replace him with another director. His hair was completely gray. His face was weathered and wrinkled. He moved slowly, like the seniors he knew in his own building.

Robert and George gave him the standard speech, "We are changing the focus of the program; we need someone with fresh ideas."

John Pierre was aging with each trip and knew if he didn't find some answers he would probably die. He agreed to clear out his desk. He would attend the Whetherbee Benefit on Friday where his retirement would be announced.

He also wanted full access to the museum and privileges to work in the conservation lab. He convinced the board he was occupied with scholarly research and anything he uncovered would be donated to the museum, including the donation he had showed them earlier. They agreed to give him an office near the conservation lab.

George added that his replacement would be announced on Friday.

He no longer cared.

Mary Rockefeller Harding hugged him. It was like getting the kiss of death. She said she would miss him and was so sorry.

Her sincerity was so disingenuousness he wondered how he worked with her or any of them for as long as he did. He didn't miss how she smiled at Leo. It was as if they won some major award.

Jocelyn invited him to spend some time with her family in the Hamptons.

Nicholas smiled as if he just won an academy award. He said nothing to him. John Pierre guessed he was throwing his name into the ring for his job.

Chapter 114

Before he left, he stopped by his office and grabbed the rest of his pertinent notes and files, the canopic jars, and lids before making his way to the Egyptian collection. He took the first lid and stuck it into the mastaba indentation and recited the words. Nothing. He repeated with the falcon and baboon head. Nothing happened. He breathed a sigh of relief. It was risky, but he had to know if it would work.

The conditions he traveled on both the first and second trips were during the full moon. He had much to do before the next full moon, which was on Friday, the day of the Benefit.

Chapter 115

"**M**r. John Pierre, I am so sorry I didn't recognize you," gasped the doorman of Whetherbee's building, who continued to apologize for his mistake.

"I'm just going to pick up some things, if that's ok."

"Don't worry, Mr. Boudreau. I was told the apartment was left to you. I thought you would have been by sooner."

John Pierre shrugged. "The lawyers were still dealing with all the paperwork for the estate. I'm sure you will see me more often."

The doorman let him pass.

You had to be a millionaire to live here. No expense was spared, and luxury was at its finest from the marble lobby, gold elevator doors, hinges – it was incredible. He quickly entered the elevator and pushed the button for the penthouse suite.

John Pierre was deposited in the hallway. He entered the main entrance with his key. Everything was as it had looked the last time he was in the apartment with Whetherbee, clean. His eyes scanned the grand foyer, living room, and kitchen. Art was scattered about the apartment. He took a closer look at the Egyptian pieces and smiled. He was sure they had been recently removed from Giza Plateau. He shook his head and grinned.

He walked toward the back to Whetherbee's office. He was shocked when he opened the door. Paper was strewn about and chairs were overturned. It looked like someone had broken in and was looking for something. Funny, none of the art, worth millions, was touched. "If I was Whetherbee, where would I hide something?" he muttered.

He went through the desk and drawers of paper but found nothing pertaining to art. It was all business related. John Pierre leaned back in the expensive leather chair and rubbed his temples. He was tired and knew time was not on his side. He sighed heavily and then smiled as he stared at various pictures of him and Whetherbee that were positioned on the corner of the desk. Most of them were of their travels together.

He reached for the one of them in front of the pyramids of Giza. It was his first archeological expedition. Whetherbee had returned with many photos and had them framed. He said, "John Pierre, when you look at the photos always remember our times together and also that the pyramids hold many secrets. The photos will one day reveal them to you."

John Pierre wondered what secrets was he referring too? The canopic jars? He bolted upright in his chair and smiled. He turned the frame over. Whetherbee had the photo matted and archival protected. The frame was sealed. He opened the drawer and found a scissor and carefully cut around the paper backing. He removed more paper and then a small envelope. Out of the envelope came a piece of papyrus with a map and instructions.

"If you have found this, take it to Abu. He will know what to do."

"That's it?" John Pierre yelled in frustration. "No note. Damn you, Whetherbee! I'm almost dead and this is all I get from you!"

John Pierre suddenly smiled as if he made an important discovery. "There are more photos!"

Chapter 116

John Pierre found more papyrus under the other photos on his desk and around the penthouse. They all had inscriptions in hieroglyphics and when put next to one another formed a map of some sort. There was one piece missing. John Pierre opened the drawer and removed a pad of paper and knew what he had to do.

Chapter 117

The museum was alive with activity. The media was everywhere, and the red carpet was rolled down Fifth Avenue and up the museum steps. Limousines were dropping off famous celebrities who after interviews and photographs made their way into the museum for the Whetherbee Benefit and Dinner. Although Whetherbee was dead, he made sure his philanthropic endeavors continued. John Pierre had aged so much on his last visit with Abu that people barely recognized him.

He heard the gasps in the audience as he was introduced and took the podium to speak. The crowd gave him a standing ovation after his decision to retire was announced. He also stated that he would be bequeathing a priceless collection of his *and* Whetherbee's art, including that of a private donor to the museum.

He smiled inwardly as he saw the stunned looks on the board member's faces as he summarized the contents of the gift. His donation included all the pieces he recently had stolen on his journeys. He had the entire collection on display in one of the galleries for all to view.

He then held up a hardcover book he had prepared, cataloguing the pieces as his final gift to the museum with photos. The collection was priceless.

He moved to the side to await the next announcement. The next item of business was who was taking his position. Anthony Meyerson had done an exceptional job at keeping it quiet. Everyone, including John Pierre, was dumbfounded when he called Montgomery Rutland's name.

"Well, now you have it all - the job and the girl," he whispered as they shook hands and smiled for photos.

Nicholas was seated with Mary Rockefeller Harding and some of the other board members. "I see right through you, Nicholas. Don't be disappointed," Mary muttered in his ear. "Montgomery understands the museum world. There was no other choice."

"I thought I had *your* vote Mary?" he said through clenched teeth. "You *promised* me."

She patted his hand and whispered back, "Some things are just meant to be, Nicholas. You just need to be patient. Your time will come."

Nicholas nodded and smiled. There were cameras everywhere and he wasn't about to let his disappointment show. Inwardly, he seethed.

John Pierre found the bar and ordered a shot of tequila and a martini. "On second thought make it two," he told the bartender. He spent the next hour, drinking, chatting with long time acquaintances, and assuring people that he wasn't ill and that he would be working on a project. Others conversed with him about the impressive collection he just donated.

It was probably the first time that he actually enjoyed himself at an event. There was no pressure to network, raise money, or make deals.

When he first took the job at the museum, he never intended on staying long. It was only temporary, but somehow he got caught up in all that he saw before him – the celebrity, prestige, power, and money. Someone was raising their glass and toasting him across the room. He smiled, finished his drink and ordered another.

He watched Charlotte, who had sent him a text message telling him it was over. She was seated across the room with a much younger, handsome man, evidently one of her model friends. She glared at him. She had told him earlier at the bar he had humiliated her, and she was the talk of the town because of their association.

"A text message? That was the best you could do, Charlotte?"

She made a scene, by raising her voice a bit too loud and told him to stay away from her.

George cornered him as he exited the restroom. "Thankfully Charlotte came to her senses and dumped you. It was about time."

"She wasn't worth it," John Pierre whispered and walked away. He was officially drunk and didn't care what he said.

He intercepted Montgomery as he watched him make his way toward a group of important donors and thrust a drink into his hand. "I just wanted to toast you," he sneered.

Montgomery was tense as John Pierre raised his glass. He noticed how J.P. slurred his words. "You may think you have it all, but I can tell you one thing - you will *never* have *all of her love*. No matter *what,* she was *always* mine. She chose a long time ago and *never* gave you a second look. No matter what, I will *always* be with her, but *you* already know that don't you?" John Pierre tapped his glass against Montgomery's as he sauntered away.

Montgomery felt nauseated for the truth the words held.

Chapter 118

$\mathcal{J}$ ohn Pierre scanned the room and headed toward Leo. "Why did you do it, Leo?"

Leo coughed nervously. "I'm not sure I understand what you are referring too?"

"Leo, it doesn't matter. You, George, and the rest of the board…whatever you're up to, it's done. I just want you to know there are no hard feelings. I'm not even mad."

Leo looked down at his feet and then back at John Pierre.

George instantly appeared and inserted his body between the two. "It looks as if our friend has had too much to drink," he announced loudly.

John Pierre swayed a bit and then leaned toward Leo. "I was out late one evening, I know what I saw. I'm sure your wife would love to know about your rendezvous and the fact that you're buying diamonds for someone other than her. Any association with Mary comes with a price," he whispered.

Leo's face turned white as John Pierre walked away.

"What's he talking about?" George demanded.

"Nothing, George; don't worry about it."

"I don't know how you did it, but I have to say the collection is outstanding." John Pierre turned and was face to face with Victor.

"Well, you better figure out how to keep it safe, for it's priceless. Why, Victor? Why do you all despise me so much?"

"You should have hired my daughter. Now with you out of the way, she will be coming home, she will take the place of

Lindsay or someone else. I don't even care. If you played politics better, things may have been different."

"Somehow I doubt it, Victor."

After more drinking and socializing, John Pierre later saw George heading to the far end of the room and followed, pulling him into one of the galleries. "You know, George, it took me a while to figure it out, but it was you wasn't it? You and Stockport were behind my termination. Why?"

Newberry laughed. "We were counting on money from Whetherbee's estate but unfortunately it went to Montgomery. We have plans to merge the institutions and needed to use that money for other interests we have. Montgomery was the best choice. He is not strong like you, before he realizes what has happened, he will be shown the door."

"Those jars were real gold, weren't they? You switched the reports?"

Newberry's eyes narrowed like a snake. "If that's what you think, go ahead and try to prove it!"

"Where does Stockport fit in to all of this? You despise him. What the hell could he possibly do for you?"

George laughed. "Let's just say the philandering playboy that he is already took care of that some time ago! Lacey is officially off the board. By the way, did you actually think I was going to let you carry on with my daughter?" He smiled arrogantly as he walked away.

John Pierre stood there fuming. He was set up and used like a pawn and Lacey would never know the truth.

Chapter 119

He caught sight of Lacey walking toward the Greek courtyard and followed. She was stunning in her off the shoulder black evening dress. She looked like a Greek goddess. "Nice necklace. Does Montgomery know you're still wearing the jewels I gave you?"

Lacey gasped. John Pierre appeared out of nowhere. She absently fingered the necklace. She couldn't part with it. "It's only jewelry; it goes with my dress," she lied.

The diamond necklace was worth a fortune. It was his gift to her on their wedding night. They were married in a castle in the Italian Alps. "You are my one and only princess," he smiled when he draped it around her neck and fastened the clasp. It was her favorite piece of jewelry. It was a mystery as to where he obtained it as he refused to tell her. So, when asked, she began telling stories. It became a game for her and John Pierre when people complemented on the exquisite jewels and asked where it was purchased. A family heirloom passed down from a French queen was a favorite. It was the one thing she could not and refused to part with after the divorce.

Montgomery saw her talking with John Pierre and downed his scotch and ordered another. His eyes blazed like fire when he saw her finger the necklace around her neck. He was not happy she was wearing it. He was annoyed that she preferred it as opposed to the jewelry he gave her. It was one of the many things she never shared with him. He continued to fume as he watched John Pierre follow her further into the gallery.

Chapter 120

Despite how John Pierre had aged, he still looked dashing in his tuxedo. They glared at one another and in that split-second Lacey could have sworn she saw pain deep in his eyes.

He tried to ignore the remark about the necklace. If he weren't so drunk, the words would have hurt more.

John Pierre raised his glass to her his words a bit slurred, "It's ironic, isn't it? After all this time *you* wound up back at this museum back right where it all began and later fell apart," he stated sarcastically. "You're right back to this dusty old building, filled with paintings and statues that *you* desperately wanted to escape from."

"I wanted a life with you, something we could build together. But apparently *I* wasn't enough!"

John Pierre moved closer. "You were all I ever needed and wanted," he whispered. His arms quickly reached out and encircled her waist as he pulled her close. He looked deep into her eyes silently professing his love before his lips found hers.

Their contact was electrifying for both. "No matter what you think, I will *always* love you," he whispered as he kissed her again. "You know what we had, and that bond will *never* be broken."

She was shocked as she felt the hardness of his erection pressed against her leg. Her body reacted just as it had done in the past when they touched or embraced. Her insides were on fire. The heat and passion between them was alive and she returned the kiss with fire then immediately froze before she dislodged herself and backed away.

"You bastard!" The slap she laid across his cheek echoed through the Greek hall. "You," she hissed, "you will not do this to me. I saw you with those women in our bed…"

"You saw nothing," he interrupted. "No matter what I say, you refuse to believe me. One day *you* will learn the truth and when you do, you'll see how wrong you were!"

Lacey was so confused. She couldn't think clearly as the adrenaline surged through her veins from their embrace and what he was saying.

John Pierre laughed. "The joke is on me. For someone who despised all this," he gestured, "you seem to be happy in your role now. I don't understand why you married him!"

Lacey wasn't sure either. She thought it would be easier. They had a mutual passion for art, and they were friends and already knew one another. But it wasn't the same love she shared with John Pierre.

He shook his head, disgusted at how he lost her. "Are you going to work side-by-side with Montgomery now? Good luck, you deserve each other!" he spat sarcastically and walked away.

Lacey wasn't sure if it was the alcohol talking or if he really meant it.

A shadow from behind the statue of Zeus watched them as they walked away. He was alarmed by what he had just observed and knew what he had to do.

Chapter 121

John Pierre staggered through the museum and toward the Egyptian collection. It was sometime after midnight and the party showed no signs of breaking up. He was officially intoxicated - more than ever - and didn't have a care in the world. He stumbled into the empty coat-check room, grabbed the two large duffel bags he had left hours earlier, and proceeded to the mastaba.

It took him a minute to find the canopic jar lid depicting the baboon head, Hapy.

John Pierre slurred the words as he began reciting the ancient text and slowly moving the canopic jar lid but stopped when he heard footsteps approaching.

"What the hell are you doing in here?"

John Pierre looked up and blinked his eyes as he tried to focus on the figure before him. The figure's face was blurred due to his own alcohol consumption. He glanced down. The mastaba was spinning; his body dropped to the floor and everything went black.

Chapter 122

The screams echoed through the museum. While the cleaning lady had never seen a dead body before, she knew when she saw his pale skin that he was dead. She was cleaning the floors and was about to enter the mastaba in the Egyptian wing when she saw blood oozing from the entrance. She peered in to see a man, sprawled on his back, and there was blood on his head and the monument. She ran out shrieking.

The authorities were called, the body was quickly removed, and it was the first time in the history of the museum that it was closed for the day.

Montgomery was not sure how he felt. His former friend and colleague, now gone, found dead in the museum and he was left to deal with the press and Lacey.

He tried calling her, but she had already heard the news on the television and raced over to the museum. "Is it true? Is he really gone?" She sobbed. He comforted her as best he could.

A thorough investigation revealed he had a habit of researching after hours and was recently found in the mastaba on many occasions and at odd hours.

His death was eventually ruled an accident. Because the alcohol content found in his system was above the normal range, it was concluded that he had been walking around during the benefit and wandered into the mastaba, slipped, and was killed the instant his head hit the stone floor.

Lacey made sure he had a proper burial and became distant in the weeks that followed.

Montgomery seethed but patiently waited while she mourned her ex-husband. With John Pierre out of the way, life would be better for them.

Chapter 123

*A*bu bolted upright in his bed. John Pierre was back. He untangled himself from the Martha Stewart comforter, threw on his tunic, grabbed his travel sack, and ran up the steps calling for Arthur.

Abu gasped in shock when he found John Pierre. He was sprawled face down in the dirt of the mastaba. John Pierre was a big man and it took some effort for Abu to roll him on his back. "John Pierre, John Pierre," he called as he slapped his face.

No response. His chest was moving so he wasn't dead, but he smelled terrible. Abu realized he was drunk. Just like the pharaoh's guards after a night of drinking with women. The sun was almost up, and John Pierre was still spread-eagled on the floor.

Abu was worried. The pharaoh was furious after the last robbery of the artifact storage. The one guard discovered inside with jewelry around his neck was immediately executed and the other was still missing. The pharaoh had his men search the entire city looking for him and it wasn't until a man pulling a barge of stone down the Nile discovered his clothing tangled in the marsh reeds, that he was satisfied that he was dead.

The pharaoh was taking no chances. He employed more men and searches continued daily. Abu knew it was not long before they would make their way to his mastaba. As the sky grew lighter, he saw the guards in the distance crossing toward the outlying sand dunes.

John Pierre groaned.

Abu quickly removed John Pierre's expensive clothing and pulled a white garment he had travelled with just in case, over him. His frail body reflected his age.

Abu gasped as his fingers touched the wetness behind John Pierre's head. It was blood. He quickly cleaned and wrapped the wound with water and treated it with a paste of healing herbs he carried with him.

He rubbed dirt on John Pierre's face and wrapped a turban around his head before pulling a hood over his head. His white hair gave him the appearance of an ancient seer. He had just finished hiding John Pierre's belongings when he heard the guards call out.

"We know you're in there, Abu," Moustafa hollered. "I know Arthur wouldn't come here without you, so come on out."

"Damn," Abu muttered as he headed for the entrance.

"Ok, Moustafa, what do you want."

"I want to know what you are doing in there all alone."

"I was in the middle of morning meditation. I pray to all the gods; it is out of respect. Why do you bother me?"

Moustafa spoke in his native tongue and indicated for some of the guards to dismount and search. They reluctantly followed the order.

Abu stepped aside, and knew he was in trouble when they started screaming.

Moustafa dismounted and approached with trepidation. He heard stories about this place and was reluctant to enter.

"Who is this?" He demanded as his guards pointed to John Pierre.

"'Tis only an old relative of mine. He was passing through…"

Moustafa cut him off. "Passing through? That is the best you can do, Abu? 'Tis clear the man has spent time with the bottle. Only 'tis not beer I smell but something stronger. I could smell the stench from outside. Load them up. We will take them to the pharaoh. He will decide what to do with them."

Chapter 124

John Pierre awoke slowly. His head was pounding, and his mouth was dry. He could barely focus as he tried to open his eyes. He needed coffee and some aspirin.

"Hello, John Pierre, 'tis good to see you again," Abu yelled.

John Pierre rubbed his forehead and tried to sit up. His entire body ached. "Is there a reason why you are yelling, Abu?"

"Perhaps if you open your eyes you will see the mess you have gotten us into," he spat.

"Spare me the dramatics, Abu, just go into my bag and get me some aspirin and coffee."

"'Tis I cannot do."

Eyes still closed, John Pierre muttered, "Tell my why you can't *do* this simple task."

"Your bag is not here."

"Because?"

"You arrived in an intoxicated state and because I could not wake you up; we were captured by the pharaoh's guards. I told them you were an old relative just passing through but Moustafa was apprehensive. The Giza Plateau is on lock down. The pharaoh is searching for the person who is stealing his art and jewels. Anything out of the ordinary is suspicious, that includes you. I hid your bags just before Moustafa arrived and took us away."

"Ok, ok. Just tell me where we are. Give me all the details about this location."

"I think they took us to one of the temples across the complex. 'Tis where the pharaoh does business while his pyramid is under construction."

The cool stone was refreshing as John Pierre leaned back and rubbed his temples. His head was throbbing. "What is this around my head?"

"When you arrived you were bleeding at the base of your head. I cleaned and wrapped it in cloth. I rubbed dirt all over your face to help disguise you. Do you know what happened?"

John Pierre was still drunk. His head was still spinning. The amount of alcohol he consumed was considerable even for him. He closed his eyes as he tried to think. Like cars on a freeway during rush hour, all he saw were glimpses of the night prior - the museum, Lacey, liquor, speeches, Newberry, Stockport, board members, Montgomery, faces of acquaintances, the mastaba, and shoes. He needed water and food.

"I can see you are weak. I have a pack of cookies and some water on me, but you must be careful not to eat in front of the guards. I don't know when they will be returning."

John Pierre quickly took the water and pack of cookies from Abu's hand.

"You look terrible. What happened to you?"

"Nothing, I was just stupid."

"I don't understand. You went back to get answers and I see what you find was only a keg of beer. You smell terrible."

He saw an image of Lacey wearing her black dress and diamond necklace. "Ok, so I had too much to drink. The only thing I discovered was I was a fool, that's what."

Abu cocked his head to the side as he tried to understand. "'Tis this um'…fool…'tis the same as the bastard Whetherbee said you were?"

John Pierre sighed heavily. "Never mind. It's not important anymore."

"Ok good, then we must figure out how we are going to get out of here and find the jar and then…"

"Abu, have you taken a good look at me? In case you haven't noticed I am aging at a rapid rate and I don't think I am going to make it," he interrupted.

Abu studied his friend. "Whetherbee said…"

"If I ever get my hands on him," John Pierre interrupted again. "Do you see the mess he has gotten me into? He couldn't just leave a nice note with detailed instructions? Instead, all I get is cryptic papyrus and tales about jars and now I'm old and…"

"So you are giving up? How could you? You promised to help me. Whetherbee was right; you are a sel-fesh bastard."

"The word is selfish."

John Pierre sighed heavily and scratched the side of his face. His beard was itching. "Alright, stop with the reverse psychology. Let's see if we can get out of here. If it's one thing I learned about your culture - there is *always* a way out."

"Oh no, the guards are coming," Abu whispered.

Chapter 125

John Pierre's eyes widened at the site of the two men who stood between him and the locked cage. They were built like professional wrestlers. Even healthy or in his best shape, there was no way he could overtake them. The guards glared at the pair and spoke in their native language.

"They are discussing how to dispose of us. One said they could pick us up and tear us from limb to limb like a piece of papyrus."

Moustafa appeared. "There will be no throwing or tearing just yet. Asim and Runihun will be taking you to the pharaoh. If you try to escape they will kill you both."

"I like a man who gets right to the point."

"Come on, you two, move; the pharaoh is waiting."

The guards walked behind and prodded the two like steers. John Pierre admired the brightly painted hieroglyphics on the walls as they walked through long corridor's that twisted and turned.

At the final turn they found themselves in a large room coved in more brightly painted hieroglyphics on every wall and ceiling. Low relief carvings filled other walls, and pottery of all sizes sat in niches while large statues lined the walls. At least he was an art aficionado. The great pharaoh himself sat on a massive throne at the end of the room. Even seated, his immense size was evident.

He was flanked by more guards, black dogs, and a scribe, who sat below the throne and was working feverishly, recording the words as the pharaoh spoke. Larger statues flanked the entrance and were spread around the perimeter. There was a table complete with food in one corner and another filled with papyrus. In the back of the room, light emanated from a hole in the wall that was cut in the shape of a rectangle. He heard the sounds of water and women.

It was the origins of the modern-day office; time had changed nothing but the decor and technology. Like a modern-day CEO, the great pharaoh was surrounded by opulence, sustenance, and physical activity. Only the modern-day executive didn't have a harem of women right in his office.

"John Pierre, you must kneel and bow before the great lord," Abu hissed.

"What…I will do no such... Ahh…," John Pierre screamed as he fell to the ground. "You didn't have to push me."

"*Silence*," roared the pharaoh.

"Abu, your presence in my chamber is disturbing. Moustafa tells me he has seen you wandering around the Giza site too many times. He thinks you are responsible for the theft of my jewelry."

"Oh, great lord, and in the name of the Gods, I can assure *you* not only 'tis *not* possible but *I* would never consider it."

"What are you doing on the Giza site? You have no business here. You are confined to the mastaba only and you know it."

"I was in the mastaba and planning on showing my friend your great complex. And he wanted to pay homage and bless your great architectural monuments. Moustafa interrupted my morning prayers."

"Who is this friend?" Moustafa demanded.

"John Pierre."

"I have never heard of this John Pierre. From the stench that emanates from him it is clear he has been living in the bottle for days. This entire room will need to be fumigated! I am a busy man and did not anticipate a cleaning today, now you force me to take my appointments elsewhere. For the inconvenience, all invaders must die."

"But my lord, he is not an invader. He is a descent of my family."

"Which is even worse. Your family comes from an old line of fragmented spiritual shamans, whose powers may have been sinister. This evil will not be tolerated in this kingdom. So you must die."

"But neither of us have any power. It is common knowledge that I abandoned my studies, as I apparently am not like others in my family. I have no powers."

The pharaoh ran his fingers through the fur of the large black beast that sat beside him. "Abu, do you think I am an idiot? I do not know what is going on with you, but I do not believe a word of what you say. I am tired of hearing about you wandering on my great pyramid complex. I will have no more of it," he shouted and banged his staff into the stone for emphasis.

John Pierre and Abu jumped as his voice grew louder and louder.

"Asim and Runihun will escort you out and take you to Xgar."

"Where is that?" John Pierre hissed.

"Not where, who. Xgar is the largest crocodile in the Nile."

"Oh great, I couldn't just die peacefully, it will be at the hands of a giant croc."

Chapter 126

"Wait! Before you take us to this Xgar, perhaps we can help you."

The pharaoh peered at John Pierre suspiciously and then began laughing. "Help me with what?"

"If you kill us then great evil will fall upon you," Abu blurted.

The pharaoh laughed again. "Yes, yes, I am aware of the legend, and that is why you have lived as long as you have. However, I have changed my mind and am no longer concerned."

"But I am sure you saw…"

"Silence," roared the pharaoh, who needed no reminder of what he witnessed in the mastaba.

"After consulting with the oracle at the temple of Horus, I realized I had made a grave error concerning you and your family. You see, as long as *I* do not do the killing, this so-called curse will *not* affect me. Asim and Runihun will take you to Xgar now!"

John Pierre and Abu were left tied back to back to a pole and set afloat down the great Nile. While Asim blew through some horn and called for Xgar, Runihan, threw two barrels of dead fish into the murky waters.

"They say its Xgar's favorite and he is sure to come," Abu said reluctantly.

And as if on cue, the giant reptile surfaced.

"He's at least twenty-five feet long," gasped John Pierre.

Abu nodded. "And he has been fed some of the most notorious criminals of our time!"

"Abu, do something! Can't you use your magic?"

"Oh, so now you believe in my magic… when I ask you...,"

"Abu," John Pierre shouted sharply. "Stop rambling and do something!"

"I am afraid I cannot. Xgar is protected by the gods. I am not powerful enough and my magic is unstable."

"But you conjured the hippo."

"The hippo is no match for the mighty Xgar. I will not put him at risk."

John Pierre was drenched in sweat. He tried to remove the ropes while Abu recited prayers. Blood dripped from their arms where the guards had made slight cuts.

"Abu, I command you to get us out of here. Try anything. Take us back to the mastaba," John Pierre screamed.

Xgar's massive head appeared and moved slowly toward the raft. His mighty jaw opened and took a huge bite out of the raft and tipped the structure under the water. The mutilated raft, and pieces of wood floated to the surface. John Pierre and Abu were nowhere in site. The guards took off to report back to the pharaoh satisfied the deed was done.

Chapter 127

ohn Pierre and Abu bumped one another as they rolled through the dirt and continued to scream before they were thrown across the rocky surface before landing on their backs.

"Abu, are you there?" John Pierre coughed as he called out his name.

"I am alive?"

John Pierre waited for the dust to settle before he rose on his elbow. "Are you ok? I said you could do it. You got us out of there. You are going to be a great shaman one day."

Abu rolled over and dusted the dirt off him. "I did nothing, John Pierre. I am not sure what happened or how we got here."

"Well, don't look at me like that, if you think I have some sort of magical power you have been in the hot sun too long. You must have done something, and don't realize it. It doesn't matter; can you just help an old man up?"

Abu rushed over and pulled John Pierre up. "It's dark and there's a full moon, perhaps I should try to return. I need to get back into Whetherbee's apartment. There may be more answers."

"John Pierre, you have aged again. I don't know if you will be able to make it back."

"Don't worry, Abu. Just take the supplies I brought and wait for my return. I have to figure a way out of this mess."

John Pierre closed his eyes as he stuck the lid in the bas-relief hieroglyph and recited the words.

"You're still here."

"Thanks for pointing this out to me."

"Something isn't right; why can't I return?"

Abu shook his head in disbelief. "The moon is still full. I am not sure, John Pierre. What do we do next?"

John Pierre slid to the ground.

"I have a plan."

Chapter 128

"Lacey, where are you going, I thought we were going out for dinner tonight?"

"I have a meeting with John Pierre's lawyer. He said it was urgent."

"The man is dead, Lacey. I know you were married to him but then you divorced and married me - enough is enough! We need to get on with *our* life!"

Lacey sighed heavily. "I'm sorry, Montgomery. I need to do this. I need to have closure. How about I go see what the lawyer wants, I'm sure it's about his estate, and I will meet you at the restaurant."

"Fine. I'll see you there."

Lacey hung up the phone. She felt bad but something wasn't right, and she sensed it. She was anxious and John Pierre's death was heavy on her heart. They had a lot of unfinished business and now he was dead. She knew she was being unfair to Montgomery in many ways, but perhaps if she visited the lawyer, she would have some closure.

Chapter 129

Lacey threw the envelope from the lawyer in her purse and raced to the museum. Once at the museum she went straight to the Egyptian collection and headed for the mastaba.

"Mr. Rutland," the voice called through the private security phone.

"Yes, go ahead, Pete."

"Your wife just arrived, I thought I'd inform you as I know you said you were going out tonight. I didn't know she was meeting you here."

"Ah yes, where is she? I will go down to join her."

"Egyptian collection sir. I saw her go into the mastaba."

Montgomery could feel the beads of sweat forming on the back of his neck. What the hell was she up too?

Lacey stood in the mastaba and tears filled her eyes the minute she walked in. She hadn't been in here since he died. It was all too surreal.

"Lacey, what are you doing? I thought you were going to the lawyer."

Lacey jumped at the sound of her husband's voice. She could tell by his tone he was displeased to find her here.

She turned slowly toward him. "I did go to the lawyer. They just had instructions for me to donate his personal art collection. I only wanted to say good-bye one last time."

Montgomery was furious. "Ok, do what you have to do." He moved toward her and put his arm around her. "I know this is hard, but you need to move on. We need to move on. Now come, let's go to dinner."

PART 3

The Incredible Truth

Chapter 130

"*J*ohn Pierre wake up, someone is here," Abu whispered. "We must be quiet."

John Pierre and Abu quietly crept from the back chamber and listened. John Pierre motioned for Abu to turn the flashlight on.

"Well, it's about time. Do you know how long I've been waiting for you?"

Lacey's head was pounding. She could barely open her eyes. As she tried to focus a familiar voice was repeating the same words over and over.

"What the hell took you so long? Abu get her some water."

"Let me help you, madam. Please sit up and drink some of this. It will help you feel better."

Lacey took a sip of the water as Abu helped her sit up. Her muscles ached as she struggled to move. The coolness of what seemed to be stone against her back was refreshing.

She stared in disbelief at the man sitting across from her. "I buried you," she whispered.

"What do you mean, you buried me?"

"You died, I buried you."

"Impossible!"

"Ok, ok, everybody must calm down. So we can figure this out. Welcome to Egypt, madam. I presume this is your lady."

"I am *not* his lady," Lacey corrected.

"I see that you received my letter."

Lacey rubbed her temples. "This can't be true. I didn't believe it when I read that document you left for me. I thought you'd lost your mind."

"Madam, you must drink some tea. It will help you feel better."

Lacey looked to John Pierre for reassurance. "Just drink it, Lacey, I promise it will help you."

"This can't be happening."

John Pierre pulled the canopic jar lid of Imsety out of the wall and held it in front of her face. His eyes sparkled with pride as he spoke. "It's *real,* Lacey. You read my letter, retrieved the lid, waited for the full moon, read the hieroglyphics, and you made it. Lacey, it's happening and its real and I will prove it to you later."

"Abu, prepare the camels; if you think it is safe, we will travel."

Abu peered out of the mastaba. It seemed like they were in there for weeks. He was happy to return to his village. "'Tis safe. Night has fallen."

Chapter 131

"Ah, madam, I hope you had a restful sleep. I have prepared some tea and sustenance for you. Please come and sit."

Lacey sat up and took in her surroundings. Brightly painted hieroglyphics covered the walls, while Abu sat at a wooden table.

"John Pierre, I saw him, I buried him."

"It will all be explained to you."

John Pierre appeared as if on cue. "She will like the raspberry Pop-Tarts and granola bars. Lacey, come you must eat and drink some water. I'll tell you everything. I'll make you some coffee."

"You weren't this old when I saw you at the museum. What happened?"

John Pierre stared at Lacey. He looked for signs of aging but didn't see any yet. I already told you everything in the letter. Basically Whetherbee left me some cursed canopic jars that allow for time travel, but for some reason one of the jars and some rings are missing and we need to find them or I will die."

"But you are already dead."

"How? Tell me what happened."

"One of the cleaning crew found you. You consumed too much alcohol at the benefit and apparently wandered into the mastaba, fell, and hit your head. The blow to the back of your head killed you."

"This explains why you can't return," Abu speculated.

John Pierre sat down. He was feeling dizzy.

Abu was concerned. "What 'tis wrong?"

"Every time I try to recall that evening, I can't. I only see bits and pieces but not everything. Someone else was there that night!"

"Think, John Pierre. Who did you talk with? What did you do?"

He looked at Lacey for help.

"I saw you talking with everyone, Charlotte, all the board members…there were hundreds of people at the event."

"Perhaps it will come to you later," Abu stated.

"Abu, tell her more about the canopic jars and show her the journal."

After listening to Abu, she turned toward John Pierre and started yelling. "How could you involve me in this? I had a life!"

"Remember, Lacey, I didn't force you. But you are the only historian I knew who would come. You are the only one who loves and knows more about Egyptian history and artifacts. You're our only hope. Abu, take her to Whetherbee's department store and make sure she gets the appropriate items to wear before we leave."

Chapter 132

"What is all this?"

"Miss Lacey, you must dress in the clothes of the time."

"John Pierre, you're a thief! You stole these from your own museum," she exclaimed in disbelief.

"No, madam, some are authentic."

"Well, it's not like I wasn't going to return them. We have to dress appropriately if we're going to survive."

Once dressed, they headed toward the camel corral. "Arthur come and sit for Miss Lacey. I will take Yasir out today, and John Pierre you can ride…"

"I will ride with Lacey," he rudely interrupted.

"Ok, ok. I see how 'tis going to be," he smiled.

Lacey looked around and saw nothing but desert. Sand, palm trees, and rock for as far as the eyes could see. "How could you do this to me, John Pierre," she hissed. "I left my life, my husband, and my work. You ruined my marriage!"

"A marriage of convenience due to my own stupidity. But you refused to believe my story." He leaned close to her face. Their lips were inches from one another. His hand reached for the side of her cheek. "Lacey, I swear to you it was all a mistake."

Lacey was hypnotized. She could once again feel the electricity between them igniting. She looked into his eyes and did not see the old man that was before her but the man she fell in love with years ago.

"Lacey," he whispered and leaned closer.

She pushed him away. Her eyes squinted as if she was going to throw daggers at him. "In case you have forgotten, I'm married and I'm not a cheater, like some people I know. I will not cheat on my husband!"

John Pierre picked her up and roughly hoisted her on Arthur. "In case *you* haven't realized, your *marriage* to Rutledge is null and void. It hasn't happened yet as its presently 2520 B.C."

John Pierre climbed on behind her. She jabbed him in the stomach as he put his arms around her and grabbed the reins. "Well, if that is the case, then I'm not married to you either!"

"She makes a good point," Abu contended.

Chapter 133

As they plowed through sand dune after sand dune, John Pierre filled her in on more of what Whetherbee was up too and how he had been able to travel back and forth in time. "Apparently we are stuck in some time warp and it all began when Whetherbee died."

Lacey was barely listening as she gasped at the giant pyramid complex that suddenly came into view. "It's incredible! To think in thousands of years man will discover its wealth, the plundering, it will then be ruined by the tourism, a road will be built and buses will come ruining the view. The salt erosion, man's graffiti…"

"Lacey," John Pierre interrupted, "you and I both know that progress comes with a price. So for once just enjoy what you are witnessing."

Lacey knew John Pierre was right.

"Do you want to see more?"

"John Pierre, we must get to the mastaba first."

"Abu, you always know how to ruin a moment, but he's right! We must go to the mastaba first. Then we'll show you around."

Once in the mastaba, Abu dug out another bag of amulets from another hiding place deep in the chamber. "You must wear these, madam Lacey. It is for your protection."

"Why do they have my name on them?"

"I do not know. Whetherbee left them for *you* and *John Pierre*. You will need to survive if you go to the Hall of Judgment. You *must never* take them off."

John Pierre's eyes narrowed sharply as he looked toward Abu. "Abu, you didn't tell me these were left for Lacey. Why… how…did you know she was coming? What other secrets have you not told me?"

Abu stammered, "Noth...ing, John Pierre, I tell you truth… Whetherbee said if she ever came…I just forgot about them until now."

"John Pierre! Stop yelling at the boy! I am sure none of this is his fault."

John Pierre waved this hand's through the air gesturing wildly as he spoke. "Not his fault? He and Whetherbee are too closely connected. And I'm going to die if we don't get to the bottom of it!"

Abu interrupted. "Miss Lacey, would you kindly wrap this around your head, your long hair needs to be covered. We do not want to draw attention to ourselves and I will show you around. 'Tis the least I can do since you have travelled all this way," he grinned.

"Like I had a choice," she retorted in John Pierre's direction. "And don't say I chose my destiny. I read your note. No matter what my feelings for you, I still came. I certainly wasn't going to let you die."

"Please, please, will everyone stop arguing? We need to go; I want to move quickly and avoid the pharaoh. Remember he thinks we are dead," Abu reminded them.

John Pierre threw up his hands in disgust. "But what about the situation?"

"Perhaps we just clear our heads and regroup and then figure out the next step," Abu interrupted again. "I will get the camels."

Abu brought Arthur and Yasir to the front of the mastaba and they hopped on and began their journey around the great Giza Plateau.

Lacey listened intently as Abu explained the workings of Egyptian life, pointed out the different buildings, their function, construction methods, and various stonemasons and artisans.

He adroitly answered questions about daily life and responded to her inquiries with the delight of a schoolboy who was flirting with a new classmate.

John Pierre rode in silence as he thought about their predicament, future, Lacey, and how they were going to get back home.

Chapter 134

"Thank you for the tour today, Abu! I would never have believed it if I hadn't seen it with my own eyes. I think it's beautiful and is why I fell in love with Egyptian art."

"If we're done eating, can we look at the papyrus map and see if we recognize any clues." John Pierre laid out the ten pieces of ancient parchment on the stone table and connected them like a puzzle. "Abu is any of this familiar?"

Abu gasped. "This is the pharaoh's temple complex. And this looks like part of the mortuary chapel."

"Just great," grumbled John Pierre. "Why would Whetherbee bring us back to his complex?"

"I have never been in this main section. It is his private living quarters."

John Pierre sighed. "There has to be a way in; we just can't walk in!"

"Perhaps you are wrong, John Pierre, perhaps we should just walk in."

"I can do it," Lacey stated confidently.

John Pierre's eye's blazed in anger. "Don't be absurd! He will never let you out. I will not allow it!"

"We can look for my mother while we are there too," Abu exclaimed with enthusiasm.

"No, no, no!" John Pierre was adamant. "You both seem to forget what era we are in. She'll be abducted, and we'll never see her again!"

"You have no say in what I do, John Pierre, and you made that quite clear some time ago. Abu, here is a list of the things I will need."

Chapter 135

The guards stared, mouths hanging open, as the woman approached the temple gates of Khafre. She removed her hooded robe and said confidently, "I have two of the pharaoh's escaped prisoners and need an audience with him at once!"

Her beauty did not go unnoticed, and the two guards were speechless as they continued to gawk at the luscious, brown hair that tumbled out from under her hood.

Abu, John Pierre, and Lacey had been watching the entrance and waiting patiently until the guards had changed shifts. They were new and were not going to argue with the long-haired beauty, who had the two men shackled in chains behind her.

The pharaoh was annoyed at the interruption and would kill the guards later for not taking care of the issue immediately.

She breezed into his private chamber as if she floated on air, removed her cloak and bowed before him, a gesture of respect as Abu had instructed.

"You may rise, madam, and state your business."

She was beautiful. He had never seen such beauty before. The multitude of jewels that adorned her almost naked body glistened like gold as the pyramid casing did in the desert sun. The red and gold silk garment revealed every curve of her body and ample bosom that could fall out of the material at the touch of a finger. And the hair, it was thick and tumbled down her backside. His body already betrayed him, and he knew he would have her momentarily.

"I travelled far to visit my friend Astiramare and found these two wandering around her residence. The village people say, they escaped your guards and I am returning them to you in exchange for Astiramare's release."

The pharaoh raised his eyebrow at the mention of the name Astiramare and studied the woman before him. He liked her spirit. She was bold in thinking she could bargain with him. "How do you know I have this Astiramare? And what are these two men to me, perhaps I just ordered them killed and do not even remember why?"

"Your villagers say otherwise," she said as she seductively walked around the men.

"This woman you seek, how do I even know what she looks like?"

"She is my mother," Abu shouted, as he removed his hood. I know you have her."

"*You two*!" shouted the pharaoh. Then to the guard, he added angrily, "Fetch me Moustafa and the woman they seek immediately!"

The guard bowed, "But how will we know who it is? You have hundreds of women…"

"Just ask who the mother of Abu is," he interrupted angrily. "Believe me, she will answer. Tell her I have her son."

He smiled confidently. The name carved on the wall in the artifact mastaba belonged to a woman and she was right under his nose the entire time. Abu's mother? He was not surprised his family was connected to the strange drawings. He would kill them all after he had what he needed.

Chapter 136

J ohn Pierre was seething. He did not know how much more he could take. Not only had he forgotten how beautiful she was, but she was playing a perilous game and the pharaoh was going to have his way with her as he could not keep his eyes off her.

"May I ask who is Astiramare to you?"

"She is a friend, we make pottery together and her family moved closer to the pyramid complex for work many, many moons ago."

The pharaoh rose from his throne and walked toward Lacey. He was over six feet tall and his muscles swelled. Each one was bigger than the next. He looked like a competitive athlete. She gasped as he moved closer. "You are a beautiful and powerful man," she whispered seductively.

The pharaoh grabbed her breasts, squeezed them and smirked. She knew the look. She would surely be raped.

"Not only are you a powerful man but you have the finest taste in art. Your palace is beautiful. I find the Khephri relief fascinating."

Everyone turned to see what Lacey was looking at. John Pierre saw it immediately. The ring that Whetherbee wore was depicted on the relief carving of the scarab. It was a clue.

"Done by my finest artisans." The pharaoh leaned in and kissed Lacey brutally on the lips and whispered, "I do not know what your game is, madam, but I know you did not come here to discuss my art collection."

At that moment Moustafa barged in the room with Asti-ramare and threw her to the floor. Moustafa looked at the two men in shackles in horror as the blood drained from his face. The pharaoh would undeniably kill him for not making certain they were dead. Sweat began pouring down his face as he began apologizing. "I saw them go in the Nile; I saw Xgar take a bite…"

"Silence Moustafa!" roared the pharaoh. "They think I am foolish and come here and try to trick the Great and Almighty Pharaoh Khafre. Remove their jewelry and kill them all…no, before you do that…bring her - he pointed to Lacey - to my private chambers and chain her to my bed. After I am done with her, then you will lock her up!"

"I'll make it easy for you. On the count of three we will all remove our jewelry," John Pierre chimed in as he looked at Lacey. Abu looked to his mother and nodded, silently communicating that it was going to be ok.

Chapter 137

The Pharaoh Khafre and his trusted guard Moustafa stood in the ornate temple chamber alone. The necklaces the group had been wearing were a pile of ash scattered and smoldering on the floor. Smoke drifted through the air past the pharaoh. All four of the figures had vanished.

"Moustafa, I do not know what just happened, but if you did as I had asked and killed those two, I believe none of what just occurred would have transpired.

Moustafa nodded knowingly and bowed.

"I am sorry I have failed you my lord."

The pharaoh's blade was swift and Moustafa was dead.

Chapter 138

The floor was cold and hard. Abu struggled as he tried to sit up. His friends were sprawled about the room on their backs. Their landing was not soft. "Is everyone alright?" Abu called out as his eyes tried to adjust to the dimly lit room.

The only light came from a slow burning torch that barely filled the space.

Everyone began to stir. John Pierre groaned and rubbed his back and then remembered Lacey. He shot up and looked about the room and ran to her.

"Lacey, Lacey, are you hurt?"

Lacey rolled on her side and slowly sat up. "Get off of me. What the hell is wrong with you? Why did you do that?"

"I couldn't stand his dirty hands on you a minute longer!"

"I had the situation under control…"

"Under control! Now that's a laugh," he interrupted. "Apparently you forgot where we are. And regardless of the century, men have not changed."

"You're so right," she interjected. "You're disgusting pigs!"

"Get real, Lacey. You were this close to being raped!"

"Ok, everyone you must stop arguing, please, we need to *help my mother*," Abu pleaded.

Forgetting about their troubles, John Pierre and Lacey looked around the dark room.

"She's over here you idiots," a gruff male voice called.

Chapter 139

John Pierre turned quickly toward the familiar voice. He was still having trouble adjusting to the darkness. "*Whetherbee*, you bastard, *you're alive*! Where are you? Do you have any idea what we've been through? How did this happen? You have a lot of explaining to do! When you're done, I'm going to kill you myself," John Pierre spat angrily.

Abu yelled out again, "Where are you, mama?"

"'Tis ok, Abu, I am over here," a female voice whispered softly.

"I have the magic light," Abu stated anxiously as he fumbled in his pockets and quickly produced the cigarette lighter. The flame illuminated the dim, rocky surroundings as Abu slowly turned in search of his mother. He quickly spotted her lying on the ground near Whetherbee and ran toward her. "John Pierre, you must help me, I do not know if she is ok. Please!"

"Put that flame out," John Pierre shouted as he pulled a flashlight from his pocket, turned it on and waved it around the room in search of Whetherbee. "The first rule of survival is to conserve supplies."

Someone began coughing. John Pierre waved the light around the room.

"Whetherbee, you bastard," John Pierre yelled again as he marched toward Whetherbee. "I could kill you for what you have done! Look at me; look what you have done to us!"

Whetherbee chuckled. "Well, its good to see you too my old friend, no pun intended."

"How the hell can you joke about this? Why did you do this? What is this all about? Where the hell are we?"

"Mr. Whetherbee was right, you are a selfish bastard, John Pierre. All you can think about is yourself when everyone else here is suffering as well," Abu stated calmly as he hugged Whetherbee. "I told you he was still alive. I told you," he smiled elated.

"Well, he certainly has you figured out," Lacey added the sarcasm apparent in her voice.

John Pierre began pacing. "And where exactly are we? Can somebody please tell me?"

"The Old Kingdom of Egypt," Lacey, Whetherbee and Abu replied together.

Chapter 140

John Pierre looked about the room in amazement. "You're all in on this together," he spat. "I planned your funeral," he stated angrily as he pointed his finger at Whetherbee. "Now that I think about it your body was never recovered, so somehow you faked your own death!"

Lacey laughed. "Really, John Pierre. Do you actually believe that?"

Upset about his mother, Abu began yelling at John Pierre for his refusal to listen and believe. "Now my mother and all of us are here and we finally find Mr. Whetherbee. I told you he was alive! You told me to believe and I did but he too has aged, and *you* are only concerned with yourself!"

"How can you defend him?" John Pierre asked as he pointed at Whetherbee.

While they were arguing, Lacey rose and made her way to Astiramare who was now nestled with Whetherbee.

Chapter 141

" Ah, Jobehar, what brings my most loyal and trusted servant to my chambers this evening?"

Jobehar immediately shaped shifted from hound to his muscular human form. "There is another disturbance in Chamber 6166."

Anubis, who had been lounging in his throne room, immediately sat on all fours at attention. "Chamber 6166 is for the worst souls," he communicated silently before shape shifting into his human form. "Tell me more."

"There are five of them now. Four arrived together – they all seem to know one another. I believe it is the group you seek. They have been arguing since their arrival. It was so bad, I had to leave!"

Anubis shook his head knowingly and smirked. "That is why they are in the predicament they are in."

"Will they face the forty-two gods and follow the protocol in the Book of the Dead?"

"No, Jobehar. This is not for the gods to decide. Because they are not of this time, they will go deeper into the cavern of death and face the wrath of their own evil. This must take place before they even go to the Hall of Judgment. Isis was kind to remind us all about the ancient ritual. It was forgotten since the many moons that have passed; we have never encountered such interference with the universal order of things. However, we must follow the rules, even the gods know this."

Jobeher stared wide-eyed in shock. "I am not sure why they would be sent, master. While they have their faults, they certainty are not the worst creatures we have ever seen. 'Tis written that nobody can survive those tests."

"Yes, I know how unfortunate, but, again, their presence violates the universal order of life and could alter history. That is their crime, in addition to the plundering of the tombs! But before they go, I must find out some information. We must find the portal and *that* group holds the key."

Chapter 142

" I s she ok?" Lacey whispered.

"She is fine, just some cuts and bruises. I think her arm is badly bruised," Whetherbee responded as he showered Astiramare with kisses and spoke in dialect unknown to them all.

"It probably happened when the pharaoh threw her to the ground," Abu surmised.

Lacey quickly removed one of the sashes dangling from the provocative clothing she had worn for the pharaoh. "Abu, hold her arm while I wrap it."

Abu followed the instructions and told his mother he was glad to see her and happy the pharaoh did not harm her.

John Pierre was sitting at a distance and observed the group. He was tired and began rubbing his temples. "This is just great, we're trapped in some type of time warp and death is probably upon us and Whetherbee has a girlfriend in, of all places, the Old Kingdom of Egypt! Nobody will ever believe this!"

"Well, John Pierre, does it really matter? By the looks of it we're going to die so you won't have anybody to tell your story to," Lacey retorted as she shook her head in disbelief.

"My life has been turned upside down and the man, my best friend, who told me he wasn't interested in anyone - has a girlfriend! And, of all places, in ancient Egypt!"

Astiramare smiled, turned her head and gazed into Whetherbee's eyes, "'Tis true?"

The pair spoke in words that John Pierre could not understand.

"What is he saying?"

"He is telling her it is true, and as he has repeatedly told her, he has never married or been with anyone but her. This, John Pierre, this is my mother and father," Abu stated proudly.

John Pierre stared at the pair before exploding. "*You* told me, no, you *lied* to me about your father and told me he was dead. You said you didn't really know Whetherbee…that you… now it all makes sense. Whetherbee told you I was coming, he made the amulets for us, he set all of this in motion…why I bet you know how to read, write…"

"He speaks many languages," Whetherbee interrupted smiling proudly. "I made sure he was well educated."

Lacey gasped as she brought her hand to her mouth about to speak but instead simply stared at the group.

John Pierre was pacing about. "Abu, why didn't you tell me Whetherbee was your father?"

"Yes, Abu, how did you find out? We wanted to keep you safe, so we never told you," his mother said concerned.

"I snuck out and followed you to the mastaba one night. I saw you with a man. I heard you talk of the danger and keeping the secret, or the entire family could be in danger. I never say a word and then he disappeared. I come to the mastaba all the time and look for him.

One day I finally see him. He found me upset. The kids told me I was strange, and I had no friends. Whetherbee was surprised and told me we would be friends. It would be our secret. I realized he was the man with my mother. I never said a word because he was my friend. I didn't want to do anything to upset my mother or bring harm to our family."

"I am so sorry, my son, that you had to learn this way."

Chapter 143

" *I* just have one question…why the hell would you send me some fake jars and not include any information about their function? There were no instructions," John Pierre shouted. "I read every piece of paper that was enclosed in those crates and that the lawyers gave me. Why didn't you just give me the jars and the information? Why go through all this trouble? Why involve Lacey? Why play such a joke sending me fake gold canopic jars!"

"Unfortunately I was preparing the documentation, but my plane crashed before it was completed. I was in the process of getting everything together and never finished sending all the documents to the attorneys with information for the codes to my safe where you could find what you needed."

Whetherbee scratched his beard and looked pensively at John Pierre before he spoke again. "What in the world gave you the idea that they were fake jars? They are real jars of solid gold. Something is wrong. Those idiot lawyers…I'll sue them. The jars are of solid gold, but the lids are what's important."

"So you didn't set out to fool John Pierre by sending him fake art?" Lacey asked.

"Don't be ridiculous. If you are referring to the conversation on fake art we had that one evening, that's was just a hypothetical discussion. I would never send him fake art. Give me some credit."

Lacey blinked with surprise. It all made sense.

"Coincidently, my team and I had been working on deciphering a dialect, which, ironically just happened to match what was on the jars. With Carter's notes, we resolved the jars were fakes. When I arrived home and was going through the mail, a copy of the authentication report was sent to me in error. When I read it, it was the rest of the proof I needed to conclude the jars were fakes. I never completed my research. I was on my way to see you when Nicholas and George called me and said they were worried about you and the new exhibit, which had problems."

"The jars are real, Lacey. Your research is incorrect," Whetherbee confirmed. He turned toward Abu. "I was going to tell you the truth; it was time, but unfortunately my plane crashed."

Abu smiled. "I knew you wore the amulets. I was sure of it. I keep telling John Pierre and he did not believe me. What happened?"

"Someone attacked me on the plane, and we crashed. During the struggle the amulets were pulled from my neck. I think it was Samir."

Astiramare gasped. "Impossible."

"I see you no longer wear the ring."

"It was lost in the struggle too; I had removed my gloves for a moment, and it was pulled off during the fight."

"I don't understand," Lacey said as she explained her findings in Carter's notes to Whetherbee.

"Look, Lacey, Carter spent years in Egypt. Who knows what he found or was studying? When he discovered King Tut's tomb, he abandoned everything. The Tut tomb was too massive for him to concern himself with anything else. The original notes were either lost, stolen, left with family…who knows. You probably stumbled on another tomb discovery. You will have to give me the details and perhaps we can figure it out later."

John Pierre was pacing back and forth. "The night at the gala. It all makes sense. My memory is still foggy, but it's starting to return. George Newberry was behind all of this. He said so himself. He forged the paperwork and said the jars were real and then later had the company send me documentation saying the jars were fakes and it was their mistake…he set me up to get rid of me…I bet he killed me!"

Lacey stared at him incredulous. "Are you crazy, John Pierre? Do you hear what you're saying? You have no proof!"

John Pierre spun around. "I told *you* the authenticity report said solid gold. George, Leo, and who knows who else had the reports altered and then switched."

Lacey's hands flew to her face as her eyes widened in shock. "They wouldn't? How can you prove it?"

"I eventually watched the security tapes. I saw Newberry in my office switching the files."

"Ok, but that doesn't mean he was the one who killed you. You need proof," Lacey cried.

Chapter 144

A slight rumbling in the wall made everyone stop speaking. Anubis and his servant Jobeher materialized through the stone. "You know what I am here for," he pointed at Whetherbee. "I need that information and I need it now!"

"Whatever it is you seek, it will not be obtained today, Anubis," voiced another figure who, mysteriously materialized in the center of the room. He was wearing a hooded cloak of shimmering white and covered in hieroglyphics of gold. He also wore a crown of plumes. Jewelry of lapis lazuli adorned his body and his flesh shimmered like the blue hues of the precious stone.

Anubis immediately bowed to the great Amun-Ra.

"You once again interfere, Anubis. They are to be sent on their journey now. You and Samir have done enough!"

"Oh exalted one, this group holds the key…"

"*Silence!*" The words sounded as if a freight train was coming through the stone. "And stop with the pretense of flattery. It is annoying and beneath you! The mysteries of the universe are not ours to change! You are dismissed!" And with the wave of his hand, Anubis and his servant had disappeared.

Chapter 145

"The test for the rest of you will start now. If you fail, life as you know it will be over. There are no choices. You each must face your deepest pain, for things you have done and things that have happened in each of your lives. Things that have perhaps shaped who you have become. Your untold pain may be revealed, and you will need to deal with it. Even I do not know the exact nature of what you will face."

"Why? Why now?" Abu stammered. His voice was yet a whisper.

"'Tis unfortunate, this cycle was evoked the moment you lost the protection you wore around your necks," Amun-Ra reminded the miserable group of creatures that sat before him.

"Now just a minute, who are you again? And what about the protection we wore. Can't you just give us more amulets or, better yet, let us leave?" John Pierre tried to bargain.

"Shh," Abu whispered as he tried to stop his friend from speaking. "You are speaking with the great Amun-Ra."

The great Amun-Ra looked John Pierre up and down and shook his head in disgust. "'Tis one like you who will never learn. You are all about yourself and your wealth, and I pity you for that. The adornments that you wore were crafted especially for you by Abu," he pointed to where Abu was seated. "But from what I understand, *you* don't believe in the magic of Abu. Since you believe in nothing, I can not help you!"

"Abu, I was told they were crafted by Whetherbee?"

Abu clasped his hands together nervously. "I said they were left by Whetherbee. You have forgotten I did study at Sarsa with Rufarron for a time."

Whetherbee gawked at John Pierre in disbelief. "Does it matter, John Pierre? If you want the truth, I suggested Abu make some charms. They were necessary."

"And the charms brought you here. Unfortunately your journey will not begin in the Hall of Judgment." Amun-Ra turned, his eyes transfixed on each of the lost souls and waved his hand around the room in slow motion and muttered an enchantment as if casting a spell before he spoke again.

A white glittery fog began to fill the room.

"You may have a moment with one another before your journey will begin." He was gone before any more questions could be asked.

The white fog was getting thicker making it impossible to see.

John Pierre shouted at the group, *"Whatever happens, be smart; remember, there's always a way out. Study your surroundings, look for some sort of key, sign, symbol, something unusual perhaps and try to escape, and let's pick one place we can all meet if we make it out alive."*

"The mastaba; where it all began," shouted Abu.

"I agree. It makes sense. We all must be on our toes, think like archeologists, explorers, use common sense. Think of every symbol we have discussed and look for signs."

Moments later, the floor opened up and swallowed the entire group.

Chapter 146

Beyond the Underworld

They all descended through the darkness at a rapid speed. Glimpses of the faces of horrible creatures and their slimy limbs reached for them as they spiraled downward through the dark, cold and then intensely hot atmosphere, before finally landing in hot sand. Each called out to one another, but only the echoes of their voices could be heard through the pitch-dark cavern. They were each alone.

Chapter 147

Temple of Isscarja

*J*ohn Pierre felt his pockets for his flashlight, pulled it out, and turned and pushed the switch. Nothing. "Damn," he muttered. He waited for his eyes to adjust to the darkness, but nothing. "I know you are here, what do you want?" he called out to the darkness as he tried the flashlight again.

John Pierre could barely stand up. The fall had aged him more; he could feel it in his bones and his entire body ached worse than before. He knew death was upon him if he didn't find a way out. He quickly turned at the sound of a hissing noise and found himself face to face with the most horrid creature.

"Welcome, John Pierre, to the Temple of Isscarja." She was illuminated in ghastly hues of green. The fat, grotesque creature was covered in scarabs. In the blink of an eye she quickly disappeared.

John Pierre now found himself alone on a dark path, more green light illuminated from somewhere in the temple. Hieroglyphic text filled the walls from top to bottom as he slowly walked down the sandy path. He stopped and began reading the text.

"Welcome to the Temple of Isscarja –Tomb of Manipulations! I am the evil, conniving, manipulative creature who pretends to be friendly, but it is all a farce. Do not mistake my friendliness, as I am really *evil*. I never knew the meaning of true friendship and manipulated *everyone* around in my quest to make every situation go my way. I steal, lie, cheat, fabricate stories to sway or hurt others. I am a *master manipulator*," John Pierre stopped reading the text, which seemed to go on forever.

"You remind me of someone I once knew."

Isscarja appeared instantly. "Really, who?"

John Pierre turned away from the vile creature.

"What? You can't stand to look at yourself and what you have become?"

John Pierre was sick for the truth she told.

"You can't even look at me? They are just scarabs; they eat away my flesh for each of the lies, deceit, and acts of manipulation I have told or done. And when there is just bone left, they eat that too. My skin grows back, and it starts again. I live in constant agony. This is exactly what is going to happen to you. I look forward to watching your pain."

John Pierre groaned as he found a large boulder on the path and sat down. His breathing was labored, and he could barely walk. He rubbed his forehead and stated, "I feel like I'm looking at myself. The things I've done in the past few years. If I could go back, I'd change it all, but I bet you hear that from everyone who comes your way," John Pierre said slowly.

Isscarja smirked as she reappeared in front of John Pierre. The scarabs that clung to her skin were reaching for John Pierre's worn body. "In a few minutes you may have him; he is almost dead," she sneered as she spoke to the scarabs.

"I would think you would want someone to talk with before you kill me, I'm sure it must be lonely down here, in the dark all by yourself?"

"So now you think you are going to manipulate *me*?" Isscarja stated irately.

"I'm almost dead; do you think I care anymore?"

Isscarja thought about that. "Well, this is true, I spend my days writing hieroglyphics on the walls detailing stories of my life. What is *your* story?"

"I studied art, ruined my life as an archeologist to run a museum, and lost the love of my life for art and money."

"So you are the one who has been stealing the art over the years?"

"I never said that. Who is trying to manipulate *who* now? Tell me…

What did you do? Why are you here?"

"I worked for the pharaoh. He raped me at a young age, I guess you could say, *he* turned me into what I have become."

"What does this have to do with me?"

"You are a foolish man."

"So I've been told."

"Look deep within yourself for your truth."

"Perhaps our stories are quite similar. I guess you could say I became someone I was not. I was an archeologist; I was pushed into something I did not want."

"You choose and…"

"Because of my choices I spent my life manipulating others for money. In return, I lost the love of my life and what I loved doing best," John Pierre interrupted.

"You lost *nothing*! You never *tried* to tell her your truth. You deserve everything you got. You wrote your future."

"You may be right, but if that's the case, then perhaps my future will not end here?"

Shrilling laughter filled the space. "Impossible! You are destined to spend an eternity with me."

It was then John Pierre saw the pharaoh's markings in the hieroglyphics, his eyes followed their path and connected them, but they were all over the walls. "Do you mind if I just keep walking? I have accepted my fate; you may do what you wish with me when I am dead."

"I know what game you play, but do as *you* wish. There is nowhere to go. I will follow you because I don't trust you. Besides if you would just tell me what you did with the art, I may let you go."

"Why would you care about such a thing? Why is it so important to you?"

"'Tis only as I have nothing to do down here, and since I have to write about your life, you could start by talking about the art," she lied.

John Pierre smirked. "You remind me of someone I know. So what's in it for you? What do you think the information is your ticket out of here?"

"No," screamed Isscarja. "I just need something different to write about."

Scarabs ran all over Isscarja's body. She was down to bone. John Pierre realized the more she lied, the quicker the flesh-eating insects ate at her body.

John Pierre knew he would not admit to anything for he wasn't about to put anyone else at risk. "I never said I took anything."

"*Liar*," hissed the evil Isscarja.

"Why do you care anyway? Your own people are going to steal it all. If I took anything it would go to the museum for people to admire and learn about your culture."

John Pierre could barely breathe, but the pharaoh's marks were guiding him toward what, he did not know. Annoyed he reached into his pocket and found what he was looking for.

"Isscarja. I have a gift for you. I wish to thank you."

Isscarja looked at him suspiciously as he opened the lighter cap and threw the lighter fluid on her. The match came next and she was engulfed in flames. Her screams echoed in the chamber. As she was burning, John Pierre ran to the wall and quickly searched for the symbol. He pushed his hands over the key and the stone moved and Isscarja's screams echoed as he disappeared into the darkness.

Chapter 148

Temple of Ehettwa

Whetherbee was greeted by Ehettwa. She announced that he had arrived in the Temple of Trickery and Deceitfulness. The old witch was covered with live sand flies from head to toe. What was once a full head of hair was now only a few strands of gray. The weathered skin had thousands of wrinkles and was so tight from time in the sun a rock could bounce off her face. She smelled and was bathed in a hue of garish-yellow and brown light.

"I understand you are the reason for your destiny?"

Whetherbee scratched his beard. "I am not sure what you're referring too?"

"I need to know how you did it. How it began. I need your story. Your secrets are many."

Whetherbee's boisterous laugh filled the cavern. "I have no story."

Ehettwa's eyes blazed and turned shades of orange. "I need to know how it all began. How did you get here? Where is all the art that you have taken?"

Whetherbee smirked, "Who said I have taken any art? Has it been proven? Did you see me take any art? Because if the answer is no, then I have no idea what I'm doing here and you need to let me go!"

Ehettwa thought about it. The dying man was right. And if that was true, she could not punish him unless he revealed the truth. "If you tell me the truth then your death will be less severe," she threatened.

Whetherbee held his ground. "I told you I have no idea what you are talking about. Obviously, the wrong man was sent. I am innocent. In fact, I think that this is a case of mistaken identity. And if you kill me by mistake, then *you* will suffer a final death."

Whetherbee wasn't sure this was true, but he tried to buy as much time as he could.

Ehettwa was not certain if the man was telling the truth. She had been content to live her life in this horrid condition alone then he showed up. Now she just wanted him gone. What were the gods going to do to her that was not already done, she pondered.

Whetherbee had been studying the walls. The hieroglyphics were running vertically with some horizontal scenes in between. He smiled when he spotted an irregular depiction and began moving toward it.

"Your entire life has been filled with trickery and shrewd cunning - cunning that has hurt those in your path and left you and many alone."

"Cunning that has kept me alive."

Ehettwa followed, trying to trick him to saying he was the art thief. "I see you have more secrets than art. Your child deserves the truth…"

Whetherbee spun around. "He already knows the truth. Leave him out of this."

Ehettwa's laugh eerily filled the space as it bounced and echoed off the walls. Whetherbee put his hands over his ears in an attempt to block out the horrid sound. The words, "Liar, liar," followed next.

Whetherbee kept moving. He was too smart. He saw the key and asked Ehettwa about it.

"It has been here as long as I have. It is written that only one know its true meaning."

Whetherbee smiled and traced the outline of the key before pushing the stone and he was gone.

Chapter 149

Temple of Nobec Gagssru

Astiramare was greeted by darkness but was not afraid. Knowing Whetherbee was alive gave her hope that she would soon see him again.

"You must return what you stole from the Temple of Sarsa."

Astiramare spoke to the darkness, "I do not have it."

The voice sounded familiar to Astiramare. "Reveal yourself!" She shouted.

She recognized him immediately; however, he was not the man she knew of in her youth. The muscles no longer existed. His skin was so fine you could see through to the bone. Spiders of all types wandered up and down and rested on various parts. Their scabs and open wounds revealed the permanent damage.

"Nobec Gagssru, is that you?" She squinted as she attempted to see through the spider webs forming across his aged face. It was so wrinkled it looked like a dried piece of fruit that had fallen off the tree and to the ground for all the bugs and insects to enjoy as the sun dried it to nothing.

Nobec Gagssru was the father of her childhood friend. He was a leader in the community.

"Welcome, Astiramare. It is good to see you, but I'm surprised as *you* are the *last* person I thought would be passing through here."

"Where are we?"

Nobec Gagssru laughed. "This is the tomb of sexual transgressions. I would have thought you would have figured that out!"

"You raped me when I was younger, and I have never forgotten it. I refuse to spend eternity with you," she stated angrily.

"Do not play the innocent, by the time I raped you, you had already been with a man. Who was he, Astiramare? I must know!"

Astiramare was not aging like the others. The walls were filled with ancient hieroglyphics; it was a resume of worlds past. She was sure her story was in there somewhere.

"Why do you care?"

Nobec Gagssru smirked. "*You* were *promised* to me and *I* was to rule with the pharaoh's court! For whatever reason the pharaoh wanted me to wed you. Without *you* I was cast out and when I searched for you, you had disappeared. Gone just like that and were never seen again."

"And what did you do? You spent your life raping others and engaging in other deviant misconduct," Astiramare interrupted.

Nobec Gagssru smiled wickedly. Astiramare knew that look. She saw it in men's eyes as they looked at other women. "No matter, Astiramare, it is all in the past. Now that you are here, I have the rest of eternity to deal with you. You are as beautiful as the day I first saw you."

Astiramare's heart began racing. She had to find a way out. "I am sure there would be some sort of penalty for another transgression."

Nobec Gagssru's eyes widened. "How could you know the laws down here? What kind of witch are you?"

"The kind you do not want to mess with, Nobec Gagssru!"

Nobec Gagssru regretted his words. She had tricked him into talking.

Astiramare began walking through the temple, her eyes searching the walls. Nobec Gagssru followed closely. "Now I remember, your family…they were shamans…well, whatever powers you have, I can tell you they are useless down here."

Astiramare glared at Nobec Gagssru her face inches from his. "How can you be sure of this?"

Astiramare saw the hint of fear in his eyes and in that split second she reacted. She closed her eyes and recited the language of the ancients and called on her energy which immediately surged through her body and out, smacking Nobec Gagssru right between the legs, leaving him howling in pain as he fell on his back. A pain, which would not subside for ages.

As he lay on the floor screaming, Astiramare, now weak from the spell, slowly made her way through the tomb looking for signs. She then saw the familiar symbol. The symbol from her grandfather's study but she could not reach it.

Nobec Gagssru was soon up and running toward her, as he grew close, she jumped as high as she could. Nobec pushed her legs into the stone and she reached higher, smashing her hand into the rock.

Nobec Gagssru fell to the ground, empty handed and howling in more pain then ever.

Chapter 150

Temple of Ararbeooka

Abu found himself lying in the hot sand. It was pitch-black. He searched his pockets and found his magic light. The small flame from the lighter only illuminated the darkness in front of him. He saw a staircase and began his descent. The walls were covered with low relief carvings depicting daily life of some unknown individual. He walked carefully down hundreds of steps, which zigzagged back and forth, until he finally reached the bottom and came face to face with a ka statue.

"Welcome, Abu, it has been a long time."

Abu jumped back as the ka statue transformed and stepped forward.

Abu stared at the short, fat woman with black hair. She was grotesque. Her face was marked with warts and her skin was shades of brown and her eyes were blazing red. A medieval type of red creature similar to an ant, but grotesquely deformed, clung to her body. Abu looked closer and realized the creatures covered her entire form, or what was left of it.

Abu shivered. She looked familiar, but he still did not recognize her.

"Our time is limited, so I will get right to the point. Why did you take the amulets from the Temple of Sarsa?"

Abu gasped. "I do not know anything about the amulets. I swear I did not take them."

"You lie!" The ugly woman shrieked, as she quickly pointed her finger toward Abu, who immediately fell to the ground.

Abu winced as he felt the pain in his left arm. "I am sorry, madam, for I do not know what happened. I feel someone is trying to set me up and I have no idea how this happened. I know I was the last in the private temple room…"

"A place you should have never been!" Ararbeooka interrupted, as she yelled louder.

Abu was pensive. "How did *you* know I was in the temple? Who are you?"

"Humph! It is no wonder you were failing your studies."

Abu looked closer and his eyes widened, "Ararbeooka, is it you? But I was told you left."

"Left?" she shrieked. "I was *banished*, you fool. *Banished* because *you* failed your studies and then *blamed* for the theft of the sacred amulets!"

"I am sorry for your misfortune, Ararbeooka, but I can assure you *I* did *not* steal them. Meretseger recently told me they were fakes and not real!"

Ararbeooka was incensed at the revelation and zapped him in the leg. Abu immediately fell to the ground.

"Fake and not real. *Impossible*! What were you doing in the room? I saw you enter. You were the only one."

Abu studied Ararbeooka. She was an ancient spellcaster who, some say, was created from a primeval spell. She could mix and make potions and her temple was lined with goblets and concoctions that were more powerful than any sorceress that ever lived. Abu did not do well in any of her classes.

Abu winced in pain as he attempted to rise. His arm and leg throbbed and the poison she had inflicted was starting to pulsate through the rest of his body.

"You are dying, Abu. Too bad, Rufaaron had great hopes for you. I can reverse the spell if you tell me why you stole the amulets and where they are hidden."

Abu studied her hideous form. "There must be a reason why you are down here, Ararbeooka? What did you do? How did you even know I was in the temple?"

He rolled to his side and grabbed for his lighter and flicked it on.

Ararbeooka laughed at his attempts to frighten her. "Ah, I see you have finally learned something; tell me about this magic stick you hold."

Abu shifted and crawled closer to the ka statue. "Can we swap stories, Ararbeooka? You tell me how you knew I was in the temple and why you were banished, and I will tell you everything. How I stole the amulets and where they are hidden. But I am having difficulty breathing, please remove the spell, and I will talk."

Ararbeooka moved about the small chamber and studied him. "You are still as foolish as the day we met. I encouraged Boutros, the master of the shape shifters, that you needed to see the amulets, as they were part of your source of power. Rufaaron discovered my deception and that is why I was banished."

"Why would you do such a thing to me?"

Ararbeooka shrugged. "Does it really matter? Besides, I need to hear your story. I have been down here so long I will enjoy your tale, as I have nothing better to do. But if you lie, your death will come quicker than you can blink."

The pain subsided. Abu sat up and began talking. He talked slow and recited detail after detail of how he entered the chamber and took the amulets. His story was long. He told of how he entered the pharaoh's tomb…"

"This is not possible; there is no light," she interrupted.

"Ah, but 'tis where you are mistaken. I have magic, here I show you."

She reached out her hand, and as soon as she was close enough, he turned up the flame and her clothing immediately caught on fire. He instantly grabbed for the necklace she wore around her neck. She screamed in pain as Abu backed away and stuck the key amulet from the necklace she wore into the base of the ka statue and disappeared.

Chapter 151

Temple of Ather're

*L*acey read the inscription on the stone of the giant temple. It was the mortuary temple of someone called Ather're. The walls were covered with low relief carvings that were brightly painted but look as though someone had chipped away at sections of the carvings. Faces and limbs were destroyed.

Figures in the next section appeared to be indulging in wine; it was like a party with the Greek god Dionysus. Nothing was familiar to her.

Ushabti figures filled roughly carved niches as she carefully made her way along the wooden walkway. Small enough to fit in one's hand, they were there to assist the pharaoh in the afterlife with all his needs. There were thousands of them.

"Why am I here? What do you want with me?" She called out into the musty air.

Lacey turned and reached for the closest ushabti figurine. "Nooooo," came a scream that echoed in the tomb. Smoke filled the chamber and Lacey covered her face. Like a genie emerging from a bottle, the smoke cleared instantly, and a figure appeared.

Red snakes of various hues covered her from head to toe. Her thinning hair was streaked with dull hues of what was once red. Her thin, boney frame was a result of partying and a life of deceit to all she encountered.

"I am Ather're. Welcome to my home."

Lacey took a step away from the creature. "Ah, you fear me!"

"What do you want from me?"

"You have ignored the truth and have run from your problems. I have paid the price because of you."

Lacey's eye's widened in shock. "What could *I* possible have done to get you here?"

"I have waited a very long time for you. I am surprised you do not recognize me."

Lacey scratched her head as she looked for a way out.

Ather're smirked. "Do not worry; there is no way out. I am surprised you do not recall, but then again, I have changed. I was an acquaintance of John Pierre."

Lacey huffed, annoyed at the mention of his name. "John Pierre had many friends, unfortunately I don't remember you!"

"Does the night of the Greek Installment Gala ring a bell? Do you remember the fight with Montgomery and your affections for Nicholas Stockport and later going home to find John Pierre in a room filled with women, beautiful women, who had him naked on the bed?"

"Stop," Lacey screamed. "I do not need to relive that dreadful night!"

"You blamed John Pierre for something he did not do. You hurt others because you did not see the truth and your own guilt."

Lacey began laughing. "You're one of those women from that night. But why?"

"Ah, finally you have time to listen. Do you remember Nicholas Stockport? He and I were to be married and then *you* came into the picture and ruined everything. After you left him for someone else, just like that!"

"I didn't love Nicholas," Lacey replied.

"How could you even know what he is about? I spent *years* loving him. We were planning a wedding. Then you showed up and he left me. Just like that. I laughed when I heard you left him and ran off with someone else!"

Lacey was dumbfounded. She didn't understand. "People date and have the right to choose who they want to be with."

The woman's laugh was sinister and then she spoke.

"I had a life! I was going to marry a great man. You stole him from me and then cast him aside like a piece of trash."

Lacey continued walking as the snake lady spoke.

"John Pierre and I were already separated, but I told Nicholas I was going to try to make it work. I told Montgomery that also."

The two were chasing after me the moment they heard there was trouble between me and John Pierre. They played on my heartache and pain and I was not interested until I resolved things with John Pierre. I was going home from the gala to talk with him and well…you already know the rest."

Ather're was astonished at the tale.

Lacey thought about what the woman said earlier. "Nicholas told me he was single when we met. I never knew there was someone in his life."

"The minute you came into his life, he changed."

"Did you ever think that perhaps he didn't really want you at all? Maybe you were just convenient for him at the time?"

The noise that came from Ather're was somewhat of a wailing scream and laugh. It echoed in the chamber. The sound was hideous.

"Do you not see? It was all a set up; I was paid a lot of money."

"Who would do such a thing? Pay you money…I don't believe any of this," Lacey interrupted.

Again with the shrill laugh. It was so loud Lacey brought her hands to her ears to muffle the sound.

"I was drugged and the addiction began, and the money enabled me to live a life of continuous partying – alcohol and drugs. You ruined my life! Choose any ushabti and meet your fate, Lacey."

"Why didn't you just tell someone what happened?"

"I never knew I would become addicted to drugs. Who would believe an addict?"

"This makes no sense. How are you in this world?"

"I died of an overdose and was cast out of the eternal realm. I was not wanted in my own world even in death and was sent to where I am now where our paths would cross."

"This entire story is ridiculous! I feel like I'm in a bad horror movie. I don't believe a word of it," Lacey spat angrily. "Besides, Montgomery was there that night I found John Pierre with you. He saw *you* and what was going on. You're lying and who knows how long you and John Pierre had been together?"

"Did you ever wonder why Montgomery was there that evening?"

"He came to apologize. And thankfully he was there. I don't know what I would have done without him. I married him. He's the love of my life!"

"You lie!"

Lacey gasped. "I do not lie. Montgomery he *is* the love of my life."

Ather're's high-pitched laugh once again echoed off the stone. "Listen to your words. You can barely speak your own truth."

Lacey studied the wall of ushabti figurines. She took a deep breath and said, "What does it matter?" And reached above her head.

Ather're smiled as if she had a secret.

Lacey smiled knowingly and moved quickly and Ather're was left standing alone.

Chapter 152

The Unknown

One by one they had each appeared at the entrance of another tomb chamber. Everyone, except for Lacey.

"How much longer do you think we have?"

John Pierre shook his head back and forth. "I have no idea." He glared angrily at Whetherbee. "This is all your fault. She's not coming back because of you and your silly games! I'll kill you if I don't see her again!"

Whetherbee was lying up against the rock wall. "Really J.P., think about it, we have aged more. I don't think the gods are going to let us out of here alive, not unless they get what they want. Now let's get to work and try to solve the puzzle. Can everyone describe whom they met and their experience?"

Whetherbee was the first to speak after stories were shared.

"These temples and the people that we met, they are not Egyptian gods to my knowledge, but instead people that have impacted each of our lives in some way exactly as Amun-Ra predicted."

"I think the gods are sending us a message," Abu said and then pointed.

They all turned to the figure looming before them. "Amun-Ra," Abu revertly whispered, as he, Whetherbee, and Astiramare immediately bowed to the almighty god.

"Pay homage, John Pierre," Abu whispered angrily.

"I see you did not learn a thing, John Pierre!" Amun-Ra's voice bellowed through the walls of the small enclosure. Within seconds, John Pierre's body lay face down in the sand.

Amun-Ra spoke, his voice reverberating through the chamber. "I am surprised but not so surprised to see you back. You are very clever but, unfortunately, you must pass some additional tests…"

"What about Lacey?" John Pierre, interrupted.

"How dare *you* interrupt *me*! Again, you have learned *nothing*!"

John Pierre howled in pain as he grabbed his right arm in agony. He could smell his skin burning. The sleeve of his right garment was shredded.

Amun-Ra pointed at John Pierre. "I would wrap that if I were you; once the creatures smell your blood, you may not make it to the end. Your journey will continue now."

Chapter 153

Astiramare helped John Pierre clean the blood from the gash on his arm and wrapped it tightly.

John Pierre stood and began pushing against the stone wall looking for a way out. "Your god said our journey would begin now, so I'm trying to help. Do you want to just sit in this chamber and wait for something to happen?"

He spoke too soon, and the group watched as John Pierre went flying through the wall as it moved forward.

John Pierre looked up at the ceiling and said, "Very funny. It's nice to know that the Egyptian gods have a sense of humor!"

The rest followed. "I am not sure what we are looking for anymore, John Pierre," Abu stated as the group walked through the sandy corridors. The walls were covered in brightly colored hieroglyphics and low relief carvings. They had removed some of the torches off the wall for light.

"Recall your studies, Abu; we must past a test, we must answer questions from the forty-two gods, and if we pass, we go to the afterlife," Whetherbee reminded him.

John Pierre stopped walking and turned to face Whetherbee, "The problem I have with all of this, is that none of us are dead."

"Well, according to Lacey, you died, John Pierre. Lacey said it herself… She buried you. So maybe you are dead?"

"I thought about that; however, while I may be dead in my time, but here," he gestured, "I'm still alive."

"What about me? How do you explain my presence?" Whetherbee questioned.

"Again, I had a funeral for you but there was no body. So let's say we all are alive. It's a fact that you and I are aging rapidly and if we don't recover something we will die. Then we need to ask *why* are we all here? The only commonality is that we removed those necklaces."

"How did you get here, Whetherbee? What is the last thing you were doing?"

"I was flying, and I think I was attacked. I vaguely remember the scuffle but have no memory of what happened. I woke up in the chamber in the Duat. So the explanation of wearing the jewelry is true. It must be worn."

John Pierre began coughing. "The dust and sand are starting to get to me. It seems like we have walked across the desert, for hundreds of miles but I feel as if we are going in circles."

Chapter 154

Fertility

"**J**ohn Pierre, you must be patient. When the gods are ready, they will reveal themselves or what they want you to know," Abu expressed positively. "The Book of the Dead says we will meet with the gods. We must be patient."

"That's part of his problem, he is impatient," Whetherbee commented.

As they rounded the path, four of the most beautiful women sat before them in golden thrones. "Astiramare approach us."

The others stood behind, while Astiramare advanced and bowed in admiration.

"Bastet, Hathor, Nut and Mut, 'tis my joy to meet you."

Bastet wore her traditional cat regalia, for the cat, which was an animal sacred to the Egyptians and worshiped throughout. Her body was covered in the most beautiful turquoise gown, while golden jewels and cat motifs covered her skin.

Hathor, was a powerful female goddess, wearing the crown of cow horns, and a gown of shimmering pastel colors.

The goddesses Nut was easy to identify in her light blue robe that depicted representations of the sky above including — stars, sun, moon phases and other unidentifiable representations of the cosmos and universe.

Mut wore a double crown and while associated with many animal attributes, the vulture feathers prominently adorned her shimmering robe of golden brown hues.

While they all had a multitude of attributes, all were linked to fertility. "Astiramare, your secrets are many, but need to be revealed before you go to the other side. Why, have you not revealed them?"

"I am not dead, so I am here only to escape the evil pharaoh. It is only love and the ways of the universe that brought me here."

The gods looked at one another and nodded before pointing, "you may pass."

Chapter 155

Geb

Whetherbee held hands with Astiramare as they walked. John Pierre was still stunned that Whetherbee loved someone from another time period. He couldn't make sense of it. And then there was Abu. Whetherbee was a father. It seems Abu was highly educated, thanks to Whetherbee. He discovered he could read, write, and knew many languages. Whetherbee had been preparing him to survive in a civilization with no modern amenities.

The hieroglyphics grew smaller and relief carvings decorated the walls. The path ended with two giant statues flanking a doorway. "The carvings depict the story of Geb," stated Whetherbee, who interrupted John Pierre's thoughts.

Seconds later, the tomb shook and the dirt from the stone above trickled down on the group. "Who dare call my name?" a deep voice bellowed.

"You already said his name, you are the one who must answer," whispered Abu. Whetherbee looked at Abu surprised. "My son you seem to know more than I suspected."

"Who called my name?" roared the male voice again.

Whetherbee stepped forward and spoke to the wall. "John Chesterfield Whetherbee."

The relief carving of the great god Geb jumped off the wall and came to life. He was dressed in greens and browns, colors associated with the earth. He was a stern authority figure, father to the gods, and provider of nourishment and linked to many other deities.

"I have waited a long time to meet the one who has had the courage to exist and continue this charade. You have upset the balance of the earth and universe."

"If I have upset you so, you could have put and end to it all a long time ago," Whetherbee stated quietly.

Geb studied the man before him. "Unfortunately, the secrets *you* hold must come forth in order for the balance to be restored. You also left your family behind…"

"I sacrificed for the safety of others," interrupted Whetherbee.

"You stole art!"

Whetherbee shrugged his shoulders. "Allegedly. But you have no proof," he whispered.

The great god nodded in confirmation. "And because of this, you may pass."

Chapter 156

Amun

"Wow, just like that he let us continue," Abu spoke. "I think the gods are baffled, as they just let us go."

"I wouldn't be too sure of that, Abu," the test is not over yet," Astiramare stated. "Have your studies not taught you anything?"

"What studies? From what I understand, he was thrown out of some school because he could not perform some silly tricks."

"Laugh if you must, John Pierre, it was not like that. I told you I left to find Whetherbee."

"John Pierre, your problem is *you* do not believe anything. You somehow think you are going to wake up and this will all be over. I have no idea what it will take for you to believe!" cried Abu.

Suddenly, a bright light shined over the group. Clouds of mist swirled about them.

"Cover your face from the light," shouted Abu.

As quickly as it appeared, it dissipated, and they found themselves face to face with statues of the almighty Amun.

"Is he alive?" John Pierre questioned as he poked at one of the giant statues of the great god.

"Of course I am alive, you foolish man!" a voice shouted and the statue in the corner instantly came to life.

Wearing colorful regalia and plumes in his hat, the magician god spoke.

"I have no time for this silliness and will get right to the point," he said as he walked toward Abu. "Did you steal the amulets from the temple of Sarsa?"

Abu bowed and stated, "No."

"He is telling the truth. You may pass. Before you go, you must discover who did. And remember, you are *more* powerful than you think!"

Chapter 157

Khepri

The group walked on further. John Pierre was breathing heavily. He had aged more, and it was getting difficult for him to keep up. More giant statues lined the path as they descended deeper into the dark tunnel.

John Pierre stopped to try to catch his breath. The group was getting further ahead, and he knew it was best to let them keep on moving.

"You may reveal yourself, whoever you are," John Pierre stated evenly as he sat down on a rock.

"My, we are just full of ourselves," a voice spoke.

"No, I am old and tired and am losing the strength to continue this battle."

John Pierre knelt before the great Khepri, the scarab-faced God of creation.

"Ah, I see you have finally listened to Abu and learned something about respect."

"What do you want of me? I care more about the others and Lacey and wish no harm to come to them. It is my fault they are in this mess."

"I like you, John Pierre. You and your friends are a welcome disruption to the same day-old issues of tomb raiding; the crazy pharaohs, and others quest for power. Besides, it is funny to see Anubis and the others running around worrying about this situation."

John Pierre smirked. "I'm glad you find this so amusing. If you haven't noticed, I'm dying and won't be around much longer for your enjoyment."

The scarab beetle laughed boisterously. "You have the power, John Pierre, and don't know it. I will give you some time to live, but there may be a price to pay."

Chapter 158

Horus and the Gods

The falcon god wearing the udjat eye, an amulet of protection, sat on a golden throne decorated in jewels of gold.

"It is about time! I have waited for *all* of you long enough."

John Pierre had miraculously appeared before his friends who were already seated in front of the great god.

To the right and left of the god, sat a tribunal of other deities also in thrones of gold, marked with motifs of animals they were associated with or amulets that embodied their character.

"What happened, you were right behind us and then you disappeared?" Abu muttered.

"Silence," a voice thundered through the chamber.

The gods began arguing with one another as to why they were summoned again. "Just kill them and be done with it," spat Seth.

Hathor and Isis disagreed. And the arguing continued before Horus put an end to it all.

"The ones before me have passed the test, but there is one who has not. Bring her," Horus shouted toward the entrance. Lacey was instantly brought into the room by one of the guards. At the same moment Anubis entered the chamber with his trusty guard Jobeher.

"Nice of you to be on time," Seth called out.

"We have a problem. There is a disturbance in Chamber 20 again.

"Chamber 20? Is that where you have Samir chained?" Seth questioned.

Anubis summoned for Jobeher with the wave of his hand and silently communicated for Jobeher to fetch the new visitor.

Jobeher, in his canine form, had carried the human and dumped him in front of Horace. The fission chain was wrapped around his body preventing any movement.

"Montgomery," Lacey cried out as she ran toward him.

"Do not touch him! You will be burned," Abu screamed nervously.

"Lacey," John Pierre screamed. "You're alive!"

"I have been roaming around these dark corridors, when this dreadful man picked me up! Let him go," Lacey cried.

"Absolutely not, madam! This man has some explaining to do," roared Anubis.

Lacey looked up at the vile god and shouted angrily, "You're burning his skin! Release him!"

"Be seated, madam," Anubis pointed. Lacey was immediately silenced, and her body was transported to the end of the room and she was seated in a box, as if she was on trial in a courtroom.

Anubis turned to face the gods. "This man was found with Samir. They are connected somehow."

Horus sighed. "First things first. You, madam," he pointed at Lacey, "you used ingenuity to escape but you failed your test. You must discover the truth or die."

Lacey could not understand what was happening.

John Pierre willed Lacey to look at him. He threw his thoughts in her direction, *Lacey think about what happened, what was your journey about?* She was not paying attention.

Lacey screamed, "Montgomery is my husband! Please let him go. You're hurting him," she pleaded. "What type of gods are you?"

"Fair, and we seek the truth. It is you who have created chaos in our realm," Isis reminded Lacey. "Are you certain you want him free? Are you *sure* this is the man you love?"

"Yes, yes. Set him free!"

The moment Montgomery was free of the fission chain he ran toward Lacey and hugged her.

Anubis whispered to Jobeher and told him to bring Samir to the room.

Chapter 159

Montgomery

John Pierre scowled at Montgomery. "It was you, wasn't it? You killed me?"

"Don't be ridiculous," Lacey spat angrily. "Why would he do such a thing? Montgomery, please *tell* me it's not true. Why and how are you here? How did you know about all of this?" Lacey pleaded.

"Yes, Montgomery, I'm curious how you knew about all of this?" John Pierre glared at his old friend. "How the hell did you get here?"

Montgomery had no idea what was going on, but he was prepared to fight for his life.

"Lacey had been acting strange and I was tired of it. I just wanted a life with her. I have been in love with her since we met in college. Finally married, I thought I had a chance, but she can't seem to escape you, John Pierre. A man named Samir approached me and said he was a friend of Whetherbee's. He sent me to his apartment to go looking for some ancient artifact. He claimed it belonged to his family and Whetherbee had stolen it."

Montgomery shrugged as if it didn't matter. "He paid me millions in advance. I thought, Who cares? Whetherbee had enough ancient things, and he'd never miss one more. So I ransacked his apartment and stole it. But Samir never returned to collect it."

Whetherbee was stunned. "It was you who has been following me and going through my things?"

Montgomery shrugged. He wasn't going to deny it. "Samir saw the photos of you on my desk. He played on my emotions and we developed a plan to obtain some dagger. He promised me he wasn't going to harm anybody. He obviously *lied* to me."

Lacey gasped. She couldn't believe what she was hearing. She backed away from Montgomery.

Montgomery shouted at her, "My life could never begin with you, Lacey, because John Pierre was always around! Once married, you found excuse after excuse to take some job out of the country."

"It *was you* who killed John Pierre," Lacey whispered. "He didn't die from a fall; you were there that night. *You* killed him!"

Chapter 160

Jobeher disrupted the stunned silence as he carried Samir into the room and dumped his body in front of Horace.

Anubis waved his hands and the fission chain wrapped around his body disappeared.

"I swear, Lacey, I didn't kill anybody. I couldn't and would never do it. You have to believe me," Montgomery pleaded.

"How do you explain his death, Montgomery? You were in the museum that night."

"So were hundreds of others, Lacey. I'm telling you I didn't do it! I swear it!"

Lacey gasped as she instantly recalled her test. It was all starting to make sense. "Ather're told me the truth and I didn't believe her. Because of my own stubborn pride, I didn't want to believe her," she cried.

"Very good, madam, you finally figured it out," Thoth nodded. "You see the truth always has a way of revealing itself," the god of wisdom announced.

Lacey, enraged, waved her hands through the air trying to get the gods attention. "No, I made a mistake. It was someone else. Someone drugged John Pierre the night of the Greek Gala year's prior. That person sent those women to John Pierre's room. Nicholas knew I was heading back to the penthouse to reconcile with him because I had told him. I told Nicolas I wasn't interested in dating him the week earlier and that night. But I also told Montgomery I was going back to John Pierre. Either could have planned this."

"John Pierre had other enemies at the gala the night he was killed. The entire board hated him," Montgomery spat. "I'm telling you, Lacey, I would never kill anyone."

"Lacey is correct; it was Nicholas Stockport," John Pierre announced. "He is the one who killed me."

"What?" Lacey cried in astonishment as she turned toward him. "Are you positive?"

Abu's eyes reflected worry. "How can you be sure, John Pierre? You need proof."

John Pierre laughed. "My memory isn't as foggy anymore; it has returned. As we are talking about the night in question the images are coming together. I saw his shoes. Those ugly black shoes he always wears. He was the only one who showed up to a black-tie affair wearing casual shoes. I was in the mastaba in the middle of reciting the words. The jar lid was already in and I saw the shoes and then looked up and saw his face. He said I had become a liability. It all happened so fast. He hit me on the head just as I was done speaking the curse. I must have made it through the portal but died in my time."

Whetherbee agreed. "It makes more sense that Nicholas is the guilty one."

"How can you be sure?"

Whetherbee glanced sideways. "Remind me to tell you the full story of one of the tragic chapters of the Rockefeller family history. Nicholas is the bastard son of Mary Rockefeller. Mary was trying to protect her family. Nicholas wanted your job and he was scheming with Mary."

Whetherbee smiled knowingly. "I bet she was angry after I left her foundation out of my will."

John Pierre laughed. "You don't know the half of it. Not that I care, but why did you do it?"

"She was misappropriating funds, or it happened when she involved Nicholas. Either way she was panicking and needed to fix the problem. I refused to help her. If her family finds out, it would be one huge scandal. Nicholas is no different than Samir;

power and money corrupted them. I wouldn't be surprised if he killed John Pierre."

"Whetherbee is right," Lacey agreed. "I, too, am positive Nicholas killed John Pierre and Montgomery was probably next because Nicholas told me about his desire for the job as the director at the museum, and he didn't get it!"

"Congratulations, madam, it looks like you put more pieces of the puzzle together and finally passed the test," the great god Horus said and looked at Thoth as they nodded in agreement.

"I swear, Lacey, I did not kill John Pierre. We have had our differences, but I would never do such a thing," Montgomery pleaded.

"Montgomery had the misfortune of getting sent directly to the Duat as he didn't have the proper amulets to wear for protection," Whetherbee added.

John Pierre glared at Whetherbee angrily. "But how was Lacey able to arrive safely. She had no amulets?"

"She was the one with the lid who started the process," Whetherbee answered. "Two can't travel together. Montgomery immediately was sent to the Duat."

"How did you get here?" Barked John Pierre in disbelief. "Do you have more jars?"

Montgomery had no idea what John Pierre was referring to. "I followed Lacey and grabbed on to her leg. I didn't know what she was doing. I never realized this would happen."

Moments later Samir stood and looked wildly about the room. His eyes locked on Montgomery and he sprinted toward him. The two circled one another like crocodiles fighting for territory on the Nile River.

Montgomery pulled a knife from the back of his clothing. "Don't even think about it, Samir. I have what you are looking for and, from what you told me, it can't harm the owner, which is me."

Samir laughed wickedly as he looked at the shiny dagger. "I dare you!"

Montgomery lunged and the two fought a vicious battle. Nobody was able to help as the gods allowed it to continue. They used some type of spell to keep everyone in their places as the fight raged on.

Blood dripped from Montgomery's face from wounds inflicted by Samir. Montgomery raised the dagger and stabbed Samir multiple times in the chest.

Samir collapsed to the floor.

Anubis shook his head and his face reflected great irritation. "Montgomery, *you* are a fool. Whatever *you* were waving in the air is *not* what Samir asked you to locate. I can assure you."

Montgomery smirked, "Does it matter. The fool is dead!"

"No, my poor friend, it is *you* who are the fool. His body will rejuvenate momentarily," Anubis warned.

As predicted, Samir was up within seconds.

Montgomery's eyes widened! He was too stunned to react.

Samir lunged toward Montgomery, grabbed the dagger, and stabbed Montgomery dead center in the heart.

Lacey screamed but still could not move to get to Montgomery.

Anubis turned to the stunned group. "As I was saying, the dagger Montgomery was holding, well, it was the wrong one. It could not kill any god."

"Ammit," yelled Horace. "You are needed immediately!"

The crocodile, hippopotamus, lion beast appeared instantly, grabbed the bloody body and dragged him away.

The other gods grumbled at the delay.

"Now we have to stop and perform the weighing of the soul's ceremony," Hathor announced.

Chapter 161

"*H*athor, we need the information! We need those jars. This has gone on long enough. It's outlandish! This group of misfits has upset…"

The chamber rumbled as Hathor spoke. "Anubis! Silence! This entire circumstance is *your* doing. If you took care of the situation as directed, perhaps none of this would have happened. But instead you sent that bumbling half-brother of yours to do *your* work. I do not even want to hear why! And now we have to stop and perform the weighing of the soul's ceremony as it is written. It will take days!"

John Pierre cleared his throat nervously. "Well, if there is going to be another ceremony, then how about we make a deal?"

Horace looked at John Pierre suspiciously. "You want to make a deal with the Gods?"

John Pierre shrugged, "What do we have to lose?"

The Gods silently communicated their discussion. "Really… it is a trick…you are foolish to think he will try to escape…I do not trust any of them…they are not stupid…"

Horace silenced them all. "Ok, let me hear it."

"You're looking for the canopic jars and this portal. You're looking at some of the best historians and archeologists of our time. Abu and Astiramare know the Old Kingdom as it exists and Whetherbee, Lacey, and I know what happens in the future. Together, we can try to figure this out and find the missing pieces. What have you got to lose? We're all going to die anyway."

Anubis sneered. "He makes a good point."

"Give us what we need to exist outside of this realm and the time to find your missing jars, if we can't locate them bring us back. Somehow I doubt Anubis is going to let us go easily anyway?"

Horace folded his hands and looked at the eccentric group before him. He knew nothing of their connection only that somehow fate had brought them all together for some reason. "Isis will place a necklace around each of your necks. You must *not* remove it, or you will permanently be returned to the Duat. Here you will meet your final death and it will be instantaneous. If you do not find the jars, death will come to all. You will disintegrate and become part of the Egyptian sand."

"How much time do we have?" Abu muttered.

"Until the next full moon; which will be upon us within days."

Chapter 162

As they walked past the gods, Isis dropped a necklace of gold and precious stones that magically sealed around their necks.

Abu was the last in line and the god Horace put his hand out and stopped Abu. "Young Abu, can you tell us where you would like to be sent to start your final journey?"

"To my home in my village."

"Very well. I wish you and your friend's good luck."

Horace reached and clasped Abu's hands and the group disappeared.

Chapter 163

*A*bu opened his hand and stared awestruck at the gold udjat ring the god had thrust in his hand before he had disappeared. He said nothing and slipped it on his finger before the others began talking.

"Abu, why did you bring us here and not the mastaba?"

"He knew we would need supplies and time to formalize a plan," John Pierre answered although the question was not directed to him.

The group walked down the deep staircase into Abu's home. Food and water were retrieved from the cave below before the planning began.

It was difficult to see Whetherbee snuggling with Astiramare. He had portrayed himself as a philandering playboy to John Pierre. He was always surrounded by beautiful women, but the more John Pierre thought about it, never once did he see him in a serious relationship. Now he understood why.

"How long have you been traveling through time, Whetherbee?"

Whetherbee smiled and kissed Astiramare on the cheek. "Long enough to enjoy and know my family. Does it matter anymore, John Pierre?"

"John Pierre, you haven't stopped quarreling since I arrived. I'm sick of it. What about Montgomery? Are you not at all sad about what happened?" Lacey asked.

"Lacey, Montgomery was my best friend. How do you think I feel about all that has happened? I shouldn't have let our relationship fail as it did, and that I'm sorry for. I'm sorry to see you're sad. But we need to deal with the current situation. If we get out, there will be time to mourn him later. Why don't we get some rest and then examine the clues that we have to see if we can get out of this mess or we are going to die also."

Lacey shook her head and glared at him disapprovingly.

Whetherbee added, "He's right. We'll eat, rest, and go to the mastaba in the morning; where it all began."

Chapter 164

"What was the point of the first journey Amun-Ra sent us on?" Abu asked.

"Someone wanted me to admit I stole art," Whetherbee stated. "What about you, Astiramare?"

"I do not really want to discuss."

"Astiramare, you must for there may be a clue."

Astiramare sighed heavily and bowed her head in shame.

"Whetherbee, when you left, I was attacked by a man, who I was supposed to marry. I refused and left. I took Abu to the temple for his protection."

Whetherbee was able to read between the lines and knew she was raped. It was the way of life here. He knew it was his fault and would carry that burden until the day he died. "What about you Lacey?"

"Humph! It was all about Nicholas, Montgomery, and John Pierre's love life! Which we have already resolved. I admit I was tricked. We all were."

"And Abu?"

Abu shrugged. "I was accused of something I did not do. I did not take the amulets from the Temple of Sarsa."

"And mine was about stealing art and all the horrible things I have been doing, the path that I've been going down. I somehow think the tombs were about the worst problems that haunted each of us but there was something, a key or symbol of some sort, that had to be familiar."

"Think of what you saw everyone," Whetherbee pressured the group.

John Pierre's eye's widened. "The pharaoh's markings led us to the sun, owl, key, and moon sign."

"The sign of the sacred amulets from the Temple of Sarsa," Abu shouted.

Whetherbee's eyes widened as he announced, "The amulets my attacker was wearing around his neck when we fought and my plane went down," he suddenly remembered.

"Do you remember who it was?" Astiramare questioned.

"I'm positive it was Samir."

Chapter 165

" *S* amir!"
"How did he make it though the portal?" Astiramare asked.

"I don't know, I thought he was dead."

Whetherbee continued grilling everyone. "Ok, and then there was the test with the gods. Abu, Astiramare, what was that all about?"

"There are always lessons to be learned in all we do. The gods want us to admit to our mistakes, but somehow we cheated our way out. They laugh at our ingenuity but know in the end it will only result in death. Their universe is out of balance; when Ma' at is out of balance, well, you saw what happened with Montgomery arriving. What if others find the way? It could be disastrous," Astiramare stated.

"Anubis is powerful and will stop at nothing to get those jars. It is what he has been after all along. The jars hold the key for all of you to return. If we do not find them, everything as we know it will be like it never existed." Abu was serious as he spoke of what was to come.

They all turned to Whetherbee. John Pierre was the first to speak. "What did *you* do with the *fifth jar*?"

Chapter 166

"Unfortunately, I never had the fifth jar. I have been searching for it my entire life. I only discovered four. Apparently, you are able to travel back and forth with four jars but must wear the ring and you will not age. The fifth jar is the *key* to the *ultimate power* of Anubis; it will somehow allow him to leave this world."

"Lacey has the last lid and if she returns…"

"Without a ring, she will continue to age and eventually die," Whetherbee finished solemnly.

Chapter 167

Khephri

The group arrived at the mastaba just outside the Giza complex loaded with supplies. Lacey retrieved her backpack that Abu had hid when she arrived. "Miss Lacey, there is one thing we have not looked at – the journal."

Lacey took the journal from Abu. "The only thing that is constant is the pharaoh's markings, jars, numbers, and the scarab beetle that is embossed on the corner of the cover."

"Scarab beetle? Show me, how did we miss that?"

"It's here," Lacey pointed. "Unfortunately you can see the likeness on the small piece left from one of the page's that was torn. He is also on the worn cover, but barely visible due to the age and how tattered the book is."

"That's it," John Pierre shouted. "The scarab beetle. The god Khepri, the one who came to see me on my journey to the Hall of Judgment! Abu, does he have a temple?"

"I do not know? He is everywhere!"

"Lacey, is there a temple dedicated to him?"

Lacey frowned. "Everyone, every kingdom and dynasty, worshiped him. There are scarab beetles everywhere. He is associated with creation, the sunrise, re-birth after death; that is the reason for putting the scarab over the heart during the mummification process. Scarab statues litter the desert. Amenhotep in the New Kingdom had statues created for the god, but that did not happen yet; we are in the Old Kingdom, but you already know this J.P."

"That's it! The mummification process, 'tis what is most sacred and Khepri is a part of," Astiramare shouted.

"And it's where the canopic jars are," John Pierre added. "The jars in the Old Kingdom were simple, but the jars I have are from a later or earlier era perhaps not known to us. Abu, when I first arrived you told me the canopic jars have magic and have been in your family for centuries, crafted for the legendary ruler King Narmer or Menes, who united Upper and Lower Egypt. You are not sure how the king obtained them or who crafted them. You believe descendants of your family hid the jars for centuries to protect their secrets. Others believe they are a gift from the gods above. The lids, as we all know, allow for time travel."

"Yes, that is correct," John Pierre. "You remember the story well," Abu grinned pleased that John Pierre had listened.

"The enchantment associated with them is the reason why Anubis wants them so bad," Lacey added.

"Yes, but Abu said his family set up their base camp or rather positioned themselves, on one side of the river and then the mastaba. I bet it was only to keep watch over the jars. As the pharaohs became more powerful…why I bet someone in your family who practiced darker magic stole them…or over time the shifting sands simply buried them," John Pierre finished.

"Whetherbee! Where did you get the jars from?"

"On a dig, in graduate school, during an internship. Eventually I made a discovery that is known as the artifact storage area. While the group slept, I went back and dug up my find. I smuggled it in my bag and packed them off and shipped them home. It was so easy. I still can't believe I got away with it. I excavated that site and we later found the mastaba. I recognized the symbols on the jar lids and became obsessed with them. It wasn't long before I learned their secret. The mastaba in the museum was my gift to your museum for safe keeping and the riches it could bring.

"Stolen, hidden in the artifact storage, covered by sand... incredible," muttered John Pierre. "The artifact storage area is what was later to become an expanded area of the mummification process. I almost forgot, the pieces of the papyrus I found from the back of your photos – the map of the pharaoh's temple and the mortuary chapel."

John Pierre smiled. "The mummification temple, or mortuary chapel, is near the Sphinx, which is not built yet. But there are more secrets to that temple's location, and we know the way, don't we?"

Whetherbee smiled and nodded. "This is true; because we were there."

Chapter 168

"Miss Lacey, perhaps you need to look at this journal again too and see if there is anything familiar. There has to be more clues that we are missing. Are you sure you can't read it?"

"I told you, Abu, I can't read any of this and there is a page missing. Let's concentrate on mapping out the mortuary chapel. There have been many sandstorms over the years – but there is an area John Pierre, Whetherbee, and I had once explored. I'm sure this is what we are looking for."

Chapter 169

The temple was busy with activity during the day, so they had to wait until night to sneak in. The secret entrance was hidden at night but already excavated in John Pierre's time, so it was not too hard to locate.

The brightly lit full moon illuminated the way toward the mortuary temple.

Armed with flashlights they moved quickly down the long, winding stairs of stone to the deep recesses of the earth, where the embalming of the dead occurred.

The smell of dead bodies was horrific. John Pierre was the first to react. In between coughing fits, he gasped, "Cover your nose with your shirt or a cloth. Look Lacey, is it how you envisioned it? One of the earliest mortuary temples? Can you believe it?"

Lacey was stunned. It's one thing to study and ready about ancient man but to witness the actual site – even she was at a loss for words.

The room was filled with dead bodies in various states of the mummification process. Colorful hieroglyphics once again filled with walls depicting the journey that would come for each traveler. The entire process was very methodical.

The body was moved from section to section and room to room for the entire procedure. Salt to dry the body, wrappings of linen, canopic jars, and fragrances in other jars, scarab beetles, medical instruments, and pigments filled the rooms.

One of the last rooms was packed with wooden coffins in numerous stages of painting, all waiting for the final arrival - the mummified body.

"Look for the symbols," Whetherbee whispered. "It has to be either for Khepri, or the amulets, or the pharaoh's markings."

"I think it is for Khepri," Astiramare called quietly.

They all joined her at the mid-sized symbol of the scarab on the wall.

"They are back there! Seize them," roared a voice.

"Lights out," John Pierre muttered.

The great pharaoh himself entered the room with three of his guards carrying torches of fire. "Someone said they saw people moving about the complex. I am surprised you are alive and have the audacity to return after *your* last escapade. But what are you after now, bothering the dead? It is sacrilegious!"

Lacey was the first to speak. "I felt bad and I am returning your prized jars that were stolen. I live in fear of the gods and do not wish to suffer their wrath."

The pharaoh turned toward her. The hot fire was inches from her face. "My golden jars? You have them?"

Lacey knelt down and opened her pack and pulled out a package. The pharaoh smiled as she unwrapped them. The gold sparkled in the light. She held them out for him. "We stole them from Anubis himself!"

The pharaoh took the jars and set them on a table. He studied each one and smiled at the shiny gold. He turned one over and frowned. "What is this language? M…a…d…e…I…n… Ch…i…n…a." He pronounced slowly.

"Made in China," Whetherbee corrected his pronunciation. "It's a secret language of the ancients."

The pharaoh laughed. "I will not ask you to explain the meaning, but I fear once again you try to trick me. You know that I cannot let you leave here. I will kill you and rape these women for what they have put me through. Guards take these men."

Whetherbee, John Pierre, and Abu were no match as the muscular men held each one tight. The pharaoh went for Lacey first, whose expression of fear changed to fierce power as she kneed him, hard between the legs. As he fell to the ground, she took out a dagger from her waist and plunged it in his heart.

Astiramare ran forward and kicked him between the legs again as he lay in the dirt. "Just in case he is still alive," she laughed.

Lacey removed the dagger and tossed it to Astiramare. "I believe this belongs to you."

The three guards quickly released the men and ran from the mortuary chamber in fear.

Chapter 170

"Remind me not to piss them off," Whetherbee said after he and John Pierre moved the dead body to an empty coffin in another room.

Whetherbee was stunned. "How did you find my dagger, Lacey? I never told *anyone* about it or its location?"

After I read John Pierre's letter. He mentioned that I should go back to your penthouse and see if I could find any other clues. He left me a list of what he had deciphered to date. When I saw the word dagger, I knew right where to look. You see, I recalled seeing a picture of it in your private study."

"But I've never allowed anyone in there, not even John Pierre!"

"Do you recall the night I came to see you after the Greek gala upset because of John Pierre's indiscretions? I couldn't sleep. I started to come down the stairs and was heading toward the kitchen when I saw light from the wall where there was no door! I stopped and saw you exit and caught a glimpse of the object. I watched how you left and never said a word. I just thought it was part of your private collection."

Flashlights back on, they went back to the door, each looking at every scarab symbol they saw. Nothing.

"I don't think it's a scarab," Abu called. He took the finger he wore the udjat eye ring and pushed it into the udjat eye symbol on the wall. The stone moved and revealed another udjat eye. The udjat eye was depicted in a circle surrounded by an owl, sun, moon, and a key. "The symbols of wisdom, perception, the universe, and power of the gods."

Everyone gasped as the wall moved. Abu smiled as he stepped back and gestured for all to enter.

The room was filled with gold – jewelry, statues and statues of the god Khepri wearing rings. "Why do we know nothing about this, Lacey?"

"Isn't it obvious, John Pierre, it has all been stolen and plundered. Just like what we're doing."

"Do not touch anything; we are missing something. We need to find a ring and there are hundreds of them. Let's think about it first. This could be a trap."

"I agree," Whetherbee said.

"I think I found the missing pages of your journal," Lacey called.

Chapter 171

She was standing by a wooden table filled with papyrus, makeshift journals, and rolls of parchment. "Somehow this was ripped out of the journal and made its way here."

"Supposedly this journal had been in your family for ages but went missing according to the legend Astiramare told me. I found it and buried it in the mastaba for Abu, but apparently I died before I could tell him about it," Whetherbee explained.

"I've been searching for the missing pages during my expeditions. Someone got hold of it and it wound up in the mortuary temple. They couldn't read the text, and the pharaoh possibly had it sent here for the scribes and shamans he employed to try and decipher and maybe forgot about it?"

"Can you read it?" Lacey asked Abu. "It makes no sense to me."

Abu scanned the page. "It is an ancient text that I have not seen before."

"Abu," Astiramare called. "Why don't you look at it and concentrate and perhaps something will come to you."

Abu took the parchment and journal and sat down on a wooden stool and joined the pages together. He closed his eyes and thought back to his teaching with Rufaaron. The moment the pages touched he could feel the heat and the words that only he could see dance in front of him.

Eyes wide in shock, he looked about the room to see if anybody had witnessed what he had.

"Well, what are you waiting for?" John Pierre said impatiently. "Time is running out!"

Abu turned his head back to the letters hovering in front of him and read,

"The one with the blood of the great shamans, the elder will return and is the savior. The one who knows the sands of time will travel to the temple and have the power to remove the ring. Only when the sky orb is at its brightest will this be achieved. The chance is many but there is only one. Death is near if you cannot succeed and the cycle of time will end ten times for one. Life will no longer be as the gods have already seen."

Abu read it again.

"It has to be Abu. He has the blood of the shamans," Astiramare stated.

Whetherbee laughed. "Yes, he may have the blood of his grandfather and others before him, but he has failed miserably; you and I already know this Astiramare."

Abu argued. "I studied with the great Rufaaron!"

"Yes, but what have you accomplished? You have learned some incantations, but it's sporadic. You have *yet* to tap into any sort of *your* real power," Whetherbee argued. "And that's if it exists at all!"

"I lost time. I went looking for you! Besides, Horus gave me this ring. He and Amun both said, 'I was more powerful than I know!'"

The arguing continued.

"Stop!" Lacey yelled. "I disagree. You're wrong."

All heads turned to her waiting for her explanation.

John Pierre was getting annoyed. "Lacey, we're running out of time. It has to be Abu. How can you not see it, all signs point to him? There is nobody else here that could have the power. I'm not saying he is the greatest magician. He is young and obviously needs more training."

"You are wrong; there is another," she whispered.

Chapter 172

ohn Pierre threw up his hands in frustration. "Well then, who the hell is it?"

"The reason for those tests the gods put us through was about truth," Lacey whispered as she glanced at Whetherbee. "Wasn't it?"

"How long have you known?" Whetherbee asked.

"It was obvious the moment I saw you all together. Tell him."

"Tell who, and tell him what?" Shouted John Pierre.

Whetherbee sighed. "Your father and mother are not dead."

John Pierre stepped back. He felt as if someone had punched him in the stomach. The range of emotions and frustrations of not having a family followed. He lunged toward Whetherbee grabbing him by the shirt.

"You're despicable! You were my friend and you knew *all* along. I can't believe you would keep something like that from me. Of all the low-down tricks…"

"John Pierre, stop! Don't even think about hitting him," Lacey yelled as she ran between them. "Let him talk."

"There is not much to say, John Pierre. I am sorry for the deception, but the truth is *I* am your father. Astiramare *is* your mother. Abu is *your* brother. Astiramare and Abu have the blood of the ancient ones and *you possibly* have it too."

"How could *you* not see the resemblance? You all look alike, John Pierre," Lacey indicated.

Abu smiled excitedly, ran over and hugged John Pierre shrieking, "I can't believe it! My brother. I have a brother! Now everything makes sense! Welcome, John Pierre, to our family!"

"You knew about this, Abu?"

"He did not," Whetherbee answered immediately. "It was too dangerous. I simply told him, you were my friend and if you followed the directions, you would come to help. Unfortunately I was killed before I could tell him and leave him and you all the correct information."

"'Tis true, John Pierre," Abu nodded in agreement, smiling proudly. "I cannot believe it! I have a brother!"

John Pierre sank to the floor. It was too much for him to take. His entire life or what he thought was changed in four sentences.

"My mother…"

"…Was my sister," Whetherbee interrupted. "She raised you. When she died, and you were on your own, I made sure your entire life was planned. Schools, scholarships, everything was paid for by me."

"The trust fund?"

"All arranged by me. I didn't want you to have to worry about anything. I later befriended you in college to forge our bond and friendship."

"Why didn't you just raise me? Why go to all this trouble?"

"It was too dangerous! Samir found us, you, me and your mother, just after you were born. I was a young boy. I met your mother and fell in love. The gods knew this was happening and Anubis sent Samir to kill all of us. Your mother gave me the dagger, the dagger from the Temple of Sarsa. She is the one who stole it.

I tricked Samir and killed him before I entered the portal with you. At least I *thought* I killed him. He somehow got through and seems to have been searching for me."

Chapter 173

"J.P. let me tell you how it began and perhaps it will all make sense to you," Whetherbee sighed. "When I first laid eyes on your mother, my first thought was she was the most beautiful being I had ever seen. I was mesmerized. The story is like any other love story. I remember the day Samir came into our lives."

The couple smiled lovingly at one another as the newborn suckled his mother's breast. The young man shook his head in wonderment at the tiny miracle. Considering the circumstances, he was surprised the child had survived. He wasn't prepared and not sure what he was going to do. The only thing he was certain of was his love for her and their child.

Footsteps from the outer chamber caused him to raise his head. He felt his hair itching on the back of his neck as a thin sheen of sweat covered his warm skin. He could feel his heart beating loudly as the blood raced through his body. He wasn't sure if the adrenaline was a result of fear, curiosity, or a bit of both.

He raised his fingers to his lips in a gesture of silence as he slowly crept in front of the woman to shield her from any potential danger. Instantly a shadow filled the small room, blocking the light emanating from the metal light-source in the far corner.

The woman's eyes widened reflecting terror at the appearance of the figure in the shadows. Instinctively she pulled the blanket over the baby and hugged him closer as she watched the man lower the hood of his dark cloak.

His neatly trimmed beard was as black as the worn cloth. His hair, a mix of black and gray, hung well past his shoulders. She could have sworn the garment had a faint glimmer of gold or silver as he moved or perhaps, it was just an effect from the lighting. Wrinkles and scars punctuated his weathered skin like the cracks on the stones of the cave walls. While shadows from the light, and his dark hair made it difficult to guess his age, she already knew he was an elder. She could see his aura permeating from his presence.

The adolescent man was on his feet instantly. "Who are you? How did you get here?" He demanded, hoping his quick movements would startle the intruder.

The older man said nothing as he surveyed the surroundings. He nodded. So the story was true. It had happened. The items strewn about the room did not belong. Impossible but the evidence suggested otherwise...it was real. He stared at the youth in awe.

"Who are you and what do you want?" the younger man commanded, his eyes never leaving the unwelcomed visitor.

The man raised the staff in his hand and pointed, "I have journeyed far and wish to sit," he stated as if he were a regular caller. He casually made his way to a stone bench across the room.

"Who are you and how did you get into our home?" The young man hissed.

"Your home," he stated sarcastically as his hand gestured in an arc around the rocks and dirt before him. "Really, do not take me for a fool. I must say this assignment was challenging. Locating you has been quite difficult. You have not made it easy."

The adolescent was irritated. He worked hard to avoid detection and failed. The discovery made him uneasy. "I have no idea what you are talking about. State your business!"

The aged man rolled his eyes and cocked his head to one side grinning confidently. Not one for endless or unnecessary chatter he got right to the point. "What you have accomplished is forbidden. The child cannot stay."

Still standing he glared at the intruder uncertain of his purpose. "I don't believe it is any business of yours," he said, his voice a low growl, as if warning his prey before striking.

"Ah, but that is where you are mistaken, my young friend. Both of you have interfered with the order of the universe."

The boy instinctively moved closer to his woman and child. Every muscle in his body tightened and he was ready to attack. "I ask you again, who are you and what do you want?"

"I am a descendent of Anubis," he gestured with both hands. "I have been sent to deal with your situation."

His eyes widened in shock and disbelief before he burst out laughing. "Anubis, the alleged lord of the underworld? Surely you jest! Next you'll be telling me Osiris and Isis are alive and well too!"

"Actually, I just saw them last week and they are happy as could be," he smirked in amusement. "Now back to our little situation…"

"There is no situation," the youth interrupted sharply. "This is my family. You are obviously in the wrong place," he stated evenly never taking his eyes off the uninvited guest. The sweat was pouring down his back as he spoke.

The ancient man glared at him; his eyes gleamed like emeralds. He removed his hands from the folds of his vestment and rubbed them together. A wand instantly appeared in his right hand. It was no bigger than an average pencil, perhaps six or seven inches in length. A stone rested at the top. The stone was held in place by some type of sturdy cloth and a band of gold links.

"If you've come to give us a magic show, you are in the wrong house," the boy stated evenly. His heart was racing as he tried to remain calm.

"I sense your distress, young man. Your attempt at humor does not hide your fear and, as you can see, I am not laughing." He pointed the object in his hand at the boy and said, "I know

who you are but I know not how you came to this place, of which I must mention has ALWAYS been understood as an IMPOSSIBLE achievement...but alas, you are here so it is obviously conceivable. How? It is a mystery, but it is not my place to question the ways of the universe..."

"Stop with your rambling," the adolescent interrupted. "I suggest you leave, or I will have to kill you."

The man chuckled at the thought. "You glare at me like that idiotic jackal Anubis," he said as he adjusted his cloak. "Kill me? Do not be ridiculous. My fate was written long ago. Any attempt at violence will only invoke others who will not be as kind as I." He sighed deeply. The situation was peculiar and highly irregular. "My intention was not to frighten you, but to warn you of the danger and ensure my instructions are carried out. You and the child...cannot stay here..."

Aghast, the young man interrupted, shouting, "What do you mean? This is our home."

The senior man twirled the small staff. The stone gleamed a brilliant green. "Do not take me for a fool. You are clearly not of this world nor is he. He will alter the future if he stays, decades of history will be modified, completely erased or changed. And if not rectified now, when you return, your life may be non-existent."

"You don't know this will happen," the youth blurted in anger. He regretted his admission the moment the words were out.

"It is obvious the prophecy is true; for here you are, one big happy family," he smirked as he pointed his wand at the man, child, and woman. "The chain of events that you started must end now. This is one prediction that must not come to fruition."

"We mean no harm," the boy argued. "You speak in riddles. How could this child possibly be a danger?"

The old man shrugged. "It is written that he will destroy the pharaoh and his kingdom."

"I don't believe you. How do I know you are not making this up?"

"Enough! How dare you doubt me," he shouted as he aimed his staff at the youth.

The boy fell to the ground groaning as he held his left arm in pain.

"Your discomfort will subside momentarily. Now as I was saying, look closely at the child. He does not favor her, does he? Once they realize he is different, his own people will kill him. This is not his world. He has no place here."

The woman sank deeper into the mound of bedding, clutching the child tightly to her breast. The two men studied one another as they each pondered the situation.

Cries from the baby broke the silence.

"Hush, little one," the old man whispered as he waved his wand in the air. "The universe will right this wrong before any harm is done." The child immediately stopped crying.

The woman gasped and pulled the blanket over the child's head attempting to shield him from the evil before her.

The trespasser smirked and waved his staff toward the infant. The blanket fell revealing his face. "Do not test me, madam, I will not hesitate to reveal the full force of my power!"

Whatever language he spoke, she obviously understood as her eyes widened in fear and tears began to flow down her cheeks. She looked toward her mate for assurance.

The young man relaxed his shoulders. He did not want to admit it, but he knew the elder visitor was right. There was no logical explanation for what had transpired. His presence was inexplicable. The child had no chance of survival here. The knots in his stomach tightened. "What do you want me to do?"

The woman screamed.

He briskly turned and silenced her with his hand.

"You need to return with him before anything happens!"

"Noooooooooo," wailed the woman who began sobbing.

"You will show me how you came, and I am to make sure you never return."

The younger man ran his fingers through his thick, brown hair in frustration, as he evaluated the situation and fought for a solution. He turned quickly to the old man. "You must let the child take his mother's milk, before I do what you ask. The child will not survive in my world without it."

The older man rested his head on the palm of his hand. He tapped his fingers gently on the cold stone as he considered the proposal. The young man had a point. What he did not know was that he and the child would be killed the moment he was shown the location of the portal.

For the first time he was uncertain of the potential ramifications and universal impact of the situation. The correct course of action was perplexing. Bargaining was not something he engaged in or was even allowed to do, but he did not want to frighten the boy. He need information and he had wasted too much time already and the consequences would be severe if he failed; however, curiosity got the best of him. Cries from the woman interrupted his thinking and he shook his head in frustration.

The young man bent down and wiped the tears from the woman and kissed her lightly on the forehead as he told her to trust him it would be ok. He turned, "You must forgive her; she is in love with her child as any woman would be. Even she does not understand the situation. Let her feed the child as needed and, I promise to abide by your wishes. Besides travel is only possible on the full moon."

"Is it true?" He growled at the woman.

She answered in the native dialect, nodding, "This he does not lie about. The moon must be full," she finished as she gestured upwards.

The old man raised his eyebrows and smiled knowingly. "So you want to make a deal? My friend, do not take me for an idiot. I have already told you I am a descendent of Anubis. You are a bigger fool than I thought if you don't realize what that means. I warn you, crossing me will only bring trouble. I will come for you and the child on the next full moon. You must not leave the cave. It is fortified with an energy force. Your death's will be instantaneous if your try."

"You have my word we will not leave the safety of this dwelling."

"I tricked Samir and lured him with the lethal dagger from the Temple of Sarsa and killed him. I disappeared through the portal with you. Unfortunately, I wasn't aware that Samir survived. Somehow the atmosphere or something else protected him."

Chapter 174

*T*he clapping of hands echoed in the room interrupting Whetherbee's tale. "Amazing! It is good to finally hear the story. I always wondered how I was able to survive," Samir snickered.

Whetherbee turned to the voice. "I returned and searched for you. I later discovered an ancient text that barely listed your name that stated that you disappeared," Whetherbee admitted. "After that, I knew I could never tell John Pierre or Abu. It was too dangerous."

"'Tis true," Samir admitted. "When Whetherbee stabbed me, I miraculously survived and have been traveling through time zones, living in the ghastliest conditions, seeking out witches and magicians, in every century. I finally met Merlin, who helped transport me to your time. I have spent years looking for you. I never anticipated you would pull my necklace off - the sacred amulets of Sarsa."

"So it was you who stole them," Abu shouted. "You and my teachers, Ararbeooka and Boutros you set me up! All this time I have been blamed."

"That makes no sense, Abu wasn't even born when the amulets were supposedly taken."

"This is true," Astiramare added.

"You idiots," scoffed Samir. "I *knew* the story of the jars and swore allegiance to my half-brother Anubis that I would help in his mission to find them. I knew the protection was needed and stole them."

"But why did Abu get blamed for the theft?" Whetherbee asked.

"After the amulets were stolen, Rufaaron had fakes put in their place, he told the story that they had been recovered to see if the real thief could be caught. Unfortunately, while Abu was training the fakes were stolen and he was immediately blamed."

"Ararbeoooka, one of the teachers, admitted to me in the test we went through beyond the underworld that she stole them," Abu confirmed.

All heads turned toward Samir. "I stole those amulets many moons before Abu! I knew they were needed for protection and if I was going to enter the portal, I knew I would need them."

"The jars you seek are on the table," Lacey interrupted and pointed toward the table.

"So you think you can trick me too?" Samir held his hand over the jars. "They are fake as I suspected. Crafted from a material unknown to me."

"Unknown because they are from another era, a period so rich in gold," Lacey cried out.

"Forget it Lacey, he would never understand you did your best. They are from her time, Samir. Worth more than what is in this room. I suggest you keep them," John Pierre stated.

Samir raised his hand and Whetherbee and John Pierre began choking.

Horrified, Astiramare grabbed the dagger hidden in her cloak and threw it across the room. As it sailed through the air, she called Samir's name. He turned toward her and the dagger landed directly in his heart. The poison from the tip of the ancient dagger from the temple of Sarsa coursed through his veins and killed him on impact.

The spell was broken and Whetherbee and John Pierre lurched forward, each grabbing their chest as they fell to the ground. They continued coughing and gasping for air before the choking subsided. The men looked at one another, astonished but secretly proud of the two women.

Chapter 175

" *L*acey, how can you be so sure it's John Pierre and not Abu?"

"John Pierre has a complete triangle mark on his back; Abu's is only partial. I noticed it when I first arrived."

"Perhaps Abu is really meant for something bigger than even we can imagine," Whetherbee suggested.

Abu frowned. "But we have never seen John Pierre do magic. He does not even believe in it!"

"My dear son, I know this is difficult for you, but the gods have other plans for you. Rufaaron *is* your great-grandfather. Your lineage is even more powerful, as my parents are descendants of the gods as well; Heka, Horace, and Isis. My father, your grandfather is not really missing, rather he is just not present. But more stories for another time. We must finish this journey and move on. I also believe John Pierre is the one."

Abu smiled he already knew the answers. "Your parents are divine gods," Abu muttered to his mother proudly. He looked at the ring on his hand, the gift from Horace and smiled.

"I'm confused about the drawings in the mastaba, and the artifact storage had the same markings on them. I understand you left clues, but the lines and shapes in the bottom corners?"

"They are like a signature but instead made reference to our family. The shapes make reference to all our names," Whetherbee drew on the dirt floor. "You will find them everywhere I've been. It was to protect everyone and hopefully you would learn the truth."

"John Pierre, time is passing. I can feel it. We will all begin to fade and become grains in the sand. You must believe. Look around the room and use your skill," Whetherbee pleaded.

"John Pierre, do you remember how we escaped Xgar, the crocodile? It wasn't me! I have always wondered how we were able to flee. I know now that it was *you* who got us out before we even hit the watery Nile. Somehow you used your power."

"I don't know, Abu. I was just concentrating very hard for a solution."

"Yes, yes, that is how you do it. You just didn't know. What about the times when you put the lid in the key in the mastaba? Light emanated…"

"Just like it did in the mastaba at the museum," John Pierre finished. "A ray of light illuminated from the mastaba." *Could it really be possible?*

"It is like an energy force that is ignited by John Pierre, who has the power when he holds it. The lid is calling for its home," Whetherbee added.

Astiramare nodded in agreement. "'Tis true, my son."

"I ate the food," John Pierre blurted.

"Food?" Lacey exclaimed flabbergasted. "How can you think about food at a time like this? What are you talking about?"

"Abu do you recall when I arrived you told me not to eat the food?"

Abu nodded.

"Well, I just remembered that I *ate* an apple, you know the fruit that was left at the base of the ka statue in the mastaba when I first arrived. Nothing happened to me. I never thought anything of it until now."

Abu gasped in shock. "Then 'tis true. Your blood and mine… 'tis the same," Abu excitedly agreed. "You would have become violently ill and died from eating the food if you did not have my blood."

"This is why I now believe," John Pierre concluded. "Who has the journal?"

Lacey immediately removed it from her bag and handed it to John Pierre.

John Pierre ran his fingers through his hair nervously and then put the book down in the sand. "Rufaaron *said* I have the power to decipher the journal."

"You must concentrate," Abu urged.

John Pierre studied the worn cover and unconsciously drew a triangle and encased the journal in a pyramid shape. He closed his eyes and let his hand hover over the book until he felt the pages open. He opened his eyes and recited the ancient text from the inside cover. Diagrams only visible to him came to life and hovered in the air over the journal. John Pierre released his hand and the text disappeared back into the book.

"Circles of gold, crafted for some
Entwined for infinity - and then some
Use them wisely for if in the wrong hands
Death and destruction will pass through all lands
The eye is watching and forever waits
The sky's above watch your fate
Find the key and turn as one Horace awaits for the one

"There are two rings that allow for travel forever but it warns to use wisely, or they could get in the wrong hands of someone like Anubis. The Udjet eye is the key to unlocking and the sky is Khephri and the Gods who are always watching. We must find the key as Horace is waiting for me," Abu said excitedly as he dissected the phrases.

John Pierre smiled as he got up and walked further into the room. He was careful not to touch anything. It was too obvious. The gold glittered, calling him to take any one of the glistening rings. But then he saw it.

A lonely scarab beetle was sitting in a niche in the wall. The carved stone was big enough to fit in his hand. It was constructed with the blue lapis lazuli stone, a reference to the sky and roughly carved. He took it and looked around the room and found the carved mark of the gods, the udjat eye surrounded by the owl, sun, moon, and key. It fit perfectly. He turned it and the wall moved. The lone canopic jar and lid of the god Horace sat with the statue of Khepri gleaming with the missing ring.

"Finally the prize is mine!"

Everyone in the room turned toward the menacing voice and gasped.

Even before the large figure removed his cloak, they knew who he was.

"It is one of two rings that exist. Whetherbee obviously had one, which is what I believe enabled him to travel back and forth through the dimensions without the rapid aging such as you have unfortunately experienced," he laughed as he pointed at John Pierre.

"Horus has kept this hidden and now it's mine," Anubis laughed as he snatched the ring out of John Pierre's hand.

"Before you kill us can you tell me how you are going to travel without the other jars?" John Pierre questioned.

Anubis' laugh was ominous as it resonated in the chamber. "The fifth jar was designed for a stone…the stone that rests on my staff… once inserted in the indentation in that jar…all the power will be mine!"

"Your sidekick Samir, will be along…"

"Enough!" The voice of Anubis echoed through the chamber. "I have had enough of your trickery. I am already aware of Samir's fate. 'Tis a shame; he was gifted and had lots to learn. Unfortunately he desired something that was unattainable – power." Anubis walked around the room as he continued talking.

"He lost his way a long time ago. I should never have trusted him with the task at hand. I told the gods he would lead me to you, and he did well. I am glad you killed him for 'tis one less thing for me to take care of. The gods will deal with him when he travels through the Hall of Judgment. The end does not look good. It never does."

"Anubis," Abu called sternly.

Eyebrows raised, Anubis turned slowly and looked at Abu. "Really, my child, what could you possibly do to me?" Anubis quickly raised his arm and pointed his finger at Abu.

Astiramare screamed and at the same moment Abu raised his hand and deflected the lightening bolt. The energy hit the powerful udjet ring and zapped Anubis sending him right back to the Netherworld.

The echoing of the ring bounced off the walls as it hit the stone and fell to the ground when Anubis disappeared. Whetherbee picked it up and handed it to John Pierre. "This is what allows you to travel and not age. You must always wear it."

"Well done, Abu," Astiramare smiled proudly as she ran over and hugged him. "It is not everyday a young boy sends a god back to the Duat. I told you great things were coming your way!"

Chapter 176

"Quickly, grab the jar, lid, ring, scarab and anything else of importance. We need to get back to the mastaba before the light of the moon fades," Astiramare yelled.

The wind and sand were whipping around the group as they jumped on the camels. "Bad sandstorm coming this way. It is a sign of things to come if we cannot finish this tonight."

"Let's go. Cover your faces and keep your head down," Whetherbee yelled as they headed toward the mastaba.

They piled into the mastaba and ran to the wall to insert the key. I don't think we can all make it together," Whetherbee stated. Two adults can't travel together. I tucked John Pierre in my jacket as I went through the portal and was lucky to have made it. If anybody must go it should be you and Lacey. I have decided to stay with Astiramare and Abu."

"But if we all hold on together," John Pierre pleaded.

"My son, it's too risky; besides, Abu and Astiramare can't travel through the portal. It is impossible. They are bound to this land. That is why Anubis wants the jars and lids so bad. The ones you now own can release him and allow him to travel to other worlds. Can you imagine the trouble he would cause?"

"Hence the reason you put the clause in your will that the jars were to always remain in the museum?" John Pierre questioned.

Whetherbee nodded. "Locked up in the museum, nobody would touch them."

"And if we decided not to take the gift."

"My lawyers were to destroy them," Whetherbee concluded.

"But what about Samir," John Pierre recalled. "He made it through the portal."

"It was an anomaly. I am guessing the atmosphere and others as he stated helped heal him. He had spent many lifetimes searching for me."

John Pierre was conflicted. "If we leave now, I will never know what happened to you, Astiramare, and Abu!"

Whetherbee put his hands on John Pierre's shoulders and spoke to him sternly. "Abu must return and study with Rufaaron immediately. He has much to learn. He, like *you,* John Pierre, has his *own* destiny. You must realize this."

Abu ran and hugged John Pierre. He did not want him to leave. "But John Pierre died in his time. How will we know if he survived? What if his death is a true death? What about his age, will it reverse? What if he does not make it back?"

John Pierre released him and grabbed Lacey's hand and kissed her on the mouth. "Whatever is going to happen, it will be fine! I just need to get Lacey back. She had a life and deserves to live it, with or without me. What's important is that she knows the truth and that I love her. I will be prepared for whatever happens. But Lacey can't stay. Even if I don't make it back, I know she will." He took the gold ring and placed it on her finger.

Lacey gazed lovingly into his eyes and swore if they could be together, they would never be apart again.

"I have left special instructions for you. Depending on how you get transported back, we will see. If you both make it, you and Lacey need to take care of one another. You always belonged together," Whetherbee smiled proudly.

"But what about John Pierre? If he makes it how will he learn his magic?" Abu questioned.

Whetherbee took John Pierre aside. "I have provided you all the tools you need, and I am happy knowing the lifetime of memories and journeys we all shared together. You know the truth. You know your father, mother, and brother. Abu will do great things and so will you. You will see."

John Pierre looked at Abu and smiled. "I will miss you, my brother. If there is a way, I will find you."

"Wait! Wait! You must not leave yet," a loud voice boomed through the mastaba.

"Rufaaron," Abu shouted excitedly.

"I heard your plea, come quickly!" He motioned to the group. "You must hurry, sand is our enemy now."

After requesting the dagger of Sarsa from Astiramare he asked all of them to stand in a circle. He grabbed their hands and slashed each of their palms. As the blood flowed, he took the tip of the dagger and drew a pyramid in the center of each of their palms then clasped them both together as one. He then chanted -

Blood of moons of ages past
Bind them forever and make it last
Earth, Air, Fire and Water - I beg you not to erase the past
Churn for ages so to learn
Revealing secrets - life, birth and death turns
Past, Present and Future unite - to protect the souls and
destinies in sight
Gods above please make it right

A mist began to engulf the group as the words were spoken.

Rufaaron yelled above the sand and wind as he spoke the words twice in an ancient dialect as the wind howled.

The group could feel the sand pelting them in the face as it blew through the mastaba.

""Tis done and up to the gods. You must go now time is running out or we will all become part of the sand. The sandstorm that is heading this way will change the landscape. Hurry, we must go."

They all hugged, and they said their goodbyes. John Pierre held on tightly to Lacey as they put the lid of the fifth jar Khepri in the carving, recited the ancient hieroglyphics for the last time, and disappeared.

The End

Author Notes

$\mathcal{T}$his story is entirely a work of fiction. Originally born from an assignment for a course in a master's program in museum studies, I later turned into a story.

The board members no way represent how a museum is run or functions. They were just created to enhance of the story and add more mystery.

While references to Egyptian art are present, such as - papyrus, canopic jars, hieroglyphics, pyramids, ushabtis, the Giza complex, gods, the entire story is truly fabricated. Dates are elusive for the ancient Egyptian world is divided in Kingdoms and Dynasties. I focused the story around the Old Kingdom when the Giza Pyramid complex was constructed and added my own twists and turns to the story.

It is a fact Howard Carter was the archeologist who discovered the King Tutankhamun (Tut) tomb and the financial backer was Lord Carnarvon; however, the theft of the ushabtis and gold canopic jars was fabricated. I read something about Carter buying antiques in a bazaar in Cairo and selling them to fund his projects for the idea. I also intrigued by artists who can create and pass art off as fake. So I added some twists about the fake jars.

The artifact storage – is also not true. Perhaps the Egyptians had some place for keeping the treasures going into the pharaoh's pyramids?

The Temple of Sarsa, the characters, the dagger of Sarsa, the amulets, the rings, and any spells are completely contrived while writing the story. Characters in Beyond the Underworld chapters are also made-up and not related to specific deities.

The Egyptian Gods were connected to everything in the Egyptian culture and some are highlighted in the story. There was a god and goddess for everything to help explain the mysteries of their world. Whether it was the origin of life, death, nature, religion, love, or simply calling upon a deity to help one get through the basic trials of life. They also had their own spirit animals and cults that they were associated with and as with any family their lineage and family tree could be traced from region to region and person to person.

I wanted to give some descriptions of the monuments and hieroglyphics, but nothing comes as close as to seeing them in person.

To study Egyptian art is fascinating. To actually go to Egypt and explore the art is indescribable. To see the slides and photographs from pages of the textbooks come to life, to crawl through a mastaba, explore the Giza pyramid complex inside and out, to enter King Tut's tomb, to stand where the Great Pharaoh Ramses perhaps roamed, to see his colossal temple – I still am awestruck and *still* wonder how they did it?

To explore the ancient monuments and wonder…wonder… who carved and painted the thousands of hieroglyphics that adorned the walls in temple after temple is astounding.

You can't help but marvel and think, what if…what would it have been like if you could go actually go back in time…

Or perhaps we are just better off visiting, reading, or studying the art in the museums?

Canopic Jars

The canopic jars were buried in ancient tombs for the safe-keeping of human organs such as the stomach, intestines, lungs, and liver. It was believed these would be needed in the afterlife. There was no jar for the heart as the Egyptians believed it to be the seat of the soul, and so it was left inside the body.

In the afterlife, it was believed, the heart would be weighed against the feather of truth by the god Anubis. If a heart was too heavy from bad deeds it would be fed to a monster that was believed to be part lion, part hippopotamus, and part crocodile.

About the Author

Michele A. Fabiano was born and raised in New Jersey. She earned a bachelor's degree in Art History from Rutgers University and master's degree in Art History from The City College of New York. She is the author of *The Agony Continues: Michelangelo's Search for Art in 20th Century NYC* and *You're Not a Fucking Bachelor Anymore*

Michele has taught art history courses at the City College of New York, The University of North Alabama, Brookdale Community College in Northern New Jersey, and Ocean County Community College in central New Jersey.

She has worked as a free-lance writer and photographer for Riverview's and Neighbor's Magazine. She also authored the college textbook, *From Cubs to Lions Your Guide to Success at the University of North Alabama.*

Michele resides in New Jersey with her husband Joe, and two dogs.

Author's Note

Dear Reader,

I hope you enjoyed reading *The Donation* as much as I enjoyed writing it. Please do me a favor and write a review on Amazon. The reviews are important, and your support is greatly appreciated.

Thank you,

Michele A. Fabiano

The Agony Continues

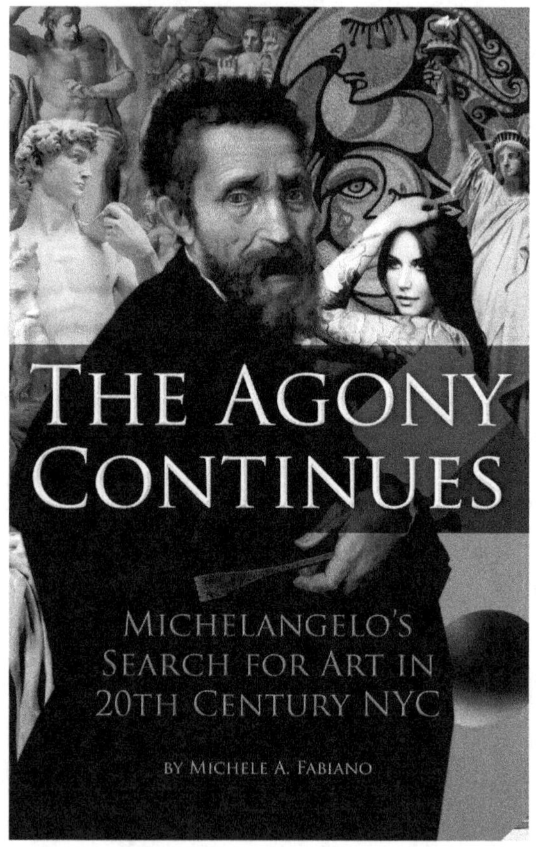

St. Peter grants Michelangelo a vacation request, allowing him to travel to the twentieth century to view art. Not only does Michelangelo want to see what artists have been creating after his death but he also desires confirmation that his own work is remembered.

As Michelangelo roams about New York City he meets a variety of people who attempt to help him make sense of modern sculpture, painting and architecture.

Michelangelo compares everything he sees to specific works he created throughout his life. He finally meets Vinnie, a tough city boy, who agrees to help with his journey.

Trying to convince contemporary society what 'real art' is becomes infuriating as Michelangelo holds amusing discussions about enlarged, abstract geometric shapes, gigantic statues rising out of the river, graffiti, tattoos, and more which he vehemently contends cannot be art.

His conversations reflect his historical interactions with political figures who commissioned art, his family and other noteworthy artists.

Time is running out as St. Peter has allowed Michelangelo to spend only three weeks in the twentieth century. Michelangelo's frustration mounts as he struggles to comprehend the modern world and educate people on the art of the past.

You're Not a F*cking Bachelor Anymore

What happens after you get married? After the wedding, after the honeymoon and you move in together? What happens when you combine assets, share space, need to make decisions together and regard one another?

My breaking point came when I ran out of the bathroom, naked, enraged and screaming nonsensically at my husband as to why he couldn't put a roll of toilet paper on the toilet paper holder! I am an educated person with a master's degree trying to debate logically about the function of a plastic roller and toilet paper! Like a lawyer I'd provide endless, rational arguments for this simple task to no avail.

In addition to toilet paper, we fought over mundane objects including, lint traps, the TV remote, coffee, money and other routine responsibilities of daily living. The quarreling and disputes became ridiculous. When had we become so unreasonable? When had I become so irrational?

This book is for anyone in a relationship or contemplating getting involved in one.